THE MACHINE

THE TEMPLE OF THE EXPLODING HEAD SAGA

A League of Elder Novel

Ren Garcia

Loconeal Publishing
Amherst, OH

THE MACHINE
THE TEMPLE OF THE EXPLODING HEAD SAGA

Copyright © 2011 by Ren Garcia
Cover Art by © 2011 by Carol Phillips
Interior Image Art by © 2011 by Carol Phillips
Interior Image Art by © 2011 by Fantasio
Interior Image Art by © 2011 by Eve Ventrue
Interior Image Art by © 2011 by Justine Marie Hedman
Interior Image Art by © 2011 by Kailey Elizabeth Hedman
Interior Image Art by © 2011 by Chantal Boudreau
Edited by Barbara Taft Verducci

Loconeal books may be ordered through booksellers, Handcar Press or by contacting:
www.loconeal.com
216-772-8380

Published by Loconeal Publishing, LLC Printed in the United States of America

First Loconeal Publishing edition: July 2011
Visit our website: www.loconeal.com

ISBN 978-0-9825653-5-3 (Trade Paperback)

THE MACHINE
THE TEMPLE OF THE EXPLODING HEAD SAGA
A League of Elder Novel

Table of Contents

LIST OF ILLUSTRATIONS

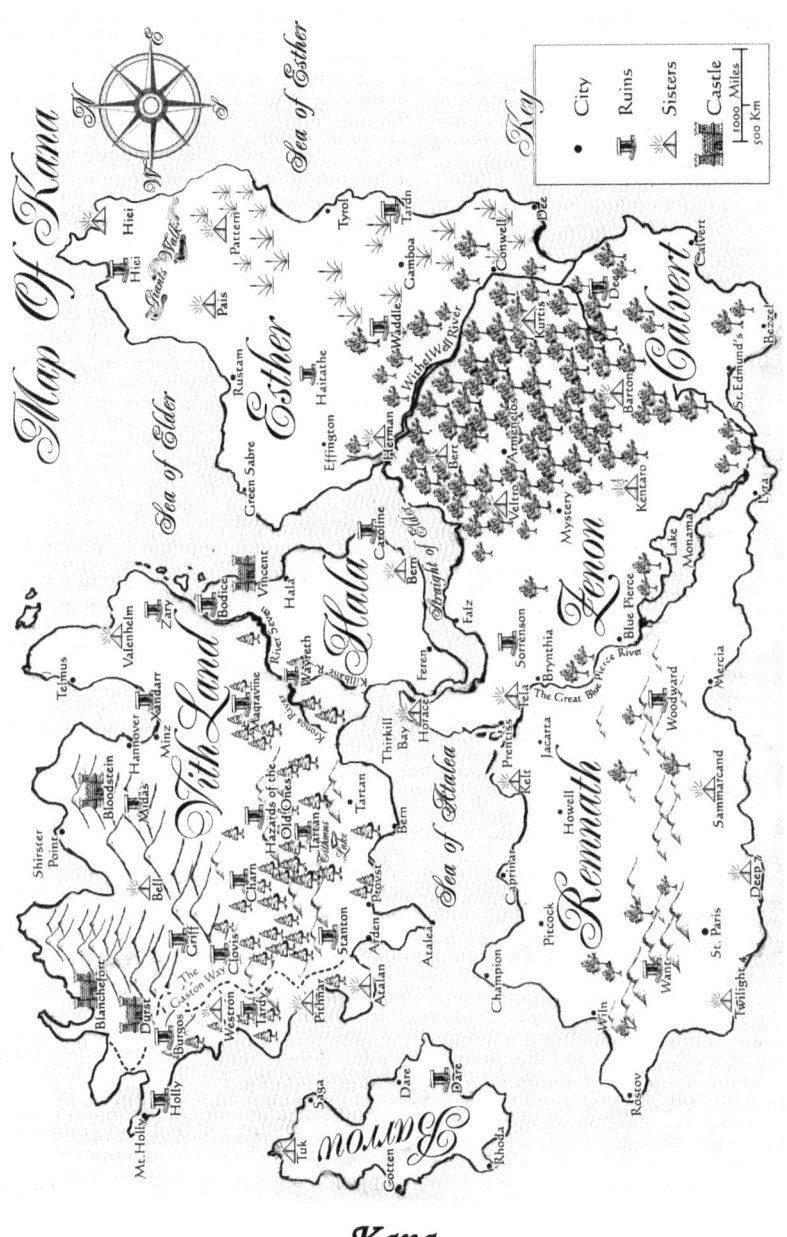

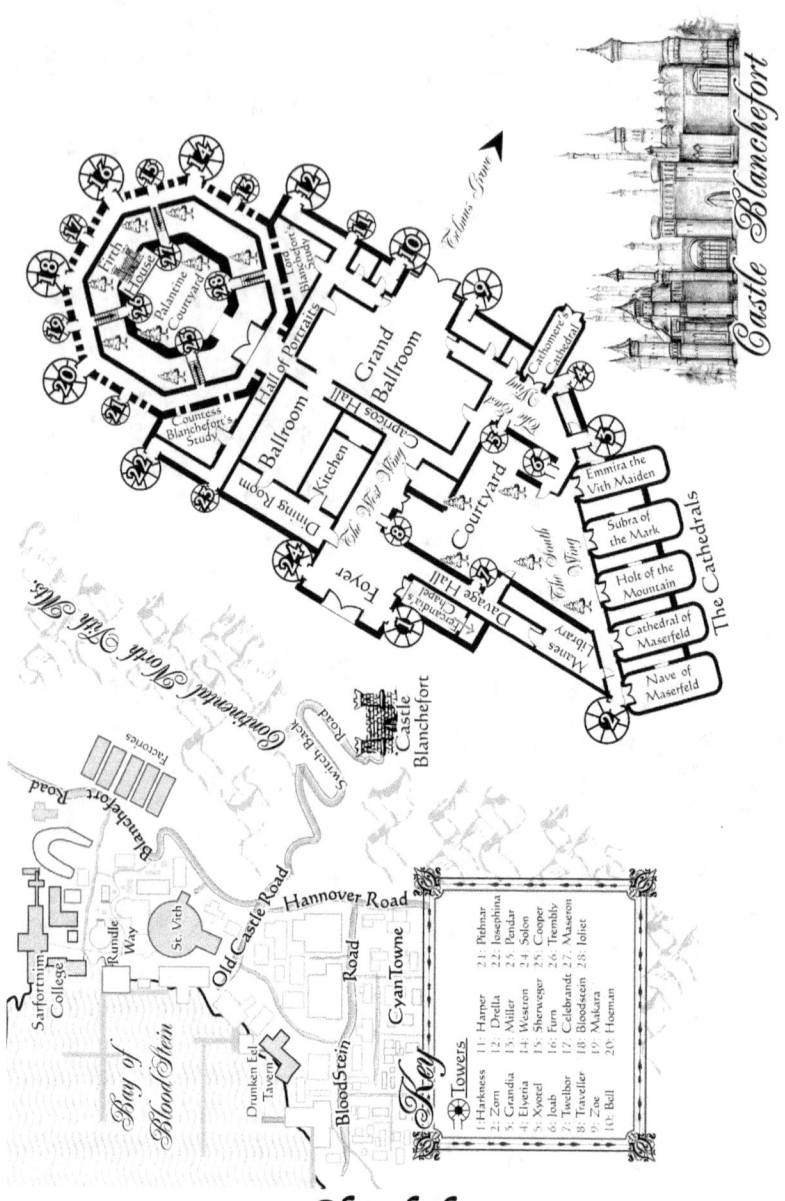

Castle Blanchefort

The Cathedrals

Emmira the Vith Maiden
Subra of the Mark
Holt of the Mountain
Cathedral of Maserfeld
Nave of Maserfeld

Castle Blanchefort

Birth House
Palantine Courtyard
Countess Blanchefort's Study
Hall of Portraits
Ballroom
Grand Ballroom
Apricot Hall
Kitchen
Dining Room
The West Wing
Foyer
Alexandria's Chapel
Davage Hall
Maines Library
The Youth
The Vand
Courtyard
The Hive
Cathomer's Cathedral
Fabinas' Grove

Blanchefort

Continued North Vith Mts.

Sarformin College
Rundle Way
St. Vith
Blanchefort Road
Factories
Stretch Back Road
Continued North Vith Mts.
Old Castle Road
Hannover Road
CyanTowne
BloodStein Road
Drunken Eel Tavern
Bay of BloodStein

Castle Blanchefort

Key

⊕ Towers
1: Harkness   11: Harner   21: Prehnar
2: Zorn   12: Dedla   22: Josephina
3: Grandia   13: Miller   23: Pendar
4: Elvetia   14: Westron   24: Solon
5: Xwteel   15: Sherweqer   25: Cooper
6: Joash   16: Furn   26: Trembly
7: Twelber   17: Celebrandt   27: Maseron
8: Traveller   18: Bloodstein   28: Ioliet
9: Zoe   19: Makara
10: Bell   20: Hoeman

Waam

PROLOGUE

Time awash and strange.

She had risen from her bed after a night of bad dreams: nightmares, *halofluges* the Vith called them. She couldn't remember them much, only that they'd been terrible, she was sure. *Halofluges* were like that—terrifying even though you really couldn't remember what frightened you so. She had a slight memory of a knife in her hand, and blood. She remembered blood.

And bugs too. There were so many bugs.

Feeling a bit shaky, she'd gone down to have breakfast in the hall and begin her day. A good breakfast would help rid her of the horrid taint her dreams had left behind. After breakfast she'd go flying; flying always remedied anything that troubled her.

And there was her brother, lying on the stones near the Grove gate as she arrived in the hall, an expanding pool of blood forming around him. She stood there staring at him. Her older sister, blue-haired and elegant, pushed past her and went to him, screaming his name, pulling him up, getting blood all over her white gown. Staff members rushing about. Her parents. The confusion.

"Hospitaler!" they cried. "Fetch a Hospitaler!"

And she just stood there and watched, numb. The halofluge returned to her fresh and whole.

The knife in her hand, the blood . . .

*   *   *   *   *

She'd flown away in her fast little ripcar as the family gathered in her brother's room to watch him die. She did not go to his room with the others. Instead she flew away, soaring high, looking for peace in the clouds. She loved to fly and she had talent, just like her father.

She found a mountainous spot, out of the way, uninhabited, unseen by any save the random mountaineer. She pushed the nose of her ripcar over, picking up speed and headed for the ground fast. A screaming, bucking power dive under full control; she was going to dash herself into the rocky valley between the mountains. Her family was to lose two children today: her brother, and herself, both by her hand.

For she had killed her brother . . . The *halofluge*.

She hit the boost and the diving ripcar pushed through the sound barrier in a flash of condensation, the mountains below coming up at fierce speed. She held the sticks in her tiny hands, perfect control, not flinching, not afraid in the least, eager for it all to be over.

The dream had been real. She held the knife that killed her brother.

The mountains, the speeding ripcar nose down at an acute angle, the trembling sticks.

She shouted her brother's name in last few moments as the rocky face of the mountain came up.

*   *   *   *   *

"My lady?" came a soft voice. "My lady, wake up."

She opened her eyes and she was back in her bedroom in Drella Tower, the stuffed animals, and paintings of her father's starship, the *New Faith* hanging on the walls, her four-poster bed draped with white veils. It was unmistakable.

What had happened? Was she dead? Was she now to become a ghost haunting her bedroom for the rest of eternity?

Would she be a good ghost, tickling those sleeping in her bed and lightly pulling their hair, or would she be a vengeful demon crawling into bed with them and troubling their dreams giving them *halofluges* like she had had?

"You're not dead," came the voice. "Just in case you were wondering, you're not dead."

She sat up. Bright sunshine, cheery through the veils. She wanted to know what happened.

"I saved you."

She was confused.

"I've made it a habit of saving you Blancheforts lately. I'll ask you the same question I once asked your brother: why did you try to kill yourself just now?" the voice asked.

She answered: blunt, the whole truth, nothing held back, the macabre details rolling out.

Halofluge. Knife in her hand.

"You think you killed your brother?"

She nodded her head. The voice didn't answer right away. She had a thought, a hope, that it would comfort and reassure her. *"Of course you didn't do it . . ."* she hoped it would say. *"It was just a dream, kid . . ."*

Then the voice spoke. "Well, even though you're just a little girl—I remember when you were just a newborn baby in your mother's arms—just look at all that red hair—you're a Vith, and you're strong too like your mother and father. I feel I can level with you: you did attack your brother, kid."

She sat there on her bed . . . and was devastated. Why? Why didn't the voice just let her die in the mountains?

". . . and you didn't do it, either. It was you, but it wasn't you. Understand?"

She didn't understand.

"Go to your mirror and take a look. Go on."

She slid off her bed, pushed through the veils and went to her mirror, gilded and full-length. The reflection in the mirror was monstrous: tall, bent, bleeding, wearing a golden mask covering the top part of what was left of her face and her red hair twisted up into a filthy beehive. And, her eyes—lusty, diabolical, demented . . . pure, restless evil.

The reflection in the mirror didn't look much like herself, but it was her no doubt about it. The stance was right, the turn of the head, the rise of the chin and so on. And, since it *was her* all the energy that she normally put into things that she loved, like flying and attending to her studies and learning Vith history, this demented version of herself would no doubt apply the same zeal to deviltry and mayhem and unspeakable crimes.

. . . her dying brother.

She wanted to put her hand to her mouth and scream, turn away and run, yet she forced herself to stand tall and appear outwardly impassive. She was only sixteen years old and just a child, but she was a Vith from a strong House. She was taught from an early age to be fearless, to face such things without pause or hesitation. Her father wouldn't shrink from such a sight and nor would she.

"There are bad folk about, my lady, and this is what they do.

They are the masters of the Horned God's temple and they are able to use its power to move back and forth through time. Moving through time is like a nice ride in the country for them. They will take you as an adult, many years from now, and, using methods that I will not tell, turn you into what you see here. They will fill your head with travesties and keep you in an evil dream, and you will joyfully do things you'd otherwise never do—like harm your brother, and his beloved. This future version of you is the servant of the Horned God and his time-travelling angels and she is evil through and through."

She put her hands to her face. She tried to be strong, but she was overcome. She couldn't look anymore and fell to her knees. She wanted to die.

Why didn't you just let me die?

Something came to her side and nudged her. Something small and silvery.

"Because, if I had done that you'd spend eternity in the gallery of the dead feeling nothing but regret. This is a moment to be strong, my lady, not to give in. Your brother right now is fighting for his life. Lady Sammidoran, at this very moment, is being pursued, by the monstrous future version of you. They need our help. Together, we can beat the Horned God and his angels. We can end this."

We can?

"Yes. You, of all people, can be of great help. Can I count on you?"

Yes, of course, she'd do anything.

But first, she needed a moment, to be weak, to be a frightened little girl.

The silvery creature next to her was tiny, no bigger than a small dog; whiskers, flippers, smoothed-domed forehead, bright, inquisitive eyes.

"It's all right, Lady Hathaline," Carahil said. "I'm here and I'm not going anywhere. You can cry if you want, and I won't tell. I promise."

She embraced Carahil and held onto him for a long time, weeping into his smooth neck; weeping for her brother, and for Sam, and for herself.

The little silver god had come again when he was needed most.

Time. He had nothing but time for her.

1—Through the Grove

K ay lay there in the morning frost. The sun was rising. The purple sky of dawn gave way in lacy veils to dark blue.

What happened? He remembered Sam, and the man and woman.

He remembered not being able to move. He remembered the woman falling on him.

Creation—things were spinning. His stomach hurt; he was in agony.

He remembered bugs, big ones, the clearing full of them.

He had been hurt by the woman. She cut into his stomach near his belly-button. He had lost a lot of blood, and he could feel it congealed around him in a dry pool. He had no idea how badly he was hurt, but it was bad.

It was very bad.

Looking down, his stomach was a mass of red. His pajama bottoms had been cut away by the woman just before she fell upon him with a dull knife and mutilated him. Despite his dire situation he allowed himself to indulge in a bit of modesty.

He was lying in the Grove in an oak clearing, not far from the Ten Gardens area. The ground was covered with morning frost. All around, ancient oak trees towered over him, the same ones that had seen war and death for ages. What was one more death to them? They were mute and indifferent to Kay's plight.

Holding his stomach, he staggered to his feet. Everything in his torso area felt loose and ready to come out. He tried to hold it all in place.

What had happened?

Sam, his love, his *Cerri-Tela*, had come to him in the night and demanded he follow her into the Grove. She had appeared to him as a wraith and floated over his bed.

Once there she put him to Trial in accordance with her people's traditions. Using the NIGHTMARE, the LosCapricos weapon of her line, she created several arcane monsters from her deepest fears to guide and test him through the Trials.

A broken, half-dead deer of sinister presence.

A golden amoeba-like creature with a humanoid skeleton for a nucleus.

A bronze, twenty foot high living metal man who took Sam's body and sealed it inside his hollow chest where she would be safe.

That's when *they* appeared—a hideous man in golden armor and a bent, skinless woman. They claimed to be Sam's tormentors and her masters, and they were pursuing Sam for tearing her control collar from around her neck. Her "Shockers" they called it which they used to turn Monamas into Berserkacides.

Sam escaped, safe within the metal man where they could not get to her. In revenge they fell upon Kay, and loudly promised they were going to kill him, and then *eat* him.

And, making a terrible noise that rendered him helpless, the woman fell upon him, stabbing him over and over.

Why was he still alive?

The man and woman were gone, and Kay was all alone in the clearing. He fought off a wave of nausea and, with supreme effort, took a step over the uneven ground toward the castle.

He took another, and then another. His heart pounded. His guts shifted.

The castle was so far away. He'd walked these passes innumerable times with his cousins, Sarah and Phillip, and never thought twice about the distance involved. He was in the back half of the Telmus Grove near the Ten Gardens. To return to the castle, he had to pass through the oak trees and enter the Inner Plaisance of the Grove, passing the Sarfortnim, Greyson, Humboldt and Telmus courtyards, and then he'd cross the bridge over Blanchefort Creek and be in the castle.

It was at least two miles.

Step after tentative step, his arms bloody from holding his stomach, he went. Through the trees, there was the Sarfortnim courtyard.

He remembered the horrid, skinless woman wearing a golden

mask sitting on him, her bloody arm rising and falling as the armored man watched. Her knife biting into him one small chunk at a time. Sam had always loved his bellybutton, and he had a notion that the woman was trying to cut it out to spite Sam. He couldn't move during the whole ordeal, couldn't fight. She was making some sort of scream that got into his head and be-spelled him. He couldn't move while she screamed. He couldn't defend himself.

Through the Sarfortnim, beech trees a canopy of green lined the path, and then the Greyson was right ahead. It was called Carahil's Walk for the great Silver tech seal Carahil who once played there. Carahil had been created in a fountain by Kay's aunt, Lady Poe of Blanchefort, and was supposedly a great spirit of some sort, a god, he'd heard, created by his smiling, humble aunt.

Carahil had helped save the planet Xandarr some twenty years prior. They loved him on Xandarr. He'd heard they carved statues of him there, and the children had a tradition of hand-writing little notes and leaving them by the statues, cradled in the stone flippers. The notes often started with the line:

Dear, Mr. Carahil. I need help.

And all that started right here near the Greyson courtyard where a god once played.

Carahil! his thoughts roiled. *Carahil, help me!*

Kay wondered how he survived. Did the woman have a sudden fit of remorse or conscience? No—no, she was spoiling to slowly kill him and then devour his sliced flesh. She said so! She was salivating in fact, drooling into his face as she filleted him alive, eager for a taste.

So what happened? Where did they go? He couldn't remember.

In Humboldt courtyard, Kay could deny the pain and sickness in his guts no longer. He toppled over like a fallen tree face first into the cobblestones, feeling a fresh flow of blood from his stomach.

This was it; he was dying. Sam's beautiful face flashed into his head. His love, his *Cerri-Tela*, now pursued by the same woman and man who had killed him.

Sam was terrified of them. Kay felt no fear here at the end of his life, only impotent dying rage and longing for his love. Perhaps he'd come back as an angry spirit and wait for the skinless, bent woman to return, if she dared. Then, he'd fall upon her with supernatural light and give back what she gave him and make a ghost out of her.

Things dimmed. Sam's beautiful pale face floated in front of him.

I'm sorry, Cerri-Tela.
I'm sorry, Sam.
The bitch killed me!

✳   ✳   ✳   ✳   ✳

BZZZZZZZZZZ . . .

Something reached into the dark and troubled him. It was a terrific buzzing sound, like that of a bee that had landed on one's ear and sounded huge.

Go away. I'm dying! Give me some peace!
BZZZZZZZZZZZ . . .

He opened his eyes. Sitting on his face was a gigantic blue bug with a sea-green belly, like a dragonfly only it had strange wings. Its wings, instead of being straight out, were swept back, like those of a fast sub-orbital, and were the most remarkable color. They were a bold coppery color, shiny and inviting like Sam's goggles from Hoban that she wore in the village to cover her black eyes.

Sam wearing her geared, copper and silver goggles, laughing, sampling delights from the shops. Pushing the goggles back and kissing him.

Kissing him.

He'd die with a happy thought in his head after all.

Things began to go blurry again.

The bug crawled a tickling course across his face, down his nose and then onto the Humboldt cobbles, standing on the strewn purple strands of his long hair. It moved away an inch or two.

BZZZZZZZZZZZZZZZ . . .

It beat its coppery wings in a shiny blur. Creation! What a loud noise, so deep, so clear.

The sound got into his head and sorted out his thoughts. Only moments before he was nearly off the coil and dead. Now, with the buzzing filling his ears, he was fully alert.

Lying on the Humboldt courtyard stones with the huge blue bug.

Wait! Bugs! Paraflies!

He remembered Paraflies, a deafening cloud of them, entering the clearing as the woman sliced him up. He remembered the man in armor being bothered by them, waving them away from his face.

The woman, ignoring them at first, got up off him and ran as they began crawling over her horrid, skinless body. She cursed and swatted at them. And they departed in a flash of green.

The Paraflies had saved his life, or what was left of it anyway.

Clutching his stomach, he rose to his knees and then stood.

The Parafly preened its face with its legs for a moment, and then took flight and buzzed away.

He exited the courtyard seeing no more bugs. They seemed to like to swarm and fly together in a cloud. Paraflies. Kay recalled his cousin Sarah, a lover of the lurid and sensational, sending him news postings of an alarming infestation of Kana by huge, previously unidentified insects called, Paraflies" by the media. Big and colorful. Loud, too. Flew in great swarms and seemed immune to bug gasses.

Why one Parafly? They liked to swarm, so why one? Almost like it was sent to him specifically to buzz in his ear and annoy him back to life.

One Parafly. One half-dead man. All right. Fine. You get your way. *I'm alive.*

Kay continued, one step at a time.

✳ ✳ ✳ ✳ ✳

The great reddish bulk of the castle studded with spires rose in the distance as he passed through the Telmus courtyard.

How far had he gone? Nearly two miles. Creation, his guts hurt.

His legs turned to stone. He struggled across the bridge. Veins empty—no blood.

He couldn't move, but there was the castle! Right there! Just a bit more.

No, no, can't move. Can't go any farther!

His heart skipped a beat.

That woman—killing him with her knife one stab at a time.

That woman!!

Shocktyte bitch!!

Rage flared through him. Hatred! Not for himself, but for Sam!

That woman! Trying to kill him and trying to kill his Sam, too. His *Cerri-Tela*. So frightened. His love looking over her shoulder, being harassed by that skinless wretch her whole life. Sam was running, and now she was all alone.

Five minutes! Give me five able-bodied minutes alone with the bitch, and I'll show her what fear is!

Everything spun, and he fell over.

Sam!

Hatred could only move him so far. He could see the gate of the castle and the dark, stony interior.

Crawling, he was there. He was just inside the castle, partially in sun, partially in shade. He'd made it all this way, only to fall to his wounds at the castle gate.

"Kay!!" He heard a hollow, echoing scream.

Rapid footfalls were coming toward him.

Everything went black.

2—Saying Their Goodbyes

"Can he hear us?" a female voice asked.

"I wouldn't think so, no," replied a male's.

He had no idea where he was, or who he was, for that matter. He'd been born, apparently, he'd lived for some period of time in luxury and peace, how long he didn't know. He had parents and siblings, and friends.

He had a pale woman who loved him . . .

Now, it was time to die.

He heard a carnival of voices all around him. He tried to see, but there was nothing but soft amber in a rippling, indistinct pool.

"Tell me what was done to him," came a somewhat familiar female voice.

"Syg, now's not the time," came another voice, male, more authoritarian.

"Tell me, Ennez!"

The folds of amber flowed. He was in pain, though nothing hurt. He was blind and deaf, though he was in a blinding and deafening cacophony.

"All right, if you wish to hear this, then I shan't deny you. Your son has suffered a severe lacerating event of the abdominal wall resulting in a partial disembowelment of the lower gastrointestinal tract. Some of his tract is missing. It appears to have been chewed through. He has been stabbed over a hundred times with a small and rather blunt metal object, like a dull knife or something of the like. The instrument used against him was filthy, full of poison. He also has been mutilated all about the abdominal area, including the carving of rune-like lettering in his flesh and the partial tearing away of his umbilicus . . ."

"His what?"

"His bellybutton, Syg. Lastly, he was sodomized about the penis and rectum."

Silence . . . flowing amber.

"Who did it, Ennez?" came the female voice, this time dark, choked with emotion. "Who did this to him? Who is going to die by my hand?"

"We're not certain. We've collected select material samples and other evidences that we shall have analyzed in our Hospitaler sanctum in Minz. We're convinced the identity of the attacker shall be made known at that time."

The woman's voice again—now ragged with fury. "I'll tell you who is was—it was Lady Sammidoran. She did this to our son!"

"You don't know that, Syg."

"Who else could it be? Bark saw her leading Kay out into the Grove, and now look at him, flat on his back, torn to shreds . . . atrocities performed upon him. I've had enough of being civilized and proper. I want her head before the sun sets!"

"Syg?"

"No, no! I want her head, and if I can't have that, I'll have the heads of her kin!"

The man's voice grew solemn. "Syg, now is not the time to crave revenge. I understand how you feel, however, you need to compose yourself. You must hear what I have to say. You need to go in there right now and . . . say goodbye to your son while you still can."

The amber bubbled. Silence for a moment.

"Goodbye?" the woman asked, her voice fearful. "What talk is this, Ennez, Beth? You—you have cleaned his wounds and closed his lacerations—masterful work. I don't understand. He's fine, the danger has passed."

"He is . . . beyond our help, Syg. His muscles we can repair, his skin and entrails we can stitch together, but, for his poisoned blood, there is nothing we can do. This is the worst case of it I've ever seen. He is well beyond Apex, even after a massive transfusion the taint remains."

Silence.

"He is gone, Syg. I'm sorry, but we've done all we can. Don't let these last few moments pass, I pray you. Say your goodbyes, wish his soul well and then take him to Dead Hill where he belongs and honor him as he deserves."

Somewhere, he could hear the woman weeping.

✳   ✳   ✳   ✳   ✳

Arin-Dan . . .

He wondered if he was dead and this was the afterlife. He tried to see, but there was nothing but amber. He tried to move; nothing.

He felt a soft hand touch his face. *Arin-Dan. Summon your strength and tell them to perform test X-452. Tell them . . . Make yourself heard, my love. Make them understand.*

Test X-452 What's that?

It will guide them in properly attending to you. He told me it would help.

Who told you?

Carahil told me.

Who's Carahil? The name was familiar but everything was a muddle.

A friend.

And who are you?

I'm the woman who loves you, Kay . . .

There were presences all around him, lurking, leaning over him. He tried to see, but it was like a dust storm, just flowing amber.

A shape came up to him and emerged through the confused murk. It was a girl wearing a white gown. Her whitish blue hair was falling all around her shoulders. Her gown was soiled with blood—possibly his blood. Mental images passed in front of him of such a girl: proud, capable, eager to socialize. His sister. Kilos, was her name. Kilos, was his sister, shopping with him in the village with Sam.

Sam . . .

Seemed so long ago.

Her lips trembled. Love and grief. None of her training in the social niceties prepared her for this, for the death of her brother. "Look what you got yourself into," she said, leaning close, stroking his hair. "You, you ruined my favorite white gown. It's from Hoban, it's . . ." She stopped and choked back a groan. "Bye, big brother . . ." Tears fell.

She vanished, replaced by a tall blonde-headed woman and a slightly shorter brown-haired man. He remembered the woman, teaching him his lessons out in the Grove. So patient and kind. All the little silver creatures she created. His aunt, Lady Poe and his uncle, Lord Peter.

Now, haggard and care-worn, the two of them.

Test X-452

"Be well on your journey, my beloved nephew. Take your place with our ancestors and share us your insight. Let death still not your voice." She kissed him on the cheek and Lord Peter led her away.

Two more figures popped up: a boy and a girl, both his age. Long coats and tall boots. Aqua blue eyes and blue hair in a ponytail. His cousins Sarah and Phillip. His best friends, come to say goodbye.

They stood there looking down on him, neither one of them knowing what to say. Then, Sarah broke down.

"I am so s-sorry, K-Kay," she stammered in-between sobs. "My big, stupid mouth is to blame for this. I'm sorry I blamed Sam and drove you apart, I'm sorry I was afraid. Stupid Jo-Boy I am!! Stupid, stupid, stupid!! I'll make it right, Kay, I'll fix this, I promise, j-just don't go . . ." She wheeled around. "Can, can he hear me?"

Somebody standing in the amber said "No." She wept and leaked slobber and possibly snot all over him. "Please don't go . . ." She pawed at him, trying to shake him awake. Phillip took her by the shoulders and led her away. Phillip hadn't said anything, but he was clearly hurting too. As always, even on his deathbed Phillip let Sarah do all the talking.

Sarah, he tried to say through the amber. *Test X-452. Quit blubbering and do test X-452. I don't know what it is, just do it.*

He tried to say the words, just nothing came out.

Another figure. A tall brown-headed lady in a uniform and a big hat held in her hands. A silver bird was sitting on her shoulder, his image burning through the murk. Lt. Kilos, family friend and mentor. Silver tech Tweeter at her side as always. Namesake of his sister. His childhood crush.

She stood there and then leaned close, her big brown eyes full of sorrow. "I'm really sorry, kid. I wish I could have been there with you, you know, to stand at your side and help when you needed me. Don't worry about your mom and dad—I'm going to take good care of them, you can count on me." She put her strong hands on his face. "Be well, and ever green. All these worlds are yours."

She kissed him on the forehead.

Test X-452 he tried to say.

Lt. Kilos didn't hear him and turned away, placing her hat back on her head.

Test X-452!

Her Tweeter bird reacted a little, just the flutter of a wing and a turn of the head. "What?" Kilos said. She leaned back down, her searching brown eyes like a pair of lanterns in the amber. "Kay did you just say something?"

I said: *Test X-452.*

"Kay?" she said again. "Tweeter here is telling me you're saying something. I don't hear anything, but he swears it!" She moved away and was gone.

A tiny woman emerged: small, green eyes framed by red hair. Shadowmark.

"Kay," his mother said in an unrecognizable voice burdened with grief. "I will have revenge for you. Revenge . . ."

His mother, full of love and brightness, her evil days as a Black Hat behind her.

His mother, watching her son die, the Black Hat returning to destroy and lay waste.

Two more figures appeared. "I'm telling you, Dav, he said something!"

Lt. Kilos had brought his father, Lord Davage.

"Ki," his father said. "He's near gone. He can't talk."

"Sight him, Dav," Ki protested. "Tweeter said . . ."

"Enough with your bird!" his mother shouted. "My son is dying!"

Ki would not be denied. "Don't accept him as a dead man, Syg. I swear he's saying something. He's struggling for life, struggle with him. Hear what he has to say."

"Do not burden me with false hope, Ki!"

"Dav!" Ki yelled. "Sight him!"

His father leaned over. His eyes lit the amber up, cutting through it, changing colors in the twilight as he tentatively probed with his famous Blanchefort Sight.

His father reacted. "God's Bodkins!" he cried. "He's Sighting. Ki's right! Somehow he's Sighting! He can see us right now!"

"Can it be, Dav?" his mother piped, the Black Hat fading a little from her voice. "Ennez said he was gone."

"I don't doubt Ennez's assessment, and I don't doubt the

resilience of our son either."

He leaned down close, close enough for Kay to feel the stubble on his cheek.

Test X-452

"Did you hear that? He spoke, just now I heard him! Faint, I'll grant you, but there it was! Ennez, Beth!" his father cried. "My son lives!"

3—A Shadow Tech Male

Voices around him, swimming in the dark.

"Test X-452," came the voice of Ennez, "is a test we of the Hospitalers use to determine the presence of a Shadow tech male—an Invernan. It's a standard test approved for use by the Sisterhood of Light, and, according to our database, it was performed upon Kay when he was two years old in Minz about twenty years ago. With Syg being a Shadow tech female, it was possible, however statistically unlikely, that Kay could be a Shadow tech male—hence the test."

"But the test was negative," his father said.

"Yes, so our records show. Case closed."

Somebody small and delicate approached and hovered over him, smelling of soft perfume and humming a pleasing tune. A whispered feminine voice came filtering down. "My training as a Hospitaler tells me you shouldn't be hearing a word I say, however my heart says you can hear me just fine. You can hear me, can't you, Kay?"

He couldn't respond. He just lay there, suspended in amber.

Warm hands on his face. "Do you remember me? My name is Bethrael of Moane. I was there the day you were born. I delivered you, I delivered your sisters and your brother too. Now here I am again, supposedly for your death. My training also tells me you should be dead, but again, I've a feeling you're not going to be dying today."

"Is the test done, Beth?" Ennez asked.

"Give me a moment," she replied. She pulled something from his face and walked away into the amber gloom. "Here. It's done."

Indistinct movement.

"Yes. Look here," Ennez said. "The test is conclusive. Kay is a Shadow tech male."

"But how can that be? He was tested negative."

Beth's voice came up. "The Ephysians say that Shadow tech males sometimes do not manifest themselves until later in life. That seems to be confirmed here."

"So," his father said, "what does this revelation mean? How does his status as a Shadow tech male assist him?"

Beth again. "Shadow tech males are said to be very resilient—able to ward off injury and Apex-plus blood poisoning that would prove fatal for any other."

"All conjecture," Ennez said.

"Here's the proof!" Beth replied. "He lives."

A form approached; his mother's. "Can this be true, Beth?" his mother asked.

"Look here, Syg. According to the Troutman, Kay's blood-poisoning level is at Apex, plus 4. He should have been dead hours ago, but, here he is, hanging on."

"Then, what are we to do? How may he be helped? Tell us and it shall be done!"

Ennez again: "There's no method of treatment for Apex blood poisoning approved by the Sisterhood of Light. It is a fatal condition."

His mother: "Then, let us discuss the unapproved ones . . . immediately."

✳   ✳   ✳   ✳   ✳

Sometime later, talking and indistinct forms moving through the amber. He recognized the voices, but the cloudy pool still veiled his eyes.

"We are risking the Sisters' punishment should they learn of this," Ennez said.

"Let me worry about the Sisters," his mother said. "Should they become involved, we'll simply say I forced you to do it on pain of death."

"Ok, ok, Syg. So, here's how we're going to proceed. We're going to introduce Kay to Beth's Silver tech. It is said Shadow tech males absorb and feed upon Shadow and Silver tech energy, and perhaps it will cleanse his blood, though I guarantee nothing. You understand that, right? This could be very dangerous and Beth might be risking her life on an unknown."

"She needn't take such a risk. I'm his mother, it should be my Silver tech offered up."

"No, Syg, it won't work. As you're related to him, he won't react to yours—Lady Poe's neither. It has to be Beth."

Beth's tiny form returned to his side and gazed down at him. "I'm going to try and help you now, Kay. I'm going to share my Silver tech with you. That is not something lightly done. When I was a Black Hat, I was taught never to allow a Shadow tech male to touch me. Never. We were told stories how Shadow tech males can dominate us, change us into a *Wandwilla*. Do you know what that is? No? Don't worry about it—I really don't think they exist, but, in any event, I would have killed a Shadow tech male before I let him get near me." He heard a soft laugh. "And now, here we are. You are the son of my dearest friends, I delivered you and placed you into Syg's arms for the first time and I'm not going to let you die. If I can save you with my Silver tech, I will do so gladly. This shall be my gift to my friends, and to you."

More people approached. "Are you ready, Beth?"

"Yes, I am."

"Are you certain you wish to do this?"

"We've little choice. I can help him, therefore I shall."

"There are dangers."

Beth became annoyed. "I'm a Hospitaler Samaritan of the Knickerbaum Order, just as you are, Ennez. I am aware of the dangers and my training and knowledge in the medical arts shall help protect me. I understand, as a Shadow tech male, he might have some minor form of control over me. As he touches my Silver tech I'll probably experience a slight elevation in temperature, a mild seizing in the joints and a dilation of the pupils. He might even be able to command me to some extent—I highly doubt it, though. I am rather skeptical of that alleged ability; my will is my own. All in all, I believe this experience might prove highly invaluable, as our knowledge in the Hospitalers regarding Shadow tech males and their effects upon Shadow tech females is suspect and incomplete. I shall try to speak aloud my thoughts and feelings as we proceed, so that we may add to our knowledge."

Ennez came up. "I think you're underestimating what a Shadow tech male can do to you, but very well. Here is how we shall proceed. Beth, you create a coalesced ball of Silver tech. Dav and I will then lift Kay's hand and place it within the ball. Syg, you shall time us. Timing is critical. For safety's sake, we'll allow Beth to remain in contact with

Kay for no more than thirty seconds. When the time elapses, we'll remove Kay's hand from the ball. If this works, Kay's B-reading might go down well below Apex and he'll be out of danger."

Things happened all around him. He saw a brilliant ball of shining, chrome-like silver form in front of him, floating, cutting through the amber, seeing it with perfect clarity; its fair moon-like shape, its flawless surface. Clouds of past and future reflected off its face as a coming storm.

Beth had created her Silver tech ball.

His hand was lifted and moved into position.

"Begin," his mother said, and his hand was slid into the Silver tech ball, the tips of his fingers breaking the round surface and penetrating it like a blob of warm mercury.

KAAAAAAAAAAY! Beth screamed in his thoughts.

A bomb went off. The world turned around him, the amber veil cast aside in an expanding circle with shocking clarity.

There was his large bedroom. He was in his bed, the old stone walls and vaulted ceiling all around carved in the Vith style. There was his terrace looking out over the mountain shelf plunging to the village far below. Proud sunshine poured in, just like any day. Scanners, rolls of cloth, medical instruments, bottles of Hospitaler "De-bug", discarded empty vials of blood, bundles of veri-plas tubes, bags full of discarded bio-materials and crimson waste were strewn about everywhere. An untidy row of empty mismatched chairs were lined-up against the wall, probably where his relatives had sat in vigil, now gone.

KAAAAAAY!

Time jumped back and forth, no longer having form and continuity.

The chairs were empty.

The chairs were full of his mourning relatives, his aunt and uncle, his sister and cousins. One sister in a bloody gown. Where was his second sister? Where was she?

There was Sarah sitting slumped, overcome with grief, Phillip with his arm around trying to console her.

The wall behind the chairs was marred with tiny defects he'd never noticed before: slight but obvious discolorations, minute scratches, the tell-tale hits and jabs from the ancient stone mason's chisel who cut it. A left-handed stone mason by the angle of the hits. All perfectly clear.

And look there; Sam had written her name on the wall in a tiny polished script, using nothing but her iron hard fingernail, sharp as a sword-blade and as fine as a jeweler's scribe; SAMMIDORAN. Her name was everywhere actually, right-side up, upside down, off-angled, on the ceiling, toward the floor—she seemed to having a liking for defacing his walls. Time disjointed, he saw her doing it, bent over, shrouded in black, as a child, as an adolescent, as a young woman, in bed with him scrawling it as they made love: SAMMIDORAN, SAMMIDORAN.

Sam . . . he loved her so.

Her name was also carved into his flesh in a different, mocking hand: SAM on the shaft of his penis in bloody black and red letters only recently repaired by Ennez.

The fleshless woman had done that to him with the same little knife she'd devastated the rest of his body with. Fresh hatred moved through him.

Nearby, his father (coatless and hatless) and Ennez were leaning over him holding his arm aloft in Beth's floating silver ball. His mother was seated on the other side of the bed gazing at a timepiece.

His large oaken dresser sat against the wall. Awash in time he could see himself and Sam standing in front of it. In the top drawer was the old note he'd receive years before—the IN LOCK note whose letters were too washed out to read. He always kept it there, a tantalizing mystery, hoping to one day decipher what it said.

Today was that day, the smeared red letters moving back in time, shrinking down into their original legible form.

Folded up in the drawer on the other side of the room, he could now read it perfectly. It said:

To: Kabyl, Lord of Blanchefort
BE WARNED . . .

BE WARNED . . . Beth, sitting on the other side of the room, shrieked and his attention was diverted away from the note. She was gritting her teeth as if she were in agony.

Bethrael of Moane. Something was wrong with Beth. Time to end this. Pull his hand out. How long had it been in there?

He was quickly overwhelmed by an intense feeling. Though Beth was seated several feet away, it felt as if she was right on top of him engaged in a bout of heated sex. He could feel her skin, the softness of her breasts and humid warmth of her ragged breath. He felt her tongue deep in his mouth and her legs tight around him, the heels of her feet going up the backs of his legs. Her pounding heart . . .

And he could feel himself deep inside her, the warmth, and the wracking spasms of her muscles tightening up, releasing then tightening again.

Flex!

She coiled up in the chair, clenching her teeth.

Flex!

He recalled her previous words:

My will is my own.

My knowledge will protect me.

Clearly Beth hadn't been prepared for the primal ferocity of allowing him to touch her Silver tech. The dry, dispassionate words on a page she'd studied somewhere in a Hospitaler sanctum couldn't compete with the overwhelming reality, and she was lost in it.

"Beth!" Ennez cried. "What are you experiencing? Should we stop?"

She grunted something in response.

"Syg, what's the time?"

"Fourteen seconds!"

Fourteen seconds? Is that all? Kay saw her body pulsing with energy and a white-light mass about her waist and legs. He could see through her body, to the balled up fist of her uterus watching it clench up, relax and then clench again like an inverted punching bag belted into a blur.

Flex! She climaxed. Flex! Again.

Kay billowed on the edge of a projectile orgasm . . . and Beth, linked to him via her Silver tech, was doing the same, over and over.

Flex! "Beth!"

Kay yearned for relief. End it, kill him, and make it stop! Time detached and wandered ahead. He saw what was about to happen.

"Enough, she's had enough! Remove his hand!" Ennez will say.

A Silver tech lance piercing his heart. Beth standing. Beth attacking his surprised parents.

I AM YOURS, KAY!

COMMAND ME!

TELL ME WHAT TO STEAL! TELL ME WHO TO KILL! COMMAND ME!

JUST DON'T EVER LET ME GO!!

She throws her arms around him and they became fluid, their enraptured bodies mingling as one. Welded together. One eternal creature, locked in ecstasy . . . forever.

Wandwilla . . . just moments away.

Just moments away . . .

"Stop!!" Kay cried.

He jolted from bed, wrenching his hand from the Silver tech ball. He fell to the floor, his parents swarming around him.

"Syg, what was the time?"

"Just twenty seconds. Was that enough."

Ennez turned to Beth. "Beth, are you all right?"

Grunting, she rose from her chair and staggered away toward the door. Her mouth was open, like she was about to sneeze or scream and couldn't get it out.

Flex! Another one.

Flex! Yet another.

Flex Flex Flex Flex Flex Flex . . . .

She threw the door open and wobbled out. "Beth!" Ennez called after her.

His heart racing, everything closed in around him.

"Did it work?" came his mother's voice. "Dav, did it work?"

And he faded into unconsciousness.

4—Trials and Wellermans

Two weeks later, Kay was still confined to his bed. Ennez and Beth had done good work. The strange swirls and rune-like carvings the woman had made in his stomach were barely visible; the other various atrocities she'd done, too, were mostly gone. He occasionally reached down through his dressings and felt his bellybutton. The woman had tried to cut it away, probably because Sam loved it, and she'd failed. That gave him a small measure of satisfaction.

He'd lost two feet of small bowel and had to be fed intravenously for a week as the stitches healed and knitted together. His blood levels were measured hourly. B-20 to B67 on average; still high, but manageable and going down by the day. He took his Cynth medication and, slowly, his blood returned to normal. Beth had reacted to him after the Silver tech incident where she'd helped save his life. She'd look at him twice when she thought he wasn't watching and she even gave him a huge, rather passionate, kiss which caused his mother to raise her eyebrows.

The image wouldn't leave his head: *Wandwilla*, welded together with Beth as one.

It almost happened.

Flex.

He began taking short walks about the castle, his mother and father at his side. His mother made few bones about her feelings in the aftermath of the attack. "Kay, you will never see Lady Sammidoran again, am I understood?"

"But why? Sam didn't attack me. She offered me the White Emilia and I accepted. I am bound to her via Trial and I must continue when I am able."

Sygillis spoke in a calm and dispassionate voice. "You will not proceed, Kay. She and her House are lucky you survived, for they would all be dead had you not. I would have killed every one of them. You will never see her again, am I understood? You shall begin seeing new ladies in the Firth House, all carefully interviewed and screened by me first. I have a young lady already lined up for you next week."

"I'm not interested. Mother, I promised Sam I'd be true to her Trials. She is counting on me."

Again, Sygillis' voice was icy and deadly calm; Kay wished she'd be yelling. "That is one promise you shall not keep. I have spoken."

"Mother . . ."

"I have spoken, Kay."

And they continued their walk, Kay stewing.

✳   ✳   ✳   ✳   ✳

He made up with his cousin Sarah. He'd been angry with her for her rude treatment of Sam and for being partially responsible for provoking the horrible fight he'd had with her prior to being attacked.

He remembered seeing Sarah sitting there in the chair, beside herself with grief, her devotion as best friend and cousin tested and proved.

She came one afternoon, meekly opening the door to his room walking over and sitting on his bed, neither of them saying anything, their body language doing all the talking.

"I'm so sorry," Sarah's body said as she sat there. *"For all of this. Forgive me."*

"It's all right," Kay's responded.

And they embraced.

After that, Sarah and Phillip came to see him often, the three of them sitting in his room with the curtains to the grand windows thrown open like they were ten years old again. Tired of holos, card and vid games, they started doing their correspondence together. They all had a lot and it took all day to catch up. Even Kay, who usually had little correspondence because Sam had been stealing it, had letters from ladies from all over wishing him well.

Sam, wherever she was, was a little too busy to be stealing letters at the moment.

Sarah, still feeling bad for her role in all of this, doted on Kay, fetching snacks from the kitchens with regularity and fluffing his pillows whether they needed it or not.

As Kay worked on his pile, he remembered the faded note sitting in his dresser drawer. "You know, the other day I thought, just for a moment, that I could read that note."

"This one? The weird one, right?" Sarah asked. She got it out of the drawer. She looked at it for a moment, lighting her Sight. "I can't see anything—just a blur."

She brought it back to Kay's bed, its pages messy with smeared ink. Phillip looked at it. "Hmmm, I can't see anything either. What did it say?"

Kay looked at the note. "It said my name; then, it said something about a warning. I didn't have time to look at the rest."

Beth . . . Wandwilla . . .

Sarah looked at it again with interest. She loved a good mystery. "A warning? That sounds creepy. Can you see anything now?"

Kay shook his head. The note was an indecipherable mess as always. "Nope. Just the same as before. This note came with the dried White Emilia flower, remember that? As Sam put me to Trial, she placed a necklace of White Emilia around my neck and said something about it being tradition."

Kay sat there looking at the note, wondering what it had to tell him.

* * * * *

Time passed and Kay had mostly healed. His blood was back to normal and no longer had to take daily doses of Cynth. He was eating solid food again. Davage and Sygillis were due to leave in their starship, the *New Faith*, two days hence, and Sygillis didn't want to go—she wanted to stay home with her son, but Davage talked her into coming. Kay was fine. The numerous Bark dogs patrolling the Grove and castle grounds found nothing. No sign of Lady Sammidoran or the phantom fleshless attackers Kay claimed had harmed him. Time for life to continue.

* * * * *

Lord Davage called Kay, Sarah and Phillip into his study near the lovely Palantine Courtyard in the northern wing of the castle.

Davage sat behind his age-old desk. It was piled high with scrolls and books. Davage had never had much time for technology, and his study was devoid of holo terminals, insta-types and so forth. The room was huge and multi-leveled, with the walls lined with thick books and shelved mementos. Portraits of Countess Sygillis and the children were everywhere. A Silver tech cat named Whiskers, whom Lady Poe had made for Davage some years ago, prowled the upper reaches on the constant lookout for StT's. A large over-stuffed chair sat to the side of Davage's desk. It was the chair Kay's mother usually sat in, though it was empty now. Through the large window, the distant village and the sea beyond could be seen. The *New Faith* sat parked in the bay on its pylons like a big blob. As usual Davage was in his wonderful blue Fleet uniform, his hat and coppery CARG resting in their usual place behind his desk.

"Well," Davage began, "we're due to sortie again in a few days and it's always good to see my son and my favorite nephew and niece right before leaving." He looked at Sarah and took in her blue-haired features. "Sarah, I must say—and I'm sure you've heard it before—as you mature into a beautiful young lady, you are the image of your grandmother, Countess Hermilane. Looking at you sitting there, it's like seeing my mother in the flesh all over again."

Sarah smiled. "Truly, Uncle?"

"Indeed. Even your shade of blue hair is the same. Astounding."

Davage turned to Phillip. "And, Phillip, what a fine young man you've become. Everything that's good about my sister and your father, Lord Peter, is doubly so in you."

"Thank you, Uncle."

"I've also heard you've grown into an amazing pilot. Is that true?"

"I really can't say, sir. I do enjoy flying."

Davage laughed. "Can you out fly my little girl, Hathaline?"

Phillip, humble as always, shrugged. "Well, I . . . Lady Hathaline has amazing talent."

"I see. Well, if you ever want to join the Fleet, your place is assured. Lord Phillip of Blanchefort, a fine junior helmsman on some lucky ship—I can see it now."

Davage then turned to Kay. "And Kay, how are you feeling this morning?"

"I'm fine, Father."

"Any pain?"

"A little, nothing to bother with."

Davage stood, turned, and went to the window. Outside it was a typical dark blue, sunny day. The sea beyond was cold and calm. "Your mother is down in the village attending to business at the factories right now, had the whole fall collection tucked under her arm when she left. 'Madam Thimble', as they used to call her, is at it again with her designs and swatches. I still recall when she sacked all my designers and took over operations herself. I thought that was the end of our family business; but no, she has done a masterful job and made us proud. Her designs are even worn on Hoban of all places, most amazing." He paused. "I wanted to take this time and talk to you, Kay, and to you as well, Sarah and Phillip, in private."

Still staring out the window, Davage continued. "Kay, I want to know what you are planning to do about the Trial Lady Sammidoran set to you."

Kay sat quiet for a moment. "Father, Mother forbade me to . . ."

Davage turned from the window and stared at him. The gold ivy and stars embroidered on his collar glinted in the light.

Kay swallowed, unable to lie to his father. "I am going to continue the Trial, Father. I am going to follow it and allow it to lead me where it will. I promised Sam, and I believe in her. She's counting on me, and I'll not fail her. I love her, Father."

Davage smiled. "I thought as much. Your mother and I have much discussing to do regarding Lady Sammidoran's status here at the castle. I'm sure you understand. She is most angry, as she loves you very much, Kay. I, however, am not as ready to convict Lady Sammidoran as she is. I am not convinced the attack on you was created by her in the least. I, too, believe in her, and in you, Kay."

Sarah spoke up. "But, Uncle, Kay's admitted that Sam said the Trial could be deadly. Kay could die should he proceed."

Davage turned to Sarah. "I've been told by your mother that you like stories, Sarah. Tales of all those old Vith heroes and what not. All the niceties that show up in earnest in the daily Posts."

"Yes, Uncle, I do."

"Then you'll know that a common theme in many of those old stories is a Vith hero facing death. Fighting a monster, performing a deed of some sort—it happened all the time back then, and it still does today. Stories are still being created. There are still Vith heroes. Sometimes, when you're a member of a Great Blue Household like this one, you're expected to act like a Blue Lord, and that sometimes means facing death."

"You cannot be serious, Uncle," she said.

"It sounds a bit bizarre, I know, but there it is. And don't get me wrong. A fair contest in which death is a *possible* outcome is a far cry from what happened to Kay in the Grove—that was outright sadism and attempted murder. And I cannot believe Lady Sammidoran is capable of such a thing. She loves him very much; that's very plain to see. From what Kay has said, she offered him multiple opportunities to bow out, and he chose not to. He promised to see the Trials through to the end. He chose to face death, for her, and he is going to live up to that promise as best he can. For that, I am very proud of him. That is what Blancheforts do. Just so I know, Kay, what is this Trial specifically?"

"She didn't specify. She presented me with the White Emilia and then said the Trial would consist of three distinct stages, each presided over by a Judge."

"A Judge?"

"She created three bizarre creatures using something she called the NIGHTMARE and said they were the Judges of the Trials."

Davage considered that a moment. "Hmmm, the NIGHTMARE is the LosCapricos weapon of the House of Monama. It's a hairpin if I'm not mistaken, and Monama women are said to be able to conjure up creations using shadow material with it. She didn't say what the object of each stage is?"

"She didn't. She climbed into one of the creatures—it was a gigantic statue-man and sealed herself inside."

"That's a weird thing to do," Sarah said. "Wish I could have seen that."

"I think she was trying to protect herself from the same creatures which attacked me. She said they were after her . . . and, before the skinless woman went to work on me she swore she was going to get Sam. I will see that monster again, Father, and next time things will be different I swear it."

"All in good time, Kay. The need for revenge is a parlor guest who will never leave your premises until dully seen, trust me," Davage said. "Let it sit and wait."

Davage paused and placed a hand on some of the old books piled on his desk. "I've been doing some reading about Shadow tech males—a fascinating subject, really, but flawed with a lack of concrete scientific data. It appears that, even in our modern League, we really don't know much about them as they are quite rare. And, it appears the Sisters and the Science Ministry, as well, have been somewhat delinquent in pursuing the subject further."

He pointed at a huge brown book sitting on his desk. "This book right here. The Sisters wouldn't be happy if they knew we had this book."

"What is it?" Sarah asked, brimming with interest in the forbidden.

"It's a book of Xaphan Cabalism. A lot of poppycock, if I'm being honest; however, there's also a good bit of useful knowledge to be had if one chooses to examine the information in the proper prism. And, Xaphan Cabalists appear to be the preeminent authority on Shadow tech males." He gave the book a rap with his knuckles. "Do you know that a Shadow tech female, like your mother, and yours, Sarah and Phillip, cannot detect a Shadow tech male? They must rely on imperfect technology; that's why your mother never knew it. We had you tested as an infant, but apparently, as we see with you, Kay, one test is not enough. Apparently many tests are needed, or possibly a better test needs to be developed. Samaritan Bethrael has repeatedly requested that she be allowed to test you, Kay, in order to increase the Hospitaler's knowledge."

"She wants to test me, Father?"

"Yes, and, if you wish to participate, that's your choice; however, I think you should give her a wide berth for the time being, Kay. She seems to have developed quite a crush on you."

Sarah laughed.

Phillip, interested, spoke up. "I have read, Uncle, that Shadow tech females—mothers excluded, of course—cannot resist the touch of a Shadow tech male. And that immunity must also pass to close relatives, as Kay has touched my mother's Silver tech many times."

Davage smiled, clearly recalling the incident in Kay's bedroom. "Yes, mothers and relatives excluded, we can only thank Creation for that, can't we? And, as far as not being able to resist a Shadow tech male's touch, it seems that notion has been validated, as I saw Beth having a bit of a . . . problem . . . as Kay touched her Silver tech. I'll say no more on the subject."

Kay thought back, the feeling of Beth all over him returned.

"For that very reason, the Black Hats go to great lengths to monitor the location and whereabouts of Shadow tech males. When they discover one, they try to abduct and hold them in stasis. Others, of lesser value, they simply kill. Apparently, the Spectres were created to assist the Black Hats in this ongoing search for Shadow tech males and keep them under heel. I must advise the three of you to keep this matter strictly under the cuff, for Kay's sake. Agreed?"

Sarah and Phillip looked solemn. "Of course, Uncle," Sarah responded.

"Additionally, it is speculated that Shadow tech males have a high degree of resistance to physical damage and the deadly effects of blood poisoning." Davage paused and looked a bit sad. "Your status as a Shadow tech male saved you, Kay. You were disemboweled and at Apex blood poisoning—the worst readings I've ever seen. We tried using one of your Aunt Poe's wondrous Silver tech Fins fish to heal your terrible wounds, but it didn't work. It just sank into the wounds and vanished. Apparently, you must have absorbed it somehow. I have already prayed my thanks to our ancestors, and to fate, that you were so ideally equipped to ward off such an attack."

Davage continued. "And, one final thing, Shadow tech males have strange Gifts—your abilities regarding Shadow tech will react with your Gifts and make them act in unexpected ways."

Kay considered his father's words. "I doubt that, Father. I do recall seeing some things in amber in my bedroom as Beth and I . . ." He cut himself off. "But only for a moment, then it was gone. I never thought I had the Sight, though Sam insisted I did. One of her manifestations claimed it was the embodiment of my Sight and was very angry with me, said I'd squandered my Gift."

"Ah, yes, amber. My reading tells me such a thing is called the 'Dark Sight'. Don't let the name fool you. It simply means that you see things in an amber sort of tint, and your eyes don't glow, as is usually the case with the Sight. According to the text, the Dark Sight is very pliable as far as time goes, and you should be able to see very far into the past, present and future. I can see a few seconds into the future and several minutes into the past, but that's all. You, Kay, might be able to look back and forth in time as far as you like— wondrous, really." He smiled but looked a little sad. "You do have the Sight, Kay, it's just an odd, different sort of Sight. I wish I had known such a thing, been more informed. We could have been exploring your Sight together for years now, and I feel that I have failed you in this regard."

Kay sat up and tried to reassure Lord Davage that that wasn't the case. He continued. "I'll tell you, when I was boy, not too much younger that you are now, I was frightened by my Sight. The things I saw, day in and day out, were things that I didn't necessarily want to see. It's easy to focus on the bad, on the frightening, and not notice the good, to not see it. Lady Sammidoran mentioned having to put you to pain. I think she said that because she wanted your Sight activated. I think she knew or was aware of your status, Kay. Monamas tend to know things that no one else can. The Dark Sight, according to the text, exacts a hefty price. It requires a strong and sustained jolt of severe pain to get it started. It might sound a bit morbid, but a healthy and controlled pain-creation session can sometimes be a positive thing."

Davage approached his son. "You'll have to work with your Gift, accept it for what it is, and with control, with discipline, you will begin to filter out the bad and see more of the good. Then, you will truly begin to appreciate the wondrous Gift you've been given. I promise you that. My only regret is that you will, most likely, have to discover those wonders on your own."

"Father?" Kay asked.

Davage stood up and went to the window again. He gazed down at the village below. The long tail of his blue hair sat flat against the center of his back.

"Your mother will be back soon, and we haven't long to talk. My son, are you aware of something called the Wellerman's March?"

Sarah's eyes lit up. "I am! I know what it is!"

Kay, who really didn't know, rolled his eyes.

Davage laughed. "Well then, Sarah, please inform your cousin."

"It's a youth initiation. Every Great Lord, as they come of age, is supposed to undertake one."

"Yes, correct, Sarah, well done," Davage said. "All Great Lords take the Wellerman's March at some point in their young adulthood. It usually is a journey that takes a fair amount of time to complete, sometimes several months, and takes one far away from where they start. Sometimes, it is nothing more than a grand, elaborate errand—the Grenvilles are famous for those—but, other times, it can be a dangerous, possibly deadly, labor. And so, Kabyl, Lord of Blanchefort, I suppose the time has come for you to go on yours, and, apparently the stakes couldn't be higher. This Trial for Lady Sammidoran is your Wellerman's March."

"Sam's life and mine."

"And," Davage stated as cheerfully as he could to Sarah and Phillip, "if I know you two like I think I do, I am certain you will want to go with him as you have a stake in this as well. This is your Wellerman's, too."

Phillip and Sarah lit up.

"I'm glad. I think that the three of you, with your various talents and strengths, can accomplish anything. I mentioned, Sarah, how you resemble your grandmother. She, too, went on a Wellerman's once—one of the few Ladies of Standing to do so. I'm certain such an added distinction will please you."

Sarah smiled and blushed.

"The three of you are uniquely placed for this adventure to come. Not only are you family, you're best friends as well, and that means something. In the years to come, no matter how far life takes you from each other, you will always have this—this Wellerman's March that you shared together, when the three of you took on the universe as one and came through triumphant. That is a bond, a closeness that will never be diminished or intruded upon."

They sat there listening in rapt attention.

"I will ask, Kay, that you wait until your mother and I leave on our next sortie in a few days. Knowing your mother, if she catches wind of this, she will don a bodysuit and tear off to try and stop you herself. What is your first destination?"

"Xandarr. The Judge, with Sam inside of it, said I was to be trained there immediately."

Davage approached Kay. "Training? It seems Lady Sammidoran is trying to maximize your potential for success. Well then, it's time for your gift. It's tradition for a Lord undertaking the Wellerman to receive a gift. I was hoping to save it for later, when you fully come of age, but it's obvious that that time has already come and gone. Look at you, a man already. And you, Phillip and Sarah, have also grown into fine young people—how time moves on. You shall have a gift as well, though I hope your mother will not be angry with me. Certainly, my gift will come in handy in your adventures to come, and I want you to have it."

The three looked at each other, and then at Davage expectantly.

"I shan't make it easy for you, however," he said. "This is a test of Sight, Kay, and of Strength and of thought, and it's a difficult one, so do be ready. Here are your instructions. Go to the southern end of the castle and locate the chapel of Lord Demophalon. When you get there, take a knee and reflect a bit. You will know what to do then. And remember that you each get one, no more; if you take more than that, I will know and will be most angry."

"Yes, Uncle!" Sarah and Phillip agreed.

They stood, and Davage embraced all three of them in turn. "Ah, my family," he said, "a better gift I could not have been given. Now go, set to it, and remember, do not leave the castle until we launch; otherwise, your toughest test, no doubt, will be surviving your mother's wrath."

5—The Old Poltava

After the meeting in the study, the three made their way to the southern end of the castle. They were eager to receive the gift that Davage had offered to them.

The problem was finding it. The chapel of Lord Demophalon? Kay knew of no such place.

"So, come on," Sarah said, her eyes wide with anticipation, her duster fluttering. "Think, people. Where's this chapel?"

"I really don't know, Sarah," Kay said hurrying to keep up, his black and purple coattails flying behind him. "Phillip, have you heard of such a place?"

"I know of Lord Demophalon, a Vith fighter of old, but I wasn't aware of his having a chapel dedicated in his honor."

The southern end of the castle was made up of a number of huge, cathedral-like structures, five of them in all. Each cathedral was dedicated to a Vith hero of the past. The largest was dedicated to Emmira, the Vith Maiden and progenitor of the Blanchefort line. There was one dedicated to Holt of the Mountain, Subra of the Mark, and two cathedrals for Maserfeld, Kay's great grandfather. One wasn't enough; apparently Maserfeld was not only a brigand but a grand narcissist as well.

The three stumped in a hurried fashion through the various cathedrals, their footfalls amplifying and echoing through the huge spaces. The local rectors, who tended them during the day, wanted to throw the lot of them out but couldn't. Kay being the next Lord of Blanchefort couldn't be excluded from his own castle. In the muted stained-glass light, they looked around.

"Who're we looking for again?" Sarah asked, her loud voice reverberating.

"Lord Demophalon," Phillip replied.

They had been through all of the cathedrals and chapels, not finding what they were seeking. They found lots of chapels crammed in all over, but none dedicated to the right lord.

"Perhaps his name is an anagram, a puzzle of some sort?" Phillip suggested.

"No, my father hates those."

After a bit, Kay had a thought. "Wait a moment. I suppose, since I am now given lease to explore the disturbing depths of my Sight, such as it is, that I should try to use it to discover this chapel. What do you think? Father did say this was a test of Sight."

"Sure, sounds fine," Sarah said. "And hurry up! I want to see our present. It will be bad—real bad—to have to walk back to Uncle's study and tell him his task was too adult for us." Kay and Phillip agreed.

Finding an out of the way pew in Subra's cathedral, they sat and Kay took his hat off.

He took a deep breath. "Before I start—there isn't any need for you two to do this. Are you sure both of you want to join me in whatever is to come? It could be dangerous."

"I ought to pop you, Kay," Sarah said, indignant.

"We are with you in this," Phillip said. "Besides, this is why we come up here—for fun, for adventure. You, Kay, are fun to hang out with, as they say."

Kay smiled, grateful for their presence and help. "All right, then we do this together. Here I go."

Kay sat back and relaxed. He closed his eyes and tried to release the amber realms that were all around him.

Nothing happened. There was only the muted light of the stained glass windows, and the small sounds of the cathedral amplified up to loud bangs and thumps.

"Just relax," Sarah said lighting her Sight and looking at him with blue beams. "See."

The Rector charged forward holding a candle snuffer. "No Gifts in this place of worship, young lady! I do not care who you are. I'll have you on my knee!"

Sarah waved him off. He turned and walked away, cursing.

Kay sat there. "No, it's no good; I can't do it."

Phillip chimed in. "Well, as your father said, you might need a good dose of pain to kick it off. I hate to say it, but that is probably the case."

Kay looked at Sarah and held out his hand. "Sarah, take my hand and start squeezing."

"You want me to squeeze your hand, Kay? I'm not going to hurt your hand."

"I'm not saying break it. Just squeeze enough to make it hurt. What's the big deal? You've never had a hard time causing me pain before."

Sarah took his hand, and Kay felt her grip turn hard and stony— the Gift of Strength. He felt a dull beacon of pain well up from his hand through his arm. His joints gave a little pop; then, he was really feeling it.

"Do you want me to stop, Kay?" Sarah asked.

Through the stony-handed wall of pain, it was easy, so easy, for Kay to fade away. The cathedral turned to amber, and things appeared to slow down around him. Glancing to his side, Sarah and Phillip appeared to be asleep. They were sitting, stiff and unmoving. He could see the cathedral filling and emptying over and over, day and night. He thought he saw his parents strolling alone up the aisle way, hand in hand, in love as always, and the brief image warmed his heart.

He then saw his mother flat on her back on the altar giving birth, a group of Hospitalers in attendance and a chorus of Sisters assisting Mother in the process.

No, on closer inspection, it wasn't his mother; it was Sarah giving birth. But, that was silly, as Sarah had never given birth. It must be Countess Hermilane, his grandmother, giving birth. Creation, she certainly did look like Sarah as everyone had always commented on; no kidding. They even did their hair the same way.

Two girls in Blanchefort gowns and a finely dressed gentleman, who must have been Sadric, his grandfather, watched the birth. The two girls were Pardock and Poe, his aunts. He was witnessing the birth of his father. Again, he felt touched by the scene. Perhaps, as his father had mentioned, his Sight, properly used and tempered, wasn't such a bad thing after all.

Continuing, the scene accelerated into a blur, moving back, back, back through time, through the ages. Suddenly, the cathedral was gone, and Kay was standing on a rocky bluff overlooking a drop to the sea far below, the sky big and cloudy overhead.

Looking back, he saw the castle, though a much smaller version of it—just a modest pile of rocks on a wind-swept bluff. He recognized it as the Firth House, the tearoom in the Palatine courtyard.

And something was moving in the sky above the clouds, something big and round like a large moon blotting out the sun.

The Elders—Kay was seeing one of the twenty-five Elders floating in the sky, now long gone in modern times. He felt humbled and a bit frightened.

Looking to his right, he saw a small chapel that was partially underground. There was a small plaque before the chapel, written in Vith, which Kay had been taught to read. The plaque read: Tomb of Demophalon.

He saw a group of ragged blue-haired people come running to the chapel. They appeared panicked and were moving about in a disordered clump. Their blue hair was filthy. The Vith. He was seeing the Vith, his ancestors. A few men and women took up a defensive position. Just then, several huge spider-like creatures appeared and began engaging the blue haired Vith in a savage battle. No, they weren't spiders—they were odd, eight and ten-armed females, all beautiful and pale-skinned, long-haired and fit, easily ten feet tall.

They savagely battled the defenders, killing a few, while one or two of their number fell badly wounded. They slung the dead over their slender but powerful shoulders and began a retreat.

One of them, a ten-armed one, looked back and seemed to see Kay. She began moving in his direction at speed. He noticed as she approached that she had five pairs of breasts to match her five pairs of arms.

She was on him and seized him in a huge, feminine hand. He could feel the warm hand, the soft but somewhat rubbery skin, and strength beyond compare.

He cried out, and the vision was gone.

When he opened his eyes, he was back in Subra's Cathedral with Sarah, Phillip and the angry Rector looking down at him. His hand was throbbing.

"I want the three of you out of this holy place, now!" the Rector demanded, holding his candle-snuffer in a threatening manner.

"What happened?" Kay asked.

"You fell into a trance for a second, then you cried out, and I let go of your hand," Sarah said.

The Rector gave them no peace, so they shuffled out of the cathedral into the hallway where he slammed the doors shut behind them.

∗　∗　∗　∗　∗

They found a quiet alcove in which to talk. Sarah was dying, as she was into this hard.

"Well?" Sarah asked. "What did you see?"

"I saw it," he said proudly. "I saw Demophalon's chapel. It's buried under Maserfeld's cathedral, I think. Yes, that should be right if I'm gauging the distance correctly."

"Which one?" Phillip asked. "He's got two."

"The bigger one."

"How's your hand?"

Kay made a fist a few times. "Hurts, but nothing's broken."

He told them how he seemed to go back in time and everything he saw—the Vith, the strange gigantic creatures, and how one saw him and attacked.

"Those are the Haitathe, the giants of old," Phillip said. "You say one of them *saw* you?"

"Yes, she grabbed me, and that's when I cried out." He thought back. "I saw the Elders, Phillip. I saw one floating in the sky like a great moon. It was humbling. How I wish they were still here with us."

Phillip was shocked and a bit envious. "That must have been something to see."

Sarah was rather impatient. "I'm sure it was inspiring. So, you say you saw Demophalon's chapel? Where was it, again?"

Kay looked around. "It was where Maserfeld's Cathedral currently is, I think. The big one."

They exited the alcove and made their way in that direction.

They entered the cathedral; again, it was a large, somber place in muted light. They looked around. Kay tried to get his bearings.

He pointed at the altar, which was, as near as he could guess, situated approximately where he'd seen Demophalon's chapel in the past.

They approached the altar and looked around, testing it, pushing and pulling; it was a good thing the Rector of this cathedral didn't appear to be around for he wouldn't be too keen on all of this. Eventually, the large altar moved a tad.

"Give me some room," Sarah announced. She rolled up her sleeves and exerted herself to Full Strength. "Wait!" she cried. "I'm not allowed to use the Gift of Strength indoors. Remember? Mother said so."

"I'm certain Mother will forgive you this one time, Sarah," Phillip said.

She was dubious. For all her bluster, Sarah was basically a good kid who did as her mother asked. "Sarah," Kay said, "as the next Lord of the castle, I grant you permission, on this occasion, to power up indoors, provided you don't tear anything up."

She nodded and accepted Kay's proclamation as valid and allowed herself to power up to Full Strength. She leaned into the face of the altar like she was wrestling with it and strained. Eventually, it moved enough to uncover a small passage. They lowered Sarah in and, lighting her Sight, she crawled off into the dark.

"What do you see, Sarah?" Kay called.

Down below, the beams of her blue light panned about this way and that. "I see the remains of an old chapel. It's pretty neat. Wow!"

"We've no time for that, Sarah."

"Hey!" she called back a moment or two later. "It's a dead end."

"You sure?" Kay called down to her. "Look around; can you Sight through it?"

"I can't see through things yet," she called back, her voice echoing a little. "There's nothing, just a solid wall at the far end of the chapel."

Kay and Phillip thought for a minute or two. "I know this is it," he said.

"Phillip, get down here and help me!" she called up.

"Just a moment. I believe your father mentioned something about taking a knee and reflecting," Phillip added. "This is a test of thought, as well as Sight and Strength."

To the far right, in an alcove, was a large painted icon of Maserfeld, their great grandfather. There he was, tall, bearded, and tipsy with ale mug in hand. Beneath his icon was a kneeling bench. Phillip walked over to the bench, considered it for a moment, and knelt down.

"Hey!" Sarah cried from under the altar. "What did you do? The wall just opened a bit!"

Kay could hear her rustling around in the dark, then:

"Hey!! Hey, you two, get in here!! You won't believe this!! Hurry up!!"

Kay found a heavy bust of Maserfeld and put it on the bench. He and Phillip then plunged into the dark under the altar. There, at the end of a short crawl, was Demophalon's ancient buried chapel, the same one he'd seen in his Sight, only now covered up and forgotten. At the far end was a hidden chamber, about ten by ten feet, lit up by the blue light of Sarah's Sight.

Inside, mounted on shelves, were about three dozen Blanchefort PtVa pistols.

The Blanchefort PtVa was a classic firearm, designed four hundred years earlier by Posnam, Lord of Blanchefort. It was a brilliant design, being fairly small, with a huge punch and an infallible firing mechanism. Its workings were still copied in modern weapons like the popular Grenville 40. The 'Poltava', as it was nicknamed, was once the lynchpin of the Blanchefort fortune, factories in the village churning them out in quantity to a clamoring market. Lord Sadric, however, despised the practice of firearm production and disbanded it, converting the factories into fabric and textile manufacturing sites. He went a step further and destroyed the back inventory of Poltavas. Then, he bought up all the surplus inventories he could find and smashed those as well; thus, the weapon virtually ceased to exist overnight. The Poltava, now rare and much sought after, was a collector's dream and worth a massive amount on the open market.

And here were dozens of them: all small, short barreled, easily fitting in the palm of the hand. And these weren't production, off-the-line models either; these were all masterpieces, each one enameled and filigreed, each one a work of art. Here, in this hidden chamber, was a cache worth a king's ransom several times over.

The three sat there feasting their eyes. Sarah, after carefully looking at each, selected a dark blue one, the handle inlaid with gold and serpentine. She held it in her hand, feeling its perfect balance. "This one's mine," she proclaimed.

Phillip took less time, picking out a green and brown specimen on an upper shelf. "Why that one?" Sarah asked eyeing the color.

"Don't know," Phillip replied. "I just liked this one. Maybe it's karma."

Kay found one that was red with gray highlights that he admired and pulled it off the shelf.

"No, no," Sarah said. "Not that one." She took a purple one highlighted in black pearl. "This one, Kay; it suits you."

Kay looked at it. "I don't want that one. I want this one."

Sarah wasn't giving up. "I really think this one's for you. It even matches your hair. Come on and take it. Just like Phillip said—it's karma."

Kay looked it over one more time. On the reverse grip, there was an enameled image, in lapis and opal, of a dragonfly-like bug with brassy wings.

He remembered the Parafly in the courtyard whose buzzing saved his life. That was the deciding factor. Smiling, he took the purple one, and it settled into his hand like it had always been there. Such a small, elegant weapon with a brutally powerful, infallible punch. Even quiet and unloaded, it made him feel secure knowing it was there. He put the red one back on its shelf.

"Good choice," Sarah said admiring his weapon. "I knew it suited you."

Sarah and Phillip had already placed theirs into pockets within their black dusters. Carefully, they exited the room and climbed back out of the altar. They moved it back into place and returned the bust to where it was, sealing up the chamber of riches.

*   *   *   *   *

After dinner, they went back to Kay's room. Sarah had gotten a box of standard ammunition from somewhere and was loading her blue Poltava. Kay and Phillip got theirs out, and she loaded them as well.

Kay walked to his dresser and got the old IN LOCK note out as Sarah slid the bullets into the clip. There it was, faded and illegible as ever. He went back to the bed and sat down.

Sarah eyed the note. "What, you want me to squeeze your hand again?" she asked wanting to know what the note said.

"Go ahead," Kay said holding his hand out. Sarah took it and began squeezing. In an amber pall of pain, the note reverted in time, the letters shrinking back down into their original form.

It read:

To: Kabyl, Lord of Blanchefort
BE WARNED:

For some time, my 72ⁿᵈ grandchild, Sammidoran, has been in love with you, and she, against my advice, is unable to compose herself and stay away. I am certain you already know that. Although you are the son of my cherished friends from the north, I have advised her to forget you and keep her heart closer to home, not only for her sake, but for yours as well.

I understand why my granddaughter feels as she does. You are, without question, a fine young man, however there are things you must know, and my granddaughter, because of our traditions, cannot mention them to you. As I shall, no doubt, be dead by the time you receive this letter, I shall speak for her. May the gods have mercy on my House.

I have included a flower you call White Emilia. It is a common plant that grows near our home. It has a tendency to kill insects that come to drink its sweet nectar. Only the right insect at the right time may drink without fear. It is symbolic of our Trials of Love. My granddaughter, should your relationship become generally known, will have to put you to Trial, as is our tradition, and, therefore, try to kill you. Your father has an understanding of our Trials, but I do not think he fully appreciates their import or gravity. Know this—should you be presented with the White Emilia, and should you accept it—then you shall face death at the hands of my granddaughter. She will have power over the NIGHTMARE, which is magic that comes to us from the Gods of Jade and Sapphire. She will use the NIGHTMARE to create visions from her deepest fears and set them against you. She has no choice in the matter, it is our way. And she has much to be afraid of; we all do. The things that haunt Monama nightmares are truly horrific.

We, of the Lake, are a cursed people, watched and kept in chains. There are things unseen that hover over us, torment us, and compel us to do things not of our choosing. We have, for ages, been slaves to demons who step out of thin air and take us from our homes and turn us into monsters, Berserkacides, at their whim. My granddaughter loves you because of her visions—she dreamed of you for years prior to your birth. I have always suspected that our visions are sent to us by the demons that confound our existence. If my granddaughter saw you in the future, then I believe that is because the demons, for reasons unknown, WANTED her to see you, and, in her innocence, she fell in love and lost her heart to an Elder boy from the north. Alas, I believe the demons haunting us and the Horned God they worship now turn their attention to you, and, therefore, we, as their pawns, shall also be set against you as well. I see a future of blood where the gods turn their attention to this place and shrink from what they see. I see the possibility of the Sisterhood of Light coming to kill us, and I cannot wholly say that I blame them. My advice, Lord Blanchefort, is to avoid my granddaughter and stay out of the troubles of the House of Monama for as long as you can. The troubles are coming sure enough, but, perhaps, if you stay away, you can remain unaware for the length of your life and pass in bliss. I pray the gods that you and your family live long and safe, unhindered by our demons.

The world is a much more dangerous place than you realize.

You have been warned.

Do not accept the White Emilia.

> *Signed:*
> *Hortensia, Countess of Monama and Astralon*

Sarah sighed and let go of his hand. "I guess she's a little late with the info."

Kay sat there and tried to absorb the information. "A letter from Sam's grandmother? Watched by demons? Is that what attacked me in the Grove? That man and woman?"

"You did mention they popped out of thin air," Phillip said.

"Over this last winter, Sam did act in a peculiar fashion. Jumpy, looking around—acting like she was afraid of being watched." Kay thought about the note. "And, one time I tried to contact her in the chapel; instead of getting Sam, I heard a voice, an angry whisper that frankly gave me the chills. Was I speaking to a, demon? I don't want you two coming with me. I don't want you to be endangered," Kay said.

Ignoring him, Phillip took his now-loaded green and brown Poltava back, went to the window and stepped out onto the balcony. He looked up at the deep blue sky. "So, Kay, when are we leaving?"

"Did you not hear me?"

"And our first destination is Xandarr?" Phillip asked, still ignoring him.

"It is."

"How are we going to get to Xandarr, if I may ask?"

"I'm going to book passage. Standard transport—first class, of course."

"Forget that," Sarah said. "We're going in the *Goshawk*!"

Phillip came back in and headed to the door. "I better preflight it. The thing's twenty years old, you know."

Kay stood there. "Sarah, Phillip, I don't want you endangered. Your souls might be at risk."

Phillip smiled. "Come on, Kay, I'll need your help with the pre-flight."

Sarah and Kay stood and followed. He was glad they were coming. Despite his protests, he didn't want to do this alone.

✷   ✷   ✷   ✷   ✷

With the usual fanfare, the *New Faith* rose out of the cold water of the bay. Countess Sygillis hadn't wanted to go. She was normally an eager cosmic adventurer, but, with the attack on Kay so fresh in her mind, she clung to him. Bethrael of Moane wearing her winged, silver helmet, decided to go with them—a huge ship like the *New Faith* always needed good Hospitalers. She gave Kay a huge hug and whispered in his ear: "*You and me, anytime, anywhere, Kay.*" She let the tip of her tongue enter his ear. "*I can still feel you.*"

He knew exactly what she meant. He had a strange dream about her—that they were standing in a vast forest, and they came together, Kay feeling the ecstasy that he felt before when he touched her Silver tech.

In his dream, Beth held onto him, not letting go. She wrapped him up in Silver tech, and they were welded together, man and woman merging as one. They became some sort of vast tree-like creature with waving vine-like branches. Though a massive tree, it moved slightly every so often—twitching in a climax that was unending.

Kay woke and had to run to the bathroom. He'd never had such a dream. He had a thought that, on the *New Faith*, Beth was having a similar dream. He splashed himself, trying to calm down—trying to get the image of Beth and the tree out of his head, and everything went to amber again, all on its own.

Unable to control it, his Dark Sight uncoiled away from him, this time, shooting forward instead on falling into the past.

What he saw was terrifying. He saw that hideous man and woman again, swooning in depravity, *eating* him. He saw Lady Poe, his loving aunt, watching with approval—she having become an evil vision. He saw Sarah and monstrous Lady Kilos locked together in a fight to the death. He saw Paraflies everywhere, crawling, stinging.

He saw a smooth silvery creature with flippers and whiskers, head bowed, being led away in chains. Was that . . . Carahil?

His aunt and sister: monsters?

Carahil imprisoned?

He saw some sort of vast, dark space, marked by stone columns at regular intervals like a poorly lit, subterranean church or temple. At the front was a platform, and sitting on it was a large, deer-like creature with a tangled crown of antlers. Bodies burned all around it. It reveled in the burning.

The Horned God has his blood.

That evening, Kay was playing with Maser in the Grove. With Kay's help, Maser had built a massive fort somewhere deep in the green. It was nothing more than a conical pile of dirt about four feet high, but Maser, clumsy, filthy, beamed with happiness in the dimming light. He had a little yellow bucket that he was using to transport loads of dirt. Kay emptied the bucket and put it on Maser's head, like a helmet. The high clouds, tinged with twilight red, were ready to give way to an open pallet of stars, the brightest of which were just beginning to come out.

"I think I hear Phillip coming," Kay said. "And he's going to want to tear this fort down to the stones. Be ready to pummel him."

Maser picked up two handfuls of earth and was ready to throw. He had a big stupid grin on his face. Being so small, he still wore kid's clothes, a miniature version of his father's Fleet uniform, only it was one piece with a trapdoor on the bottom in case he soiled himself. With his mother gone, aloft in the *New Faith*, one of his nannies would be looking for him soon.

Kay was far too old to be playing in the dirt, but, he couldn't help himself. He loved roughhousing with his brother and his cousins and, for that matter, he was only twenty-two. He was still just a child, too.

Everybody seemed to forget that.

Lady Kilos strolled into the clearing, heading back to the castle for the evening. She was holding a handful of flowers she'd picked from the Ten Gardens. "Kay, there you are. We need to get Maser into the castle for the night."

She saw them playing in the mud. "Oh, for Creation's sake," she said looking at Kay in the dirt, disapproving. "What are you doing?"

"What's it look like, biscuit-face!" Kay said, noting Kilos" unfinished, puffy face still locked in her childhood.

She turned red with anger. "That was so mean! You know I hate that!" She dropped her flowers, put her hands to her face, and began to cry.

Immediately, Kay felt bad and jumped down off of the dirt mound. He thought of Ki's bloody gown, and how she had wept over him on his deathbed. "Hey, Ki, I didn't mean that. I'm sorry. Really, I'm sorry." Making sure to keep his muddy hands away from her green Blanchefort gown, he gave her a hug and, after a moment, she buried her face into his shoulder. "You can put my hair into your mouth, if you want, Ki," he said. "Remember how you used to do that?"

She laughed, and he helped her pick up her flowers. He looked at her, his little blue-haired sister. Though her face was puffy and unfinished, it didn't take much imagination to picture her as blossoming into a true beauty. Sam had predicted the future and said in five years her "Puffies" would be gone and she'd be a beautiful young woman. Soon, very soon, there would be gentlemen calling on her from all over the League, waiting to see her in the Firth House.

Sam also predicted she'd be taken by the enemy in 003256.

A monstrous Lady Kilos and Sarah of Blanchefort, fighting to the death . . . an evil Lady Poe watching with glee. He'd seen it. A dark vision where House Blanchefort and the League falls. Carahil in chains. It was in the future. How could this be?

"Sam is fine," Ki said.

"I have to believe so," he replied.

"She is Kay." She considered her words. "You know our great-grandmother Christiana was a Bloodstein witch, right? She had a secret collection of arcane books that are passed from the eldest female to the next. Aunt Pardock presented me with the collection a few years ago—she and mother thought I was old enough to have them. So there I was with all these, spell books" sitting around supposedly able to do all sorts of bizarre feats of magic."

"I remember you showing me those."

"Yes. They can do some pretty nasty things, but I'd never used them. No, I take that back. I did hex Lady Togstra with a case of uncontrollable profanity once after she spread a rumor about me."

Kay laughed. "Did it work?"

"Sure did, caused a real commotion, too."

"Well then, score one for our departed Bloodstein great-grandmother. Ever use them on Sarah?"

"Been tempted to, but no. Good thing, now that we're friends and all." Ki became serious. "There is a litany in one of the books that allows one to, look in" on another from afar if you have something personal of theirs; it's nothing overly specific, just general impressions and such. I have plenty of Sam's hair in my brushes, so I used a strand or two and spoke the litany."

"And what did you determine?"

"I determined that Sam is fine at the moment. She is in a safe place, though she cannot tarry in any one spot for too long. She sleeps inside of a metal man and dreams of you, Kay, and, as soon as she can, she will return. She is eager for that time."

Kay closed his eyes. "What an amazing sister I have. Thank you for this news, Ki. I've had to put Sam out of my thoughts as of late; if I hadn't, I'd be mad with worry. Now I can, at least, look to this Wellerman's March and be a little less troubled."

Maser climbed down from his mound of dirt and tugged on Kay's pants leg. Kay looked down at him.

"Can I come with you?" Maser said in his tiny kid's voice.

Kay knelt down and picked him up. With Kilos standing there and the sun setting, he felt like this was the last day of his childhood, the waning moments of his innocence. Tomorrow, the sun would rise, and he would be a man, the Lord of Blanchefort, with all of the worries and troubles that came with it.

The loaded Poltava in his coat emphasized the point.

"Hey, chief," he said to his brother. "I'll be back before you know it. Take care of our sister here, all right? You have to protect her while I'm gone. Can I count on you to do that?"

"Yeah."

Kilos stood there, and Kay thought he saw her begin to tear up. "The Wellerman's March can last a while so I'm told. Do you know when you'll be back?" she asked.

He realized how much he loved his sister, and his brother.

"No, I don't, Ki," he said softly. "I am going to take this march, and I am going to make sure that all the things you want, all that you hope for, come true. I know you are soon to be a fabulous beauty, just like you have always wanted to be."

Kilos reached out to him. "Then take my hand, Kay, and walk me back to the castle. Let's find Hath, so you can say goodbye to her, too."

Kay was about to take her hand when he remembered his own hands were muddy. "I don't want to get you dirty, sis."

"I don't care, Kay," she said. "I expect you to be careful on your journey. You are my brother, and I shall think of you every day until you return. I honestly can't recall the last time I told you that I love you. I suppose, being my brother, it should be understood, and I also suppose that saying it should be easy, but it's not. I love you, Kay."

"I love you too, Ki."

Kilos took his hand and, with Kay still holding Maser, they walked back to the castle, reveling in the last few minutes of Kay's childhood. The stars leapt out, unmindful of the scene below.

6—The Demon's Identity

Bright and early the next morning, Kay, Sarah and Phillip headed out to the black, bat-like *Goshawk* parked deep in the Grove. Xandarr was a two day flight away, so they told their mother, Lady Poe, who seemed rather tired, that they'd be gone on an outing for several days. She was, of course, full of questions, but Xandarr was now a League world, and the route to get there was well-patrolled. There was no danger. Additionally, the Blancheforts, due to their efforts in defeating the Black Hats twenty years ago, were well favored in the court of the King, Balor I and his queen Zoladerra. Lord Peter was actually quite excited—he wanted Phillip to test out some of the new gadgets they'd installed. They had checked the old ship over, and it came through just fine, a tried and true design, sturdy, fast and reliable.

Lady Poe, looking haggard, kissed both of her children and gave Kay a large hug.

Carrying their bags packed with a few days changes of clothes and a healthy supply of food, mostly snacks, they headed out for the ship. Kay, initially wanting to go alone, was glad for the company. He wasn't looking forward to the trip—space was not a pleasant thing for him.

They were so far out past the Ten Gardens that the castle was low and far off in the distance. Only the tallest of spires were visible over the horizon, like a cityscape of tall buildings. Nearby, beyond the walled outer-rim of the Grove, a gallery of steep mountains loomed—the vanguard of the northern Vith range, a bumpy carpet of sheer mountains that extended for thousands of square miles all the way to Minz in the east and south to the Tartan headlands. Mt. Vith, its peak bathed in clouds, rose like a gnarled finger to the east, just the first of many towering, monolithic peaks lurking in the range.

∗　∗　∗　∗　∗

The *Goshawk,* sitting there in the tall grass like a bat sunning itself, wings outstretched, was over twenty years old and was once used by Peter of Ruthven in his alleged pirating activities with the Duke of Oyln. In the intervening years, the Duke had, allegedly, given up pirating, instead going on the occasional space-faring adventure with his Duchess, Torrijayne of Oyln. He also had built a faster more modern ship called the *Windhawk,* which was a true marvel, and sold his obsolete *Goshawk* fleet to Balor I who used them as a template for a new Xandarr Starfleet. The ships now sat in a lavish park on Xandarr, where they were venerated as the Defenders of the Planet during the Black Hat cleansing scourge of twenty years ago. King Balor was always hoping to add the *Seeker* to his collection when she was retired, but she still flew, soaring through the skies with Captain Gona of St. Paris in command.

Peter of Ruthven, however, had bought his old ship from the Duke and kept it in perfect working order. While he was courting Lady Poe, he used it to take her on exotic outings, the fast black ship sailing at speed too far off places, and it was said that Phillip and Sarah were conceived on one of the couches in the rear area of the ship while on one of these frequent outings. It was a prized hot-rod that Peter kept for special occasions.

The *Goshawk* was a black, barrel-shaped vessel, about fifty feet tall and a hundred and fifty feet long. It had a large, swept-back wing with no tail. It was agile and fast, small enough to be able to land just about anywhere, but large enough to support several people in space fairly comfortably. It was brimming with once illegal scanning technology, now commonplace in the modern League. The pilot section at the front of the ship was flared out a bit, giving the whole thing a rather bat-like appearance from a distance. It had a few small crew quarters and a fair-sized cargo hold. Lord Peter had removed the old shock-skids and replaced them with a knobby set of cranked, semi-retractable wheels. With all of the modifications Peter and his gifted sons Milos and Phillip had made to the ship, it was twice as fast as it once was—a true speedster.

∗　∗　∗　∗　∗

When they got to the clearing where the *Goshawk* was parked, its black metal surface crawled with shiny, rust-colored life. They could see their reflections on an undulating surface.

It buzzed.

Sarah gawked at the scene open-mouthed. "Look—Paraflies!" she exclaimed. "I've read about these. The whole planet's infested with them."

Phillip squinted to get a better look, but kept his distance. "I heard they're supposed to be stowaways from another planet and are running rampant."

"Lt. Kilos seems to think they're from Bazz," Kay said.

"Creation, they're huge, but I read they're not supposed to be dangerous," Phillip replied.

"No, but look at them—probably could sting your eyes out," Sarah said, rather morbidly.

Kay remembered the cloud of them, buzzing as he was attacked in the clearing. And, he remembered the one Parafly that helped save his life as he struggled to return to the castle afterward. He admired the shiny carpet of their coppery wings and wasn't worried in the slightest.

"They're not going to sting you, Sarah. I consider them good luck."

"Yeah," she replied. "If they decide to come after you, good luck."

After a moment, the huge insects took flight, buzzed in the air in a swirling, droning mass, and departed to the north.

A bit put off, Phillip got a small controller out of his duster, and the hatch slid open. They all piled in and selected quarters—Phillip and Sarah picking quarters with windows, while Kay took a small interior room. He didn't want to see the stars. They would make him sick.

All moved in, Phillip plopped down into the pilot's chair and began the complicated process of starting it up.

Sarah, always a good planner and packer, checked all they had brought to make sure they hadn't forgotten anything.

"Phillip, how many SAPPs did you bring?" she asked.

"I packed three," he replied.

"Three, and I brought two—that should be good. Kay, you have your CARG?" she asked.

"You saw me walking out here with it, Sarah," Kay responded.

"Where is it now?"

"In my cabin."

"And does everybody have their Poltavas?"

Kay and Phillip both nodded.

"Let me see them. I don't trust you two."

Kay and Phillip reached into their coats and brought out their guns. Sarah was satisfied, and they replaced them in their pockets as she loaded the food they'd brought into the cooler.

"Oh, what about money?" she asked.

"I've got several bags of haders here."

"Ok, good. What if we head out to Bazz, we'll need a Cred Stick."

"Bazz?" Kay said with dismay. "Well, if we end up on Bazz we'll just go to the SBL and buy a Cred Stick. No big deal."

Kay sat there, a bit nervous—space travel, he hated it. The *Goshawk* came to rumbling life as Phillip slowly powered it up, the metal floorboards thrumming underfoot.

Sarah took a look around and was giddy. "Oh, I hope we end up on Bazz—I love Bazz. You know, I think this is going to be fun. Thanks, Sam, for doing whatever it is that you're doing. It'll be a great adventure. What do you think, Kay?"

"I think I'm not going to like this one bit," he said quietly. "I hate space travel."

"Oh, you big sissy. Hey, if you think you're going to be sick, use a bag. There are plenty of bags back there, so use them if you need to; that's important. Father will kill us if we bring the ship back soiled with your sick, okay?"

She got her blue Poltava out of her duster—she liked to admire it still. Kay sat there and looked out the open hatch to the sunny wilderness of the Grove, wishing he was outside.

Phillip finished preparing the vessel and, with a clank, he hauled it into the air, quickly gaining altitude and pinning Kay into his seat. Kay watched the ground quickly fall away as the nimble ship climbed. The open hatch made him quite queasy. "Phillip, will you shut the hatch, please!"

"I'll shut it later. I'm going to do a lap down the Gaston Way; then, we'll climb up and out into orbit. I'll shut it then—promise."

Through the hatch, the familiar mountainous passage of the Gaston Way came into view, moving by fast as Phillip hugged the mountains. Sarah unbuckled and went to the hatch, fearlessly leaning over the edge, her blue pony tail and coat tails taking flight in the slipstream.

"Oh, there's Clovis down there!" she cried pointing. "We'll investigate Clovis for the Wraith next!"

Kay, despite his clenched up stomach, chuckled a little. Little did Sarah know that the fabled Wraith of Gaston was actually Sam in disguise all this time.

Moving fast, they were out of the Gaston, and Phillip rapidly pulled into a climb, shutting the hatch at last.

"Roll it!" Sarah shrieked. "Roll it, Phillip!"

Kay went through every sick bag they had.

✳ ✳ ✳ ✳ ✳

That evening, as they set the ship to auto-pilot and shadowed, with permission, a four-ship convoy of Gioma spice merchants, they changed into their pajamas and readied for bed. As usual, Sarah had the Aire-Net blaring as she watched her favorite programming, munching on some sweet snacks. Though they were speeding through the dead of space, it was just like being at home.

A message chattered in on the Com. It was from Lt. Kilos far away across the League on the *New Faith*. She looked serious. "Sarah, turn it down, I need to take this," Kay said.

Sarah muted the Aire-Net, and they settled in front of the screen. Lt. Kilos was sitting in her quarters on the *New Faith*, coat off, Tweeter fluttering around. "How you feeling, Kay?" she asked.

"I'm fine, thanks."

"Your mother is driving me crazy and I'm ready to get her in the gym and beat the daylights out of her. Seems all the Barks she's got running around aren't seeing you anywhere in the castle or out in the Grove and she's freaking out over it. Where are you?"

"We're on an outing."

Ki was skeptical and saw right through him. "An outing? Ok, what's going on? You can tell me. Wait! Let me guess—you're out after Sam, aren't you?"

They looked at each other. "Why tell you something you already know? I made her a promise," Kay said.

Ki ran a hand through her long, somewhat windblown brown hair. "Gods—if your mother finds out about this, I wouldn't want to be you, let's put it like that. You Vith, I swear . . . You know, Kay,

I've made lots of promises in my hundred-plus years that I've not kept for one reason or another and I got over it!"

Kay fired back. "This isn't just about keeping a promise, Ki. It's about trust and loyalty, and yes, keeping a promise falls into that, I suppose. It's also about not failing the person you love most when they need you most, and seeing that person safe in your arms once again. And, it's about revenge, as the woman who nearly killed me is out to get Sam too, and I'm eager to see her again and spill her blood. Does that spell it out for you, Ki?"

Ki sat there and shook her head. In the background, Tweeter was pecking at variously-sized brass bells mounted on a stand, making a twinkly sort of free-form music.

"Yes, Kay, yes it does. Well, don't worry about me, I won't say anything to your mom. I'm assuming you father knows about this, right?"

"He does."

"Ok, good. Well, it's about the person who attacked you as to why I Com'ed tonight. I wanted to tell you that we know who did it, Kay."

"Pardon, Lt.?"

She took a look around and leaned closer to the screen, Tweeter's bell pecking bright and clear in the background. "Ennez took the material samples he gathered back to Minz and had them analyzed. It wasn't too conclusive at first; there was Sam's DNA all over you—that's no surprise, Sarah and Phillip's also and a little from your parents. It was the . . . bite on your entrails, that's the one that was conclusive. The Hospitalers got a match on the DNA samples taken from your guts."

The three of them listened in rapt attention. The auto-pilot controls clicked in the cockpit beyond. A rush of hatred welled up in Kay.

The skinless woman with the golden mask.

The man in armor.

The Demons. Sam's tormentors and nearly his murderers. He seethed with rage.

"Who? Who was it? Who's going to die the moment I get back to Kana?"

Kilos looked around again and continued. "It's your sister, Kay."

They were shocked. Kay was opened-mouthed. Sarah and Phillip, too.

"You're saying Lady Kilos attacked me in the Grove?" he said with disbelief. "It wasn't Ki, Lt. I got a good look at her—she was tall and miserably thin. She was also bent at the torso in an odd fashion. She had no skin for Creation's sake."

"I didn't say it was Bottle, Kay." Lt. Kilos always called his sister "Bottle" as they both had the same name. "It was Lady Hathaline. Your youngest sister, Lady Hathaline, nearly killed you in the Grove."

Kay didn't know what to say. Phillip and Sarah looked at each other and shuddered.

"Lt.," Kay said, "Lady Hathaline is sixteen years old and is still rather small. This woman was adult and tall. She was a perverted monster."

"I didn't say I understood how or why, Kay, but the fact remains. Her teeth marks and her spit were on your guts that she chewed off."

Kay was aghast.

More bells twinkled in the background as Tweeter fluttered from one to another, pecking at them in a pleasing fashion. "Look, I was pretty freaked out when the Hospitalers told me—I mean, it doesn't make any sense, right? I mean, Lady Hathaline couldn't possibly have attacked you, so I went on a Manhunt to find out the truth myself," Ki said.

"A Manhunt?" Sarah asked. "With what?"

"With Tweeter, who else." Tweeter's glowing silver form fluttered up on the screen for a moment, and then resumed pecking.

Sarah was skeptical. "You know, I've asked my mother if Tweeter has all these wondrous abilities you claim he does, and she says no. She created him after all, she should know."

Ki was visibly perturbed. "You know, girlie, if you were standing right here in front of me, I'd sock you one. He's not like the other crappy Tweeters your mom creates—he's special. I think Carahil breathed something into him way back when before the three of you were born. He can do anything I ask him to do and he heard you, Kay, as you were lying on your death bed, so you have him to thank for your continued well-being today. With that in mind, let's not harsh on my Tweeter again, Sarah, ok?"

"All right, all right, wow you're touchy."

Appeased, Ki continued. "So, I went out into the Grove and found the spot where Kay got attacked—Tweeter showed me where it was. I let him root around for a while to get the feel of the place, and then I told him to point me out the guilty."

"He can do that?"

"Yes, he can. They don't call me, Manhunter, for nothing. Usually, manhunts take a while as I have to follow the subtle hints and clues he gives me. It's a slow process. This time, though, he hopped off my shoulder and started flying, which told me the guilty party was fairly close by."

"So, what did you do?"

"What did I do? I followed him. Tweeter zeroed-in on Lady Hathaline. She was out messing around at an old fountain in another part of the Grove and he nearly got stuck in her hair. Gave her the fright of her life. So, there it was—proof the Hospitalers were right. Tweeter put the finger on her."

"No, no, it can't be."

Lt. Kilos looked down. "Look, here's another thing. The other day, when the Sisters came to the castle and Stared everybody down over the theft at Hiei, they nearly took Lady Hathaline to Twilight 4 with them. They said she had something 'bad' about her. They didn't know what it was, but they were eager to find out. Only thing that saved her was your dad. He talked them out of it. I mean, we've all seen strange things in our day: Alteration, Transformation, Cloaking, all that other stuff I don't understand. Changing one's appearance isn't all that difficult if you have the means to do so."

Kay thought about it, and something told him that she was right—that his tiny, red-headed sister, Lady Hathaline, was the one who attacked him.

He became confused, his shock and hatred mixing together. He had no idea how to feel. He loved his sister. "Do my parents know about this?"

"Creation no."

"What are we going to do?"

"I don't know. I've asked some of my contacts in the Blanchefort Magistrate's Office to keep an eye on Lady Hathaline. Now, here's the really weird thing. The night you were attacked, Lady Hathaline was asleep in her tower the whole time. I reviewed the security logs myself. I can tell you how many times her heart beat, if you really want to know. She grinds her teeth, and she gets up to pee fairly often."

"So, what are we to make of this then? How can my sister be in two distinct places at once in forms both fair and foul? And who was the man in armor? And, according to Sam, those two had been secretly tormenting her for her whole life. As Sam is quite a bit older than Hath, how did she manage that?"

"You got me, Kay. Don't know, but we've all seen weird things before, haven't we? Things that nobody can explain properly. You know we have stories on Onaris, of skinless kin who come and terrorize their household, causing strife and destruction. We call them 'Jennybacks', just folklore for a dark night around the fire with a jug of moonshine, but look what we have here. The lady you described, Kay, sounds like a nasty Jennyback to me. The Xaphans, too, have stories about such things. I've no idea how this has happened, and I don't pretend to understand it, but I intend to protect both you and Lady Hathaline. The arcane is at work here, and I don't like it one bit."

Tweeter tired of pecking the bells and flapped up onto her shoulder. Ki gave his beak a loving rub. "Listen, I'm going to send you a code via your personal holo-account. When you get home, use it. It might help. Make sure it's midnight when you do, okay?"

"What is it?"

"You'll see—and don't take no for an answer. I've got to go. Be safe, and do not let your mother find out about this. Oh, by the way, your honey, Bethrael of Moane, says hello."

"Thank you, Lt., and good night."

"Goodnight." She screened off.

They looked at each other. "Well, I'm good and creeped out," Sarah said. She peered around at the darkened interior of the ship and the stars shining through the cockpit glass. "What does that mean? How could Lady Hathaline have been the one who attacked you?"

Kay closed his eyes, feeling sick again. "I don't know, but it feels right. The woman was a monster, thin, bent like she'd been broken and then crudely put back together again. Still, she seemed like Hath, had her presence now that I think on it. And, let me tell you something else . . ."

He told them of his vision, of the evil Lady Poe, and Sarah and Lady Kilos locked in a terrible battle.

Sarah laughed. "Me and Lady Kilos in a fight? That wouldn't be much of a fight!"

"It wasn't just a fight, Sarah, it was a struggle to the death, and my sister was doing just fine. She's pretty tough—you've never given her the credit she's due, and, like the image of Lady Hathaline, she was ugly—monstrous."

Phillip went to the cockpit and checked the auto settings. Outside the Gioma ships flew nearby, their running lights winking in a comforting fashion.

"What does all of this mean? Do you really think you're seeing the future, Kay?" he asked.

"No clue, Phillip. All I know is that, if it is the future, I'm not going to let it happen. I'll change it somehow."

They slept, and Kay had nightmares. The skinless woman came and tormented him. She ripped off her golden mask and there, mutilated and aged, was what was left of Lady Hathaline's face. He wanted to hate her, as he did before, but couldn't. His heart broke as she got out her knife and began stabbing him again and again.

7—Xandarr

Two days later, Phillip set the *Goshawk* down in a lovely forested area south of Xandarr Keep. The Keep had been completely rebuilt since the infamous Black Hat attack twenty some years ago. It was a large, domed palace built in the opulent Xandarr style of polished marble and hammered brass, but it was nowhere as big as the former structure had been. It was surrounded by a large wooded park, mostly open to the public so that the citizens could enjoy it; however, the wooded sections to the south of the Keep by the banks of the River Torr were private for the King and his House.

Balor I, the king, and his wife, Queen Zoladerra, never forgot the promises they made after the attack. Balor was a good king and, slowly, Xandarr had built itself back up to prominence. Fifteen years prior, Xandarr had petitioned and been admitted to the League, the first Xaphan planet to do so. As such, Xandarr was a target for ambitious Xaphan warlords and led to an acute uptick in League-Xaphan space battles, all of which the vastly superior Fleet won. The great northern city of Zamma was a major League outpost and ship berth.

They were greeted by several footmen who were dressed in colorful veils and light vests—typical Xandarr clothing. Kay announced himself, and the footmen immediately escorted them to the king and queen.

They were sitting in a landscaped garden terrace out in the purple sunshine and big sky of the afternoon.

"Lord Blanchefort!" the King exclaimed. "You have been too long in visiting us. You will find that you and yours are always welcome here! Always!"

Kay bowed, and Sarah and Phillip did the same. Balor's children of various ages surrounded Kay, fascinated by his purple hair. Of course, all of the Xandarr children were blue-haired.

Queen Zoladerra smiled at him from her couch. An ex-Black Hat, she had the Shadowmark on her face, just like his mother and aunt did. As per usual with former Black Hats, she was very pretty with a long, ringed head of blue hair. She wore a small silver charm at her throat in the shape of a seal. Her charm had an embossed "1" in the center.

* * * * *

Kay's father had often told him of the Xandarr 44. During the Black Hat attack, Carahil (yes, he again) had helped save forty-four Black Hats during a pitched battle inside the Keep. Being a god, Carahil was able to free the Black Hats of their thrall to the Black Abbess, and King Balor took them in. In time, they formed a sorority, calling themselves the Xandarr 44 and living in a grand marble villa off the village square, with Queen Zoladerra as their tacit leader, hence her "1". The `44, he'd heard, were key in thwarting Xaphan spies, assassins and subversives sent to create chaos on Xandarr. Throughout his childhood, Kay recalled occasional female guests in the castle from time to time, all wearing veils and sporting little numbered seal charms about their necks. They came to the castle to go to the Greyson courtyard and pray, offering their thanks and hoping to commune with the little silver god in the form of a seal who, in kindness, had saved them years ago.

*　*　*　*　*

"We were there on the day you were born as honored guests of your House," the queen said. "You have grown into such a handsome man. Why have you not visited us sooner?"

"I am sorry, Great Queen." He looked around, admiring the ornate architecture and the mountains in the purple distance. "It is a breathtaking place to be certain."

"Thank you, and please, simply call me Zoladerra."

"Thank you," Kay said, feeling shy about addressing a queen by her name.

As Sarah and Phillip offered their greetings to the King and Queen, several veiled females Wafted in with aplomb. They were shoeless, dressed in the usual Xandarr style, Shadowmarked, and wearing charms with the numbers 6, 14, 26 and 33; more of the Xandarr 44. They laughed and seated themselves in a gregarious manner as servants brought them a variety of iced drinks.

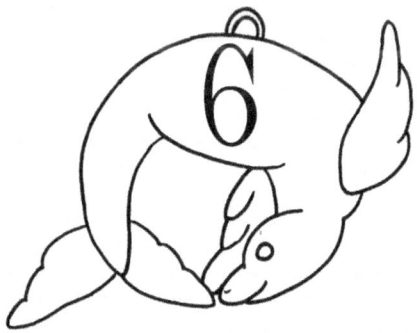

"Well," 33 said, "who do we have here today, Zol? What attractive young people."

"This is Lord Kabyl of Blanchefort and his cousins, Sarah and

Phillip, here to visit us, Willa," the queen replied. They all turned to Kay.

"They're too over-dressed," 14 stated. "They need to relax and be comfortable. Are you not hot, dear sir?" she said to Kay taking a sip from her sweating ruby drink.

"I'm fine, Great Lady," Kay replied.

"Oh, listen to him," 6 said holding her drink. "I'll wager he's sweating buckets under all those Vith clothes. Now there's a young fellow worth seducing, wouldn't you say, Gal?"

"Yes, I'd slip a love potion into his tea, I would," 26 added.

"Actually, I'd take all three of them," 14 said, and they all giggled.

Number 6, a small, handsome woman with ringed brown hair, stood and made her way to Kay, still holding her iced drink. As she approached, Kay noticed her garb was rather transparent, and he could, if he wanted, see every bit of her down to the ring on her bare ankles. He was disciplined enough to keep his eyes locked with hers and not waiver. That seemed to impress her.

"Domeneau of Xandarr, formerly of Holly and number 6 of the Sisterhood of the Xandarr 44, at your service, sir." She bowed and Kay followed suit. "Had I but known you were coming, I'd have baked you a cake, but perhaps a kiss will do instead."

Kay turned several shades of red as Sarah gave him a chiding elbow in the ribs.

She continued. "These cretins here are my sisters. 33 is Willa-von-Tapmos of Hoban. 14 is Zagamoria of Gulle, and 26 is Galla-Metra-Forna of Tudor. Don't worry about them; I'm much more skilled in bed than they are."

"You are not," 33 said.

King Balor laughed. "Oh, Dom, such a lady you are! Give the boy some space and leave your door unlocked tonight. Perhaps you'll have a visitor! So, Lord Blanchefort, to what do we owe the pleasure today? Do you bear any official dispatches from your parents, perhaps?"

"No, Great King. Under unusual circumstances, I was told to come here for training."

The King lit up. "A lesson? You're here for a lesson? That is wonderful news! You have had an open invitation your whole life, but your mother would not allow it. I am pleased that she finally has agreed."

Domeneau, number 6, persisted. "I've a lesson or two for him I'd like to teach, King."

Kay tried to maintain his bearing. "Lesson, Great King?"

Zoladerra laughed. "You needn't be shy; many come for lessons. It is a much sought-after service that we offer, usually at great expense to the trainee. For you, no monetary payment will be accepted. However, you will be expected to offer a small gift of some sort. You shall see."

The King poured two glasses. "Lord Phillip, Lady Sarah, please sit and relax. You'll have your turn later."

Kay still stood there, not quite sure what to do.

"Take the path a short way to the river," the King said. "We shall wait for you here. Don't forget you will be expected to offer a gift of some sort."

"Yes," 6 said, "And I shall still be here when you return." She licked her lips.

Sarah sat down and picked up her glass. "Well, Kay, go on."

Kay tipped his hat and started down the path, his elegant boots crunching on the pebbles as he walked. The path twisted and turned through a stand of dense trees. He began to feel a bit hot and loosened his collar. Xandarr was a warm world—far warmer than he was used to, coming from the cold Kanan north. There were statues mounted at various points along the path cut into pebbled nooks, backlit and well-tended. One particularly large statue was the likeness of a seal—Carahil. Kay smiled and looked at it for a moment. He loved Carahil. Everybody did.

Carahil . . . being led away in chains . . .

Carahil's front flippers were littered with little folded scraps of paper. Kay stopped and picked one up. It was a hand-drawn note written in colored pencils by a child. It had a fanciful drawing of Carahil on it followed by a short, heart-felt note.

Kay put the note back where he found it. Whatever the child had requested, he was certain Carahil would answer. He was a friendly, accommodating god.

He had the feeling that he'd just recently seen Carahil, but couldn't place it; it was one of those déjà-vu feelings.

He continued on down the path. Eventually, the trees opened into a small clearing by the banks of a broad, lazy river, the Torr, no doubt. Beyond, he could see the valley below and the mountains in the distance, all tinted in purple. Very pretty setting. Several moons hung in the sky.

A small, long-haired woman sat by the edge of the river. A canvas was set up in front of her, and she appeared to be sketching—lost in concentration. She was wearing light blue and purple veils, just like the King and Queen, and her blue hair was set and ringed in a similar style to Zoladerra. Her leg veils were pushed up to her knees, and her feet were submerged in the cool river water. A dusty box of colored chalk sat at her side.

Carefully Kay came up to her side, trying to be quiet.

"Have you come to help me finish my drawing?" the woman asked in a breathy, dreamy fashion, not turning around. "I've been working on it for awhile now, and it's almost finished, but I just can't seem to know where to stop."

Kay looked at the canvas. It was nothing but a scrawl.

He had heard of Princess Vroc of Xandarr often while growing up. His father talked about her every so often. His mother despised Princess Vroc. He had heard how she was responsible for nearly killing his mother. He had heard how she nearly managed to blow up

Castle Blanchefort and how she was under the sway of the Black Hats. He had heard she was nearly responsible for killing every living soul on Xandarr, her family included.

He had heard, also, how she was insane, a tormented Eleventh Daughter of House Xandarr, worthless and hounded, always at fault; how her father, King Hezru, had sold her into prostitution and then to a meat market in Burgon to be consumed. He had heard how the Black Hats drove and tortured her until she fell into utter madness and killed her entire family, except for Balor who hadn't been home that day. And, he had heard how King Balor had taken his mad sister back to Xandarr and, through love and care, had restored at least a hint of her sanity. At last, she was now at peace.

And, one more thing, he had heard that, for whatever reason, Princess Vroc of Xandarr was one of the greatest swordsmen his father, Lord Davage, had ever faced. It was at first thought that the Black Hats, through sorcery or via chemical means, had enhanced her physical strength and her fighting abilities. But, through the years, her skills and her amazing strength never faded. She was reputed to be a genius, her small but lethal sword arm legendary. She was the tutor of many, many League Lords daring to seek out training. Much of the considerable income derived from these tutoring lessons had gone to help rebuild Xandarr.

Now Kay fully understood. He was here to fight the legendary Princess Vroc of Xandarr. His mother, should she become aware of this development, would be livid. It was a good thing his father had chosen to be discreet.

Kay took a good look at the Princess in the purple afternoon sun. Her physical appearance had been related to him many times, and he always wondered what he might do if he ever stood in her presence. She had achieved a larger-than-life stature in his mind, rather like her older sister, Princess Marilith, another legendary princess of Xandarr.

She was small, not much bigger than his mother, but not nearly as diminutive and bone skinny as she had been described to him. She appeared trim, but well fed enough to not be overly thin. Her straight blueberry hair was down to her waist and ringed in the Xandarr style. In years past, her hair had been cut short in an unflattering crop.

He had been told that Princess Vroc was rather homely—his mother had said that, and his father hadn't disagreed. Her sister, the famous Princess Marilith had been a rare beauty, but Vroc, it was said, was plain and mannish in the face to the point of being ugly. However, in seeing her in person, her face painted and her hair done up, she certainly wasn't homely or mannish in the least—she was no raving beauty like the Xandarr 44 up on the hill—or like Sam, for that matter, but nor was she ugly.

Her left arm, covered with a veiled sleeve, bore a ragged, chewed-up scar, a reminder of her long ago battle with Kay's mother where they nearly killed each other.

And, true to the Xandarr style, her veils were light and see-through. Her nude body underneath was plain to see if he wanted. He tried to be demure and avoid looking at the private areas of her body.

She looked up at Kay, her fingers tinted with chalk. "Would you like to help me finish my drawing?"

Kay knelt down and selected a piece of chalk out of the box. He surveyed the scribbles on the canvas and scratched out a few lines of color. "There," he said. "A fine sunset."

She looked at what he had drawn. "You are an artist, sir." She glanced at the CARG saddled at his side. "CARG," she said. "LosCapricos weapon of House Blanchefort. I've never faced a CARG before."

Kay didn't bother to correct her; it wasn't prudent, for Princess Vroc most certainly had faced the CARG before.

She looked at the weapon and sighed. "I suppose it is too much to hope that you are here simply to sit and chat with me." Her eyes moved to his purple hair. "I like your hair. I wish mine was purple, too."

Kay took his black triangle hat off and let her look at it. After a time, she spoke again. "I have a price. I require a payment."

"Payment for what, ma'am?" Kay asked.

"Payment for fighting me. That's why you are here, to fight me, isn't it?"

Kay smiled. "No, actually I came to help you finish your drawing."

Vroc's face lit up. There was no chair for Kay to sit in, so Vroc scooted over, and she shared her chair with him. Together, they spent the rest of the afternoon scribbling on her canvas, the only sounds being the occasional gurgle of the river and the back-and-forth scratching of the chalk on the canvas.

Later, as the day grew old and the sky darkened to a deep

cranberry, Kay stood to take his leave.

"You're going, sir?" Vroc asked.

"I am. I've a long journey home."

Vroc gazed at him with her deep blue eyes. "I have enjoyed sitting with you."

"And I with you, ma'am."

She stood up and dried her wet bare feet on the grass. "Are you certain you don't wish to have a match with me?"

Kay placed his hand on his silver CARG. "I feel shy, ma'am."

"Why?" She drew a BEREN from the side of her chair. It was a sham BEREN, a mock up—the slim, fluted blade was visible, not the real thing which, if his knowledge of LosCapricos weapons was accurate, was invisible. Now that she was standing, he could see the real thing saddled to her left leg. "You needn't feel shy, sir. I can handle myself, I assure you. Please, I want to see your skills and offer advice if any is needed. I wish to have a match with you."

Kay sighed and unsaddled his CARG. "What about your price?"

Vroc thought a moment. "My price? Very well, here is my price. I demand a lock of your purple hair. Will you agree?"

"Is that all?"

"Yes, that is what I wish of you." She raised her fake BEREN and assumed a classic fighting stance. "Please level your weapon, sir."

Kay readied the CARG. He held it one handed in a fencer's pose, as he usually did. His father would never approve.

Some of the cloudy dreaminess left her eyes. She appeared ready, focused, and eager to begin. She neared him and crossed his weapon, taking an aggressive posture. "You hold your CARG one-handed, why is this? With the CARG"s advantage in weight, a two-handed grip shall maximize your capabilities. I will allow you a moment to change your grip, and I highly advise it."

"No need, I am at ease."

Vroc smiled. "Then, be at your guard."

They lightly clanged weapons, Vroc twisting the blade of her fake BEREN, Kay matching with the CARG.

With a strong thrust and septime, Kay turned Vroc's weapon, and they exchanged positions, weapons still crossed. "Yes, excellent, you fence well," she said.

Vroc came again, feinting and thrusting, Kay foiling her strikes with beat and opposition, the shaft of the CARG ringing and scratching with each hit. Suddenly, Vroc swept his legs out from under him and had him on the ground, her wet and slightly muddy foot placed on his throat. "Recall, sir, that I have feet, that I can move around. A fencer standing still is greatly disadvantaged by an opponent who moves laterally. Again, please, you are doing quite well."

She let him up, and they started again, and, as before, Kay fenced one handed with his CARG.

Vroc side-stepped, and Kay drew back to adjust. He had an opening but didn't take it. Vroc, with a hard block, moved his CARG aside and hit him in the face with a right cross, easily the hardest punch he'd ever felt. He hit the ground with a thud, his lip starting to swell.

"And I have hands as well. I gave you the opportunity to hit me; why didn't you?"

"I'll not hit a small woman."

"I am a small woman who could kill you in many different ways," she said. "Again, and this time if you choose not to fight me, I will bleed you deep."

She became intense and highly aggressive. She pressed him with the BEREN, forcing him this way, then that, pushing him back into the river. She hiked her veiled leggings up and followed, her bare feet splashing.

Their weapons moved in a blur and then locked. "Put both hands on your weapon!" she said, her voice a growl. "Do it now, or I'll kill you!!"

Kay, swallowing hard, put both hands on the hilt, the CARG feeling strange in his hands with this grip. His father had wanted him to fight with two hands for years, but had, obviously, never threatened to kill him during a practice.

Vroc came, and she seemed to be fighting for keeps. Cross, thrust, heel, bite, bang, BANG! She drove into him, trying to move his CARG aside and belt him again, and this time he side-stepped, releasing his CARG and seized her by the neck. He easily lifted and threw her into the water. After a bit of splashing, she surfaced, her blue hair a wet mop. Her veils were like drenched tissue paper around her. She looked up at him and smiled, all of the fierce intensity gone. "Excellent, sir. Very well done."

Kay helped her out of the water, and they sat down to dry off.

"I've hurt your lip," she said tenderly. She dipped a cloth into the water and sat next to him, dabbing his bloody lip.

"I hope I didn't hurt your neck. I shouldn't have done that."

"My neck is fine," she said absently, continuing to dab his lip.

She put the cloth down and looked at him. "Now, for my payment," she said. She sliced off a small lock of Kay's purple hair, which she coiled up and set aside.

In the twilight, Kay saddled his CARG and picked up Vroc's chair, her canvas and the box of chalk. Vroc took his arm, and together they walked back up the path. She hummed quietly as they walked.

At the top of the path, King Balor and Queen Zoladerra sat where they were previously, their terrace now lit up in soft lighting. The ladies of the Xandarr 44 were gone.

Sarah was rather salty. Her duster lay over the arm of her chair, and her boots were removed. "What in Creation took so long? It's getting dark. I'll not have my turn!"

The King laughed. "All in good time, my Lady. Tomorrow you'll get your turn—we've fine accommodations awaiting you all. Well, Vroc, what do you think of young Lord Blanchefort here?" he asked cheerfully.

She looked at Kay, still holding his arm. "He fights well. Needs a bit of work, and has several bad habits to correct, but very talented. I am quite pleased."

"Vroc, you seem to like Lord Blanchefort," Queen Zoladerra said.

"I do, Zol. I am going to marry him."

Kay's jaw dropped.

Balor laughed. "Did you hear that, Lord Blanchefort? My sister likes you. What do you say to that?"

Kay blushed. "Princess Vroc is a genius—every bit as skilled as her reputation dictates. I am glad I did not embarrass myself."

Vroc slowly approached him. "I will expect to see you again, Lord Blanchefort; we have much to train. I offer you another blade. And my price will be another lock of your hair—and a kiss. What say you?"

Balor, Zoladerra and Vroc all stared at him.

"I do not wish to intrude on the Princess's valuable time."

He bowed and turned to leave. When he stood, Vroc quickly drew her BEREN and laid it on his shoulder.

"I would not have invited you for a second lesson if I didn't have time or the inclination."

Kay, feeling on the spot, bowed again. "Then, yes, I am honored, and I shall meet your price."

8—Racing with Waft

K ay settled into bed. The King had given him a large room in the eastern wing of the Keep, with Sarah and Phillip in adjacent rooms. The room was lovely, all polished stone, hanging veils and lofty worked brass hammered out in the intricate Xandarr fashion. A large curtained terrace looked out over the valley, sparkling with lights and the rising bulk of the mountains in the far distance. There was no glass or window pane—Xandarr's warm, dry climate made such a thing unnecessary. Two bright moons hung quartered on the horizon.

Kay was drifting to sleep. Sarah, now snug in her bed in the next room, had given him no peace. Sitting there in her pajamas, she demanded to know all of the details of the encounter with Princess Vroc, as she was eager to take her on in the morning and didn't think she'd be much of a challenge.

Poor Sarah. She was in for a real shock for Vroc had controlled Kay in their duel like he'd never been before. He'd been in lots of duels with his father, but of course, Lord Davage had never tested him to that extreme. And, his father had never belted him across the face or stepped on his neck.

He thought about Princess Vroc. Now, no longer a character in a fable, she was a living, flesh and blood person, and not the monster she'd been made out to be. His mother had a small stained glass window built in one of the corridors of the castle depicting the battle with Princess Vroc. The images of Vroc were less than flattering—some were rather monstrous. He must admit that he felt quite glad at the attention she'd shown him. Sitting there by the Torr, scribbling with her on the canvas, he felt a real kinship with her.

He felt he liked her. Such skill. The things she'd endured and overcome.

He thought about Sam. He was still so young. This was the first time he'd really been away from home on his own—Sarah and Phillip were with him, but still. There was so much out there, so much he'd not experienced. Sam had, to a greater or lesser degree, been with him his whole life and had taken aggressive steps to ensure he was isolated and alone. He thought of his sister, Lady Kilos, standing with him atop the Firth House, voicing her views about Sam stealing his correspondence and haunting the Gaston Way, preventing her rivals from visiting.

Aren't you curious as to what else is out there? she had asked.

Had he given his heart to Sam too soon? He had never thought so, until now.

He thought he heard a rustling on the terrace and sat up. He saw the tall, slender figure of a woman standing by the rail. The woman glanced back at him.

"Sam?"

The figure turned, exposing a grotesque bend in the torso. She suddenly cringed and raised her hands.

Roused to wakefulness, he grabbed his CARG and went to the terrace. "Hath!" he yelled. He threw open the curtains.

The figure, if it had ever been there at all, was gone.

In the far distance, he saw something moving through the air. A chariot, floating on the wind, pulled by three naked women and driven by a tall, statue-like bronze man, approached.

Soon, Kay was backed into the room, the tall man looming over him in his chariot. The orange eyes of the three women pulling the chariot glowed in the dark.

"It is time for your first test," he said in a flat baritone. One of the women unharnessed herself from the chariot and stepped forward. "This will be a test of Waft. Remember, Lord of Blanchefort, this test tonight is a mortal one—fail, and you will die."

"Where is Sam?" Kay asked.

Without answering, the chariot turned, and the remaining two women pulled him back out into the night air. He was gone as quickly as he came.

Kay and the woman stood there staring at each other. Her mud-like appearance cleared up. Now, with the exception of her orange eyes, she looked just like Sam. Her mane of black hair went down to her ankles, and her naked body was inviting if he allowed his mind to wander.

"Get dressed," she said finally. "Or we can do this naked; it's your choice."

Kay, remembering the night in the Grove, started dressing.

"She must really like you, to go to this extreme," Waft said watching him dress. "In any case, make no mistake, I really don't care whether you survive this or not—it makes no difference to me. I am here to test and expand your abilities with the Waft, and I will not be a gentle teacher. You will progress to my satisfaction tonight, or you will die. I hope that's clear to you."

"I'm not helpless," Kay said pulling his boots on. "I'll defend myself."

"Oh, going to fight me with your CARG are you? Go ahead, take my head off with it—won't make a difference, I'll just put my head right back on. I am a creature of the NIGHTMARE, and you cannot harm me with your weapon. The only way you're going to beat and be rid of me is with your Waft. Understood?"

Kay finished dressing and saddled his CARG. She looked him over.

"Now," she said, "your test has begun. First, I want you to Waft out to the courtyards below."

Kay went to the terrace and peered over the side. He was two stories up, about sixty feet to the grass below. He decided it was best to try and get this over with and comply with her wishes. He stood straight and began to Waft. Slowly, he could feel the usual funnel of air begin to build up around him.

"No!" Waft screamed, incensed. "Too slow! Too clumsy!" She strode up to him as the wind began to blow and punched him hard in the stomach, doubling him over. She then picked him up with one arm and threw him over the side of the terrace like a sack of laundry, where he landed in the grass below with a cry.

Kay lay there blinking up at the stars and moons in a daze. He was in great pain, but he didn't think anything was broken. After a moment, she appeared in front of him, naked as ever. "Your Waft is pathetic," she said standing over him. "Your concentration is terrible, and your technique is laughably bad. This could very well be the last night of your life, and that will make her very sad. She's doing this because she loves you. Why, I really don't know."

She helped him up. "Anything broken?" she asked.

Kay checked himself over. "No, I don't think so, but . . ."

She took his left hand and savagely broke his pinky. Kay reared back and choked down a scream.

"I'd Waft away if I were you," she said breaking the next finger in a grotesque fashion. Kay tried to pull his hand way, but her grip was unbreakable.

"Waft, Kay!" she yelled. Pain and nausea flowed through him. Just as she was ready to break his long finger, there was a rush of wind and Kay was gone. He had Wafted back up to his terrace. He stood there holding his hand, agony throbbing through him. The room began to fall to amber. He could see his broken fingers. He could see the snapped bones under the skin—nice clean breaks. Nothing that couldn't be repaired. Incredible pain. He concentrated and pulled his Sight back to normal. Now wasn't the time.

She appeared a moment later and smiled. "That's better," she said. "Pain, unfortunately, is a fine motivator. I'm sorry, and there's nothing personal. Look how fast you Wafted up here—that's what I'm looking for: fast, effortless, with a minimum of wind and noise. A lot of wind and noise is the hallmark of a bad Waft, contrary to popular belief. Let me see your hand."

Kay didn't want to give her his hand, but she took it anyway, examining his broken fingers. "Good. In the morning, should I not have to kill you, the King's Hospitaler will be able to fix you right up. For now, you need this dose of pain. If you can do what I think you can, then you can virtually fly. Great Wafters can Waft so fast, they can fly through the air—you can do that. Not even your father can Waft that fast."

She stepped out onto the terrace and pointed to a distant mountain. It was the tallest of a sturdy range, shaped like a crooked shark's snout. Kay thought he could see a dusting of snow at its gentle rounded peak. "You see that mountain, the big one?" she asked. "We're going to have a race right now, you and I. We're going to race to the top of that mountain, and either you beat me to it, or you're going to die. Understand?"

Holding his hand, Kay walked to the edge of the terrace and gingerly looked out. The mountain seemed far off in the night. "How far away is that mountain?"

"About sixty or seventy miles—what difference does it make?

Here, I'll give you a head start." She picked Kay up with one arm and threw him off the terrace again. This time he Wafted with a quick blast as he tumbled through the air and appeared several hundred feet away, landing on his feet. He looked back. She was standing there on the terrace, her pale body framed by her black hair. "Better move!" she yelled, her voice echoing.

He was standing on the ground, surrounded by tall trees, he couldn't even see the mountain from where he was. Using the moons overhead as a directional guide, he started running. He'd taken a few steps when he was roughly clothes-lined by Waft's soft but strong arm. He hit the ground holding his throat.

She was irate. "If you're going to waste my time running, I think I'll just go ahead and kill you now!"

She pulled a medium-sized tree out of the ground and made to slam it down on Kay. He jammed his broken fingers, creating a spray of pain and Wafted several hundred feet away to the top of a distant tree. She threw the tree aside and followed in a blast.

Ahead, the copse of trees ended and opened up to a broad, hilly plain that spilled out into the night like a vast, shallow bowl. He could see little huddles of glittering light—small hamlets and villages sprinkled about, and far away, the looming range of mountains. Taller than the rest, there was the big snowy mountain, his destination. Picking a point fairly far away, he Wafted in a blast, then he did it again and again, moving in little stages, always stopping to mark his bearing and continue. As he progressed, he was dimly aware that he was Wafting in mere seconds, whereas before he needed every bit of a minute. His heart pounded with excitement. He was doing things he never thought he'd be able to do.

Waft—to a distinctive hill in the distance in a cone of wind.

Boom!—to a windmill.

He was really covering the distance. He figured he'd gone about ten miles so far in a matter of only a few minutes. Incredible. He didn't see Waft and was feeling rather proud of himself.

As he made his rapid but jerky progress along the ground, he saw a black figure moving at speed across the sky framed against the stars. It was she, with her naked body and mane of long black hair, she looked like she was swimming across the sky. He could feel the wave of her blasts drift into him.

He decided that this was a race he could possibly win. He gauged her speed and her height and Wafted.

He appeared behind her in mid-air and grabbed her by the hair. Spinning round and round, he sent Waft rocketing, arms and legs splayed, toward a farm house where she smashed into it with a satisfying crash. Feeling himself beginning to fall, he righted himself and found a distant landmark in which to Waft.

With a sharp boom, she appeared under him and sent a fist into his chin. After another moment, she was far away, heading in the direction of the mountain range that was getting closer and closer by the moment.

As Kay fell, he lined her up and Wafted. When he emerged, he put a boot into the back of her head, sending her spinning.

The mountain range began unfolding in front of him. He could see a confusion of small foothills and minor mountains spreading out beneath him along with little populated hollows and small points of isolated lights. He had to be at least three hundred feet in the air. He had no idea how fast he was moving, but it was fast.

She appeared about two hundred feet in front of him. Finding that he enjoyed putting a beating to her, he lined her up and Wafted, aiming to put a hard elbow into her back.

She Wafted when he got there, again appearing about a hundred feet ahead.

He Wafted.

She Wafted. Over and over. Gravity no longer had any meaning—Kay was a creature of the air. He had no idea how high he was, possibly a thousand feet up moving who knows how fast, the mountains streaking below at a blur. He found, as he appeared, that the cushion of air he created supported him for a good two or three seconds before he started falling. Such a span of time was an eternity. He could leisurely pick his spots, whether on the ground or at the heights, and instantly go there.

He was, for all intents and purposes, flying.

Snow. He must be getting close. Where was she?? Head on a swivel—there she was! He Wafted and was at arms with her. They struggled in space for a moment, then she had him by the scruff of his shirt, hauled him around and sent him spiraling down where he crashed into the snowy ground. Things spun. His fingers ached.

She appeared in front of him, the fresh snow coming up to her calves. She seemed unfazed by the cold of the snow.

"My Lord," she said. "Look where you are."

Frantically he looked around. He was on a high, uneven bit of ground that was deep in snow. In the far distance, he could see the valley below lit up with bluish moonlight. Far away he could see the blinking, pearly complex of Xandarr Keep. There were mountains all around.

He was on the summit of the large mountain.

"You won, my Lord," she said bowing low, arms outstretched. "The race is done."

"You threw me down here. You could have won if you'd wanted."

"Maybe and maybe not. I never said that my goal was to win the race at all costs. My goal was to determine if your Waft could be expanded, and if so, to develop it—and look where you are. Look at the ground you have covered with me at speed."

She put her hands on his face. "You have passed my test. Maybe she was right to believe in you after all."

She stood him up. "Remember what you've accomplished tonight. Your Waft can save your life if you let it. I'm sorry I broke your fingers and caused you pain."

"I'm sorry I kicked you in the head."

She smiled, and they stood there in the snow, looking at the surrounding mountains and distant lights. "Embrace me, if you will," she said. "My time is done."

Kay opened his arms and gave her a long hug, which she returned. "Are you not coming back to the Keep with me?"

"I am returning whence I came. Fear not, though your lady sleeps, she dreams of what we have done tonight, and I am certain she is proud of you, as I am."

They stood there and enjoyed the night for a bit longer

9—Admiral Carfax

The gigantic *New Faith* was snug in low orbit over the south of Kana, a few bars north of Dare. Captain Davage, Lord of Blanchefort, had been in command of the vessel since its launch twenty years prior. His arguments for the command chair before the Admiralty had been half-hearted. He hated leaving his old vessel, the much smaller, *Straylight*-class *Seeker*, but he had been told, in no uncertain terms, that the time had come to move on.

His initial reaction to the ship had been tepid at best. He was in love with the swan-like *Straylight* class of ships that his *Seeker* belonged to, this new *Triumph*-class ship being like a double-tiered slug in comparison. He found the ship too big, too slow with a turning radius the size of a small moon. He demanded speed and agility, as the *Seeker* had given him. He pestered and tested the patience of Lord Probert, the designer of the vessel, and that of the Lady Branna, Probert's new bride and designer of its weaponry. Davage demanded changes and, by Creation, he was going to have them. How could he fight the Xaphans in such a lazy beast? It couldn't turn; it rolled only under protest; and it had the heft of a large elephant.

Captain Davage wanted his *Seeker* back.

Lord Probert and Lady Branna threw their hands up in dual frustration. So, back to Provst the ship went. Probert re-ducted the entire ship. He tripled the amount of thrusters and vents and added mass drivers at key points along the ship's length. He also stiffened the superstructure and altered its center of gravity. The result: the *Faith* variant of the *Triumph*-class of Main Fleet Vessels became the fighting standard. Now it could turn almost as tight as a *Straylight* and could barrel roll even better. Lady Branna's much contested Sar-

Beams proved to pack a tremendous punch and, armed in concert with canister missiles, the *Triumph*-class ship was the most heavily-armed vessel the League had ever seen.

Such weaponry and performance, as it turned out, was needed. With the entry of the planet Xandarr to the League, the Xaphans shook off their melancholy and fear of the League, and began a protracted campaign to forcibly seize Xandarr and re-claim it as Xaphan territory. Camilla, Baroness of Sorrander, declared herself the Queen of Xandarr in exile, and demanded tribute and fealty, and offered rich bounties to any who could deliver her fiefdom to her. Xaphan warlords answered her ridiculous charge and schemed to unleash hell on Xandarr. They began designing new warships in far-away yards. A new Xaphan mastermind, Lord Verd of the old House of Charn, appeared to be quite skilled, and this latest generation of Xaphan vessels was comprised of very competent designs. And the Charn ships weren't all that was coming fresh off the Xaphan yards. They were flying around in damn bizarre ships, if one could call them that. These new ships looked like giant statues, like works of fine art at a museum. Davage had never seen anything like them. The old *Merci* and *Ghome* vessels, once used by the Xaphans, were gone and quaint in the memory. Now they roamed aloft in bug-like Charn ships and bizarre flying statues that actually performed quite well; and, like in the days of old, Xaphan warlords openly took on the League and its mighty Fleet in grand, swirling battles in space.

The *New Faith* and Captain Davage, with his fighting Countess Sygillis at his side, was right in the middle of it, engaging them time and time again, the double teardrop silhouette of his ship becoming a dreaded sight for the Xaphans all over again.

∗ ∗ ∗ ∗ ∗

A recurring theme in the Xaphan's attack plan was not only to reclaim Xandarr by force but also to take a League world in retribution. The obvious choice was Hoban. Proximity-wise, it was near to Xaphan space, and several Xaphan Great Houses had close ties to various Households located on Hoban. Historically, one of the Xaphan's greatest heroes, Princess Marilith of Xandarr, had centered many of her schemes around Hoban, so it was a "hot-spot," so to speak, in their activities. The Lords of the Fleet weren't overly concerned, though the Xaphans were re-motivated and re-equipped, they were still no match for the Fleet.

Still, a troubling series of events on Hoban had bubbled to the surface and needed to be dealt with immediately. Several prominent Households on Hoban, including the Governor's, had fallen into madness and melancholy. Captain Davage wasn't completely clear on the details, but whatever had happened was certainly traumatic and had the Governor of Hoban fearing for his life.

The Governor called for the Fleet. He wanted it there at all costs, and a grand task force was being assembled at once.

Parked off the *New Faith's* starboard was the *Bethel,* commanded by Lord Harrison of Dare, 3rd Order, and the flag vessel *Westerville* under the command of Admiral Carfax, Lord of Woodland. All three were *Triumph*-class, three cities in space.

Admiral Carfax was quite a rarity—a *fighting* Admiral. He had been appointed to the *Westerville's* chair some years ago and led it with fine skill. For his ability as a ship's captain and his Admiral's polish as a diplomat, he commanded great respect from the Fleet Captaincy, Davage included. If only there were more like him.

Coming in from the northern pole were two *Straylights* on loan from the 3rd Fleet: the *Twilight* captained by Lord Van of Mystery and the *Halo Dawn* captained by Lady Strella of Jacarta.

When the ships assembled, all the captains were due aboard the *Westerville* at once for a meeting with Admiral Carfax. The old practice of using ripcars to travel between ships in flight had largely been discarded. Instead the *Triumph*-class of ships made use of an electro-matter teleporter. It had been refined greatly over the years and forced to comply with a number of stringent regulations to prevent unwanted incursions, as with the *Triumph* incident of twenty four years ago. In its original incarnation, one simply teleported anywhere one wished and appeared there in a ball of light. Now, the places where one could teleport were quite limited indeed. Also, now, the teleporter consisted of a long dark hallway. One could only go to the end of the hallway with no variation allowed. Usually the two teleporter areas of the various ships were linked, and nowhere else.

Davage and Countess Sygillis, arm in arm, walked down the teleporter hallway, the *New Faith* at one end, the *Westerville* at the other.

Syg sighed in her wonderful gown. Davage gave her a hug and smiled. "Worried about Kay, Syg?"

"Yes."

"I know, to have such a thing happen. But, he's fine—and he's a big fellow now. You can't stand guard over him forever."

"Watch me. We should have stayed home, Dav. None of the Barks I asked Lady Poe to set out are seeing him. I think he's gone away somewhere."

Syg looked up at Davage and kissed him. "I guess I'm getting to be an old pest, huh?"

"Well, you're my old pest, Syg, and I love you. Do you want any more after all this?"

"Absolutely," Syg said. "They're all getting so big. Soon Maser will be going off on his own."

"Syg, Maser's barely twelve."

"Yes, and he's getting older every day."

"I was thinking, Syg. It's been a while since we've been off on an outing, you and I. How about, when this business is concluded, we take a trip, just the two of us? Perhaps to Bazz?"

Syg smiled. "Dav, whenever we go on an outing alone, we usually end up with another child. I know what you mean, though. I sometimes miss the days when it was just you and me. This business with Kay, I feel very much older in the aftermath." She took his arm and snuggled into him, enjoying the privacy of the teleporter.

Davage thought about the horrid shirts Duchess Torrijayne of Oyln had saturated Blanchefort village with. "Syg, did you ever get even with Torri for the shirt thing?" he asked.

"I did, actually. You'd be proud. It was rather fun, and I intend to continue. I find I enjoy pranking that miserable bitch—I mean duchess."

Davage laughed. Syg and Torri continually sought to humiliate the other.

As they walked, a light appeared in the distance. "I suppose I'll need to be a countess again. The things I do for you, love." Syg stiffened and assumed her rigid public appearance.

"Love you, Dav," she whispered as they entered the *Westerville's* teleporter room.

After the usual greetings were exchanged, Davage was quickly ushered to the *Westerville's* massive main conference room. Waiting for him were captains Harrison, Van and Strella. In the corner, three Sisters sat along with a flanking contingent of Marines. Orderlies shuttled back and forth, fetching them drink and plates of tasty hors d'oeuvres.

"Did you see what the Xaphans threw at us at Two-Pitch Nebula last month?" Captain Harrison asked, holding a drink. He was a mountain of a Barrow-man, broad and blonde-headed, even taller than Davage. "It was a starcraft of some sort that looked, for all accounts, like a naked woman. I mean it had no discernable bow, stern or beam, no lights, no dorsal or ventral. I really didn't know what to make of it. It was a pity to put it to the sword actually. It was quite a lovely statue."

Captain Strella, wearing a ladies *Tremblar* uniform, stirred her coffee. "That is a new thing among the Xaphans. They call it 'Bondarism' or 'Bondarunga'. It's an artistic movement where they eschew standard and practical construction techniques in favor of bizarre, functionless forms and unlivable structures. It's their hope that these oddities will accelerate their evolution to a higher form of life."

Harrison laughed. "That is the stupidest thing I've ever heard."

Strella blew and took a drink from her cup. "They're Xaphans, sir, not known for overly sane thought."

Eventually, Admiral Carfax and an orderly appeared, and the meeting began.

<What are they saying, Dav?> Syg asked via telepathy, always chatty.

<The meeting has only just begun,> Davage replied.

The Admiral was doffed out in his huge blue coat with knee-britches, leggings and black buckle shoes—an admiral's outrageous uniform was one reason why Davage had never wanted to become one.

<I want to know what they're saying, Dav. Why can't I just come in?>

"Thank you all for coming," Admiral Carfax said. "These are exciting times, I must say. Though nobody likes to see the daily horrors of armed conflict in space, the recent upswing in Xaphan aggression has me feeling as I did in the days of old, when we had an enemy to fight and lives to save. We are in a second Golden age of the League/Xaphan conflict, and every day glory awaits, but I digress."

They all, with the exception of the Sisters and their Marines, seated themselves at the large conference table. The Sisters sat out of the way, like an all-powerful chorus in an ancient play, sitting with their plates of hors d'oeuvres, silently watching from the wings of the room.

The Admiral's orderly dimmed the lights slightly. In workman-like fashion, the orderly then pressed a few buttons, and a holo-map of a large planet appeared over the table, hovering in mid-air. Davage looked at it: average land-to-water ratio, three distinct continents, a fierce-looking mountain range to the south, long, flowing coast-line to the north. Clearly, it was a map of Hoban.

"Yes, as you may or may not know by the look of it, this is a holo-relief map of Hoban. What can any of you tell me about the latest doings on Hoban?"

Captain Harrison spoke up. "Lots of Xaphan activity, especially from the combined Houses of Sorrander, Woodward and Midas equipped with new Charn cruisers and those outrageous statue ships."

"Aye," Carfax agreed, "there has been that. Most of their current activity has been funded by the wayward Camilla of Sorrander and by the Vorsham Consortium selling Gifted Xaphans to Ming Mooreland, so our spies tell us. Excellent, what else?"

Captain Vann chimed in. "I have heard that the House of Elam suffered a recent tragedy. As a result, the Elams have withdrawn from League society and have hermited themselves in their holdings in the south of Hoban."

"Ah, yes," Admiral Carfax said. "That is true." The orderly pressed a button, and a blinking red light appeared on the map's southern continent, indicating the location of House Elam. "Pray, have you heard what had happened to them, good Captain?" Carfax asked.

"I have not."

Lady Strella stirred. "I have heard that the House of Gregory also suffered some sort of tragic event. Something to do with Lord Gregory's youngest son, I think."

Again Admiral Carfax's orderly pressed a button, and a blinking red light appeared in the central area of Hoban's main continent.

The admiral turned to Captain Davage. "And you, Lord Blanchefort, have you also heard similar stories coming from Hoban?"

"I haven't. I'm afraid I've been consumed with matters at home as of late."

"Oh, well, I hope it's nothing too pressing."

The orderly pressed buttons, and twenty more blinking lights appeared. They seemed to be arranged in such a way across the face of Hoban that they formed some sort of character or symbol.

"As you can see, there have been a number of such recent incidents on Hoban—all of the blinking lights here denote where a similar incident has occurred. These incidents have a usual thread or pattern. Usually, and this is not generally known to the League, the lord or countess of the Great House in question is brutally attacked by a member of his or her own family."

The captains looked at each other.

The Admiral called up a list. "Let's see: Lord Carlisle attacked and killed by his son, Lord Derth. Lord Hisborough attacked and wounded by his youngest daughter, Lady Carbina. Lady Derlith molested by her own mother. And, just a few days ago, Lord Nels of Crossland was attacked and mildly wounded by his youngest son, Lord Mervin."

Davage sat there and listened. His thoughts became dark, recalling the attack on Kay.

"Admiral," he asked. "Are there any reports of these attacks occurring outside of Hoban, possibly on Kana?"

The Admiral paused a moment, considering his words. "Yes, Captain, with increasing frequency, though nothing approaching the levels we see on Hoban. As I said, a common theme in these attacks is that the perpetrator is invariably a beloved family member—a son, a daughter, a parent. A passed-on ancestor in some cases. Let us take the case of Lord Hisborough. He was attacked by his own daughter, Lady Carbina—the DNA evidence is conclusive. However, and please stay with me, Lady Carbina is naught but twelve years old and is safe and sound at this very moment in her home. The creature that attacked Lord Hisborough was a twisted, mutilated monster, at least one hundred ten years old, according to the Hospitaler report. A monster certainly, terrible and hideous, yet it was Lady Carbina. A parent always knows their child, no matter what form they might take."

The captains looked around at each other. Davage listened with rapt attention seeing patterns forming.

Kay.

<What's going on, love?> came Syg.

<Nothing, darling. Just boring stuff,> he lied.

<Are you going to be done soon? I'm feeling a bit hungry.>

<Yes, yes, just bit longer.>

The Admiral continued. "The effects of these attacks are demoralizing and heartbreaking, as you might well imagine. Lord Hisborough killed himself in grief for his daughter. With the number of these bizarre attacks increasing, Hoban is slowly dying of a broken heart, one Household at a time. And, friends, we have got to put a stop to it. We have been tasked by the Governor himself to investigate this matter and bring it to an immediate close."

Strella looked at her hands. "But, how—how it this possible?"

"Clones, no doubt," Van said.

Admiral Carfax shook his head. "No, sir. Clones, although created from like DNA, show clear deviation and are rather easy to detect. The creature that attacked Lord Hisborough was not a clone."

Captain Harrison thought a moment. "Then it must be a flesh replica—a robotic construct covered in flesh. I recall a ring of them in the Calvertlands of Onaris some years back. Yes, the Drury Matter, as I recall."

Again Admiral Carfax shook his head. "An interesting thought, Captain, but no. A flesh replica is still a robot at its heart. This creature had no robotic parts, no synthetic parts either. I am afraid, at this point, our thoughts are leaning toward the most improbable of all choices regarding these monsters."

"And that is?" Van asked.

The Sisters, sitting in the corner, stirred. A Marine spoke up. "We, of the Sisterhood, know of the possibility of time travel, in various forms, some more problematic than others. We know, theoretically, that it is possible to travel back in time if the flesh has been properly treated, and a temporal anchor-point has been established. There, with the anchor-point in place, a person could interact with himself or herself and not create a temporal schism. We believe that these people, these bizarre attackers, at some point in a theoretical future, have been abducted, held, tormented, mutilated and then released into the past to wreak havoc."

Captain Harrison objected. "Are we speaking seriously? The mechanics of time travel are plain and clearly possible; however, the issue is not connecting two disparate points in time—the issue is bridging a member of one continuum to another. The effects of temporal gravity are impossible to defeat. It cannot be done."

"Again," Marine said for a Sister, "the anchor-point is the key. Travel to the past, free of bridging, is possible up until the point that the anchor-point was enabled. It is a finite tunnel to the past, allowing easy passage from one temporality to another, free of temporal gravity."

Harrison still objected. "Such an 'anchor-point' as you put it, Great sister, will require a device colossal in size and draw ruinous amounts of operational power. I doubt the whole of Kana generates, at any given time, enough power to fuel such a beast."

"Agreed, but nevertheless . . ."

"How are the Xaphans doing this?" Strella asked. "It must be the Xaphans behind it, correct?"

The Admiral shook his head. "It doesn't seem like a usual tactic or technology they would choose to employ. Additionally, we have spies in their midst, just as they do in ours. Through our spies, we have heard of similar instances happening with great frequency in Xaphan space as well for years and years. We assumed that it was a byproduct of their madness."

The Admiral pulled a kerchief from his pocket and wiped his brow. "The Xaphans even have a name for these monsters: *Killanjo*, the bringer of sorrow and chaos."

"So then," Davage said, "assuming you are correct, who is doing this future abducting and tormenting? Who is responsible for this?"

The orderly pressed another button. A few bits of old-looking holographic pottery appeared next to the Hoban map. Carfax: "We have always assumed, and our scholars have made no clear distinction, that we were the first inhabitants of Kana, that Kana was a vast, uninhabited paradise just waiting for our arrival with the Elders ages ago. Doesn't really make sense, does it—a bountiful world like Kana having no intelligent life prior to our arrival? Recent scholarly teams from the Science Ministry, working in close cooperation with the Sisterhood of Light, have made remarkable discoveries in recent years. We have discovered evidence of an old precursor civilization vastly predating us on Kana. We have found bits of odd, petrified technology, traces of ancient cities, and fragments of pottery. And, this one here . . ."

One of the pieces of pottery expanded in size. Davage could see it was decorated with tiny symbols. The Admiral highlighted and expanded one of the symbols in size.

"We have found similar glyphs carved into the flesh of Lady Carbina's *Killanjo*. Like a chill wind from the past, whoever these people were, or possibly are, they are our enemy, not only of the League, but of the Xaphans, too. Any who are Elder are in their gaze. We are all under attack. Perhaps they fear our Fleet—fear to make a public statement of war and face us in open battle. Perhaps it is their intent to strike at the soft tissue beneath the armor. In any case, our mission to Hoban is thus: identify and thwart the attackers, discover their purpose, create some sort of dialog if possible and determine the location of this theoretical temporal anchor-point."

"So, we're operating under the assumption that such an improbable device exists?" Captain Harrison asked.

"We are, Captain. We are dealing with the improbable, as with these *Killanjo* monsters. We have already eliminated the impossible, cloning, flesh replicas and so on; therefore, the improbable is all that is left to us, and that is how we shall proceed until evidence dictates otherwise."

"Tell me our mission again," Harrison demanded. "The short statement."

"Very well. We are to defeat these fiends and put their temporal anchor-point to the sword. Simple enough?"

The Sisters stirred. "Tell them the rest, Admiral," a Marine said.

The Admiral winced and shook his head. He squeezed his kerchief. "I protest, Sisters."

"Do it, sir."

He struggled for words, then: "Another common feature of these Hoban attacks, as the Sisterhood wish to point out, is that they come with the presence of Berserkacides."

The captains stirred. "Berserkacides," Harrison said in a dry voice, "are a construction of lurid posts and imaginative journalists looking for a sensational story to frighten the public."

"I agree," Davage said. "I have seen odd things recently with my own eyes, however, I shall not subscribe to superstition and folklore."

"I understand how you feel," Carfax said. "Berserkacides, however, are very real. And, wherever we have seen these attacks on Hoban, the Berserkacides are present to add a further touch of terror. Firstly, let us make sure we are speaking on common ground. The term, 'Berserkacide' refers to men, women and children hailing from various tribes of Monama. Somehow, some way, they become enraged, four-armed beasts, never to return to the shy, quiet folk they were before. We currently have no information on how or why a Monama becomes a Berserkacide, but, once they do, there is no going back, and they must be killed. A massive nest of them was found in Vithland recently, stashed in the ruins of Clovis. We have the Sisters to thank for the discovery and eradication of this nest."

Admiral Carfax looked down at his shoes for moment. "Due to these recent events and the increasing propensity of Monamas to become dangerous Berserkacides, the Sisterhood is considering performing the rite of *Shuw-shun* against the House of Monama."

Davage stood up, outraged. *Shuw-shun*—the utter destruction and killing of all members of a particular House. To wipe them out to the last man, woman and child. The Sisterhood hadn't done such a thing in ages.

"That is barbaric!" Davage said to the Sisters. "The Monamas are a good people, and they are citizens of the League. This cannot be done! They do not deserve this!"

"The Berserkacides are real, Lord Blanchefort," a Marine said. "And the Monamas pose a clear and present threat to the safety and well-being of the League. We believe that the recent theft at our stronghold at Hiei was perpetrated by a Berserkacide. The evidence is overwhelming."

"Yes, yes, back to that again," Davage said. "Sisters, I am sorry somebody stole a piece of your property; however, you cannot use that as an excuse to wipe out an entire House. You cannot!"

"We have hair and bits of skin from a Monama perpetrator. Unfortunately, we do not have a comprehensive database of Monama DNA on file. However, the evidence is clear that it was a Berserkacide who did it, or it was a free Monama, and that makes the crime even worse. We shall keep the League safe from this menace."

"All right!" Davage shouted. "Assuming Berserkacides are real, then clearly the condition is a malady of mind and body that must be examined and treated. They are our friends, and we must help them."

"There is no helping a Berserkacide. Only death. And the only clear preventative step is eradication," a Marine stated.

Davage slammed his hand onto the table. "I recall leather-bound Sisterhood dogma stating that a Xaphan Black Hat could not be turned from evil. For thousands of years that's what was said, but, look,

Black Hats fall from evil with regularity now. We have found a solution to what was once accepted as impossible!"

The Sisters rustled and appeared perturbed. "Then, we suggest, Captain, you set to it and discover this cure for yourself. Whether or not the tribes of Monama live or die depends upon the success of this mission and the useful information that is gathered from it. We will be watching. If you cannot uncover the true perpetrators of this growing conspiracy to undermine the League, then the Sisterhood will have no choice in the matter and personally intercede—and our first step will be to partially disarm the attackers and declare *Shuw-shun* against the tribes of Monama and destroy them. Of course, we will not do such a thing lightly; however, if it must be done, than it shall be done, and it will be on our conscience and ours alone."

"You are not thinking clearly. You are reacting to a situation, not responding to it."

The Sisters stood. "This conversation is at an end. If you do not wish us to 'react', as you put it, Lord Blanchefort, then 'respond' with results." The Sisters then left the room, with the Marines following.

The captains sat in silence for a bit. "Admiral," Davage said. "I will not allow this. I will not allow the good people of Monama to be laid waste like a tainted crop."

Admiral Carfax darkened. "Then, as the Sisters said, it is up to us to save them. What we do in the next few days might determine not only the fate of the tribes of Monama, but possibly the course of the League itself. I pray the Elders that we are successful."

10—An Afternoon with Cloak

The following morning, every bit of Kay hurt. His body was stiff as a board, and not even the fine Xandarr sheets of his bed could comfort him. His ribs were sore from getting punched by Waft, and his back was a mess from getting thrown off the terrace by her. And his fingers, broken clean, were two spindles of pain.

He might have thought that last night was a fantastic dream—that he dreamt the entire race with Waft, but his aching body and broken fingers bore proof that it had, in fact, happened. As he stiffly dressed and exited his room, he tried testing himself just to see if last night was a mere fantasy. He Wafted once or twice and was astounded. As he recalled from last night, he could now Waft in a mere blink of an eye—truly remarkable.

His fingers becoming unbearable, he found a porter and requested to see a Hospitaler as soon as possible. He was taken at once to the King's personal Hospitaler where she began working on his painful fingers. Halfway through the procedure, Sara and Phillip walked in, and he told them what had happened. Sarah didn't believe it, of course, and it wasn't until he showed her with a demonstration of Waft, after his fingers had been fixed, that she believed.

"Didn't you hear the commotion? I was making a lot of noise."

"Didn't hear a thing," Sarah said. "Did you, Phillip?"

"No, I didn't."

Sarah, as usual, was fascinated. "You went all the way to that mountain?" she said, shading her eyes against the morning sun. "That big one way over there?"

"Yep," he said, hungry for breakfast, his aching body beginning to loosen up.

"Why didn't you come and get me so I could watch or help?" she wanted to know.

"Because there was no helping, Sarah, and she didn't give me any time to fetch my cousins to watch the spectacle."

"Damn!" she cried. "I would have loved to have seen that."

$$* \quad * \quad * \quad * \quad *$$

Sarah was the first to see the Princess that day. Holding her SAPP, she marched down to the river, the tails of her duster blowing majestically in the breeze. She came back about an hour later an awful, soaked mess; apparently, the Princess gave her a rather rough way to go. Phillip asked her what happened, and she said she didn't want to talk about it.

Phillip took his turn. He, too, came back up the path about an hour later also looking to have been roughly dumped into the river, but he took it in better stride. "That was amazing," he said. "Truly."

Finally, it was Kay's turn. He strode down the gravel path and made his way to the river. There, sitting alone in her little chair, was a small, veiled female, as before.

Kay smiled and walked up to her. "Good morning, Princess," he said cheerfully.

The woman who looked up at him was not the Princess; it was another mud-like naked female wearing a veil over her bushy head.

"Hello, Kay," she said softly. As with the previous one, her rather muddy appearance changed to that of Sam's—with the exception of her eyes, which remained orange. She transformed into the pale likeness of Sam.

"Where am I?" he said.

"You're in a Painted illusion. Right now, you're wandering around in the woods somewhere. I've got you. I have been looking forward to our meeting." She stood up, stark naked, her veils falling to her feet.

Kay raised his fists and made to fight. She raised her hands in a defensive fashion. "Please," she said, "I'm not going to hurt you. I don't wish to fight. I'm not going to attack you or cause you pain, I promise." She stood there smiling at him.

Kay lowered his fists and suddenly felt a bit awkward speaking to a naked woman, even if she was in Sam's image. "May I please offer you my coat?"

"Oh, yes, thank you."

Kay took off his coat and draped it over her, expecting at any moment to be attacked. She stood there and held the coat shut with her hand. "I think, of all my sisters, I'm the most like your lady. I suppose that means that I love you because she does, and I have no intention of harming you."

"So, what are we going to be doing? You're here to test me, yes? And if I fail, I die?"

"That is how it works, I'm sorry to say." She held out her hand. "But, you're not going to fail. I'm going to teach you until you pass. Please, walk with me."

He took her hand, and they strolled down a path until they arrived in a large clearing full of white marble statues frozen in various poses, all nude. Some were standing, some were sitting, and others were engaged in what appeared to be wrestling matches of some sort. In one hand, they were all holding little wind chimes that tinkled in the breeze in a pleasant fashion, and, in the other hand, they held small torches. Orange fire cracked and spit. The statues were arranged in a rock garden of colorful gravel and calm reflecting pools. A very peaceful setting. Cloak escorted Kay through the rows of statues.

"Your Cloak isn't something that I can shock into service with pain or aggression, like Waft did with you last night. Rather the opposite. You need to be relaxed—at peace. The Cloak takes years of study and mastery. You couldn't hope to perform a fully Painted Cloak in just one night, and it isn't realistic or fair of me to expect that from you. Invisibility, however, is another story. Once you master invisibility, then the other various disciplines of Cloak will follow in kind. You, Kay, are going to make all of these statues disappear, and I don't mean just visually—you are going to Cloak them thermally and audibly as well. When you can do that and hold it, then you will have passed my test."

"And, if I can't?"

"Then I'll have to kill you, and I don't want to do that. That would break my heart. That's not going to happen though. You're going to do just fine."

They sat down in the grass with the statues laid out before them in a gallery of white-marbled poses. Cloak got very close to him and began playing with his hair.

"Now, I want you to relax, Kay. Just let your mind be at ease."

She whispered into his ear. "Just pretend that I'm Sam. Pretend that it is she whispering into your ear and that you'll get a kiss when this is all over, possibly more. Pick a statue and Cloak it, Kay. Come on; it's not hard."

Kay was heavily distracted. Cloak's mouth was so close to his ear he could feel her breath and her lips brushing past his earlobe.

"Just relax."

He allowed himself to relax and, sure enough, the statue vanished, a full visual Cloak.

"Very good, Kay." She reached out with her foot and kicked in the direction of the statue. He heard the jingling of chimes, held in an invisible hand. "Now, let's Cloak it at an audible level, too. Just keeping doing what you're doing." She began kissing his ear. He tried to move away from her, and she followed, matching his movements.

"Don't worry about what I'm doing, Kay. Just concentrate and be at ease."

He concentrated. "No, it's too much. My head feels as if it's going to crack open."

Her tongue wandered into his ear. "That's natural," she whispered. "It'll feel odd at first, but just let the initial discomfort pass by. Go on, Kay, Cloak it audibly."

He struggled, feeling a great fist of pressure building in his head. Cloak started kicking at the statue, and, slowly, its chimes faded into silence. Soon, the heat from its torch was gone, too.

She stopped kissing him and gave him a large hug. "Very good, Kay. See, it's easy." Kay stood and paced about, examining the remaining statues in detail. They were an assortment of male and female statues—the female ones all looked like Sam, and the males all looked like Kay. And, though he previously thought some of the statues were carved in wrestling poses, on closer inspection, that's not what they were doing.

They were having sex, some in demure basic poses, and others in tangled-up challenges of form and flexibility, all locked in a screaming, ecstasy-filled moment. Meanwhile, to his shock, some of the Sam statues elsewhere were performing acts upon the Kay statues best left for closed doors. Kay blushed.

"You're so funny. You needn't be shy, Kay. It's pretty clear she likes you," Cloak said. "This is what's on her mind much of the time. Monama women enjoy their sex and she thinks it's so funny how demure you are. She's baffled by it sometimes. I like you, too, Kay, and I want you to be at ease."

"I'm having issues concentrating with all of this."

"So shy. Sit down, Kay," Cloak said.

He sat down, and then Cloak quickly climbed into his lap, putting her legs around him and pushing his face into the dip between her breasts. "Now, back to your task," she said. "I want you to Cloak all of these statues at once, visually, thermally and audibly; then, we'll be done. Take your time as I'm in no hurry. Take all day if you need to. You're going to pass my test with ease."

"There are too many statues to Cloak—my head will explode," he spoke muffled into her chest.

"No, it won't. You'll feel the strain for a bit at the beginning, but then you'll forget all about it. Just forget about it." She began rocking back and forth, his face between her breasts. "Just forget about it . . ."

A sarcastic voice rang out from a distance. "Why are you being so nice to him, Cloak?"

At the far end of the grounds, the last female, still in her mud-dabbed appearance, came striding in. The final female: Sight. She crunched naked across the gravel, looking rather surly.

"I will conduct my test as I see fit," Cloak said. "Kay is doing quite well. There is no need for anything more."

Sight walked up and moved Cloak aside. She picked up Kay and pushed him down roughly in a clatter of gravel.

"Sight, leave at once—I'm warning you!" Cloak demanded.

Kay got up, and, giving tit for tat, pushed Sight down hard, her feet flying into the air as her head hit the ground. She sprang back up and tackled Kay. They rolled around in the gravel.

Calmly, Cloak separated them. Sight sputtered with rage, and Cloak slammed her naked body into the ground once or twice; then, spinning Sight around by her hair, Cloak sent her spiraling away, where she disappeared through the clouds and was gone.

Cloak knelt down next to Kay. "Are you all right?"

"I'm fine."

Cloak kissed him. "I'm afraid Sight doesn't like you very much, Kay. I think she feels you've ignored her for your entire life, and she's very bitter. Very angry."

Throughout the rest of the afternoon, Kay, with Cloak's patient guidance, Cloaked every statue, muffled their chimes and cooled their thermal images. He passed his test with a fair amount of ease, though his head pounded with the strain of Cloaking all the statues at once. Cloak gave Kay a large hug and a kiss, and she gave him back his coat.

She seemed sad. "I've enjoyed our time together, Kay. I wish I had more time to teach you. You're a good student. And, like I said, I love you because she loves you."

"What will your fate be?"

"My task is done. I'll go back to the nothingness from whence I came and be forgotten."

Kay embraced her. "I'll not forget you. I thank you for your kindness today—I wasn't expecting it."

"Just remember," she whispered into his ear, "tomorrow, when you face Sight, stand up to her. She wants you to look at her, to acknowledge her. Don't let her push you around. Whatever she has in store for you, I know you'll be up to it. And, wherever I am tomorrow, I'll be rooting for you."

Kay looked at Cloak. "You are just like Sam, in every way."

"Am I? Will you do me a favor then?"

"Name it."

"I have a few hours left. Will you sit here and share this time with me? We can enjoy the remainder of the afternoon together."

"I'd like that."

Cloak transformed the Painted rock garden into a lovely sea-side at dusk. Sitting down, Cloak tucked her knees up into her chest and laid her head on Kay's shoulder. Together they watched the sun go down.

She was so much like Sam.

She was so much like Sam.

She was so much like Sam.

11—Brawling with Sight

A raging storm, a rather unusual occurrence on Xandarr, pelted the Keep that night.

Kay hadn't bothered going to bed. He figured his sleep would be rudely interrupted, and he wanted to be ready.

Sight was coming for him, and this was going to be his toughest test.

He didn't have long to wait. Through the rain, he could hear a taunting voice filtering in from outside.

"Kay, little Kay . . ."

He heard a wry giggle. *"Wanna' fight? You're going to die, Kay."*

He got up and went to the wind-whipped terrace. Outside, through the roaring rain, he could see a solitary figure standing in the grass beyond the Keep.

He felt a little relieved that it was finally here. He saddled his CARG, and, without thinking about it, Wafted down to the wet grass and the rain.

Her hair was alive with movement. "So," she said, her mud-like appearance gone, "you actually showed on your own without me having to collect you. This is the prize event; make no mistake. Waft was indifferent, and Cloak liked you. Me, I'm going to tear you apart! I'm not here to help you. I'm here to win this!"

"Cloak said you are angry with me, that I've ignored you my whole life!"

"And haven't you? Sight is your most powerful Gift, and you have frittered it away. Hiding from it—shrinking from the wonders that were yours for the taking! Enough! Fight me, and pray I don't choose to break you in half immediately!"

"What is my test?" Kay asked as Sight assumed a fighting stance.

"Figure it out for yourself!" she yelled, charging.

An odd thing happened. Sight, raging, a creature of the arcane and incredibly strong, missed. Kay, calm and collected, simply Wafted behind her.

She snorted in anger and charged again. Again, Kay Wafted, and this time he put a huge, thudding blow on the back of her head with his CARG.

She fell to the ground and immediately sprang back up. Kay Wafted again, but this time she anticipated where he'd come out and put a massive left hook right on the button, dropping him. Savagely, she pushed his face into the wet ground. "I have the Sight, remember. You want to Waft again? Then do it, and I'll be waiting. I know your every move!"

She grabbed him by the leg and lifted him into the air, where she then slammed him back down with a splat. She took his CARG and threw it off into the darkness.

Dazed, Kay looked up and took a foot to the chin.

He was just about done. He was in agony.

WHAM!! She struck a terrible blow to the back of his head.

And everything went to amber. He could feel his Sight open up and detach, like a thistle seed from its husk, and float around him. He could see everything clearly. He could see past the driving rain and the thick vault of clouds. He could see the stars laid out in their unfamiliar constellations and the moons. He could see his CARG coursing with Silver tech energy lying in the grass some distance away. He could see the Keep and Sarah and Phillip asleep in their beds.

The Keep? The Keep was behind him. Creation, he was seeing out of the back of his head!

Time seemed to come to a crawl. He could see Sight planning to hit him with a fight ending—and possibly life ending—shot to the neck. He could see her anticipating his counter-move, and he could see himself anticipating her anticipation. On and on, ruse after ruse, until she reached her limit. He, however, had not.

He blasted into the air, hovering at about a hundred feet, and then Wafted down at speed, mashing Sight into the drenched ground.

Another round of ruse and counter ruse, and Kay put his elbow into Sight's chest as she didn't know which way to turn.

He took a good look at Sight standing there in the rain. Her body seemed whole and normal, but in just a moment of observation, he had a wealth of information. Deep down, she was made of some sort of smoky substance—the NIGHTMARE material that Sam used to create her. And deep within her chest was some sort of hollow spot.

He gazed at it and saw that, at one time in the past, there was a gold medallion there, filling up that space. The medallion wasn't there now, but it *was* there yesterday. He was, again, seeing into the past.

The medallion, he Sighted, had an embossed image of Sam's smiling face.

As he and Sight began grappling in the rain, he was fixated on the medallion that was once there but now gone. He recalled the giant, multi-armed females he saw in the distant past—how one of them saw and actually seized him. He had a notion that he could somehow interact with objects in the past, and possibly in the future as well. Perhaps that medallion was his test, to reach out into the past and get it.

After the usual bit of ruse and counter ruse, Kay Wafted to his CARG, lifted, and presented it to her. It looked strange in his Sight, coursing with energy from the Silver tech flowing within it.

His Sight fell backwards, and there was the medallion mounted in her chest.

She charged, and Kay, with a direct thrust, pushed the horn of his CARG through her chest and out the other side.

Lying in the muddy grass was the medallion. It wasn't there now, but it was there once. He picked up the medallion from the past, held it, and gazed at it. It felt solid in his hand.

He showed it to her. "Here, Sight, is this what I was after? Is this my test? I have looked back through time to present you with this medallion. I have used my Sight to accomplish this." He looked away, and the medallion vanished, falling back into time.

She looked at his hand, then lowered her fists, the hole in her chest closing up. "Yes, you have passed your test."

She appeared incredulous. She lowered her head, turned, and began walking away through the layers of rain. All around him, his Sight hovered and spun like an uncaged gyroscope. It was freed from the constraints that had held it his whole life. Nothing could hold it back now.

"Sight!" Kay called to her through the rain. "I want to thank you. Thank you for opening this Gift to me and showing me what is possible. You were right. I ignored my Gift; I was afraid of it. You have helped me to face it, and I thank you."

Slowly she turned to him, and her face softened. In the rain, she approached Kay and put her arms around him, pressing her forehead against his. "I guess she chose well, after all. Use your Sight, Kay. Don't be afraid of it. It will bring you back to her, and it will save your soul if you let it. Pass your Trials, and be one with her." She looked at him in the rain. "Go back to your bed, Kay, and wait. Our master will be by soon, and you will receive your instructions."

Sight then kissed him on the cheek, walked off into the rain, and was gone.

12—Over Hoban

The Fleet task force of three *Triumphs* and two *Straylights* travelled at a leisurely pace. Hoban was a rather long slog from Kana, taking at least three days at a good pace and four, at worst, if at half-sail. Once in the Hoban area, they were to link up with a detachment of Marines from the 22nd division flying *Trelaine* attack ships.

Captain Davage surveyed his bridge. How big and modern it was in comparison to his old *Seeker*. The bridge overflowed with scanners and sensing stations, all laying out the surrounding space in bold holos and vivid displays. The navigator's chair, once a horrendously simple set up, now had a colorful array of holos floating around it, including the clock, the AM/PM orientation dials and stellar charts. The sensing stations, once manned by seven people, now only required one person with a battery of holographic and printed out displays. The old Missive station was gone altogether. He still recalled the *Seeker* with its primitive bridge and sensing equipment—the ship was virtually blind. He always stood there behind the helm wheel, his lit Sight, seeing through the hull, quite literally using his own eyes to pilot the ship. He still missed it to some extent.

His countess Sygillis, as usual, sat in his chair. For twenty four years she had fared the stars at his side. Together they shared in many adventures and built a family; Syg never changed. She had grown a bit Bluer as time progressed, taken to bowling and had a superior bowling average of 177-180, but he could live with that. She loved their home at Castle Blanchefort and their children and was loathe to part from them, but she never allowed Davage to sortie without her. Their youngest daughter Hathaline, to Davage's delight, loved coming with them on their missions. She even had her own room on the ship, permanently set aside for her use. They had always hoped Kay would want to join the Fleet, but he was rather insistent that he didn't enjoy space travel, so that was quite a disappointment for them. But little Hathaline, always trying to impress her father, was a natural. Davage was certain she would want to join the Fleet someday. Perhaps she'd follow in his footsteps and become a junior helmsman. She seemed to have all the tools required, and her pedigree couldn't be better. Lady Hathaline was her father's daughter.

Lt. Kilos, Davage's ever-present friend and first officer, was also on the bridge standing at her station. She'd been at Davage's side for over thirty years, starting out in the Stellar Marines, and then changing to the Fleet. She'd had plenty of chances to strike out on her own and command a vessel, but she had always declined. She knew her limitations, and she considered herself a much better follower than a leader. At least she was honest about it.

As the Fleet arrived near the outskirts of the Hoban system, Davage felt more and more uneasy. The meeting with Admiral Carfax and the Sisters kept flashing through his head. The poor families of Hoban, attacked by their own kin—and not just by their kin—but by bizarre, tormented visions of their kin, along with packs of snarling Berserkacides.

That's what bothered him the most. The Sisters, watching and waiting, were considering the *Shuw-shun* against the Monamas.

To level their homes.

To destroy their property.

To kill every last one of them, down to the very young without trace, as if they'd never been there at all.

∗   ∗   ∗   ∗   ∗

Shuw-shun

The Sisters hadn't done such a thing in hundreds of years. It never looked good for the Sisterhood to flex their muscles in such a way, and, obviously, it made the Great Houses of the League quite nervous. Normally, the Sisters liked to stay in the background and allow the general League leadership via the Ex-Commons to address a pressing matter. But, apparently, they were concerned enough about the situation to pull out all the stops and involve themselves directly, and that could mean *Shuw-Shun*.

Nobody was quite sure how the Sisters could accomplish such a thing; they were more powerful than they let on. They wisely kept such power hidden.

The most recent House to feel the *Shuw-shun* was the lowly House of Mutt, a wretched Calvert House whom nobody was sorry to see go. The Sisters occasionally punished unruly Great Houses and wayward cities which they felt had strayed too far into decadence, but they normally informed the victims first, giving them time to up stakes and vacate. Then, at the appointed time, the Sisters literally blew the House or city off the face of Kana in a cloud of destroyed debris and scorched earth. The House members or city inhabitants, now destitute and penniless, rolled about the landscape, humbled and contemplative. It was hoped that such a public punishment would teach whomever a lasting lesson and cause them to grow from the experience.

The *Shuw-shun*, however, came without warning in a flash of destruction and death leaving no survivors, no bodies to bury, and no earthly possessions to distribute.

The *Shuw-shun* left nothing behind; everything was ground into dust and thrown high into the air.

And the *Shuw-shun* was coming for the House of Monama. To save the League, they will genocide the tribes of Monama and close their eyes forever, unless he and the rest of the Fleet task force could come up with something conclusive—provide the Sisters with the identity of the true attackers, for the Monamas appeared to be nothing more than pawns. Dangerous, rabid, slavering pawns.

They must not fail.

✶　✶　✶　✶　✶

"Syg," Beth said, "The Hospitalers have tasked me to obtain permission to perform tests on Kay—a Shadow tech male. Think of what we could learn. It's not an opportunity we should allow to pass by."

Lt. Kilos took a big swig from her tankard. "Beth, what is it with you in the last few days? Kay this and Kay that. Heck, I like the kid too, but . . ."

"Beth?" Davage asked, "Are you still addled from the Silver tech incident ? Of course you know we're in your eternal debt."

She sat there and stared at her coffee cup. "Syg," Beth said, "have you ever allowed your Silver tech to touch Kay?"

Syg took a drink of coffee and stared at Beth. "Of course I have, I'm his mother after all."

"Well, apparently, his power doesn't work on you—and that is a very good thing, Syg, because let me tell you—you don't want to feel what I felt, he being your son and all. I'm still having chills."

Kilos laughed. "Kay gave you *chills,* Beth?"

"You laugh, Ki, but you don't understand. He gave me more than just that—a lot more."

"Did it hurt?"

"I wish all it did was hurt."

Syg shook her head. "Beth, you're a Hospitaler—you said you knew what would happen if you allowed him to touch your Silver tech. You said you were prepared for it."

"I thought I was. I knew from a forensic, textbook standpoint what would happen, yes. I knew he could control me if he had wanted. But—to feel it, to actually experience it. Nothing could have prepared me." Beth took a drink of coffee, her hands shaking slightly.

"Prepared you for what, Beth?" Ki asked.

"Come on, Ki—use your imagination for Creation's sake. It's no wonder the Black Hats are so afraid of Shadow tech males." She turned to Davage. "Sir, you said you're in my debt?"

"Yes, you know that. You saved his life."

"Then I'd like permission to court Kay—will you take offense to that?"

"What?" Kilos cried.

Syg interjected. "Why, yes, Beth, I think so. I think we would."

"Why? He's a man now. He can make his own decisions."

"He's only twenty-two. Besides, Beth, you're like family. It's a little creepy to think about it," Syg said. "You delivered him. You slapped his little naked bottom, remember?"

"So? Why don't you allow the two of us to decide what's creepy and what's not. This really doesn't concern you, Syg, and I was only asking as a courtesy."

"Beth, you're scaring me," Kilos said.

She took a drink of coffee. "Yeah? Scares me, too."

Hoban was a distinctly brownish-colored world with a single moon. The larger cities of Brindecea and Crossland stood out against the dark landmasses. Its single moon Lauralea was distinctive for having its own atmosphere. Its largest city Synthmere also stood out in the darkened sky.

The Fleet task force settled into a high orbit along the equator, spacing out so that they could cover the whole planet.

As planned, a Marine contingent of twenty-five *Trelaine* attack ships came in from 4:45AM and took up station around the huge Fleet vessels.

And, there they waited.

13—Lord Christopher Park

It was getting dark. A man wearing a long coat and a scarf sat in Lord Christopher Park, a lovely wooden area outside the southern city of Lyra, one of the larger cities in the Zenon region of Kana. He'd been there all day. He was far from home.

As the sun began to go down, several sets of people who had been enjoying the park saw him, stopped and advised that he should take his leave. The park wasn't safe at night as of late, they said.

Berserkacides, they said.

The man thanked them for their concern but didn't move. He simply sat there on the bench and got out a portable holoterm and did some reading to pass the time. Eventually, as the bright southern stars came out, he sent a Com to his wife.

She was lying in their bed. She looked thin and bone-tired. She said she was very worried about him. He said he was fine and that he loved her. She begged him to be careful.

She said she couldn't live without him.

He put the holoterm away and sat some more.

After a time, a slight buzzing came from his coat pocket. Looking around, he opened his coat and pulled out a small, robotic animal in the shape of a large bug. He held it in his hand for a moment, made a fine adjustment to it, then let it go. It flew on its metal wings, hovered in the air, then landed on the bench, its jewel-like green eyes alert and watching.

The man had been at this for two days with no success. He was tired and he wanted to go home to his wife. Perhaps tonight would yield results.

As if on cue, the robotic bug became agitated and took flight, moving down the path to the south.

The man got up and followed it, walking at a brisk pace. Perhaps now his patience would be rewarded.

The path took him into a deep copse of trees, the canopy of green blotting out the stars. The robotic bug flew a bit farther, and then it landed on a tree branch.

The man stopped walking. He knew how to read the robotic bug's movements. He had perfected it in the last few weeks, and it was finally working like he'd hoped it would.

His wife, his beloved wife, couldn't take much more. He had to get it right and gather just a little more information. Then, it would be perfect. For his wife's sake, it had to be perfect.

The robotic bug beat its shiny wings, making a rather loud BUZZZZZZZ . . . .

It was time, the man knew to be at his guard.

Coming down the path in the opposite direction was a person walking a large dog.

The person and the dog approached the man. As they got close, the dog was revealed. The dog had six legs.

The person walking it was a hideous monster, skinned and dripping bile and gore.

The dog was a Berserkacide, naked and ravenous for blood and walking on all sixes—four arms and two legs. It was held on a bloody chain.

The monster and the Berserkacide looked at the man for a moment. Then:

"Our first catch of the night. Kill him," the monster said unleashing it. The monster watched the Berserkacide lope ahead a few paces, and then it vanished in a green flash.

The Berserkacide roared and sprang as the man, ready, took his black scarf off and laid it out in front of him. As the Berserkacide charged, he skillfully got his scarf around it and, like a great constricting snake, the scarf moved on its own, wrapping around the Berserkacide in a tangle of thin, gangly limbs and hair, and commenced to squeezing the life out of it.

The Berserkacide struggled as the man watched. It was very strong, and it rolled about on the ground, trying to free itself.

But the black scarf was strong, too, and it squeezed even harder. The Berserkacide's bones began to crack under the pressure as the scarf relentlessly constricted. One of its black eyeballs popped out and hung there. It moaned and wailed—the man hadn't expected that. The man, watching, felt sorry for it as it died. The agonizing process seemed to take forever.

When it was at last still and newly dead, the man took his scarf back and said a short prayer for the Berserkacide's soul. He then dragged its crushed, pale form off of the path, and, taking a small kit full of instruments from his coat, set to work on its dead body, the robotic bug watching silently nearby from a tree.

He carefully collected the samples he needed. Finally, they would be whole and ready.

Finally, his wife might have peace, for she couldn't take much more. The man collected his robotic bug and began the long journey back to home and his wife.

14—Rostov

The Great metal man appeared the next night, his chariot moving on its own without Waft, Cloak and Sight to pull it. They had returned from whence they came. He landed in the green and, with thunderous strides, dismounted. Kay sensed his presence and Wafted outside to stand before him. Towering, the metal man looked down at Kay, and appeared neither impressed nor sympathetic that Kay had passed the first portion of the Trials.

Inside his great chest, Sam slumbered. Kay Sighted his chest but could see little within.

"You have bested my horses," he said finally. "You have proved your Gifts are now of a suitable level that you have a reasonable chance of surviving the Trials to come. The Lady of Monama's preconditions have been met in full. Very well, it is time for your first Trial."

"I want to see Sam," Kay said looking up at him.

"Not possible. She slumbers within, safe and unharmed. If you wish to be reunited with her, I suggest you proceed with your Trials at once."

Kay didn't give up. "Sam is pursued by something—those creatures that attacked me in the Grove. I want to know who and what they are."

The metal man didn't answer Kay's question. Instead, he continued. "The House of Rostov is built on lies and stolen goods. Their House sits upon blood-stained ground. A wondrous device rests within a vault at House Rostov. You will remove this device and keep it safe with you."

A shimmering object appeared before the man, spinning, floating on air. It looked like a smallish, rather organic-looking ring made of silver. It had a hole in the center, like a silvery doughnut.

The shimmering image faded. "Remove this device and keep it safe, and you will have passed the first Trial. You will not see me again until you pass all three of the Trials set before you. If you succeed at the House of Rostov, Bathloxi will seek you out and continue."

The man climbed back into his chariot.

"Wait!" Kay cried. "You're certain Sam is all right?"

The man turned the chariot and began climbing into the sky. "Safer with me than anywhere else."

✴ ✴ ✴ ✴ ✴

"So, what the hell does that mean?" Sarah asked as she pulled a drink from the _Goshawk's_ small fridge.

They were all sitting by the _Goshawk_ in the purple evening under the rising seven moons. They'd all come to like Xandarr, its King and Queen, the 44, and its remarkable princess. They would all leave this place truly enriched.

The next morning they said goodbye to King Balor and Queen Zoladerra. Kay took the long walk down the path and said goodbye to the princess. She didn't react at first, just sat there by the river and drew on her canvas. After a bit, Kay turned to leave.

Hearing rapid footsteps from behind, he turned and saw her running toward him. She was holding her canvas. "I made this," she said, panting. "I made this for you."

Kay looked. On the canvas was a very accomplished portrait of him, done in pleasing pastels. His eyes were deep and roving.

As he held the canvas, she put her arms around him and wept.

Had Sam not been in his thoughts, he felt sure his heart would have been lost to Princess Vroc right there and then. How his mother might have reacted to that.

Then, with heavy hearts, the group boarded the _Goshawk_ and flew off, all vowing to return someday.

✴ ✴ ✴ ✴ ✴

Two days later, they tucked into orbit and barred in on Rostov.

Rostov was a sea-side city on a small peninsula jutting into the southern Sea of Esther. It was perched about as far west as was possible. To the east of Rostov were the warm lands and rolling hills of Remnath. There wasn't a whole lot beyond the outskirts of the city, just a series of green steps and hills. The nearest city was the Remnath bastion of Wiln about a thousand miles to the northeast. A little farther east was St. Paris, that fine, trendy city of quiet manors and sprawling castles. The Sisterhood strongholds of Twilight 4 and Deep 7 hugged the coast to the southeast.

Though Rostov was technically in the Remnath region, it was not a Remnath city. The Rostovs, the founders of the city, were notorious of the Calvert line, hailing from the seedy city of Bezzel. Censured by the Sisterhood of Light for the crime of wife-swapping, they were finally chased from their ancestral holdings by the Sisters when they continuously harassed the chapel of Barton, deep in the Great Armenelos forest. Though the House of Rostov, led by their scabby patriarch Nouables hadn't broken any laws, the Sisters had had enough and forced them from their dreary holdings in Bezzel. Smiling and polite as always, the Sisters informed them that their House would be completely and utterly destroyed, and they advised them to not be present when that happened. Flying away in a rickety transport, they prowled the southern coastline trying to squat in the Zenon city of Lyra. However, being made to flee, they eventually settled on the rocky finger of land in a barren area of Remnath that eventually became the city of Rostov.

There, isolated and left alone, they flourished, though they didn't really create anything productive. Rostov became a haven for sportsmen, with most if not all of the more notorious sportsmen on Kana either hailing from or having trained extensively in the city. Dirty courtesans also seemed to come out of Rostov with frequency. In fact, the dirty courtesan's trademark fungus, "The Weed" had been elevated to new heights in the moist hot houses of Rostov.

✳   ✳   ✳   ✳   ✳

With the *Goshawk* safely in orbit around Kana, Kay, Sarah and Phillip began working on a plan. Kay, though still a little shaky in space, was much more able to endure a long space flight than he was before leaving for Xandarr. They thought it best to check into a quaint inn somewhere in the city and use it as their base for the duration of this unusual operation. Rostov was a dark, dirty city of narrow streets and seedy shacks. The city itself was, with the exception of a few outlying structures, comprised of one, huge, walled-in structure. It was built villa-style, in a vast spread-out design of confusing courtyards and galleries.

As the *Goshawk* descended, an automated message popped up, informing them that the airspace over the city of Rostov was restricted and advising a more southerly course. Phillip veered to the south and settled at fifty thousand feet. They tuned the ship's scanners and took a look. From the air, they could see many people moving around in the open spaces. They could see the piled up stacks of refuse that passed for buildings. There were barred windows and black stone. In a courtyard, they thought they saw someone getting executed.

After witnessing that for themselves, none of them really wanted to stay in Rostov, so they found a suitable establishment in a hamlet outside of Wiln near the sea. It was far away from Rostov, but it was better than actually having to stay there.

Sitting in Sarah's room that evening, they stayed up late and formulated a plan. Sarah was basking in this; she loved hanging out in nice inns and ordering room service, and she loved planning things.

"So," she said, relaxed in her pajamas, "we're looking for a small, doughnut-shaped device that is hidden in a vault? Why's 'Sam's Doughnut' so important?"

"I don't know, and yes, that's what he said."

"Did you write his clue down word for word?"

"For one, Sarah, I didn't have anything to write with, and two—it doesn't sound like a clue, per se, to me. He told me exactly where it is."

"Can we get him back here to ask questions?"

"No, Sarah, we cannot."

They tried calling up detailed maps of the House of Rostov's manor, a black-stoned heap of rocks by the sea called Leap Manor—many such places, including Castle Blanchefort, were detailed in the Holo-net. But, like Castle Blanchefort, none of Leap's secret locations were revealed, just holos of it from various angles and the barest of maps.

"I think," Phillip said turning away from the Holo, "that we're going to have to fly over it and make our own detailed maps."

"It's restricted. They'll probably try to shoot us out of the sky."

"Not if we're Cloaked."

Kay and Sarah listened. "Kay, you said that on Xandarr your Gifts were expanded, including your Cloak. Is that correct?"

"Yes, but I'm still pretty raw. Just a few forms of basic

invisibility. I can't disguise myself yet, and I certainly can't Paint an illusion."

"Invisibility is all we'll need. But, we'll need to Cloak not only ourselves, but the *Goshawk,* too."

Kay shook his head. "The *Goshawk's* too big. It'll give me a headache."

"So, you get a headache. Endure it." He got up and went to the terrace. Outside, beyond the tended gardens of the inn's back lot, was the usual ship park. Several ships, a few mid-sized transports, and a number of land cars and floats were arraigned in a row, including the black *Goshawk,* which was off in a corner by itself.

"Try to Cloak the *Goshawk,*" Phillip repeated.

"It's too big," Kay insisted. "And it's too far away."

Sarah shut down the Holo. "Well, how about we work our way up to the ship. Start off by Cloaking yourself, and then us. Then, when you get used to that, Cloak the ship."

For being an impulsive hot-head half the time, Sarah could, at the strangest of moments, demonstrate flashes of jaw-dropping, cool, collected reasoning. Kay couldn't argue.

Kay recalled his training session with Cloak. He recalled how nice she was—how much like Sam she was. He relaxed, and after a moment or two, he was Cloaked, falling easily into its invisible embrace, his head hurting with the initial strain.

"That's pretty good," Sarah said looking around. "I can't see you at all." She reached out and touched his arm. "And I can't really feel you too much either. It's like you're there, but you're made of clay." She lit her Sight and panned around. "My Sight is starting to improve. I can see your outline a little if I really concentrate."

Phillip lit his Sight, his eyes glowing silver. "I can see him well enough."

Kay dropped the Cloak, and he reappeared—his head throbbing.

"Now do all three of us," Sarah commanded. Kay took a moment to allow his head to stop hurting, then he cleared his mind.

"All right, we're Cloaked."

Sarah and Phillip looked around. "Everything looks the same." She looked at her hands. "And I can see myself."

"Of course you can see yourself—that's how a decent Cloak works. We can even talk to each other, but nobody outside of the three of us can hear or see."

"Really?" she said.

Before they could stop her, she bolted out the door in her pajamas and went hurtling down the stairs to the pub. The impulsive Sarah was back in earnest.

"Are you feeling any strain?" Phillip asked.

"Yes. My brain feels like it is being wrung dry."

"If you can keep this up, then we should be able to penetrate House Rostov and be off with the device in no time. We just need a little recon to gather insight on the floor plan, and that means Cloaking the *Goshawk,* too."

He went to the terrace again. "Come on, Kay, Cloak it. You can do it."

Kay sat down on the bed and concentrated. After a minute or so, the *Goshawk* faded into a Cloak. The strain was terrible. To Cloak the three of them and the ship as well was too much; it was overwhelming. From downstairs they could hear Sarah whooping and hollering joyously in the pub.

"Good, good," Phillip said.

"I should drop it on Sarah while she's down there running around like an idiot and give her a thrill," Kay said. "I'm going to let it go," he said, holding his head.

"No, leave it up. In fact, keep the ship Cloaked all night. That'll be a good test. I've heard from Duchess Torrijayne that good Cloakers can keep things Cloaked for a long period of time, and without really having to think about it. Since I can't Cloak, I can't confirm or deny that."

"My head will explode, Phillip. I'm dropping it. It really hurts."

"If you drop it, I'm going to punch you in the neck," Phillip said in a serious tone, pointing at him. "Keep it up." He kept looking out the terrace.

It appeared Phillip was a sterner taskmaster than Cloak was. Kay lay back on the bed and held his throbbing head, convinced he was going to die of an aneurism at any moment.

Although the first few minutes were terrible, after a bit, he had to admit he felt a second wind coming on. His head began to feel better. Even though he was Cloaking all three of them and the *Goshawk,* it was almost as if he could hold the Cloak and not think about it. After a while, the pain vanished, and he forgot he was doing it at all.

Sarah came dashing back into the room, out of breath. She was holding a half-full bottle of spirits.

"You two!" she yelled, excited. "I took this bottle of spirits right off a man's table, and it fell into Cloak with me!"

Phillip was cross. "Sarah, put that bottle back where you found it, right now!"

She turned and bounded back down the stairs with a bumpy fuss. Kay got up off the bed, and he and Phillip left the room and went down the stairs.

"You all right?" Phillip asked.

"Fine, I'm fine."

It was a strange thing to move about unseen and unheard. Inn guests and staff were going about their business, unaware that Cloaked people wandered about. Kay recalled, as a young boy, his parents taking him to fine restaurants in Minz and Hannover. As they sat eating their dinner, his father sometimes mentioned to his mother that Cloaked people were walking about the floor. At some of the finer restaurants, the establishment actually employed Cloakers to covertly remove dirty dishes and silverware from patron's tables, thus enhancing the illusion of near miraculous service. Lord Davage often enjoyed speaking to the Cloaked people as they approached the table, seeing them in his Sight, and watching them jump in surprise. In the north it was considered incredibly rude to Cloak one's self into invisibility—only people who had something to hide Cloaked themselves. To be caught while under Cloak could be a serious occurrence, and, sometimes, Cloakers who over did it found themselves in prison or in a bad way with the Sisters.

Kay and Phillip spilled into the pub. Tables full of people were scattered about. They saw Sarah sitting at a gentleman's table. She was holding the long blue length of her ponytail and was going to tickle a man's nose with it as he dined.

"Sarah!" Phillip yelled. "What are you doing?"

"I'm doing something I've always wanted to do, and don't try and stop me!" She waved her hair and the man brushed his nose absently. "Haha!" she cried.

Phillip moved to the far side of the pub. "How're you doing, Kay?"

He seated himself at the bar. "I'm fine."

Sarah again. She'd moved on to another table and it looked like she was about to pull something off of a lady's plate.

"Sarah, if you're hungry, get dressed and we'll come down and eat!" Phillip shouted, heard by only the three of them.

"You're no fun," she said getting up.

✶ ✶ ✶ ✶ ✶

Later that night Kay dropped their Cloak and they went outside onto the terrace, Sarah eating a plate of something she'd gotten from the pub and rubbing her tired eyes. Phillip sat down in a chair and enjoyed the night breeze.

"What are we doing out here?" she asked, tired, wanting her rented bed.

"Making a fool of yourself in the pub tires you out, doesn't it?" Phillip asked.

"It does."

Kay turned. "We're going to begin our recon."

"How are we going to do that?"

Kay allowed his newly activated Sight to roam. "I'm going to look in on them."

"From here?"

"Yep. You see Cloaking the two of you and wandering around in the pub reminded me that my Gifts are now working a lot better than they were. And, I now have access to my Sight. I'm going to test it. I'm going to look in on Rostov. If I'm able to see it from here, that'll keep us from having to fly over it and risk getting shot down."

Sarah, becoming interested, rustled in her seat and set her plate aside. "Ok, that's about a thousand miles from here, right? You really think you're up to it?"

"We'll see in a moment, I suppose."

Kay allowed his Dark Sight to stretch out.

"So your eyes really don't glow?" Sarah asked, looking at him.

"Apparently not."

"Kay," Phillip said, "you're facing the wrong direction. Rostov's that way." He pointed to it.

"It doesn't matter. I can see out the back of my head, too."

Phillip and Sarah looked at each other, impressed it seemed.

The amber passes of his Sight reached out from their little inn at Wiln and moved, slowly expanding in all directions. It was hard—the concentric bubble of his Sight expanded in stages and then stopped, only to expand again in regular hops. His eyes strained. Just when he thought he'd reached his limit, he'd hop out again, like a person holding his breath under water to see how long he could go, *just a few more seconds, just a bit longer.*

And soon, the walled fortress of Rostov came sprinting into view, perched on its nook by the sea. It was an irregularly shaped citadel of black rock, bastioned at various points with turrets and watchtowers. The keep was a confused collection of buildings in the far western section of the fortress. The eastern part was open within the walls, and many shacks and other ill-constructed buildings were piled up in a haphazard fashion. There, amidst those seedy surroundings, Kay could see many people milling about. They were at sport, betting money on this game of chance and that. Farther away, under the keep, was a huge treasure vault guarded by many men and a few bizarre-looking creatures. Heaped about in the treasure room was an assortment of artifacts and other valuables. With regularity, people came into the vault, either removing an item, or depositing one.

There, mixed into the pile, was the twisting, doughnut shaped device—Sam's Doughnut, Sarah called it.

"I see it. There it is."

"Where is it?" Phillip asked. "Is it guarded?"

"It's in a large treasure room several levels below the ground. A vault of some sort. It's guarded by many men. I see patterns of energy. The vault appears to be Waftlocked, and there are numerous arcane devices scattered about to detect the presence of invisible beings, no doubt. I also see a host of strange creatures roaming about the vault."

"Creatures!" Sarah exclaimed.

"What do the creatures look like?" Phillip asked.

"They are rather snakelike in appearance, about fifteen feet long, with tiny lizard-like arms and six tails that are barbed. They appear to be green on their dorsal quarter and are yellow with black spots on their bellies."

"Those sound like mickalmicks—woodland creatures from the Armenelos forest area. They can be tamed and trained to perform all sorts of functions. They are said to be able to see Cloaked people, so, given that, the Waftlock and the other arcane instrumentality in place, our infiltration into the vault will be greatly complicated."

Kay had a sudden thought. He recalled the Haitathe warrior who saw him from the past. What if he could simply reach out and grab the piece and pull it back?

He turned around to face in the direction of Rostov, then he reached out with his hands, and sure enough, he could feel the smooth, cool sides of the device. He pulled it back, his hands shaking with new confidence.

"Look, Sarah, Phillip, I got it!" He looked away for a moment in triumph, and the device was gone. It fell back into the vault in Rostov. Kay shut his Sight down in bitter disappointment.

"What?" Sarah said.

"I had it. I had Sam's Doughnut in my hands. But, the moment I looked away, it was gone, right back where it came from. Oh, that's frustrating."

"Try it again," Sarah said, excited. "Maybe you messed something up!"

Shooting Sarah a dirty look, Kay tried again. Once again, he held the device in his hands, and, once again, it fell back to the vault the moment he turned his gaze away.

"I saw you holding something!" Sarah said. "It was round, about a foot and a half wide, right?"

"That was Sam's Doughnut. Again, as soon as I looked away, it fell back to where it came from. Creation!!"

Phillip remained calm and empirical as ever. "Where is this vault?" he asked.

"It's in the western-most point of the keep. And it's under heavy guard with those monsters as well."

"That would be Leap Manor, per my reading on the Holo-net here," Phillip said.

"Bring one of those monsters back here so I can see it!" Sarah demanded.

Not bothering to acknowledge Sarah's ridiculous request, Kay took one more look. As he spied in on House Rostov, his Sight tended to wander into the past and the future. Going back into the past revealed little. The House, after a few bouts of destruction and recreation, simply disappeared, and an uninhabited bit of windy land, grazed occasionally by wild animals, appeared.

Going forward, however, was illuminating.

He could see multiple possibilities for House Rostov. In one future, they continued as is, being a cradle for sportsmen and courtesans, falling further and further into vice and decadence. He saw the city being destroyed once or twice, by raiders and rival

Houses. Eventually, he could see the Sisters once again chasing them from their rocky perch, leaving a crater of scorched earth where the city now stands.

However, in a radically different path, he could see House Rostov being transformed, the House reforming and fully embracing Elder teaching. He could see Rostov becoming a real city by the sea, led by a man in white with a large triangle hat. At his side was a small woman with long, curly amber hair and a Shadowmark adorning her right eye. Behind them walked the people, and the city rose. In this path, Rostov became a place of great learning and enlightenment—a place where Great Houses wanted to live, where inspiration and new ideas flourished. He could see the black eminence of Leap Manor failing down, being replaced with a white stone castle of a new House Rostov without walls—a place where the Sisters would never come in anger again.

All this, Rostov could be. The central figure in determining which way the House went appeared to be a huge, scabrous man in a long, dark coat holding a sinister rifle-like weapon.

He was the key. If he lived, the House would fall into ruin and be destroyed in a flash of fire. If he died, it would be reborn.

Hmmmm, Kay thought, interesting but immaterial.

He quieted his Sight and told Phillip and Sarah what he'd seen

"I think," Phillip remarked, leaning back in his chair, "that the easiest course to us is to simply go in, Kay. You Cloak yourself, sneak into the vault, deal with the mickalmicks and the machines, and grab the piece."

"That's a novel plan," Kay said.

"Sometimes simple is better."

Kay shrugged. "We'll tarry here a day or two and continue to observe Rostov and get a feel for their schedules, if they maintain any. Then, we move. You're not in any hurry, are you, Sarah?"

"Nope," she said.

The night was lovely, and they continued to sit outside, listening to the gentle sounds of the sea and feeling the cool breeze. Eventually, to appease Sarah, Kay pulled back one of the mickalmick creatures, and she gasped with delight.

15—Message From The Cat God Pub

"**C**an you believe, Beth?" Syg said in their quarters, getting ready for bed. She sat at her mirror in her favorite nightgown.

"I guess touching Kay with her Silver tech was a pretty jarring experience, much more so than she expected. It's a good thing she's out here with us instead of wandering around Blanchefort on her own— might keep her out of trouble. Still, Syg, Kay's old enough to pick his own relationships. If he wants to court Beth, who are we to stop him, though I don't think he's got eyes for anybody other than Sam."

Sam. Syg bristled at the sound of the name. "Yes, well," she said, brushing her hair, "that relationship is at an end. I have already forbidden him to see her any further, and, if I catch her on our grounds ever again, I will kill her without question."

Davage struggled, wondering how much he should tell Syg about the attacks on Hoban, and about the attack on Kay. He wondered if he should tell her that he, more and more, believed that the attacker was a demented, twisted version of Lady Kilos, his beloved daughter. He didn't think Syg would take it very well; he himself was barely square with the thought.

She put her comb down and turned to him. "What are we doing out here, Dav, far away over Hoban? We should be home defending our own."

"The ship still sails, Syg. We've a duty to accept the charge appointed to us. All is well at home."

"Is it? I have not seen Kay about the castle for days. I had Lady Poe release Barks all over the place and I haven't seen Sarah or Phillip either and, coincidentally, the *Goshawk* is missing. Seems to me that they're on an outing. You wouldn't happen to know anything about that, would you?"

"I know all about it," Davage replied. He had to be careful, as Syg could determine truth from lie (and little white lie) with ease. A generous helping of truth, misdirection and a dash of obfuscation was the best course of action when dealing with a potentially unruly Syg.

"Where did they go?"

"Xandarr, I believe."

Syg considered that. "Why in the name of Creation did they go to Xandarr? The place is so bloody hot no Vith goes to Xandarr on a whim. You complained until my ear fell off the last time we were there."

"Xandarr was his destination."

"He should not be going to Xandarr. He's still recovering."

"Syg, our son survived and is well. You cannot treat him like he's infirm, or dead for that matter—that is not our tradition. He cannot become a hermit in our castle, stashed away like a scared rabbit, and I have encouraged him to resume his usual activities."

Syg flushed up. "He went to Xandarr to see Lady Sammidoran, didn't he?"

"I'm not aware of that."

Syg stood and approached him. "Do not attempt to skirt around the question, Dav, or bend the truth to your liking. You know exactly why he went to Xandarr, and it wasn't for the beating sunshine and salt breezes. Now, let's have it, all of it, and if I don't like what I hear I'm taking an immediate transport to Xandarr to confront Kay and drag him home by his ear myself."

Being married to an ex-Black Hat had its disadvantages, as Syg could detect truth from lie, and she was skilled enough at debate to know when he was attempting to divert to course of the discussion or cloud the issue entirely, and, he had no doubt she wouldn't hesitate to personally fetch Kay in an embarrassing public spectacle.

He decided to simply lay it out and appeal to her using logic. He composed his thoughts and readied to reply when the Com rang in.

"Com," he said in answer, thankful for a momentary respite.

"Sir, you have a pending message."

Davage looked at the clock—it was well past the evening bell. "At this hour? From whom?" It couldn't possibly be from the Fleet. "Is it live or pre-recorded?"

"The message is unregistered from a live source. The sender does have a valid code."

Unregistered? They forgot about their discussion. In the old days, he was used to getting mysterious messages. He frequently received odd messages from his old antagonist, Princess Marilith of Xandarr. But, he hadn't heard from her in twenty years—she was dead.

Syg killed her.

Davage had a feeling that the unregistered message, whatever it was, had an ominous portent, as did Syg. They approached the large desk where the Com terminal was placed. They seated themselves, Syg taking Davage's hand.

"Fine, Com. I'll take the message here."

"Aye, sir."

"It must be regarding Kay, Dav," Syg said, concerned. "What if it's from Sam and she wishes to gloat? What if she wishes to boast and threaten another attack?"

The cone lit up.

A woman wearing a lavish black evening gown appeared. She was sitting in a grand smoking room. It reminded Davage of a particular officer's lounge in the north wing at Fleet that he favored; it was a large, craggy sort of room lined with shelves and old books. There were leather chairs all about and credenzas topped with sparkling glasses and bottles of aged spirits. He thought he could almost smell the fine tobacco floating on the air. The room on the cone was different from the one at Fleet in that it was decorated in a greenish sort of motif; rich green carpeting, green accent lighting and tall green vases containing leafy green ferns. There were also cats all over—ceramic cats hidden in the corners, paintings of smoky cats with alluring green eyes, pearly cats nestled up in the shelving.

The woman seated before him herself seemed rather catlike, with that ubiquitous feline aloofness. Her long hair was a catlike mackerel color with black tabby stripes. Hanging from her throat was a black charm embossed with a large capital "M".

Apparently, Syg was seeing something completely different from what Davage was seeing. "Who are you?" she said, somewhat incensed.

She smiled. "My name is Mabs."

"Why are you sitting in my personal study? I'll ask you to leave my study at once! That room is to be locked at all times unless I am present."

She shook her head. "I am not sitting in your study, Countess. This is a small establishment I run. I call it the 'Cat God'. Different people see it as different things. Each to his or her own."

<*Is she telling the truth, Dav? I see my study redecorated in green,*> Syg sent to him via telepathy.

In the background Davage saw waiters moving by, transporting trays of drinks to indistinct people seated all over the room. *<I don't see your study, Syg. I see something that looks like a smoking room I favor at Fleet—also done up in green with cat statues in abundance.>*

<I too see cats. So, what does this person want?>

<I suppose she'll make that plain momentarily.>

Davage, Syg and Mabs stared at each other for an odd, awkward moment.

"I have been asked to help you, and is what I intend to do," Mabs finally said. "I am sorry for the hour."

Davage was mystified. "You want to help us in some fashion?"

"Yes."

"Who, by chance, made this request?" Syg asked.

"Carahil."

Davage and Syg knew Carahil well. Carahil, protector of Xandarr and a god—supposedly—created in tree-filled passes of their own Telmus Grove by Dav's sister, Lady Poe of Blanchefort. Lady Poe considered him her son, and therefore Carahil was their de facto nephew. Davage recalled with a smile that Carahil was a notorious prankster. Now that Carahil was mostly gone from the Grove, away to who knows where, Davage missed his pranks to some extent. He also liked to think he was somewhat of an authority on Carahil, and if this woman was familiar with him, then he should know her as well. He didn't.

"How do you know Carahil?" Syg asked.

"I am very close to him. All the gods have their secrets, and I am honored to hold his." Several children came into the cone and played at her feet. They appeared to glow with a silver radiance. "You go and play," she said to them. "If you're good you'll all receive a special treat." Chattering, the children streamed away.

"Were those your children, ma'am?" Davage asked.

"Yes," she said with pride. "I have news for you, and guidance."

"News and Guidance? From Carahil you say? Where is Carahil? Why isn't he here giving us this news himself? He's hardly a stranger and he does get around."

"He is far away, Captain, doing things he feels he must."

"What things?" Davage asked.

"He is defending the life of Lady Sammidoran."

Syg spat. "He defends the attacker of our son. How could he?"

"Lady Sammidoran did not attack your son, Countess, and you

needn't me tell you that. Your mother's heart is full of rage and the need to strike out for your son whom you love. I know that feeling well. For ages I lamented my lost children. You knew me then, Countess. You knew me once when I was full of rage."

"I did?"

"Yes. And now, thanks to you and Carahil, I am at peace with new children to warm my heart."

Davage interjected. "I am glad you have found solace. Now then, you have news for us?"

"Your son is making great strides and is becoming a powerful Vith lord. You would be very proud."

"We've always been proud of our son," Syg said. "Is he still on Xandarr?"

"No."

Davage thought about it. Kay must be having success in his Wellerman's March. That was good news indeed. "Thank you for this news, ma'am. You also have guidance for us?"

A waiter came by and she took a drink from his tray. "Your guidance is to stay your course, for you shall soon have answers, though they might not be what you wish to hear. You wish to help your son, Countess, then you are ideally placed at Hoban. Hoban is where you may serve your son best."

"Here, at Hoban you say? I don't see how I can help my son so far from home."

"You shall soon see." She turned to Davage. "Lord Blanchefort, are you aware of the ancient hero named Atrajak of Want?"

Davage thought a moment. "He . . . was a Remnath, I believe. A berserker from antiquity."

"Do you know anything further?"

He tried to remember, to recall his studies of the Kanan past. He had volumes of knowledge in his head of the history of Kana, unfortunately, his studies were dominated by Vith teaching and Vith heroes. Atrajak was a Remnath, and the Vith never gave them much due. He felt rather embarrassed for his lack of knowledge.

"I'm afraid not, ma'am." Syg sat next to him and was rather shocked—Davage not knowing something. It was astounding.

She smiled. "That's all right. There is a volume you will want to look up: '*The History of the Hidden Wars and the Long Journey of Atrajak of Want.*' It will be of great use, I promise."

"What does this volume tell?"

"It contains crucial information." Mabs stood and approached the cone. "Now then, I must be off. Be true to yourselves and always know that Carahil, and I, are with you. Farewell."

The cone went dark.

Syg was incredulous. "What was all that about?"

"I really have no idea." Davage turned to the terminal and called up the ship's library.

"What are you doing?"

"I'm looking this fellow Atrajak up. I feel rather ashamed. I suppose we of the north do tend to look down on the Remnaths quite a bit. I shall make it a point to correct that error in the future."

Information flowed in on the holo-cone and Davage was disappointed. "Oh, look at this, Syg?"

"What?"

"Apparently, Atrajak of Want was labeled a traitor by the Sisterhood of Light after he attacked their strongholds of Twilight 4 and Deep 7 in 000004ax. Quite a long time ago. There isn't much here, most of it is restricted, including the book she suggested."

"So, what are we to do? Do you really think this book will help us somehow?"

"Hard to say, since we can't see it to find out." Davage suddenly felt very tired. "Well, let's sleep on it. Perhaps fresh ideas will present themselves in the morning."

Davage stepped into the lavatory while Syg went to the bed and removed the top cover. He loosened his collar and removed his shirt. "Perhaps I'll inquire with Captain Strella of the *Halo Dawn* in the morning. She's a Remnath and might have familial ties to the old House of Want. It's too late to inquire with her now, she's probably off to bed."

"Davage, come here, please," Syg said.

Yawning, he returned to their bedroom. "What is it, darling?"

Syg pointed at the bed. Something rectangular and rather large was placed under the covers. It made a pronounced box-like bulge in the center of the bed. "This. What is this?" She pulled the bedcovers back.

A large book was revealed; old, leather-bound, and creaky with vellum. The cover was lettered in fancy writing which neither one of them could read.

"I suppose Carahil couldn't resist giving us a gift," Syg said.

The book smelled of cream pie, Carahil's usual calling card.

16—The Tombs of Crossland

Orders came down from Admiral Carfax the next morning. The *New Faith* had been assigned the task of investigating incidents in the North Croatoa region of Hoban, starting with the influential House of Crossland. The Lord of the House, Nells, was reported to have been attacked by a monstrous version of his son, Lord Mervin. Additionally, the monster was said to have been slain by the House staff and was kept on ice for inspection.

The teleport tube came down on the trimmed lawn of Crossland Manor. Captain Davage, Countess Sygillis, Lt. Kilos, Bethrael of Moane and Ennez the Hospitaler walked out into the balmy Hoban afternoon. High above, sitting in the command chair of the *New Faith* was the dashing Paymaster Stenstrom, Lord of Belmont. He was the son of the venerable Captain Stenstrom of the *Caroline*, a warbird of great respect. Although Stenstrom was a Fleet Paymaster—a glorified legal observer and civilian clerk—he had his father's gift of command and had become a Paymaster merely to appease his mother, Lady Jubilee, as she didn't wish to fear for her son as she had through the years for her husband.

Paymaster Stenstrom was gifted, willing and eager, and Davage felt perfectly at ease giving him the ship.

Samaritan Ennez hadn't initially come on the journey to Hoban. He'd been Davage's Samaritan for thirty years, but, as Hospitalers weren't members of the Fleet, their participation was on their own initiative, and Ennez's verve for sailing had diminished a bit as of late. Davage had heard Ennez was finally ready to settle down and seek out a bride, but had had no luck as of yet. Fortunately, Bethrael was available and willing to fly. Still, after they sailed, Ennez, cantankerous as ever, changed his mind and booked passage with a fast transport in Atalea, linking up with the *New Faith* just short of Planet Fall. Beth and Ennez were a matching set, both Hospitaler Samaritans. They wore the black uniform with silver instruments sticking out of the pockets. Also, the two wore their little winged silver helmets and carried the jet staff which they could use with lethal efficiency.

Ahead was Crossland Manor. It was a big, provincial estate built in Remnath style, full of lacy stone-work, statues and fluted rails. A host of local Hobans tended the meticulous grounds, trimming the bushes, watering the flowers and raking the pebbled drives. The manor was built of some sort of burnt umber stone which matched Hoban's odd amber sky. In the late afternoon the sky was decorated with its lone pearly moon.

They had announced their arrival some hours earlier. Their plan was to interview Lord Nells of Crossland, his Countess Alberta, and have a look at the remains of Lord Crossland's attacker.

They needed something—anything to give to the Sisters. Davage was desperate for information. What they discovered here on Hoban could either save or condemn the House of Monama. The Sisters would not wait much longer.

The atmosphere inside the manor was surreal—the recent attack on Lord Crossland had apparently sucked the life out of the place. The staff seemed sad and dour, going about their duties in a strange, pre-programmed sort of fashion. The Crosslands themselves all seemed to be rolling about in shock, like they were stuck in a bad dream. The Countess of Crossland, Alberta, greeted them in her brown, jeweled gown and, of all people, seemed the most lucid, though her sadness was thinly veiled. Her lips trembled as she spoke; her little hands shook.

"We are so glad that you are here and bid you welcome," she said.

The Crosslands had fourteen children, three of whom still lived there in the manor. Mervin, the boy in question who had supposedly attacked his father, was safe and sound in his wing. The Countess took them upstairs and admitted them into his room. There Mervin was, wearing a miniature version of the long Crossland coat. Only fourteen years old, he played with his toys, oblivious to the maudlin atmosphere around him, to the sorrowful, somewhat suspicious, somewhat fearful eye with which his mother looked at him. Lt. Kilos, proving to be great with children, approached and played with him—the poor boy seemed starved for attention. Beth carefully scanned him as he played, and he came out clean. Just a happy, healthy fourteen year old boy. He appeared to want his mother, but she didn't approach. She just stood there and looked at him, her horror thinly veiled.

Then the Countess took them into the depths of the manor, to the body that was waiting there. She had the clear sense to keep it on ice, to preserve it for just such an investigation. Of all the Crosslands, Countess Alberta appeared to be the only one who'd kept her head, the only one who had not given up in sadness, though just barely.

"I'm sorry for the dark," Countess Alberta said lifting her skirts as she went down the stairs. "This is our wine cellar and there are no lights—it's bad for the wine, so I'm told." She looked at the rows of stored bottles sporting the cheerful House label of vines and rolling meadows, they seemed to remind her of happier times. The Countess stopped at a cubby and produced several small lanterns that she turned on and passed out. "This way, please." Holding the blue, flickering lanterns, they continued into the depths of the cave-like cellar.

The frozen corpse that emerged in the bluish lantern light was truly monstrous.

It was of bizarre and tortured proportions. It was about eight feet tall—its body somehow elongated and stretched, painfully so. Its joints were all distended and fused in an unnatural way. His skin, if one could call it that, was a mauled, sliced patchwork partially covering his thin musculature. His face had no skin at all. Several portable freezing units were placed next to his body, keeping it rock solid.

Kilos looked at the thing on the slab. "Elders balls," she said.

Sygillis, thinking back to Kay, put her head into Davage's chest as they looked at the creature's dead face.

"Great Countess," Davage said quietly. "How was it that you were able to determine that this was your son?"

Without missing a beat she answered: "It feels like him. It has his presence—I cannot explain further—I just know. A parent always knows his or her child."

Without saying it, Davage fully understood; Syg did, too.

The lantern light was dim, and Davage lit his Sight.

There were obscenities carved into his flesh from top to bottom, vulgarities and profanities, the graffiti of the dead written by an insane hand.

The creature's face was truly terrible. His eyes, nose and ears had been removed—in their place was a travesty of male organs stitched into position and jutting.

Beth couldn't look any further, and she turned away. Ennez, stalwart as always, got his scanner out and examined the hideous corpse in workman-like fashion.

"Who could do this?" Ki asked.

Ennez waved his scanner around. "Five penises on his face, attached by some sort of fusing process that I'm not familiar with."

"There are only four, Ennez," Ki corrected. "Isn't that enough?"

Ennez continued. "I repeat. There are five attached to his face. There's one in his mouth as well."

That was all she could take. Even the iron-nerved Kilos, a former Marine who had seen it all, turned away.

Ennez carefully scanned the ones attached where his eyes should be. "The ones here have some sort of sensory structures built within—again, I've not seen anything like this before."

"This can't be their son; it just can't," Syg said.

"It is," Ennez said. "The DNA is a perfect match. No hint of 'Blanding' as one sees in a clone, and I detect no robotic parts, so it cannot be a flesh replica either. This is Lord Mervin of Crossland. Only, it is much older. I'd say he's at least a hundred years old, his blood is poisoned, and I see indications of rampant decay throughout his body."

Syg stared at the body. "How is this possible? How can he be upstairs playing in his room and be here as well, dead, in a monstrous, aged form all at once?"

Davage adjusted his hat and looked at the thing on the slab. "Time travel—the Sisters believe it to be a possibility."

Ennez agreed. "His tissues show damage consistent with theoretical temporal travel, as described with the various writings put out by the Sisters. The time travel aspect itself isn't all that difficult to achieve; it's the temporal anchorage that is the key. Without it, bridging from one temporality to another would be impossible."

Syg snapped out of her funk. "You're saying this—thing—is from the future?"

"I am. What other option is there? Make no mistake, Syg—this is Lord Mervin. His tissues are much older than he currently is, and this isn't a clone or flesh replica. His DNA would show signs of that, and he's not a robot. He is from the future. At some point, Lord Mervin will be transformed into this creature and then sent back and turned loose on his family."

"Talk sense, will you?" she replied.

"Here it is, Syg, right in front of you. What do you want me to do?"

Lt. Kilos returned to the table. "It's like the old stories we have on Onaris, the Jennybacks. They're evil versions of kin that return to plague their House."

"This has happened on Onaris?" Syg asked.

"Sometimes."

Davage stood there looking at the thing and felt his heart break.

Kay.

He'd had his suspicions, his simple theories as to what happened to Kay in the Grove. Was something similar to this what attacked Kay? It had to be. One of his daughters, in a monstrous exertion like this one, had done it and is still on the loose.

Davage was a fearless man . . . for himself. He found as time passed that his fearlessness didn't necessarily extend to those whom he loved. He worried somewhat about Syg, but she could handle herself. What of his children? What of Kay, and Ki and Hath and Maser? How would they measure up to the dangers of the world? The world had almost been too much for Kay.

And now here was this monster, and his girls and young son, home alone. He felt himself panicking. Home, that's where he and Syg should be, defending their children from monsters such as these.

Mabs . . .

You are where you need to be.

Shuw-Shun. The fate of a whole people depending on this investigation. He stared at the creature on the table, his thoughts far away.

You are where you need to be . . .

The Countess Alberta stared at the abomination lying dead on the table. "My son," she said.

Davage composed himself. "Your son is safe and sound in his wing, playing with his toys. We are going to get to the bottom of this—rest assured of that. But, first, you must protect your son and do your best to keep him from this fate."

She looked at the creature with horror.

"You must steel yourself, Countess. You must be his mother and not fear him, as I detected you were doing earlier. Do not let this—thing on the slab—alter or color your love for him. Someone or something did this to him with the express purpose of shocking you, of breaking your heart. Don't allow their efforts to be successful. You, with diligence, might save him from this."

The Countess nodded. "I am trying. Of course, you're correct. I am trying."

"Countess, were there any Berserkacides with this monster?"

The Countess thought a moment. "I do not know what a Berserkacide is, Captain."

"A Monama. Naked, rail thin, black-haired, black eyed. Most of these attacks that we've seen across Hoban have been accompanied by Berserkacides."

She shook her head. "No—just this. Is that not enough? I—I think we surprised him. I don't think he was ready to encounter us so quickly."

Davage nodded. *No Berserkacides.*

Unable to view the creature any further, they took their leave, went back upstairs, and saw the lord of the manor—Lord Nells.

On the way Davage pulled Lt. Kilos aside. "Ki," he said. "I need you to do something for me."

She could see he was serious. "Name it," she said.

"I want you to return to the ship. Apprise Paymaster Stenstrom of our situation and take a *Trelaine* back to Castle Blanchefort immediately."

"I'm not leaving here, Dav," she said. "The Jennybacks . . ."

Davage lost his composure for a moment. "You must, you . . ."

He took a breath and calmed himself. "Ki, our girls are at Castle Blanchefort undefended. I need you to go there and protect them—Lady Kilos, your namesake, my little angel Hathaline. Our little boy, Maser. I need you to do this for me, Ki, please!"

"But what about Lady Poe? She's there."

"She is not well as of late, and I fear for her. Please, Ki. My children."

Kilos could see how serious Davage was—how desperate. Desperation wasn't a thing she was used to seeing from Captain Davage.

"All right, Dav. I'll do it. I'll go there at once, and not leave until you return. I'll not let anything happen to them; you can count on me."

They embraced causing Ki's Tweeter to dislodge from her shoulder. Tweeter flapped up and landed on Davage's hat. Davage, pulling free, reached up and gave him a pat on the beak. He then returned to Ki's shoulder.

Giving Davage a last look, Ki turned and exited the manor.

Davage took a deep breath, Ki will protect his home. He felt reassured and then joined the rest in the study.

Lord Nells of Crossland sat in his large study. He had been attacked several days prior while walking in his garden with his Countess. A monster had appeared from thin air and had got him in the leg. The couple appear to have surprised it—like it wasn't ready to encounter them so quickly. The monster was then was killed by one of the staff. Though it was hideous and tortured of form, they instantly recognized it as their son Mervin. Parents always know their child, even in such a state. And Lord Nells fell into a deep melancholy, sitting in his study oblivious to everything.

He hadn't bathed or eaten in days. He just sat there, shell-like and morose, his cheeks stubbly and drawn. He was thin and gaunt.

Countess Alberta admitted them, and she tried to pull him out of his daze. "Nells," she said. "Darling, the Fleet is here. They are going to investigate this matter and give us answers."

He barely seemed to recognize her.

They interviewed Lord Crossland, and he mumbled his way through it, staring off into space, answering the questions that he had only half-heard. His mind was elsewhere—still grappling with the beast in the form of his son. Afraid of the innocent boy playing upstairs.

"We, with your permission, sir, will search the grounds and look for clues," Davage said.

Lord Crossland didn't respond.

"You have our permission. The grounds are yours," Alberta said. "I will show you where the attack happened."

She began showing them out of the study.

"Lord Crossland," Davage asked looking back, "are you drugged, sir?"

He didn't answer.

"Lord Crossland, I understand how you feel, but this is not the time to . . ."

He rousted out a bit. "Lord Blanchefort, Captain of the Fleet," he said. "I have been attacked by a monstrous image of my son who tried to kill me and my wife—his mother. Additionally, the next day, I saw my Countess standing in the fog, beckoning, arms wide, for me to come to her. I was about to but remembered that my Countess was inside the manor."

Davage, Syg and Beth looked at each other.

Nells sighed. "What was that I saw? A ghost—another monster? What would have become of me had I gone to it? We are surrounded by evil here. Our home is no longer ours. The League is no longer safe. By your leave, you cannot understand how I feel, Captain."

"With respect, sir," Davage said, "I know exactly how you feel. My son—our son—was attacked and badly wounded by a monster similar to the one in your basement, a monster whom I am convinced is a member of my own family."

Lord Crossland stirred a bit at this news.

Syg turned to Dav, shocked. *"What?"*

Davage continued. "So, forgive me, sir. I know exactly how you feel."

Crossland rustled uncomfortably. Alberta looked at the floor.

"How I wish that it had been me attacked, and not my son," Davage said. "That such a thing could happen to one so dear to me, and I wasn't there to assist him, to help him. However, I am not going to sit back and fret and feel sorry for myself. I am here, on Hoban, far away from my home, trying to discover who has authored this attack, and I am going to discover them, sir—make no mistake! I am going to discover them, and I am going to make them pay—make them rue the day they chose to come at my son. Meanwhile, you've your family to think of and defend. You've your beautiful Countess and your young son who needs his father, and I suggest you set to it and protect them as best you can. In any event, you may either assist me in this endeavor, or you may get out of the way."

Crossland didn't respond.

Countess Alberta approached. "Please, come this way, I will show you where the attack took place. Please . . ."

As they readied to leave the study, Crossland stirred and called out to them. "The tombs, Captain. Check the tombs, I hear them there. I hear my wife's voice calling to me there."

✳   ✳   ✳   ✳   ✳

Far back from the manor, past the lovely manicured gardens, pebbled walkways and service structures, was a huge, walled-in space encompassing several square miles. The Countess, using a large, ancient key ring, opened the rusty gate, and they all went in.

Within the wall was the Crossland graveyard. The interior was vast, housing an uncountable number of fallen tombstones, vaults and mausoleums. The ground was lumpy and somewhat moist with undrained, standing water. The air felt thick and humid, and patches of fog reached up from the tussocks.

Centuries of Crosslands and their staff were buried here. The place had an unnatural, ominous feel to it.

The Countess took her leave, and Syg immediately confronted Davage about his theory that either Lady Kilos or Lady Hathaline had attacked Kay.

She was close to hysterics. Davage told her it was only a hunch, but the evidence was mounting, and Syg nearly collapsed, weeping into his shoulder.

She turned an angry eye to Beth and Ennez. "Did either of you know about this? You ran tests. Did you know about this?"

Beth looked down and adjusted her little silver helmet. She didn't say anything. Ennez spoke up. "Yes, Syg . . . We did. Lady Hathaline's DNA was all over Kay. Our samples were conclusive."

Lady Hathaline? It was Davage's turn to be shocked and wrecked. He was certain it had been Lady Kilos. His little girl, Lady Hathaline, had done it??

"And were you going to say nothing? I thought you two were our friends. Beth, how could you?"

Beth managed to find her courage and spoke up for herself. "And what were we to say, Syg, that your daughter nearly murdered Kay, and ate a bit of him as well? We were trying to spare you until we knew more. We're searching for answers too. The both of us . . . didn't know what to say. I'm sorry, Syg."

Syg flopped down onto the wet ground and began to weep. Recovering from his own momentary funk, Davage pulled her back up.

"Syg, you're not going to do this—you're not going to tuck in like Lord Crossland sulking in his study."

"I want to go home and protect our children! They need us! Take me home, Dav!"

"I already dispatched Lt. Kilos, before our audience with Lord Crossland. She is on her way there with speed, even now, and she will protect our Household. Syg, we are where we need to be—right here investigating this plot and determining the attacking parties. You heard Mabs, we must put an end to this, not only for the sake of our children, but for the sake of others as well—for that little boy playing alone in his room, feared by all."

She listened to him and calmed. "Ki's going to watch out for our children?"

"She is, Syg."

Syg nodded and felt assured. After a bit, she, showing a lot more guts than Lord Crossland, stood tall and assumed her place at Dav's side. "Whoever is behind this, Dav—they're going to die. I am going to kill them, and don't try to get in my way."

Beth stood there, sheepish under her winged helmet. Davage and Syg approached her and gave her a grand hug. "Thank you, Beth," Davage said. "For being a friend."

Syg smiled at her. "I know that was difficult, Beth. Thank you, I'm sorry I yelled at you just now. You still do not have permission to court Kay, by the by."

Beth laughed.

They separated. Ennez had already started sweeping the area with his scanner. Heading north, they followed him into the rows of the dead.

"What are we looking for?" Ennez said waving his scanner around.

"I'm not sure," Davage said. "The fact that there were no Berserkacides present during the attack troubles me. According to Admiral Carfax, all of the attacks on Hoban have featured the presence of Berserkacides. As they seemed to have surprised the monster, perhaps it didn't have time to properly deploy them. Also, Lord Crossland is convinced that a monstrous version of his Countess is roaming the cemetery, calling to him. We must search for sequestered Berserkacides and a phantom countess."

"Wonderful," Ennez said.

Syg, standing close to Davage, threw up a blob of Silver tech and created her usual *Seeker* familiar.

✳ ✳ ✳ ✳ ✳

Syg's Silver tech familiar was a four foot long, one foot high miniature version of their old ship, the *Seeker*. Externally it looked exactly like the *Seeker*, being rather swan-shaped, with wings, turrets, a tower and a roving, light-emitting sensor mounted on the frontal section. It could fire little guided canister missiles that exploded with a massive punch, and could lay down a blistering wall of Battleshot fire from tiny gun batteries arrayed along its length. Soaring overhead, Syg could see what it saw with its roving sensor, and she could speak and hear through it as well, it having a much greater range than mere telepathy. The light from its sensor could also destroy and clear out StT's, which was handy.

Syg liked to say that there was a tiny crew roaming around

inside: a tiny Dav and a tiny Syg. She'd tinkered around with it over the years. She added a feature that she could expand it in size and get in, like a ripcar. She even had space for two—she liked to take Dav for rides in it.

The *Seeker* familiar took shape and soared about like a model spaceship, loitering about, its cyclops eye panning this way and that casting a strong beam of silvery light—Syg able to see what it could from its overhead vantage point. Its high-flying presence and roving eye was comforting. Syg's little silver *Seeker* could do a lot of damage in a hurry if it needed to.

Beth looked up at it soaring overhead. "Syg, you're still using the *Seeker* as your familiar? You don't fly in the *Seeker* anymore. Why don't you redesign it to look like the *New Faith*?"

"Because the *New Faith* is ugly," Syg said. "I like my *Seeker* familiar. It has served us well for twenty years now, and I've no intention of changing it."

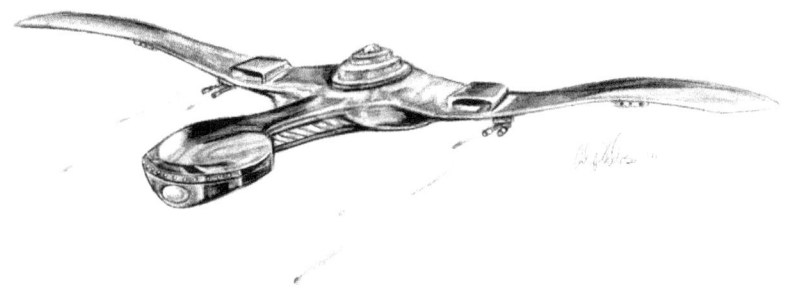

"Ah," Beth replied. "Here's mine; let me show you." Beth tossed out a large blob of Silver tech of her own, which twisted and turned into the shape of a huge, long-legged frog with bulging orange eyes. The frog shifted in color from silver to green, to a lit-up blue, to a pearly pink and back again. "It took me the longest to get the colors right," Beth said happily. "I call him 'Bernie,' after Lord Bernard of Hopkins—that man could eat."

They moved on, "Bernie" hopping along at their side, the *Seeker* loitering overhead.

They began passing many vaults—row after row of moss-covered Crossland vaults, old and nameless.

Beth had advanced several rows into the graveyard, using her jet staff as a walking stick to get through the sucking mud. Her Silver tech frog became interested in a flooded furrow. "Bernie! Bernie!" it said in a froggy voice. Beth knelt down next to him.

"Hey, come here!" she called out.

They made their way to her. There, partially submerged in the furrow, were four badly decomposed bodies. They pulled them out and laid them on top of a small vault. Beth and Ennez poured over them with their scanners.

"Four bodies," Ennez said. "Two adults and two juveniles. They have been lashed together at the wrists and ankles. Apparent cause of death—exposure, starvation and neglect. Somebody tied them up and left them here."

"Are they Hobans?" Davage asked.

"Nope," he said. "They appear to be Monama. The bone composition looks like what we know Monama bones to be. Notice the higher presence of cartilage in the joints, ribs and chest cavity— that's a Monama hallmark. Also, and we of the Hospitalers have suspected this, they appear to have an under-developed, extra pair of cartilaginous arms here, a vestige from the past, as, apparently, they were once four-armed. Monamas do not appear to be Elder in origin. They have very alien physiology."

"That is still in debate," Beth said.

"Look for yourself, Beth. Do these scans look Elder to you?"

Beth didn't answer.

Davage looked down at the sad, lashed skeletons. "Berserkacides always seem to have four arms."

"Monamas can't survive long away from Kana," Beth said. "Remove them from Kana and all their Gift-like powers vanish, and they soon grow sick and die. Also, if it gets too cold, they quickly take ill."

"Again," Ennez said, not letting the matter drop, "confirming that they are of alien origin."

Davage felt sorry for them, these forlorn bodies. "These poor people were scooped up from their homes, left here and forgotten— probably by the monster now rotting in the Crossland dungeon."

"These poor souls were intended to be Berserkacides?" Syg asked.

"Probably, why else would they be here? I want these bodies attended to and brought back to Kana where they may be identified and returned to their tribes. They'll not be left on Hoban."

They heard a muffled groan in the distance. Drawing their weapons, they made their way to the source of the sound. Syg lifted her *Seeker,* and opened its tiny Battleshot ports, putting it in a good position to cover them. Its spotlight shown down.

A few rows away, they came across a large vault. The sound they had heard came from within. Ennez tried the door, and it was locked. Davage Sighted into the vault.

"I see six people grouped together inside!"

Another groan.

"Syg," Davage said. "Deal with this lock, please."

Syg went to the door and, drawing back, blasted the door off its ancient hinges with her Silver tech.

They pushed the door aside and went in.

Within the vault, leaning against the wall, were six naked people, all tied together—four men and two females. Clearly, they were Monamas. Their skin was dead white, their hair black and bursting down to their feet. Their black eyes were pallid and a rather unhealthy gray in appearance. They were bound together at the wrists and at the ankles. They appeared to be in bad shape. Beth and Ennez quickly began scanning them.

One of the Monama females was moaning.

"Five are alive, one of the females is dead. Dehydration, hypothermia, and acute malnutrition," Beth said.

"I'm reading an excess of gamma, Dav," Ennez announced.

"Gamma?"

"Yes, and it seems to be coming from these Monamas."

"Beth," Davage said. "Find Countess Alberta and tell her we need water, blankets, anything she has, here immediately. Then, contact the ship and inform Paymaster Stenstrom of the situation, and tell them we will be back directly with wounded!" Beth ran out and Wafted away. Bernie hopped after her.

"We'll need to get these people back to Kana as soon as possible—Monamas don't do well away from there," Ennez said.

Ennez tried to cut their bonds with a scalpel pulled from his pocket, but the cords refused to break. "These bonds resist cutting."

Syg came forward and started working on the bonds with her Silver tech. Even with Silver tech, she appeared to be having a hard time.

"What is this? It's like jelly."

Syg finally got the bonds off, and they fell to the ground wiggling like snakes. Ennez carefully picked one up and put it into his pack for study later.

The Monamas were in bad shape. The bonds had been so tight that two of them had broken wrists; another one's hands appeared to be dead from lack of circulation.

The survivors appeared to be in a funk. Their eyes were open, but their expressions were blank.

"They're in Head Swarm, Dav," Ennez said.

"What is that?" Davage asked.

"A state of waking catatonia. They have seen their deaths and fallen into Head Swarm—sort of a defensive mechanism they have. I don't know if it's possible to get them out of it."

Davage tried to stand them up, but they were flaccid and uncooperative. And, somehow, they still appeared to be bound together though their bonds were cut.

"We are facing a serious conundrum here, Syg," Davage said. "Clearly, these poor souls were left here by the enemy for the purposes of changing them into Berserkacides. So, here's our problem—we cannot leave these people here to die, however, we invite disaster upon ourselves as they could transform on us at any given moment."

Syg struggled with the limp bodies. "So, what should we do?"

"We have got to determine how and why they become Berserkacides. If we know how it's done, then we can stop it. Ennez, what data have you?"

"Very little. Your guess as good as mine. If it's not simply related to mental illness, it could be a chemical reaction, a response to stimuli, or possibly a drug-induced or a surgical enhancement. I doubt it's a chemical reaction and surgery is not practical. It must be a result of direct stimuli—something they see or hear."

Davage thought a moment. "I recall Kay mentioning something about a red light—seeing a red light at Castle Durst, and that Sam was mortally afraid of it. Sam is a very courageous woman, and for her to be so afraid of something that she was unable to stand at Kay's side and fight means her fear was primal—deep-rooted. Perhaps a certain frequency of red light is the stimuli used to turn a Monama into a Berserkacide."

"Sounds reasonable, Dav," Ennez said, "but where is the stimulus? I don't see any red lights around here."

"Ennez, you said to saw an excess of gamma band energy around them—perhaps that's where we should look." Davage adjusted his Sight on the Monamas and struggled. "Gamma is so difficult to see."

Davage focused in. "Syg, Ennez!" he cried. "Look here! I can see they are wearing some sort of necklace or collar!"

"I don't see anything," Ennez said.

"I see it in Sight, Cloaked in the Gamma band."

He saw a thick, black cord wrapping around their necks, lashing them together though it could not be seen without Sight. Davage tried to break it, but the cord resisted.

"Ennez, raise the ship and tell Paymaster Stenstrom that we need precision cutting tools down here as soon as possible now!"

"You need to start carrying a communicator, Dav," he said. Ennez put his scanner away and ran out.

Davage looked more closely at the cord, straining to see it. A number of oblong objects sprouted out of their collar. They were smooth diamond-shaped crystals covered with arcane writing. "Syg," he said, "I see prisms of some sort studding the collar. Red prisms. These prisms at their necks must be what turns them into Berserkacides. They must!"

Davage tugged at the bizarre necklace of prisms. "Help me get them off. Hurry! We can prevent this from happening!"

Syg started pawing around. "Why can't I see it? Is it Cloaked?"

"Sort of. It's not like a standard Cloak though. It's some sort of Gamma-band distortion field. I'm having a difficult time seeing it myself."

Davage and Syg struggled with their necklaces. As he concentrated and tuned his Sight, he could see them clearer and clearer in the Gamma spectrum. He saw, to his disgust, that the necklaces were stitched rudely into their flesh. As he tried to dig them out, the surviving girl began to stir in muddled pain. She looked at them with groggy eyes and struggled. She cried out.

"It's all right, ma'am. It's all right. We're here to help you."

The girl cringed in fear. She mumbled a few words, but, they were in Monama.

"Oh, Creation," Davage said. "Ma'am, do you speak the

common League tongue? I'm sorry; I don't know your language."

She didn't respond. Davage continued to work at pulling away the prisms as she struggled weakly.

He managed to pull off the prisms studding her collar, there were six of them. He threw them to the floor and kicked them away. The last one he placed deep within a coat pocket for study later. "Our ship is nearby. We are going to take you there and keep you safe."

Syg managed to cut the fibrous lash binding their necks, freeing the girl. She said a few more words. "Ma'am, I can't understand you. Oh, where is Kay when we need him? I'm certain he'd understand."

She struggled and began speaking in broken League common with a bad accent. "Vot . . . vafe. I . . . vant to get `house . . ."

"You want to go home? We are going to take you there. Safe and sound. You and these fellows here shall be our special guests."

As he tried to calm the girl, he saw a flash of Gamma waves coming from outside the vault. It snaked through the air like a green cloud.

Someone walked in just then. It was Countess Alberta.

But it wasn't Countess Alberta—it was a hideous monster in her guise, half skinned, dripping blood, wearing a crown of fingers and ears. She was capering about, holding a prism in her right hand, glowing red. "Kill them!" she screeched. "KILL THEM!!"

The monstrous Countess then began to scream something in a hideous, high-pitched bark, as if she were casting some sort of spell.

Syg, sensing danger, pumped her fist and blasted the creature with a stream of Silver tech, blowing her jaw off. She dropped the prism she was carrying and held her face.

Syg blasted her again—this time blowing her out of the vault.

"Dav!" Syg screamed. "I can see from the *Seeker* that there's movement all over the graveyard!"

A din of growling and screaming filtered into the vault from outside.

The prisms around the Monamas necks all burst into a rosy red glow staining the walls of the vault as blood. Davage took the girl's face and pushed it into his breast, keeping her from seeing the light. She struggled feebly.

The four remaining Monama men came to life in a roar. Where, only moments before, they were languishing on the verge of death, lost in "Head Swarm" as Ennez had called it, now they were fully energized. Their already formidable-looking claws lengthened, and as Davage watched, they sprouted an extra pair of arms, delicate and studded with black claws. Slavering like raging beasts they hacked at the fibrous rope binding them together .

The girl, her face shielded by Davage's chest and coat, whimpered in terror.

"Creation, Berserkacides!" Syg screamed as she readied to box them into a Sten.

Cackling with delight, the monstrous image of Countess Alberta came running back into the vault—missing her lower jaw, an arm, a shoulder and a good portion of her chest. She grabbed Syg from behind and pulled her outside.

Holding the girl to him, Davage unsaddled his CARG and, one-handed, swept the thrashing Monamas—now raging Berserkacides—back, holding them temporarily at bay.

He glanced outside. There, he saw Syg struggling with the monstrous countess. He saw a sort of feathery door open behind the monster in a green flash of Gamma, and she pulled Syg into it. The door then closed and Syg was gone.

17—The Berserkacides

Davage stumbled of out the vault and ran in the direction of the manor. He ran like he never had before, jumping over the jumbled obstacle course of gravestones, tombs, and vaults, the drenched ground sucking at his boots, slowing him down. The terrified Monama woman was cradled in his arms.

Syg was gone, and he feared for her. Beth and Ennez weren't anywhere around.

Behind, Berserkacides pursued in a snarling mass. The ones from the vault came tearing out after him. They ran on all fours, like apes, holding their extra pair of clawed hands over their heads, ready to slash and tear. Others came howling in from all over the graveyard—apparently a whole host of them had been stashed there.

Overhead, the Silver tech *Seeker,* without Syg to control it, sauntered about mindlessly.

The Berserkacides shall soon overrun him. They were so fast.

He tried to Waft away and get the girl to safety, but couldn't. It sputtered and coughed around him. He couldn't Waft!! What was happening?

The Monama woman! Holding her was somehow counteracting his Waft! He recalled Kay and Sam talking about such a thing once—how Sam thought it was funny that her touch disrupted his Gifts, and how it took practice for him to overcome the odd phenomena.

Davage didn't have time to practice.

He didn't have a communicator; he couldn't contact the ship. His telepathy was terrible other than with Syg and Ki, so he didn't bother trying.

Instead, he ran, leaping over the vaults, springing off the

tombstones as fast as he could, the shrieking, foaming Berserkacides howling in from all sides hot on his heels.

One stumble, one misstep, and they would be on him.

Syg—where was Syg? What was happening to Syg?

There was no escaping the ones from the vault; they were simply too fast. They were mere moments from bringing him down. In desperation, he dropped the woman with a splat into the muddy ground, and he Wafted just as the Berserkacide claws were about to find his neck.

Confused, they skittered to a halt and turned their attention to the woman.

With a blast Davage reappeared behind them, CARG at the ready. He took the top half off one Berserkacide and lopped the head off another.

Snarling, the last two sprang.

Davage Wafted second time and again appeared behind them. With one swing of his famously heavy CARG, he bisected both, cleaving through flesh and bone alike.

The graveyard was alive with noise and movement, closing in fast. He picked the girl back up and began running again.

He reached a small clearing and Sighted a mass of Berserkacides coming in on his position from ahead. He was about to be cornered.

He veered to his right and found a large vault with a recessed door—a good place to make a stand. He dove into the recess and put the girl down.

"Don't look, ma'am! Whatever happens, don't look!" She curled up into a ball and whimpered, covering her face with her hands, her long black hair, rather like Lady Sammidoran's, thick and all over the place.

Davage raised his CARG and readied for the onslaught. He drew his MiMs pistol and cocked it. He didn't really think the tiny MiMs could do much to stop these Berserkacides, but it couldn't hurt. This girl, this Monama, had information he needed. Willing or unwilling, she was in the service of these monsters, these "Jennybacks" Ki had called them. She was therefore the key to understanding this mystery. If only to get her to safety, he would hold this position until he could do so no longer.

She had to survive and tell what she knew. She had to. The fate of her people possibly depended on it. Davage had to give the Sisters information; otherwise, they would wipe the Monamas out.

And the Berserkacides came in.

Davage's Sight gave him a great advantage, and he could see when the Berserkacides would attack a few seconds before they actually did it, giving him time to ready his CARG or fire his MiMs.

Swing after swing, he laid into them, hacking off arms and legs. One Berserkacide put his claws into the stone of the vault just before Davage chopped his arm off—the appendage hanging there, disembodied and still struggling. The Berserkacides were savage in the extreme, incredibly strong and fast, outdoing even the terrible, foam-flecked Hulgismen. Gravely wounding Berserkacides did little good, nor did lopping off their arms and legs, as, wormlike, they would crawl back into the fight. The only thing to do was take off their heads.

And Davage did that, swing after swing, the pale naked bodies piling up to either side of him; heads lopped off, faces cleaved in two. He emptied his MiMs and dropped it—the tiny gun having no effect.

The torrent did not yield—Berserkacides kept pouring in. Davage Sighted them overwhelming his position in a few moments, their sheer weight of numbers taking him down and the girl with him. He Sighted their claws tearing out his throat. He could Waft away, but then the girl would be lost.

This was it.

"Ma'am!" he yelled to the cowering girl behind him. "I want you to climb up over the top of the vault and run. Run to the manor, as fast as you can! Keep running until you get to safety! I'll try to hold them here!"

The girl, in terror, didn't move.

"Ma'am!"

Davage picked her up by the scruff of her neck and threw her up and over the top of the vault. Recovering her senses a little, she began scrabbling away.

Lowering his guard and tossing the girl was costly. The Berserkacides came in a killing wave, and he couldn't possibly stop them all. He didn't have time to build a Waft.

From a distance came a sharp: CRACK! CRACK! CRACK! CRACK!

Four Berserkacides" heads exploded, and they fell in a heap. Beyond, standing on the distant outer wall, was the thin, coatless form of Lord Crossland holding the SMOKELESS, the LosCapricos weapon of his House—a long rifle that never missed. His triangle hat was huge on his head. Countess Alberta, the real one, stood next to him. Apparently, he had recovered from his funk, or she had rousted him from it.

Countess Alberta held the small form of their son to her breast. Lord Crossland reloaded his SMOKELESS. The Berserkacides regrouped and continued the assault.

Momentarily clear, Davage Sighted for the girl.

She had covered a fair distance in the direction of the manor but ran right into a pocket of charging Berserkacides. She screamed in terror as they fell upon her.

SNAP! SNAP!

With a lightning fast Silver tech tongue, the Berserkacides were pulled off their feet and into the huge, waiting mouth of a giant, orange-eyed frog lurking in one of the trees—a frog of changing, scintillating colors.

"Bernie! Bernie!" the frog said as he ate one Berserkacide after the next, his insides apparently mystically pocketed to allow him to devour impossibly huge things.

After a moment, Beth and Ennez appeared and, with their whirling jet staves and lances of Silver tech, fought the remaining Berserkacides in the area with devastating skill.

SNAP! SNAP! "Bernie! Bernie!"

Back at the vault, another wave came in, and Davage readied himself for the killer assault.

A shaft of light shined down from above and, just then, the silver *Seeker* roared into the clearing, banking gracefully at an acute angle. Its tiny Battleshot batteries opened up, mowing down a large group of incoming Berserkacides—their crazed bodies collapsing under the weight of its minute but withering shot.

With a blast, Syg Wafted into the doorway. Covered in sticky-looking blood, she quickly threw up a Sten field across the vault and, though it wasn't killing the Berserkacides, they couldn't get through it. They pawed at it in a fury, their clawed hands sparking as they painfully raked at it. Taking a moment, Dav and Syg fell into each other's arms, grateful that the other hadn't been killed.

In the usual "Baaaaaaaaaa!" sound, the *Seeker* familiar blasted the Berserkacides leaning against the Sten into paste.

Then, overhead, five Marine *Trelaines* came diving in from the heavens, ordered down by Paymaster Stenstrom. They raked the howling Berserkacides with passing fire and then set down with ranks of red-coated Marines quickly piling out and forming defensive lines. There, they engaged the remaining Berserkacides and secured the graveyard. Their Marine SK pistols were easily large enough to bring the Berserkacides down.

Soon, as quickly as it began, the battle was, thankfully, over, Davage holding the bloody Syg to him. She dropped the Sten, and they came out, joining with Beth and Ennez. Bernie, full of devoured Berserkacides, leapt down from the tree and followed her.

They went a distance, and there, huddled against a tree stump and lit-up in the *Seeker*'s spotlight, was the Monama girl—sick, terrified, naked, but very much alive and in her right mind.

18—Sam's Doughnut

Two days later, Kay, Sarah and Phillip dressed, had breakfast in the pub, and checked out. They went outside into the warm Remnath sun, and, at first, thought the *Goshawk* had been stolen, for it wasn't there in the ship park where they had left it. Kay had forgotten it was Cloaked—had no idea he was still doing it. Truly, as Cloak had said during their afternoon together, the more relaxed you were, the better the Cloak worked. When they thought nobody was looking, Kay dropped it, and the *Goshawk* appeared as if from nowhere, black and bat-like.

They then mounted it and headed west for Rostov. Phillip flew low, hugging the rolling grasslands, causing herds of wild animals to flee as they passed; the fast ship nimbly following Phillip's control. When they neared the city, Kay Cloaked it, and Phillip set it down a mile or two away near the sea.

On foot, following the rocky coast and the crashing waves of the sea, the sound of the breaking waves loud, they walked into Rostov.

The looming black gates, lined with stone and watch towers, were open, waiting for them. They passed through, and inside was a collage of noise and activity—a whole seedy world in miniature. Within the black walls was a patchwork of thrown together structures and fallen debris, all pushed up against one another with little thought paid to design, visual appeal or function, forming a nonsensical, drunken grid of threadbare streets, metal-strewn yards and dead-ends. Due to the roughshod and non-permanent nature of most of the structures, the layout of streets and alleys often changed daily. There were makeshift marketplaces, made from the rusty hulls of old, scrapped Fleet ships, selling all manner of questionable items from illegal pharmaceuticals and counterfeit dura-techs to low-end

finished goods. There were banned substances being bartered about a-
plenty, home-made spirits of questionable levels of toxicity, and they
even came across an alley full of venders selling various incarnations of
"The Weed" to hopeful courtesans of all shapes and dispositions. Sarah
saw a stand selling Remax to a clamoring crowd. Remax, as Sarah knew
from her avid reading, was a dangerous painkiller and stimulant from
Bazz, easily leading to addiction, spontaneous deformity and death. It was
supposed to be illegal in the League.

There were small, walk-up diners selling noodles, dried fruits
and fried savories designed for the eater on the go. There were flop-
houses and cricket huts to crash in, dingy residences and flesh
peddlers out and about in unabashed force. There were even areas of
greater and lesser prosperity—some of the nicer structures appeared
fairly well built and semi-permanent, while others looked to be, quite
literally, falling apart at the rusty seams.

And, by far the most plentiful and omnipresent, there were sports
houses—places of gambling and lost money where, for a price, you could
risk all and lose everything at the throw of the bones or a pull on the
wheel. Every sort of game and entertainment was available to be tried,
from modern holo-shunts and needlers to ancient games of chance. All
one needed was a little money and the hard stones to give it a toss.

All of this, this cornucopia of depravation, was a sure-fire way to
get destroyed. The whole place was just crying out to receive a fiery
visit from the Sisters.

Huddled up against the western wall and watching over the whole
odd mess was the keep—Leap Manor—the seat of House Rostov, a
menacing collection of buttressed towers, dark windows and
impressively sharp-looking spires, seeing everything that happened
below and nothing at the same time. It looked like a collection of
variously-sized black spears stacked up and piled in a corner.

Underneath that pile of black rock was the vault and Sam's
Doughnut within.

Marching proudly through the masses was the Watch—roving
groups of House Rostov guardsmen wearing checkered tunics, making
sure that the House got its coin. They milled about, armed to the teeth,
and holding those odd mickalmick creatures at leash. The mickalmicks
wore a type of harness just behind their heads. Attached to the harness
was a checkered House Rostov flag on a short, waving pole.

Casually making the rounds, they saw all sorts of things they wish they hadn't. They saw dirty, impoverished mothers betting—and losing—their children at games of chance; the weeping children being carried off by the Watch after the dice or needle-cast failed them—no doubt a career in prostitution awaiting them. They saw a gentleman betting his mechanical arm and his artificial groin, but, fortunately, he won them back plus a big score. They saw a lady betting the clothes off her back, and soon she was wearing nothing but a dirty blanket.

Sarah, always hungry and ready to try new things, bought something fried on a stick from an eat shack. Apparently she liked it, as she bought two more. "So, how are we going to do this? What's our plan?" she asked getting her teeth into the fried morsel.

A solitary member of the Watch approached them. He was a smallish fellow, sandy haired under his large triangle hat, and quite young. He was wearing a white tailed coat and matching pants with a pair of black Calvert boots. He didn't have the scarred, burned-in look of the other Watch they'd seen. He had a Dare A-H gun holstered at his side and a second one tucked into his checkered sash. In his left hand, he held a leashed mickalmick. His mickalmick seemed friendly and tame—almost like a reptilian dog. Its spotted belly shown in the sun, and its little checkered flag waved in the breeze.

"Greetings, strangers," he said.

"Well met," Kay replied.

He looked them over. "Nice clothes," he said referring to Kay's Blanchefort coat and hat. He glanced at Sarah and tipped his hat. "I believe, good sir, that there are a number of nicer places to take such a fine young lady besides Rostov. There's nothing to do here but waste your money. I suggest Wiln, nice scenery, fine dining . . ."

"Good sir," Sarah said. "Do you know that there are people bartering Remax down the street?"

He sighed. "Again? All right, I'll go down there and break them up. Won't do any good. They'll just re-surface somewhere else."

He prepared to leave, and then stopped. "You three have the Vith look—you look like Vith to me. That's fine, the sportsmen here just love the Vith—always come with a lot of coin, they do. However, allow me to give you a bit of friendly advice. With Vith comes trouble—that Elder razzle-dazzle they like to pull—and the Watch are extra vigilant against such antics. You're probably being watched even as we speak. If you try to turn invisible, or Dirge somebody, or try to Waft away, they'll be on you in no time, and the laws can be pretty harsh about certain things here in Rostov, the use-of-Gifts being one of them. Please, enjoy yourselves—assign yourself a limit on how much you're willing to lose and stick to it. When you've met your limit, take your leave. Go to Wiln or St Paris and have a good dinner. It's just a bit of friendly advice; take it as you will."

"We will, sir," Sarah said. "And thank you," she added petting the mickalmick on the head.

With that, the Watchman tipped his large hat again and he and his friendly mickalmick made their way down the street. Kay watched him for a bit—he seemed familiar for some reason.

Continuing on, Kay saw a stand down the street that looked a bit nicer than most of the others. It, like many of the other sporting establishments, flew a white and black checkered flag—the crest of House Rostov. The presence of the flag indicated that the House and not some urchin or chump was running that stand. Without consulting Phillip and Sarah, Kay walked up to it.

A small sportsman dressed nicely in the Calvert fashion, sat behind the counter and regarded Kay for a moment.

"Good day to you, fine sir," he hissed. "What's your game?" Kay asked.

"Shell game, nice and simple," the sportsman said.

He produced, as if by magic, a small dried pea and three similar-looking turtle shells on the countertop.

Kay smiled. "How much for a game?"

"How much you want to bet, dear sir?"

Kay produced a Blanchefort hader and set it on the counter. The sportsman looked at it and seemed satisfied. He produced a few Rostov solaris and placed them next to the silver hader. "We start nice and easy—2 to 1, how about that? That all right?"

"Fine."

With that, the sportsman covered the pea with the turtle shells and began skillfully moving them around on the countertop. With his Sight, Kay could see the shell with the pea under it dancing around gracefully on the countertop. Suddenly, he Sighted a pea under each of the shells. Clearly, the sportsman's dexterity was without peer and wanted Kay to win this opening "teaser" round. A classic ploy.

The shells came to rest. "Please choose, sir," the sportsman said.

Kay sighed and pointed at the middle shell—he knew he couldn't lose. The sportsman turned it over, exposing the pea. "Looks to be a winner." He slid the solaris and Kay's hader back to him. With incredible skill, the sportsman made the other two peas disappear. He showed Kay the single pea again and covered it. "This time, we play 3 to 1—that all right?"

"Sure," Kay said, putting his hader back on the counter. The sportsman put more solaris next to it.

The sportsman started moving the shells quite a bit faster this time. Again, toward the end of the shuffle, two more peas appeared under the shells. Again, Kay couldn't lose. He picked one and won. The sportsman then reset the game. "This is your lucky day, sir. Now, we play for 5 to 1. How about that?"

Kay shrugged. "I think I'm done, thanks."

The sportsman reddened in the face. "Now, just a moment, lad. You've gotten pretty lucky so far. I'd like a chance to win my payout back. Come on—I'm paying 5 to 1 this time. You're on a hot streak; you can't stop now."

"Frankly, I'm a bit bored. Haders and solaris—big deal."

The sportsman leaned forward, intrigued. "Ahh, a high roller, eh? Well then, name your score. We aim to please here."

"I want to play for an item in Rostov's vault."

A few dirty courtesans saddled up to the counter to watch. One began touching Kay on the shoulder. The sportsman shooed them away.

"That a fact? Want something from the vault, do you? There's some wondrous things in there, no doubt about it," he said watching the courtesans depart. "But swag like that doesn't just come up for just anybody, or anything. The spice needs to be right—see, you've got to put something nice on the table first; then, if it is agreeable, we can possibly deal. So, with that in mind, let's see the color of your money."

Without missing a beat, Kay reached into his coat pocket and pulled out his Poltava, Phillip and Sarah's eyes growing wide. Slowly, butt-first, he put it on the counter, the enameled dragonfly on the grip flashing in the sun.

The sportsman, skeptical, picked it up and looked it over. "What's this?" he said as he turned it around in his hands. He blinked and looked it over again, his interest growing by the second. "This looks to be a Poltava. Not a knock-off. This seems to be the real thing. A rare beauty, too." He whistled. "You kill somebody for this?"

Kay shook his head.

"Ah, well, none of my business who you killed over a treasure like this one. So, you'd like to bet your Poltava against an item in the vault, would you? Very well; I think we can deal. Any particular one strike your interest?"

The dirty courtesans returned, and this time, the sportsman was too absorbed to run them off. They looked at Kay's Poltava with wonder. One of them skillfully tried to steal it, and, with a click, the sportsman drew a long dueling pistol and put it up her nose. She skulked off. Before long the Watch converged and had her in chains, dragging her off to who knows where.

Kay, a bit put off, began describing the piece he wanted—a small, silver, doughnut-like device. The sportsman dispatched a runner and, soon, a contingent of the Watch approached the stand. They had several items from the vault matching Kay's description. They displayed the items for Kay, and he pointed; the Watchman on the right had Sam's Doughnut—just as Kay had seen it from Wiln, small, silver, made in an organic-looking, twisting sort of design. It wasn't really much to look at in person.

"That look to be the one?"

"It does."

The sportsman smiled and turned his head. "Looks like you've got an esteemed audience." He nodded away toward Leap manor and, standing on one of the flat-topped terraces, there was a huge man in a long black coat.

"That's Lord Xerin up there a-watchin', our goodly host," the sportsman said. "He's interested in how this plays out. He's never had a Poltava in his vault before."

Kay and Sarah looked up. He recognized the man from his vision of the future. The dark lord of Rostov who will lead the House in ruin, again. There he was, right up there on the terrace.

"So then," the sportsman said. "Are we agreed, the Poltava against this device? Winner take all?"

Kay thought a moment and shook his head. "I have another thought. My Poltava is quite valuable—a real find and probably worth twenty-times the value of the silver item. What say we simply trade up—a straight swap of goods and be done?"

The sportsman was disappointed. "I'd say be off. This isn't a market or a pawnshop. If you want to trade, go down the street and bargain for tissues to cry into. This is a place of sport. We bet— winner take all."

"I imagine, sir, that, at this point, any shell that I pick will not have a pea under it."

The sportsman was enraged. "You calling me a cheat, boy?"

"I'm calling you a businessman. Mere chance is bad for business."

The sportsman's ire diminished a little. He chuckled and leaned back. "Now, sir, are we going to play, or are we not?"

Some of the dirty courtesans watching became restless. "C'mon, Charlie, play. Play!"

Kay ignored them.

"We are not." Kay pulled his Poltava off the counter and put it back into his pocket. The courtesans gasped. The sportsman was shocked and drew his dueling pistol again.

The Watch surged forward and seized Kay by either shoulder. "You are under arrest!" one of them said.

"For what?" Kay cried.

"For theft. You cannot take an item off the table once bet—that is the law! The Poltava now, by law, belongs to House Rostov. You will be taken for trial, and then executed."

"What?" Kay said struggling.

As the Watch began trying to chain Kay up, the young Watchman they had spoken to earlier with the large triangle hat returned, his mickalmick making barking sounds like a dog. "What's going on here?" he asked.

"This man's to be tried and executed for taking a bet item off the countertop."

"Come on, Jessum," the young Watchman said. "The gentleman here is obviously new to Rostov, and wasn't aware of the serious nature of taking a bet item off the table. Give the 'Charlie' a break, how about it? He's probably got a lot more coin to spend, which he won't be able to do so if he's dead. Right?"

"Phender," the Watchman spat. "You milquetoast whore-seed. I'd expect such womanly behavior from one such as you! The Poltava now belongs to House Rostov, as does his un-spent coin. He will be tried and executed—no exceptions."

Phillip and Sarah pulled their Poltavas and got the drop on the Watch.

"More Poltavas!" somebody cried. "Look!"

Guns: pistols of all kinds, energy weapons, rusted Dee-Dees, sonic lashes and a whole host of other nasty-looking weapons emerged from everywhere and were leveled at Kay, Phillip and Sarah.

The young Watchman named Phender rolled his eyes. His little mickalmick made a small barking sound again.

19—Tellerran of Monama

Under Ennez's care, the Monama girl improved a bit. Her system, though, was in turmoil. So far from Kana, her body was slowly shutting down. He, with Davage's help, managed to remove the invisible collar stitched into her neck and gave it to the Sisters for examination, along with the prism Davage had collected.

She hadn't said anything since being brought aboard the *New Faith*. They gave her clothes to wear, which, she put on and a blanket for her to wrap up in—Davage and Sygillis knowing from Lady Sammidoran that Monamas liked it warm. Ennez brought in a small heater, and she sat next to it in her baggy donated clothes, shivering under her blanket.

After a day, Davage and Syg joined her in her room.

She hadn't slept in the bed, and the food that the orderlies had brought in for her sat uneaten. She just huddled in a corner next to the heater, curled into a pathetic ball.

Davage sat down and looked at her. Syg also sat.

They noted her plates of uneaten food. "Ma'am, you've not eaten since you've been aboard, and who knows how long before that even. You must be hungry. Please eat."

She didn't react.

"You needn't be frightened. You're safe here."

She gazed at them from under her mane of black hair and said a few words in her Monama language.

"Can you understand us, Ma'am?"

She shook her head. "Only . . . few vords I know."

Davage stood and went to the holo-terminal. He pressed a few buttons, and a woman in a Fleet lieutenant's uniform appeared.

"Fleetcom," she said.

"Fleet, well met. We have with us a guest who does not speak much of the common vernacular. We require a translator, please."

"Aye, sir. Can you tell us what language your guest is speaking?"

"I'm not entirely certain. Our guest is a Monama, if that helps." The Lt. punched a few buttons. "Aye, sir, stand by." The Fleet header came up for a few moments, then a crewman sitting in a crowded cube room somewhere at Fleet popped up.

"Crewman Laval here, sir," he said in a distinctive Zenon burr.

"Well met, crewman," Davage replied. "We have a Monama guest here who does not speak League common. We are hoping you might translate for us."

He saw the Monama woman huddled in the corner and spoke up, speaking some sort of Monama tongue. Upon hearing more familiar words, she pricked up her ears and became a bit more lucid. She said a few things back to the crewman on the screen.

"Captain, she is speaking Conox. It's one of a family of related languages spoken by the Monamas. I am most proficient in Anuie, but I can get by well enough."

"Excellent. We appreciate your help. Can you ask the lady her name, please?"

They exchanged a few words. "Her name is Lady Tellerran of the Fphenook tribe. She would like to know your name, sir."

Davage turned to her. "I am Davage, Lord of Blanchefort, and captain of this vessel. With me here is my countess, Sygillis of Blanchefort." Syg bowed to her.

Though fearful, she smiled a little in response and pushed her hair out of her face.

"Crewman, can you ask her why she's not eaten? We are very concerned about her."

More banter back and forth. "Captain, she says she doesn't feel good. She says she thinks the Elder foods presented to her will make her sicker."

"Then please ask her what we can bring her that she will eat."

The crewman and Tellerran exchanged more words. "She says she would like some Gesser. She thinks she can eat that and not get sick."

Davage smiled. "Com," he said looking up.

"Com here, sir," came the business-like reply.

"Com, please ask Lord Ottoman to prepare a fine dish of Gesser as soon as possible. Have it brought to room 10-6 when it's ready."

"Aye, sir."

The crewman on the screen began punching more buttons. "Sir, as Conox isn't an overly exotic language, I'm uploading the programming for an endecar that you may use to speak directly to her. It should be ready for you in a few minutes. They're very simple to use. It will create two voice cones, one in League common and the other in Conox. All you need do is speak into it."

"Thank you, crewman; if we require anything further, well com the Fleet."

The Crewman's image disappeared from the screen, and Tellerran appeared to panic for a moment. She cringed and huddled back into the corner, shivering under her blanket again.

They spent an awkward few minutes in silence as they waited for the endecar and the food to arrive. At last, the door opened, and an orderly brought in the endecar. It was a small device composed of a black disk with two trumpets, one red, the other blue, protruding from either end. The orderly turned the device on and showed them how to use it.

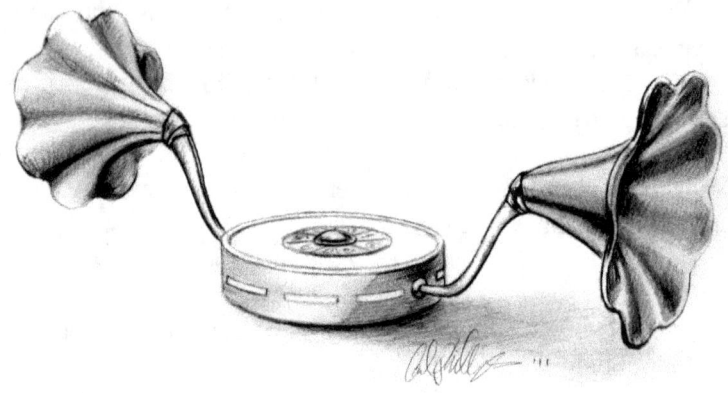

"The blue end will accept sounds and repeat back in League common; the red one will do the same in Conox." The orderly then left. Davage placed the endecar on the table and pointed the red trumpet toward her. He leaned down and spoke. "Can you understand me, Lady Tellerran?"

She seemed surprised and fascinated at the same time. Slowly, she got out of the corner and seated herself, still huddling under her blanket. "Yes. Yes, I can," came a slightly synthesized voice out of the blue trumpet. "What wonders you Elders create. I've never seen anything like this."

"Yes, quite. I've never used a device like this either. It seems to work well enough. Are you cold, Lady Tellerran?"

She nodded. "I'm freezing."

Davage got the portable heater and placed it near her on the table. "Does that help, ma'am?" "Yes. Thank you."

"So," he said, trying to break the ice. "You speak Conox; is that right?"

"Yes."

"I've not heard of Conox before."

"My tribe speaks it, and a few others do as well. Do you speak any languages, other than the common?"

"I speak Vith. I can write in it as well. Does Conox have its own alphabet?"

She shook her head. "No. It didn't used to have an alphabet until only recently. And we use the common alphabet."

Davage then tried to deepen the conversation and capture her full attention. "My son's *Cerri-Tela* speaks Anuie, I believe."

She seemed quite astonished. "*Cerri-Tela?* I know that word. Your son is seeing a Monama girl? Is she a Zerb or Minzer? No, she must be a Cardinal."

Syg seated herself at the table and spoke into the trumpet. "No, ma'am, she is an Astralon."

Tellerran thought about it. "Astralons are mean. They don't like other Monamas. Think they're better than the other tribes, like mine who speak Conox. I'm sorry. I didn't mean to speak ill of your son's *Cerri-Tela.*"

She sat there and puzzled for a moment. Davage could see she was full of questions. "Your son's *Cerri-Tela?* How did they come together?"

"She said she'd dreamed of our son since she was a little girl. Her grandmother was our personal seeress, and we gave her permission to visit whenever she wished."

"And she sought him out?"

"She did."

Tellerran looked dumbfounded. She grappled with the notion. "I once dreamed of an Elder boy, but I never had the resolve to leave the fog." She seemed lost in remembrance.

A moment later, several orderlies brought in a large plate of steaming hot Gesser, silverware and a tankard of water. Davage thanked them, and they left.

The Gesser looked like a pile of black beans on a hot bed of something dark and fibrous. Davage secretly hoped he didn't have to eat any now to get her to start.

"Come now," Davage said. "You'll want to eat it while it's hot. I'm told that's how it is best. Our chef made this just for you. I'd hate to see it all go to waste."

Tellerran picked up her silverware and scooted in front of her plate. She then looked over her shoulder once or twice.

Syg pitied the poor girl. "Please, miss, eat. You're safe here, we promise. Nobody is going to hurt you."

She grabbed the endecar and slid it a little closer to where she was sitting. She then began eating, trying to hide the fact that she was ravenous.

Clearly famished, Tellerran finished the first plate in no time, and Davage called for another serving. A second plate soon arrived, and Tellerran tucked into it. As her hunger was slaked, she became a bit more talkative. The endecar seemed to be a security blanket for her, as she kept touching and adjusting its position on the table.

"Thank you for the meal, my Lord. It was very good," she said into the endecar.

"You're welcome. Are you still feeling sick?"

She nodded. "It's space, being so far from home. My people don't live long in space."

"We're going to arrange transport for you back to Kana, and we will return you to your home. Would you like that?"

She looked at her hands. "My family won't accept me. I was taken, and I am considered dead. They will consider me a Berserkacide, whether I'm one or not. There's no place for me there anymore."

She looked up at them with her black eyes. "You shouldn't have brought me here. It's not safe. I don't want to hurt anybody. Better to have left me where I was and let me die."

"What sort of talk is that?" Davage said. "If you're worried about becoming a Berserkacide, I can assure you that won't happen. We've removed the prisms that were attached to your neck—we've learned a great deal in the past few days."

Again, she sat there astonished. "My Shockers, you took my Shockers off?" A mixture of wonder and fear filled her face. She felt about her neck and shoulders with her hand.

"Shockers?" Davage said. "Is that what you call them, those odd prisms?"

"We're not allowed to take those off. We're not allowed to touch them. That's an unforgivable sin. To remove the Shockers means instant death."

Davage smiled. "Instant death? Yet, here you are." "They'll come for me. You can't stop them."

"'Them?' You must be referring to those monstrous beings that attacked Lord Crossland and my Countess."

"Yes. They watch us all the time, and they make us do terrible things. We are their slaves. We have always been their slaves. I can say no more."

"No longer, for you are free."

"I'm not free. None of us are free. I am a slave. Your son's Astralon woman—she is a slave, too. They came and pulled me and my sister and my brothers out of our warm beds, and they brought us to this place and left us there, tied together. There is nothing we can do. They watch us—always. They'll punish us. They'll shock us!" She cringed in sadness. "My poor brothers! My sister . . ."

Davage tried to comfort her. "I saw them when they tried to turn you into a Berserkacide. I saw them open a Gamma-band portal, step through it, and then depart. I know where they hide now. We are wise to them and have set up defenses. The Sisters aboard this vessel are on vigilance for them, even at this moment. Those people cannot harm you any longer. My heart is with you, and your departed kin, but, perhaps, something good may come of this." Tellerran looked around, looking for hidden people who weren't there.

"So, please, Lady Tellerran, it is very important that you tell us anything you can. We do not wish to see any others harmed by these fiends, but we are sorely lacking in information, and we need your help."

"They'll punish us!"

"There will be no punishment. We will protect you."

Tellerran looked like she wanted to start talking, but she stopped herself. "You can't fight them. They cast spells which paralyze you. They cannot be fought."

Syg moved around the table and put her arm around Tellerran. She adjusted the endecar. "Lady Tellerran, our son was attacked by these creatures, and I blamed Lady Monama. I was angry and frightened, and I blamed her. I see now that I was wrong, that it wasn't her fault. In the graveyard, they came at me, and pulled me into their horrid realm. It was a dark, an alien landscape, the sky full of stars that I didn't recognize. I could barely see, and there they were, several of them—monsters and demons all. They laughed and were eager to have at me. They tried to cast spells, and there, alone, I fought them. I fought back, and I killed them—I killed every last one who was there. These beasts are not invincible, they can be beaten. Look at me—I am small, and I beat them, and I made them fear me as I did it."

Tellerran gawked at Syg with a mixture of fear and disbelief.

Syg gestured towards Davage. "My Lord knows what to look for now, and he will see if they dare to come. He can see anything. He saw the prism around your neck and got it off. He watches over you and, if they come, we will take care of them. So, please, trust us. We want to help you. You are our friend, and we want to help you, to free you."

Tellerran turned to Davage. "You can do that? You can see them?" Hope began welling up in her face.

"Yes, I can," Davage confirmed. "I promise you."

* * * * *

Clutching her blanket, speaking slowly into the endecar, Tellerran began a long oratory, and Davage and Syg held her long-nailed hand as she talked.

"We have been slaves to the Golden People and their fleshless demons for ages. They once roamed Kana in great, mirthless cities. The Golden People pretend to be beings like us, but they are not. They are shapeless and changeable, making themselves into whatever they want.

"Long ago, we were evil, and we worshipped a Horned God deep in the earth. Then, the Gods in Jade and Sapphire came and took the evil from us in exchange for our second pair of arms. We turned our backs on the Horned God and lived by our lake where it is warm and we were a happy people. The Horned God was angry and cursed us, setting his angels the Golden People against us. They took our people into their windowless laboratories and experimented on us—

tortured us. Treated us like cattle. They built into us the Heart Trigger, a genetic code in our tissues that, once activated, turns us back into what we once were—Berserkacides. They sew the Shockers into our flesh and tell us never to take them off on pain of death. They come and take us, use us as warriors in faraway places against enemies whose names we do not know. Worlds have fallen under our claws, all for the sake of these angels, these Golden People who make others do the fighting for them. We prayed for deliverance, but the gods told us we were evil, and this was our punishment."

"But," Davage said, "your people are so strong, so fast. Why didn't you fight back?"

"We cannot. The Golden People and their demons cannot be beat. They killed the Anuians, the greatest among us."

Davage knew what this was: conditioning. They had been conditioned to be afraid of these beings, whoever they are, over many millennia. And that hold, that conditioning, was not going to be broken easily.

Tellerran continued. "Then you came with your Elders, and they were afraid. They destroyed their cities in clouds of fire and fled. They left us on Kana near our beloved, warm lake and we rejoiced at our deliverance. But they came back, watching us, hiding in the shadows, telling us to do things. They watch us always, and if we told and gave away their secret, they swore to kill all of us—every last Monama. And so, under their heel, we have lived keeping to ourselves, doing what we are told by our tormentors from afar.

"There were centuries when they didn't come at all, and we rejoiced. We forgot the terror under which we had lived and the Horned God in the ground. We began to stretch out our hands, to embrace you Elder people, for you appear to be good folk, and we find you so beautiful. We began to share our gift of prophesy. We wanted to seek you out and share our dreams with you—love you, like your son's *Cerri-Tela*, who did something few of us have the courage to do. But, in the last few decades, the Horned God's angels began coming again with frequency, taking us from our houses, from our beds. And they make us become Berserkacides. They make us spy on you—lie to you, take you to the City of Many Forms. When they come for us, like they did for me and my sister and my brothers, we never come back. I saw my death at their hands, tied up in the vault with my sister and my brothers. My soul died into Head Swarm.

I was resigned to it though I didn't want to hurt anyone. All I wanted to do is go home, and now I can't even do that."

Davage lifted her chin. "These monsters that they send—Lord Crossland's son, the Countess, what are they?"

"They are demons that Golden People create in the Tank; they are their generals and their soldiers—laughing and chiding. They torment us, kill us for pleasure, use us and then discard us."

Davage gave her a pat on the head. "We will take you home, Lady Tellerran. You have given us much useful information. We will discover who these people are, and we will put a stop to it. Get some rest and fear not. We will protect you."

Davage and Syg started to leave the room. As they approached the door, Tellerran ran forward, dropping her blanket. She put her arms around Davage's legs. She started speaking, but it was in Conox. Syg picked up the endecar and handed it to her. She held onto it with both hands.

"I saw my fate, and that of my brothers and my sister. We always know when we are going to die. I saw myself dying as a Berserkacide, and I was resigned to it. I was in Head Swarm. I never saw you coming to help me, to risk yourselves for me. Thank you, my Lord, Great Countess. Thank you for protecting me, for standing over me . . ."

She wept and they knelt down and comforted her.

20—The DEATHLOKK

The standoff in Rostov seemed to have lasted quite a while. Phillip pointed his Poltava at one of the Watch, who had a throbbing Tartan energy gun pointed at Kay. Sarah had her blue Poltava pointed at another Watchman, who had his dingy-looking pistol pointed at Phillip.

"So, what's going to happen here?" one of the Watch said. "There's no way out of this; why not lower your weapons?"

"Why not lower yours?" Sarah asked.

"You have broken the law."

"It's a stupid law. You've got people here betting their children over a throw of the dice and selling Remax tablets to addicts, yet you're willing to get into a shootout with us over a breach in betting protocol?" she argued.

The young Watchman named Phender again tried to diffuse the situation. "Look, Jessum, if we keep imprisoning, trying and executing visitors to Rostov, well not have any customers left. I say let's let these people be on their way."

Jessum scowled at him, raised a small holocam, and took a scan of Kay, Phillip and Sarah. He then backed away into the crowd of people with drawn weapons.

Kay, standing there by the counter, was the only one in sight without a drawn weapon. Slowly, he picked up Sam's Doughnut and held it in his hands, feeling its weight.

Sam's Doughnut.

Once again, the sportsman pointed his dueling pistol at the back of Kay's head. Sarah covered him with her Poltava.

"It might seem odd to you now," Kay said studying it, "but one day, this could be a place of great learning and enlightenment. A place where people will come from all over and want to live and raise their families—not to fester and throw their lives away. A great city of white stone could stand here one day," he said.

"How do you know that?" Phender asked.

"I've seen it. More 'razzle dazzle' that you touched upon earlier."

"Rostov is as it is. Who are you to judge us?" the sportsman asked, angry.

"Me? Nobody. I'm nobody at all," Kay replied. He looked at the sportsman. "You want to make a bet? I'll bet I can do something you've never seen before."

"Slim chance of that, Sonny-Jim," the Sportsman replied.

Kay set the silver device down and allowed his Sight to fall away. Back in time it went, through the ages.

He turned his gaze north. Eventually, he found what he wanted. It didn't take him nearly as long as he thought.

With an odd movement, Kay reached out, as if he were pulling on something. The Watch tensed, and one of them cocked the hammer of his weapon.

Suddenly, two huge creatures emerged in the dingy street in front of Kay. They were at least fifteen feet tall, female, mostly naked, and multi-armed and multi-breasted. One had twelve arms, the other eight.

Haitathe, from thousands of years ago.

They looked around for a moment, perplexed. The people on the street turned their gaze to them and were shocked. The sportsman screamed as they towered over him.

One of the giants heard the scream and kicked at it, leveling the stand, causing Kay to leap out of the way, his gaze almost faltering.

All at once, the giant, multi-armed females and the crowd began flailing and shooting, most of the Watchmen scattering. Soon, the entire city was in turmoil as the giants roughly mopped up the place. They splintered the drab structures with their delicate, yet brutally powerful fists. They swung boards, knocked down shacks and tossed people high into the air. They roared with fiendish delight as bullets and energy beams bounced off their slender, pale bodies. Occasionally, they picked up struggling persons and devoured them. The whole walled enclosure was like a huge playpen for them.

In a killing frenzy, they both began growing. Soon, they were nearly twice as tall as when they started, looming, stomping, smashing and devouring.

Kay kept his gaze fixed on them, not taking his eyes off—not blinking. As long as he kept his gaze fixed on them, they would remain. They would remain until he wished them gone and looked away. It was hard work, though, draining and easy to let slip.

The sportsman came up from behind his newly destroyed counter and pointed his dueling pistol at Kay. Kay couldn't look away; he had to concentrate on the Haitathe, or they would vanish, and the three of them would be surrounded in a hostile city focused on them.

POW! Sarah gunned him down.

A Watchman made to shoot Kay with an old Hit-Six frag-lock.

POW—Phillip got him with his green and brown Poltava.

Bullets started flying from Sarah's and Phillip's tiny but powerful guns. People dove for cover. As incoming and outgoing lead and energy lances whizzed by, Sarah was sure she saw Kay get hit once or twice, but he didn't seem fazed. He concentrated hard on the Haitathe.

The two Haitathe headed west, toward Leap Manor, destroying everything in their path, a fireworks display of energy shots and gunfire following them in a colorful cloud.

Sarah and Phillip pulled Kay away, toward the gates.

One of the remaining Watchmen drew a bead on Kay with his Redwagon energy gun and aimed at his head.

There was a shot, and the Watchman fell dead, the Redwagon clattering from his hand.

Phender, the young Watchman, stood there holding his smoking Dare, and quickly put it away. "That true, what you said?" he asked Kay.

"Yes."

He looked around watching the two Haitathe giants tear up the city, killing and stomping with every step. "Did you summon these beasts?"

"I did. I'm sorry."

He looked around at the destruction. "I can't say that I blame you. My older brother was going to have you killed simply because you didn't want to get cheated by my uncle Ebenezer who's never run a fair game in his life. I can't say that we don't deserve it. It's not like this place hasn't been leveled to ground many times for one reason of another—be it by monster, brigand, lout or infuriated Sister. I'm getting sick of this, embarrassed by it. Maybe a fresh start will do this place well this time."

He picked up Sam's Doughnut and handed it to Kay. "Take the piece and get out of here. You better run, and you better watch it. Lord Xerin of Rostov is not a forgiving, or a forgetting, man."

Somebody fired a Dee-Dee, blowing off one the twelve-armed Haitathe's arms. She bellowed in rage and trawled the street for the culprit.

Another Dee-Dee shot took the head off of the other Haitathe.

Headless, she staggered for a moment, then a new head grew back in place of the old—a totally different-looking head with black hair.

Like two huge spiders, they began scaling the black walls of Leap Manor.

Activity on one of the high towers of Leap Manor caught Kay's attention, and he almost let his gaze slip again. The large man in the dark coat stood on the tower, apparently quite agitated. Someone joined him on the tower roof—it was Jessum, the Watchman who had tried to arrest Kay. He handed Lord Xerin a holo-viewer and pointed in their general direction.

Four servant girls, each holding onto the corners of a large red pillow, appeared on the tower and approached Lord Xerin. He reached down and pulled a huge, nasty-looking black rifle off the pillow.

"You three better get out of here!" Phender said. "That's Lord Xerin up there, and that's the DEATHLOKK he's holding. All he's got to do is want to hit you with it, and he will. Jessum just showed him your picture. You could be a continent away, and he'd still hit you in the chest with it."

Phender unchained his mickalmick. "Gersey," he said to it, "get them to the city gates. I'll do my best to cover you—my very best!" With that, the mickalmick reached out like lightning and seized the three of them with three of his six tails. He held them aloft, and they struggled for a moment, Kay concentrating on the Haitathe.

"Who are you?" Phillip asked as Gersey began bearing them away.

"I'm Lord Phender of Rostov," he said drawing another Dare from his sash. "Maybe I liked the sound of what you said. Maybe we can be something after all."

Gersey began moving, slithering on his belly like a greased rocket, through the chaotic crowded street and throngs of panicked people, toward the gates of the city. Watchmen converging from all sides began taking potshots at them as they passed, and Sarah and Phillip, held aloft, returned fire.

Kay concentrated on the Haitathe and held onto Sam's Doughnut.

Far away, Lord Xerin, holding his DEATHLOKK, fired it into the air with a deafening, mortar-like report. After a moment or two, one of the Haitathe fell dead, struck to the chest, the shot having made a terrible hole there.

Nonchalantly, he reloaded, and fired again. Another massive report, and the last Haitathe fell dead. Kay quieted his Sight and let them fall back, dead, into time.

Ahead, several of the Watch had created a barricade in the direction of the city gates. They were cutoff.

A Watchman with a DeeDee rifle laid a bead on Sarah. There was a CRACK, and he fell, taken down by Lord Phender some distance away.

Gersey extended his three remaining tails, running on them in stilt-like fashion. He cleared the barricade and continued.

Kay, free of the Haitathe, concentrated and Cloaked all three of them, Gersey, too.

Ahead, the city gates, were not a hundred yards distant.

Kay Sighted and was appalled. He saw the man in the dark coat holding the DEATHLOKK.

Then he saw bullets zeroing in on them.

"Phillip! Sarah! Get your SAPPS out and make a shield. Hurry!!"

Phillip and Sarah took off their SAPPS and quickly formed them into two broad, semi-convex shields. They pointed them skyward just in time for a massive shot to come raining down on them from above. Even though it was just a rifle bullet hitting the shields, it hit with the explosive power of a large grenade. Gersey was knocked off balance, and he skittered to a stop just short of the gates.

"Creation, that just about broke my arm!" Phillip said, trying to hold up his shield.

Gersey released them and slithered away, falling out of Cloak.

Another shot came in, and Sarah screamed with the blow. Even Cloaked, it didn't matter. All Lord Xerin had to do was want to hit them, and the DEATHLOKK would connect—no matter where on Kana they were. This was a gun from which one couldn't hide; as long as one was outside, one was vulnerable.

Another shot. "Kay, we need cover! My SAPP can't handle much more!" Phillip yelled, struggling to hold his SAPP up. They were pinned down, unable to advance.

Kay rolled out from under the shield and allowed Lord Xerin into his Cloak—such was the improvement of his skill.

Now Lord Xerin could see him plain as day. From a distance, they stared at each other.

Kay set down the silver device and zeroed in on the man

standing on the tower. Lord Xerin saw him and laughed. Casually, he loaded the long DEATHLOKK with a fresh bullet. Apparently, it was a single-shot weapon.

Kay drew his purple Poltava and aimed. Lord Xerin again laughed out loud, seeing Kay point the tiny gun at him. Xerin probably knew his weapons, and he probably had heard about the power and accuracy the Poltava was reputed to have. But still, it was nothing more than a short-barreled pistol that probably had an accurate range of fifty feet.

They must have been at least a half mile apart. He finished loading and held his arms out to his side, inviting Kay to fire, giving him a free shot, with the DEATHLOKK clutched in his ham-like fist like a huge, black matchstick. Then, once Kay fired and missed, he would pull the DEATHLOKK"s trigger and blast Kay into yesterday.

Kay zoomed in, adjusted his gun, and pulled the trigger.

POW!

Lord Xerin was hit right between the eyes. The power of the Poltava's shot was such that the bullet entered his skull, scrambled his brains, and exited the back, where it continued on and eventually fell into the sea. Arms waving, Xerin stumbled backwards and, doing a half-back flip, went over the side of Leap Manor, down several hundred feet into the crashing waves of the sea below—his DEATHLOKK falling with him in a lazy twist. Jessum, the Watchman standing nearby was stunned. He looked over the side to see where Lord Xerin had fallen.

POW!

He, too, was hit in the back of the skull by a second shot from Kay's Poltava; a few moments later, he, too, was falling over the side of Leap Manor, eventually his body floating in the surf, nudging against Lord Xerin's.

Kay put his gun away. The three of them left the city as fast as they could, just as a contingent of the Watch came surging out of the city gates looking for them. The Watch had mickalmicks with them that, supposedly, could detect Cloaked people; however, they were looking in the wrong direction, the wide open space outside of the walls being too much ground to search.

As they made their way from the black city and its dead patriarch, Kay was satisfied that the House of Rostov had, most likely, a better future ahead.

21—The Trouble with Lon

They made their way back toward the *Goshawk*. Moving in what they thought was a clever and silent fashion, they approached the waiting vessel and went in with their prize, Sam's Doughnut, safely in hand.

Somebody was sitting inside waiting for them. Trigger happy after Rostov, three Poltavas came out of their coats.

They couldn't believe it. Sitting there on the back bench was Lord Lon of Probert, Kay's and Phillip's friend from Arden, his little triangle hat in his hands, his leggings and hose-socks, his buckle shoes splayed apart at an irregular angle. He was wearing his usual big Probert coat—green this time.

He was asleep, mouth open, snoring.

"Lon?" Sarah called, putting her Poltava away. He didn't react.

"Lon!" she yelled, kicking him.

He woke, snorting to life, looking around in a daze. He focused on them and smiled. "Oh, hello—I must have nodded off." He stopped suddenly and checked his breath.

Shaking his head, Phillip dropped into the pilot's chair, shut the hatch, and began firing the ship up, eager to put some distance between them and Rostov.

"Where in Creation did you come from?" Kay asked.

Lon smiled, feeling proud of himself. "I heard you were in the Wiln area. I was keen to speak to you, Kay, and I inquired at the various inns and so forth to see if you had checked into any. I had the good fortune to locate the lovely inn you had checked out of this morning. Then, as it happened, I saw the *Goshawk's* departing silhouette against the sky and, using simple arithmetic, zeroed in on your approximate location. I then hired a coach to bring me out here."

Phillip jerked the ship into the air and banked east. "You saw our silhouette, Lon? But how did you find the ship? It's Cloaked."

"I know—I was wearing my No-Cloak goggles."

Kay stood there and shook his head. Only Lord Lon. "Anyway, it's good to see you, Lon."

"And you, Kay." He put his hat back on. "Which brings me to my point. I was wanting to discuss something with you, if I may?"

Kay went into the cargo hold and put the silver piece into a small chest. He then came forward and sat down across from him. Sarah opened the cooler. "You want anything to drink, Lon?"

"Whatever you're having, Sarah, is fine. Thank you."

Sarah pulled out a few cans of red Gasol and handed one to him and Kay. Lon popped it open and began drinking.

"So, what's on your mind, Lon?"

He straightened up a bit, swallowing his drink. "Kay, I want to discuss Lady Sammidoran of Monama with you."

Sarah's ears pricked up, and Phillip turned his head a little from the cockpit, trying to listen.

"Lady Sammidoran of Monama?" Kay said. "What about her?" Kay had a sinking feeling. Whatever was on Lon's mind it couldn't be good.

"You mean the creepy lady in black I was going to beat up at the 'Falling in Love' ball a few months back?" Sarah chimed in, playing dumb.

"Yes," Lon replied laughing. He put his drink down and darkened a bit. "I want to know what your relationship with Lady Sammidoran is, Kay. I want to know what there is between the two of you. There is something, I know there is."

Sarah cut in. "Well, Lon, she wanted to get with Kay, but, when she found out that I was going to knock her teeth out if she tried, she backed away, and we haven't heard from her since."

Lon wasn't buying. He sat there with his drink and looked at Kay.

Kay stammered—Sam had sworn him to secrecy. "My relationship with her, Lon? My relationship with Lady Sammidoran of Monama, if any, is rather private."

Lon wasn't going to be denied. "I demand to know, Kay. She has sought me out several times—she has a wonderful mind and a keen interest in technical matters. I believe that I find her lovely, intelligent, inquisitive and enchanting."

"Lon, what are you saying?"

"I'm saying that I have allowed myself, after a bit of introspection, to fall in love with Lady Sammidoran. Yes, not only is she an exciting intellect, but she is most beautiful as well, and I wish to formally court her. But first—I know there is something between the two of you, and I want—*I demand* to know what it is."

Kay made to say something but stopped—Sam's promise holding him back. Sarah chimed in. "Lon, Kay and Lady Sammidoran have been actively seeing each other for five years."

A frustrated wave passed over his face. He gritted his teeth.

"Five years?" he said. "Five years? I suppose, then, that the prospect of getting beaten up by you, Sarah, wasn't much of a consideration, was it?"

Sarah's mouth fell open in shock.

Lon focused on Kay, his face turning red. "Then why have you not announced yourselves? By the Elders, you looked like you were going to vomit at the ball when she started making eyes at you, Kay."

"Yes, Lon, I was just acting. I'm sorry."

Lon looked at his shoes. "You've been seeing her for five years, and you've not done her the courtesy of announcing your intentions to the League?" Lon was positively livid. "Are you ashamed of her, is that it? Does her lowly status as a Monama give you pause? Is she not good enough for the mighty Lord of Blanchefort? Is she your secret whore, Kay?"

Kay's eyes flashed. "That will be quite enough, Lon."

Lon considered his words and continued. "I'm still waiting, Kay. Answer my question, or do you require Sarah to do it for you?"

"Yes, yes, we have been seeing each other for quite a long time. And I wanted to announce ourselves to the League long ago; if it were up to me, we would have been announced properly by now, but she never let me. She insisted that we keep it to ourselves, and I honored her request. Believe me; you don't want to know why she wanted it kept secret."

"It's a Monama thing, Lon," Sarah said.

Lon sat there in frustration. "Phillip, please land the ship. I don't think I fully believe you, Kay. And, for that matter, I'm not backing down. I have always been the novel friend, the nice, silly boy hanging in the wings—the person everybody likes but nobody loves. You and Phillip—you two could have virtually anybody you wanted—daughters of Great Houses lining up to throw their lot in for your hand. And what do I have—

nothing but a shiny pin from my latest scholastic achievement. I want to be that person. I want to be the man who gets the girl. And I have my hopes set on Lady Sammidoran, a Monama who couldn't hope to be on the same social level as the Great House of Blanchefort."

"Lon, what do you want me to tell you? I don't care about her standing or her House," Kay said, pleading.

Lon stood. "Phillip, in the Name of Creation, land the ship! I don't want you to tell me anything, Kay," he said reaching into his coat and pulling out his CEROS. "When Phillip lands the ship, we will step out and present our weapons."

"Lon!" Sarah cried. "You can't be serious!"

Phillip looked back, the *Goshawk* wobbling a little as he did. "Lon, I'm not landing the ship for this foolishness."

Lon was determined. "Then present, Kay. Do it now!"

Kay and Sarah were stunned. The ship lurched a little as Phillip whipped his head around again. Lord Lon, their friend from the time they were kids, the fellow who helped him design his CARG, now wanted to duel with Kay over Sam.

"Please put your weapon away," Kay said.

"Present, Kay, or I'll kill you unarmed. By Creation I will!"

Kay stood up. "Then kill me."

He was enraged. "The last time I spoke to her, she was in tears. She was inconsolable. What did you do to her? You must have done something!"

The thought of Sam in tears banged his heart. "We had had a fight, Lon. I accused her of all sorts of crimes. I was unreasonable, and I made her cry."

Lon's hand, the one holding the CEROS, shook. He then dropped it and sat back down on the bench. He looked angry, sad, and embarrassed as well.

Kay took Lon by the shoulders. "Was she all right, Lon? Was Sam ok?"

"She was upset about something—she avoided saying what."

Kay picked up his CEROS and handed it back to him. "I'm sorry about all this, Lon, and I'm sorry I couldn't bring you into my confidence. If I had known what you were feeling, I would have told you in advance. The last thing I want is for you to suffer. Sam wouldn't want that either; she likes you. In fact, she is keen to find somebody out there worthy of you."

Lon looked at his CEROS and gritted his teeth.

They sat there and stared at each other in silence—the only sound being the steady thrum of the *Goshawk's* engine.

After awhile the ship gave a loud thump, and Phillip moved some levers on the pilot's dash.

"Water," Lon said quietly.

"What?" Sarah asked.

"That thump—it probably was the super-condenser. It engaged, meaning the air suddenly became much more humid, which means we're over water."

Sarah shook her head. "Phillip, are we flying over water?"

"Yes," he responded.

Lon suddenly seemed consumed with emotion. It all came spilling out of him. "Look, all I wanted was someone I was sure nobody else did. A beautiful, intelligent woman, consigned to the dregs of League Society. I thought that nobody could possibly want her."

Kay leaned forward. "Don't sell yourself short, Lon, ever. You have talents and skills that few in the League could rival. I think you've convinced yourself that you loved Sam because you thought she was a safe choice—that there was no competition. If a Monama is what you truly want, then pursue one. They are good people, a strong people. Sam sought me out as a child, and I had the good fortune to win her love. Perhaps the same will be for you, if that's where your heart truly lies. A Monama girl could be dreaming of you right at this very moment, like Sam did with me. She has over twenty sisters, you know," Kay said.

Lon seemed to brighten a little. "I've . . . I've been doing research on Monamas. It's a fascinating House. There isn't a whole lot out there regarding their private ways and habits. I, I even picked up a little Anuie to attempt to impress her."

Kay responded to him, in Anuie. *"Sam loves speaking in her mother tongue. She taught it to me."*

Lon replied. *"A pretty language to speak."*

"Sometimes she refuses to speak anything else. I never knew I could pick up a new language so fast. In fact, now that you're here, maybe you would like to assist us. It's one of those, Monama habits', as you put it, that we are investigating even as we speak."

"You'll pardon me then, Kay, for being angry? For presenting my CEROS? Are we still friends, or have I ruined our friendship?"

"Of course I will, Lon; it's already forgotten. And, no, you could never ruin our friendship."

They embraced, Kay playfully jabbing Lon in his round Probert belly like he did when they were kids.

Sarah intervened. "Hey, what's going on? And, for the sake of those here who don't speak 'Sam', can we please talk normal?"

"Sure, Sarah," Kay said, still hugging Lon.

Phillip looked back and smiled. "It's a good thing you're making up back there; otherwise, I was going to have to knock some heads together."

"You fly the ship, Phillip, and I'll do the head knocking," Sarah replied.

Kay re-seated himself. "Now, let's to it. I know that Sam came to you some time back for assistance. What was she wanting specifically? Anything you could tell us will be of great help."

"She wanted detailed technical information on a lost machine that she'd been researching."

"Which machine?"

"A legendary machine built by the House of Want long ago. A machine called the *Oberphilliax.*"

"What does the machine do?"

Lon settled himself and began chirping happily. "We had a spirited debate on just that very topic. Supposedly, and this is merely coffee-table conjecture, the machine creates a singularity between two or more separate points of temporality."

"What?" Sarah said.

"A time machine," Phillip said from the cock-pit.

Lon giggled, his belly rumbling. "Yes, that is the modern conclusion, though the machine's use is rather mysterious. I must say, Lady Sammidoran strongly disagreed. She said, in so many words, that the *Oberphilliax* is a device that allows degrees of separation in disjointed continuums to be thwarted safely and rejoined elsewhere without the benefit and limitations of a temporal anchorage. A theoretical impossibility. That is simply too ridiculous to contemplate, but she was adamant."

"I disagree," Phillip commented from the cockpit. "The Mana of Kind in a vacuum, states that two separate continuums may be bridged should degrees of separation be properly severed and rejoined."

"But," Lon said, his excitement and enthusiasm growing, "but the degrees of separation have not been proved as an Actuality by the latest thoughts on quantum mechanics."

Kay felt his head starting to spin. Sarah also looked confused. "Gentlemen—a fascinating topic, but food for a later conversation. Can we sum up somehow? What did Sam say the machine does, in ten words or less?"

"By her account, it supposedly allows objects from separate time continuums to seamlessly merge, but that is just not possible. Such a thing would make it the Golden Goose of time travel."

"How on earth would Sam know something like that? So, it is a time machine?" Kay asked.

"No, Kay, that would make it a temporal bridge—very different and much more complex and desirable than a mere time machine. However, Lady Sammidoran's speculation is, at best, a fanciful bit of conjecture," Lon said.

Kay shook his head. "Is that all you talked with Sam about, Lon?"

"No, she wanted to know if such a machine could be built."

"And what was your response?"

"I told her no—impossible. The House of Want used an assortment of unique materials and machining methods that were lost when the House left the League centuries ago. Such a great loss of knowledge. Also, I told her that the power source for the unit is not generally known. I could see she was disappointed; she started crying right there at the cafe. I tried to cheer her by stating that there currently is an *Oberphilliax* already in existence. Its current location and the detailed specifics of the machine are manifested in a book, property of the Sisterhood of Light at Hiei, though that particular book is not available for research."

"There is?"

"Yes. Over lunch we did some Holo-research. The Science Ministry has a complete manifest of all printed materials in the Sisterhood's possession—as the Ministry often works hand-in-hand with the Sisters regarding various projects. I know my mother's Science Ministry codes, and I accessed their database."

"And you gave Sam the information?"

"I did. The name of the book and its exact shelf location at Hiei. I told her not to bother—the book's not available for reference. It's restricted for the time being."

Kay recalled the visit from the Sisters. Could Sam have broken into Hiei and stolen the book in question?

"Did she say why she was so interested in this particular machine?"

"She refused to say. Quite the secretive thing, isn't she?" Kay smiled. "She sure is."

Lon sat there with a look of longing for a moment.

Sarah opened the *Goshawk's* holo-terminal and started a session. The familiar holographic gentleman popped up, wearing his long black coat and holding the red staff of knowledge.

"Access history: *Oberphilliax,*" Sarah said. Working the holo-terminal took practice. Kay, not much of a lined-in researcher, usually let Sarah do it. His sisters, Kilos and Hathaline, were expert at it. Sam, with practice, appeared to have gotten quite good as well.

The gentleman waved his staff and spoke in his slow, elegant voice. "*Oberphilliax,* ancient machine designed by Lord Revis, House of Want, 000009ax."

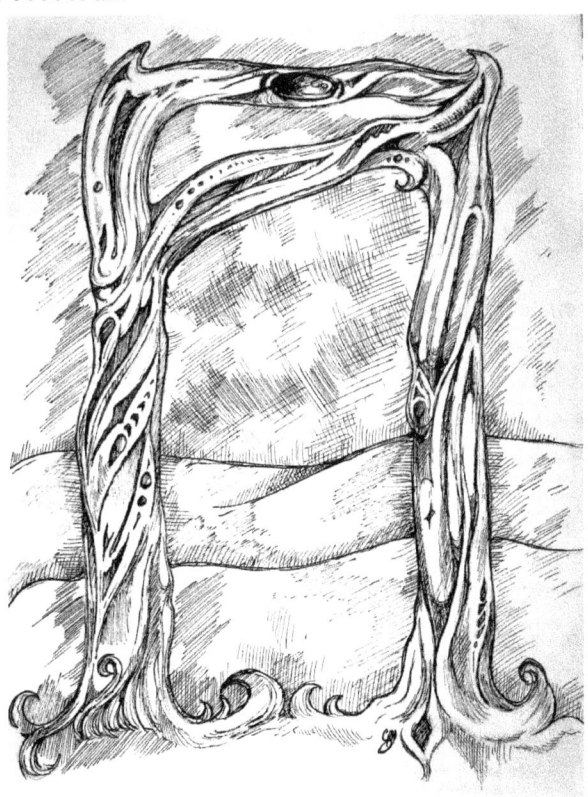

Next to the gentleman, a shimmering image of a dainty silver machine appeared. It was a slender archway about seven feet tall and three feet wide; its silvery legs and twisting crosspiece were designed in an organic, sinewy sort of style. It looked fragile—like something that should be used as a decoration in a garden path.

"What is function, *Oberphilliax?*"

"Query suspended—function *Oberphilliax* in contest and denied access."

"Countermand."

"No countermand possible."

Sarah huffed. Certain Ministries and, on occasion, the Sisterhood restricted information regarding various topics, and using the Holo could be a tiring and frustrating adventure. And, if you pushed the matter too much, said Ministries and, likely, the Sisters might become wise to your activities. A visit from the Sisters could be a possibility. Kay would rather look up information in old books.

"What is current status, *Oberphilliax?*"

"Current status, *Oberphilliax* . . . Status—in dispute. One known unit constructed."

"Status, *Oberphilliax* known constructed unit."

"Status—unit thirded by order of the Sisterhood of Light, 000570ax."

Sarah was perplexed. "Thirded? The Sisters broke it into three pieces? Why didn't they just destroy it?"

"They probably couldn't—the House of Want was near Elder-Like in their knowledge. It was a great loss for the League when they left," Lon said.

"Where did they go?" Sarah asked.

"Unknown. I think they went to Cammara, you know, the old home world during the CX Epoch. I think they went back there."

Sarah returned to the Holo-net. "State location, thirded pieces of *Oberphilliax?*"

"Query suspended. Location of *Oberphilliax* restricted."

Sarah turned away from the terminal. "Well, that's that. Looks like we've run into a dead end."

Kay sat back and thought. "Sarah, I think the three portions of Sam's Trial are to recover the pieces of the missing *Oberphilliax*."

"Sam's what?" Lon asked.

"She is putting me to a Trial, Lon—it's some sort of Monama

tradition. We've already accomplished one portion of the Trials, and two more await. I'm not clear as to her ultimate intent, but I believe she is guiding me into recovering parts of a strange device: a machine of some sort. Three parts to be precise. I am now convinced she's guiding us to recover the three pieces of the *Oberphilliax*."

"How could Sam know where they are?" Lon asked.

"There was a recent theft at the Sister's stronghold of Hiei. They weren't happy about it; they even shut Hiei down for a bit. They came to us asking if we knew anything about it."

"They came to our House, too," Lon said. "I was really scared. The Sisters scare me. I got sick."

Sarah laughed. "You got sick in front of the Sisters, Lon?"

"I did."

Kay laughed and clapped Lon on the shoulder. "Lon, I now believe that Sam was the perpetrator of the break in at Hiei. I believe that Sam, craving information, stole the book you mentioned to her."

Lon shook his head. "I won't believe that—she'd be throwing her life away."

Kay stood up. "You require proof? Sam is a stubborn little pistol. If she gets something into her head, there is no stopping her. Allow me." Kay went into the *Goshawk's* cargo hold and brought out a small chest. He opened it. Inside, the doughnut-shaped metallic piece he'd retrieved from the House of Rostov sat on its cushion. "This is the first piece, Lon—we just now retrieved it. Take a look. What do you think?"

"We've been calling it 'Sam's Doughnut'," Sarah added.

"Yes, yes, I see that."

Lon carefully took it into his hands. "Oh, this is most definitely a House of Want construction. Feast your eyes on the detail, the craftsmanship. This metal—it's an alloy of some sort. Wondrous." He pulled a set of goggles out of his green coat and adjusted several prisms. He then examined the device again, turning it over in his hands. "Yes, indeed, this is a treasure. Where did you get it again?"

"The House of Rostov; it was thrown in a vault full of gambled booty."

"Can you make anything out of it?" Sarah asked, sitting down next to him.

Lon sucked in his breath as he carefully looked over the device's silvery surface. "It's an alloy, as I said before. It's a solid piece, yet its construction is not solid—it's made up of millions of tiny interlocking pieces—amazing. Amazing!" He looked up, flabbergasted. "I must have this for study."

"After we're done with it, you can have it," Kay promised.

Lon adjusted his goggles. "I believe that twisting in this direction and applying a bit of pressure here . . ."

Suddenly, as Lon worked the device, it began to grow. Like a plant sprouting up out of the ground, it expanded in size until it was about six feet long. Lon had to turn it lengthwise so that it didn't go through the top of the _Goshawk_.

In comparing it to the flickering holo image on the terminal, it was clearly one of the legs supporting the machine's elegant arch. Without question, this was a portion of the legendary _Oberphilliax._ Lon worked the device, and it shrank back down to its former configuration.

"So," he said with sobriety, "you appear to be correct. Lady Sammidoran must have stolen the book from Hiei. I cannot stress the need for secrecy—should the Sisters find out, they will bring their wrath down upon her and her House."

"Yes," Kay said. "I'm certain all here can be counted on for our discretion."

Phillip turned from the cockpit. "Now that we know this information, if the Sisters ever Stare us, the jig will be up."

Lon smiled. "Oh no, there are ways around the Stare. My mother taught me. You think my mother, as a top scientist—an Imperator of the Science Ministry—contents herself with sticking to Sisterhood dogma and restrictions? If the Sisterhood knew what was rolling around in my mother's head, oh boy!"

Lon suddenly fell silent and looked around. "Forget I said that, okay? Anyway, there are techniques that can be applied to defeat a Stare. We'll discuss that in further detail later. "Now," he said in full discovery-mode, "what about power?"

"I don't know. I suppose well handle that issue when we get to it."

"What is to be done with this machine once it's reassembled and properly powered?" Lon demanded.

"Unknown. With luck well have Sam back, and she may explain herself in more detail at that time. I don't know what Sam wanted with it."

"Where is Lady Sammidoran at the moment?" Lon asked, and Kay filled him in on the proceedings to date. He listened and nodded.

He looked at the piece of the *Oberphilliax* and seemed to burst with excitement. "May I come as well? I would greatly enjoy fetching the parts, and you will probably need my help during the reassembly."

"Glad to have you, Lon," Sarah said.

"So, let's get me up to date. You have the first portion; where is the next one?"

"Don't know. I haven't been told yet. We're going to fly to Esther and await further instruction."

"And the final piece?"

"We haven't been given that clue yet, either."

"Oh, I see." He sat there for a moment, his mind spinning. "Power will be the big thing. It will be a crystal stone, about the size of my fist."

"I disagree," Phillip said. "Many known devices of the House of Want were solar powered."

"True, but this device is unlike many of their previous creations. I recall seeing a large stone mounted in the centerpiece of the machine on the Holo-display. That must furnish its power."

"What if it's just a decoration?" Sarah asked.

"A decoration?" Lon said, aghast. "I suppose that's what Lady Sammidoran was asking about when she came to me that second time."

"Come again, Lon," Kay said,

"She came to me and was very sad. My heart went out to her—that's when I decided that I wished to pursue her. After she calmed down a bit, she showed me a holo drawing of a large crystal and wanted to know if I thought it looked correct. I made some minor changes to it, and she thanked me."

"Did you ask her what she was doing with such a thing?" Kay asked.

"She said something about saving her heart for the future."

22—The Horned God

With Lord Lon now in tow, they decided to head to the Esther region and await Kay's next set of instructions. It was maddening not knowing what was coming next or when the information would arrive. Kay felt a little nostalgic for the Gift trials, and he found himself missing the three Gifts who helped to train him, especially Cloak, who was the most like Sam—the things he had shared with her.

Before they could go to Esther, they had to bear north and make a quick stop in the city of Arden. Lon, never really straying too far from home for any length of time, had to stop in and let his parents know what was going on and get a few things.

Probert Manor was partially a Vith ruin, partially a modern, progressive structure on the cliffs by the sea. Lon's father, Lord Milos of Probert, loved to keep up on the latest in styles and trends; in so doing, he kept adding onto the manor turning it into a mishmash of form and function. The newest structure on the grounds was a large lab he had built for Lady Branna, his wife.

Phillip set the *Goshawk* down near the cliffs. They all piled out, and Lon lead them into the manor. Sitting them down in a comfortable study, he bolted up to his wing to get a few "essentials." When he returned to the study, his mother, the Lady Branna of Probert, was with him.

Lady Branna was one of the League's top scientists—she being one of the four Grand Imperators of the Science Ministry. A tiny, blue-haired woman of the House Pitcock line, she struck a regal figure. A scientist through and through, she was also a prolific inventor and innovator, and her contributions to League technology could not be denied or easily calculated, her lab often crackling with strange sounds and glowing with an odd light. Formerly, when she was still married to Lord Timon of Fallz, her battles with Lord Milos of Probert, the Stellar Fleet's chief engineer, were legendary, and rather humorous—she wanting to incorporate new technologies into his grand Fleet ship designs, and he telling her, publically, to buzz off. She always swore that she'd have Probert rotting in her dungeon sooner or later, and he always replied that she was soon to have a lengthy stay in prison for war crimes for her stupid ideas.

The dungeon for Probert.

Prison for Lady Branna.

The fact that she didn't have a dungeon in House Fallz didn't matter. She swore to build one just for him and stock it with all manner of blood-thirsty worms, lice and vermin to feast specifically on his flesh.

When her husband died, she found an immediate kinship with Milos of Probert, her old rival. Despite her combative relationship with him over the years, she'd always greatly respected him and admired his intellect—one to rival her own. He had been politely rejected in courtship by the Lady Poe of Blanchefort, and the two of them, lonely and evenly matched intellectually, soon struck up an unlikely friendship that blossomed into romance and then marriage. Relocating to Probert Manor, Branna and Milos had four children— with the Lady Branna already having twelve from her previous marriage. Lon was their youngest and final child, so she swore.

Lord Lon had his father's mechanical and engineering skills and his mother's insatiable curiosity and need to constantly innovate. He, also, though a bit on the roundish side, had more of a Pitcock look to him than a Probert—which was a House known for their minds, not their good looks. In time, Lon, no doubt, would be a fine handsome fellow, but, at only seventeen, he still had a lot of the "puffies" and wasn't overly suave with the ladies—another of his father's traits that he'd inherited.

He was the delight of his mother's eye. Countless times as he was growing up, his mother dragged the tiny Lon into the lab to show him something she'd created, and she was amazed how many times Lon instantly grasped what she had made and, sometimes, even improve upon it, to her delight. Though a mother would never admit to having a favorite son or daughter, Lon was clearly Lady Branna's favorite—her pride and joy, and she doted on him in an embarrassing fashion.

"Lord Blanchefort," she said to Kay. "Your mother and father are aware of this 'field experiment,' are they?"

"Yes, my lady," Kay replied.

"And how long will Lon be gone?"

"Oh, it's difficult to say. Pending on our . . . 'results' . . . we should have him back in a week or so."

Lady Branna looked skeptical. "I see. Knowing you Vith like I do, I expect you'll be taking my Lon off somewhere to perform some brazen and foolhardy act. Will you assure me that whatever you are doing is perfectly legal?"

Kay laughed. "Oh, most certainly, my lady."

"Yes or no will do."

"Yes, our activities shall be perfectly legal."

"And, you will guarantee his safety, Lord Blanchefort, will you? You will personally look after him?"

"I will, my lady. I promise."

Lady Branna seemed satisfied, and, after a round of hugging and tossing his hair, she led him away to pack.

Sometime later, Lon returned, lugging a few small suitcases and a fresh blue Probert coat and freshly polished buckle shoes.

Lon endured a final round of hugging from his mother, and then they went outside and climbed back into the *Goshawk*, Lady Branna waving a hanky as Phillip lifted the ship away. Inside, Lon took over Kay's tiny room—Kay opting to sleep on the couch.

They then headed east to Esther to whatever awaited.

∗   ∗   ∗   ∗   ∗

They didn't have long to wait. As the *Goshawk* soared at altitude over Thirkill Bay near the mouth of the Kronos River, the ship fell into a thick storm cloud that brewed up out of nowhere—one that caused the *Goshawk's* screens and instruments to go totally dead.

Flying blind in the unnatural dark, Phillip struggled to keep the ship level.

Then, the hatch flew open, and several snaky tendrils of black twisted their way into the cabin. Quickly, one of them located Kay, wrapped around him as he drew his Poltava and pulled him out of the ship, the scrambling Sarah and Lon unable to get to him in time.

Outside, in the moving, streaming dark, Kay was held fast. He couldn't breathe, couldn't get a lungful of air. Desperate, Kay Sighted, looking for the *Goshawk,* but he couldn't see it—it just wasn't there. He looked down, seeing through the murk, and didn't see Thirkill Bay below.

The dense mist parted, and he found himself standing alone in an immense room, like a vast, squared-off cavern plunged in darkness. It was huge, the ceiling being so high off the stony floor he had to use his Sight to see it clearly. The room was rectangular in shape, with the distant walls being lined with the fallen remains of huge idols, all toppled over and broken. In front of him, far away, was a platform or stage lined with stone pillars that went up to the ceiling. The place was oddly quiet. For some reason, he imagined this quiet space should be filled with savage, pounding noises: whoops of lust, screams of pain—a din of commotion that had known no end in ages.

There was something large in the darkness ahead, something big, like a huge animal resting on the ground.

He heard the rustling of heavy chains, and saw a large silvery beast shackled from top to bottom. It had a smooth-domed head and whiskers. It turned its head and gazed at him, bright eyes blinking.

"Carahil?" Kay asked, "is that you?"

He's after me too, kid, came a reply and the beast vanished.

"Carahil?"

No answer.

Kay detected movement on the platform in front of him. Sighting, he could see a sorrowful figure lashed to a pillar on a distant platform. He couldn't quite make out what it was. It looked like a dead body, flattened, trembling ever so slightly against the pillar.

Unsaddling his CARG, he continued toward the platform, the gritty, crunching sounds of his footfalls quite loud.

He approached the platform and climbed up. Tied painfully to a pillar before Kay was what appeared to be a dead deer, its body smashed and broken beyond repair. He recalled seeing it along with the others that night in the Grove. Sam had created it. Though it hung there unmoving, legs dangling, its eyes were bright and quite alive.

Kay looked at the poor creature. "Are you the Judge of my next trial? I remember you from the Grove." His voice echoed.

Without moving its head, it spoke. *"Aye, I am."*

"Where am I?"

"Over Thirkill Bay. This is simply a NIGHTMARE illusion. This is a representation of a place your lady fears most. This is a place where her people go and never return. She has seen it many times in her nightmares."

"Where's Sam? Is she all right?"

"She is safe where she is."

"Do you know my next step?"

"I do. You will go to the University of Dee. There, in the library, is an item that you shall seek. Secure it, and you will have passed the Second Trial."

The glowing image of a device identical to the first piece from Rostov floated in the air before Kay and shimmered.

"Where is this device?"

"Use your Sight. It will become obvious. It shan't be hard. You will succeed, no doubt."

"Thank you for the vote of approval."

Kay looked at the smashed deer in front of him. "Sir, may I ask—Sam created you, yes?"

"She did—using the NIGHTMARE. Monama women can do quite a bit with it, though if they use it too much, then they mark themselves for death."

"Death?"

"Yes. They will, no doubt, come for her when this is all over— thus the importance of your passing the Trials. They cannot get to her where she currently is, but they will once the Trials are concluded."

"The machine—the *Oberphilliax*, I know Sam is making me seek the pieces of the *Oberphilliax*. Why does Sam want it? What is its purpose?"

The deer considered his words. *"To circumvent a dark future."*

"Can you elaborate?"

"No, I must take you back now. I have given you your instructions. You will now pass your Trial, or, when next we meet, I will kill you."

"If I may ask? Why are you like this? Sam created you—why did she make you in such a state? There must be a reason for it."

"Because I am in the image of the Horned God whom your lady fears. This is his temple that his angels use to cross the stream of time and place. It is his power that gives this temple life. I am the image of He whom she fears and hates."

Dark tendrils formed around Kay. "Wait! Who, who is that?"

As Kay faded into the dark, he heard one last thing before he was put back into the *Goshawk*. He heard the deer say: *"The library, Lord Blanchefort, your trial awaits."*

23—The Battle of Hoban

Over the next few days, Lady Tellerran of Monama improved greatly. Since her ordeal in the Crossland cemetery, she had gained a bit of weight and shed most, if not all, of her initial fear. As a Monama, she shared much in common with Sam. She had the Monama pallor, and was extremely chalky and pale, she had the usual black eyes and thick head of black hair, and her fingernails were long and pointed, like a set of daggers. However, there were significant differences from Sam as well. Sam was a buxom six feet tall, while Tellerran was much smaller and less-full than Sam, standing only about 5'4", though her thick mass of hair gave one the impression that she was much bigger than what she was. Her black eyes were tiny compared to Sam's. She was dressed in a warm set of crewmen's clothing, furry boots and a flight jacket that she got from a Marine. She carried the endecar with her everywhere, and she even made a little decorative bag to carry it in out of scraps of cloth she found in the laundry area. She slinked about and flirted with the crew, soaking up the attention she was getting. She didn't even want to return to Kana anymore—she was having too much fun.

It was said that, when a Monama saw his or her own death, that their personality died; Lady Tellerran's, however, appeared to be reborn with a vengeance. She smiled and laughed. She was intelligent and interrogative, flirtatious, a bit catty and somewhat prone to a touch of arrogance. With her massive head of black hair now combed and cared for, she was quite pretty, though not quite as attractive as Lady Sammidoran, if a comparison had to be made. Davage had heard she'd won her flight jacket by oiling up and wrestling a Marine for it. She was a great hit with the Marines. She took great delight in hanging out with them in the mess, arm wrestling and beating them; her wiry, freakish Monama strength, even in space, was surprising. Her prize for beating a Marine—he had to show her his bellybutton, which seemed to excite her. She even took to drinking with the Marines, though Ennez made her stop—her metabolism couldn't handle it.

Ennez had initially wanted to get her on a fast *Trelaine* back to Kana as soon as possible, as Monamas didn't do well away from there. As Ennez observed her, he discovered that her system didn't appear to absorb nutrients very well in space. As his findings became clearer, Ennez conjectured that he should be able to keep her fully healthy with augmented nutrients, though her Gift-like powers, except for her tremendous strength, could not be restored. With frequent check-ups, a regimen of vitamins, and a shot of iron every once in a while, he was satisfied she could remain in space indefinitely and not suffer any ill effects.

She took her vitamins and flirted with the crew, becoming saucier as the days went on.

This one Monama woman, Lady Tellerran of the Fphenook tribe, had provided a wealth of useful information.

She developed an undeniable crush on Captain Davage, she following him about, insisting that he take her arm as he showed her the huge workings of the *New Faith*—batting her black eyes at him. Countess Sygillis, at first, was patient and accommodating, allowing Tellerran to occupy a spot at Davage's side that normally she filled, but, she eventually, and politely, told her to back off, and Tellerran did.

The Fleet was still in orbit around Hoban, doing dry laps around its coffee-brown equator. The information Tellerran had given them was insightful, but not definitive. They'd been in orbit for five days, and, since the attack in the Crossland cemetery, nothing further had happened. The swarm of Marine *Trelaines* had thinned a bit—several ships had been dispatched to quell nearby Xaphan activity. Captain Harrison of the *Bethel* was beginning to make noises about wanting to leave and press on to other matters, but Admiral Carfax ordered him to stay.

The Sisters had been hard at work going over some of the items collected in the attack: the prism, cords and the gate device that Syg had used to return after her attack. They found that the prism resonated at an extremely high, very complicated frequency in the Gamma band. The red light they created was due to the glyphs carved on the surface, which resonated at a much longer wavelength, appearing red. How or why such a frequency could turn a Monama into a Berserkacide eluded them. Ennez and Beth hypothesized it was the combination of gamma and the red light that created the Berserkacide change.

The cords were fashioned from some type of charged, resinous, polymer that had the Sisters baffled, as did the device that Syg had brought back with her. Those things they took with them into the ship's Priory, and they were not seen again. No doubt, they were spirited away to Twilight 4 or Valenhelm for intense research.

They did, however, come up with a potential fix for the Monama/Berserkacide issue. The Sisters created a thick black paste that effectively filtered out both Gamma-band wavelengths and red light. Ennez put the paste into capsules fired from an air gun. The paste then came bursting out of the pellet, totally covering a target's face, and it was so sticky that it refused to come off without a reactant being applied to it. It was also semi-porous, so a person having his or her face covered with it could still breathe, though it was rather labored.

Ennez rigged up an air gun and test fired it at Davage. Sure enough, it covered his face and wouldn't come off without the reactant being applied. He reported it wasn't quite like being smothered to death, but it was close. But, Davage agreed that the paste did make an effective barrier against Gamma-band and red light. It should work. It should protect the Monamas from being transformed into Berserkacides, provided it could be applied in time. Davage ordered a great many air guns be prepared and distributed to the Marines, and he gave one to Lady Tellerran and told her to carry it at all times and to shoot herself in the face should an attack happen, which she thought was very funny. She wanted a holster to put her air gun in, and she got a neat-looking Marine holster, with which she loved to walk around with.

* * * * *

As the sixth day wore on, Davage, true to his word, kept looking for Gamma band. It was tiring and hard to see—his eyes ached. For days he'd seen nothing. The Sisters, too, looked, though they couldn't see Gamma like Davage could. They could, however, tune their thoughts and "hear" it as noise. But, they, as well, had heard nothing.

* * * * *

Davage sat in the mess with Syg having breakfast. Lt. Kilos' usual seat was empty—she was back on Kana, watching Lady Kilos and Lady Hathaline. She Com'ed in daily, giving Davage and Syg detailed reports. Lady Kilos and Hath were safe and sound. She mentioned something about Lady Kilos giving her a hard time during her tutoring sessions but nothing more distressing than that. Kay, Sarah and Phillip were still gone.

All was quiet on the home front. Just like it was over Hoban.

They were joined for breakfast in the mess by the lovely Captain Strella of the *Halo Dawn*. She had been good enough over the last few days to take a look at the odd book they had recovered in their room. Sitting at their table, Strella was dainty and regal, a typical Remnath woman, complete with their south Kana accent. She wore the *Tremblar* version of the standard Fleet uniform, which was designed specifically for a lady: a light coat and white blouse, demure skirt, knee boots and an odd Remnath hat that could be folded up and placed in a pocket. It was something worn more often by land-locked female officers at Fleet HQ and was generally eschewed by ship-borne ones, like Lt. Kilos, but Strella wore it well.

She pushed the book across the table returning it to Davage. "You know, books like these don't surface much outside of old southern parlors and dusty libraries." She had a pronounced south League Remnath accent, rather like his friend, Lt. Verlin of the Stellar Marines. "These books are considered contraband by the Sisters. A stern talking-to could be in order or, at worse a censuring and confiscation or property should they discover you have it." She sniffed the cover. "And, why does it smell like pie?"

He laughed. "Long story. Now, these books are censured because Atrajak of Want attacked the Sisters'' strongholds, is that right?"

"Yes, near the end of his life. He went mad after he lost his wife. This book details all of that. It's written in a very old form of Remnath and some of it is beyond me, frankly. Atrajak was a man of remarkable power—a male Sister it was said. He fell in love with an Anuian Monama woman, a princess of Nebulon named Tiverlan. He then led the Monamas in a long series of battles called the, 'Hidden Wars', hidden because few people, including the Sisters, knew of their existence."

Davage shrugged. "I've never heard of these battles myself. Who was being fought?"

Strella opened the book, flipped through the thick vellum, and came to a page with a rich illustration. It depicted an armored man battling a creature that was in the process of stepping out of a smoky slit in midair. She pointed at the drawing. "A mysterious group of beings he called the Kestral Oligarchy, or, more simply, the 'Golden People'. According to his writings, they could simply step out of thin air whenever they wished and vanish just as quickly. They watched our doings, past the Sisters vigilance. They, according to Atrajak, preceded us on Kana, a very heretical conclusion."

She turned the page to another illustration; fleshless monsters covered in depravity and nude, four-armed Berserkacides. "These Golden People were very powerful and could become anything they wanted. They worshipped some sort of Horned God who lived in the ground and had many slaves working in their thrall. They had demons that Atrajak called *Killanjo* who did most of their work for them. He mentions something about time travel with these *Killanjo*, that they were treated and made resistant to prolonged exposure to traveling through time. I don't know, I couldn't understand that part very well. Also, there were the Monamas themselves. The Golden People and their *Killanjo* lieutenants could transform them into Berserkacides at their pleasure. Atrajak speaks of them taking the Monamas away into windowless cities and experimenting upon them, creating the Berserkacide and triggering them at will. They made use of their strength as warriors. It was for the love of his wife that Atrajak began the Hidden Wars against the Golden People and their *Killanjo*, to free the Monamas, and they followed and called him, 'father'."

Davage was interested. "Well this is a revelation, and I believe I recall Lady Tellerran mentioning something about Horned Gods and Golden People tormenting them. We can use this information with the Sisters. Clearly these Golden People are behind the attacks on Hoban and elsewhere. What did these Golden People want? What was their objective?"

"Atrajak never knew, he simply thought they were deranged and evil," Strella said. "Tiverlan, his wife, thought they were parasitic, somehow feeding on them."

"What became of the Hidden Wars?"

Strella flipped through the book. "Here. It mentions Atrajak and his Monama army had great success and routed the Golden People and the *Killanjo* from the south of Kana, however, their ability to come and go as they pleased meant that victory could never be fully achieved; they'd just pop up again sometime later. He writes of having two choices. The first choice, as advised by his friend and great general, was to quest across the cosmos and engage the Golden People on their home soil. The second was to locate a mythical temple somewhere on Kana and destroy it. That's what his wife wanted to do, but he chose the former. Atrajak then went on a long journey across the cosmos, to confront the Golden People and defeat them for all time." She opened to a chart of a ten-planet solar system. A vast nebula bisected the system. "He has all sorts of maps and charts in the book detailing his stellar journey, and this one here is where his general thought the Golden People came from and that's where Atrajak and his army went in an Elder ship. However, his army grew sick in space and died, including his wife. He returned to Kana a broken, deranged man."

"What became of him after that?" Syg asked.

"His wife, before dying, told him again of a temple deep in the ground somewhere on Kana where a fearsome Horned God lived. She believed this god and his temple granted the Golden People much of their power over space and time, and over Kana itself. She said to be rid of the Horned God's temple would rid Kana of the Golden People, and she begged him to seek it out. Returning to Kana, he did so, mistaking Twilight 4 for the elusive temple and bringing the Sisters wrath down upon him."

She closed the book.

"A Horned God? Well, this is informative," Davage said. "I think we might have something here."

Captain Strella finished her coffee. "True, however, this book is contraband, and the Sisters will not take council from its teaching."

"The Sisters are well known for holding grudges. Look at this knowledge that has been kept from sight for centuries because a broken man dared attack their holdings. Our stated mission is to locate some sort of improbable 'temporal anchor point', discover its use and destroy it. You mentioned time travel in Atrajak's book, and that this Horned God's temple is said to provide the Golden People with access to Kana. Perhaps it is the anchor point we have been tasked to locate. This book is therefore key in our mission here and can help save the Monamas, and I will gladly risk their displeasure. We should convene a meeting at once."

Strella stood and checked her timepiece. "Oh dear, I need to get back to my ship. I'll contact the Admiral and arrange a briefing as soon as possible. Then, you can slit your throat with the Sisters. Good morning, sir." She pulled her tiny hat out of her pocket and popped it on her head. "Countess," she said bowing to Syg and took her leave, exiting the mess.

Alone at the table, Syg, wearing a lovely cream-colored gown, called for a fresh cup of coffee. "You really think the Sisters will be upset we have this book?"

"Oh, without question. They don't forget such things. Look at the theft at Hiei—they're still up-in-arms about it. They're simply going to have to sit down and see reason. I'm convinced that this temple, whatever it might be, is our objective."

The door to the mess opened, and Lady Tellerran came through in her borrowed clothes, the wrestled-for jacket and holstered air gun, followed by Ennez and Beth in their black uniforms and silver helmets. A group of Marines hoisted their mugs and cheered as she entered. She saw Davage, waved, and headed in their direction. Syg scowled and rolled her eyes.

<Well, there goes a quiet breakfast with my husband,> Syg shot him with a bit of scorn.

<What?> Davage replied.

<Your girlfriend has arrived. Oh, I swear she's going to step on my last nerve again.>

Tellerran strode proudly up to their table and sat down, carrying herself in that distinctive Monama way. She got her endecar out of its bag and set it down, adjusting its positioning for optimal effect.

"Good morning, Lady Tellerran," Davage said standing.

"Good morning, my Lord," she responded happily through the device. She turned to Syg. "Countess . . ."

Syg nodded in a courtly way. Ennez and Beth sat down—they could see the annoyed state Syg was in and smiled. "You seem a bit—agitated this morning, Countess," Ennez said.

"Do I?"

Tellerran took a deep breath of Davage's coffee. "My, that smells good," she commented. "Countess, do you mind so much?"

Beth started laughing. Syg put down her cup and looked ready to explode.

Suddenly Davage sat bolt still. Everyone noted him and watched.

<Syg!> he telepathed to her. *<Don't move! Don't react!>*

<Dav,> she replied, *<I'm not going to rough her up too badly. I'm just going to hit her in the . . .>*

<Syg—a Gamma Band just opened up, near the aft wall!>

Syg started to turn around. Beth, who could hear Davage's telepathy, looked as well.

<Don't look—don't react! I can see several foreboding shapes staring through it. They're looking at Lady Tellerran.>

<What should we do? Should we attack?>

Davage looked around. *<Syg—I see several more Gamma Bands opening up all over the ship, and I also see several openings outside. Big ones—big enough to drive a starship through.>*

Tellerran could see that something was wrong. "Captain Davage, is everything all right?" she asked.

"Com!" he said.

"Com here, sir," came the reply.

"Has Captain Strella arrived aboard her ship?"

"Aye, sir, she just checked in."

"Good, good—thank you."

<Syg—contact the Sisters. Tell them that the fleet is under attack. We need them to alert the other ships. Also, well need the Marines deployed in Sections 4, 7, 15 and 22 at once. Hurry!>

Davage saw a grotesque figure emerge from out of the Gamma Band and shamble in their direction. It was a man, about eight feet tall. He was thin and shirtless and rather gray of skin tone. Somehow, attached to his chest—possibly bolted or sewn on—was a lower torso and a pair of female-looking legs that went up over his head like a pair of antennae—the legs waving about in a sinister fashion, the torso's crotch ending just below his chin. Tied to both ankles were a pair of odd devices, apparently some sort of advanced Gamma Band emitters keeping it hidden from sight, except for Dav's.

And that wasn't all. At first Davage thought the man was wearing a broad, stiff skirt of some kind, cone-shaped, that went down to his ankles, but it wasn't a skirt. It was a multitude of female legs attached to his waist, at least twelve of them. The legs all moved in a semi-organized trilling fashion, like a centipede.

Eyes lamp-like and wide, he confidently strode toward Lady Tellerran.

In one of his hands, he was holding a diamond-shaped prism. Back to their standard repertoire, Davage thought. He was going to turn her into a Berserkacide right here and now.

So, here they were, just like the lurid illustrations in Atrajak's book, *Killanjo* appearing from thin air at their leisure. The Hidden

Wars apparently had never ended. Here the enemy was yet again, hidden and malevolent, confident and unchallenged.

Just like the ones who nearly killed his son.

Not this time! Atrajak the Remnath had begun the Hidden Wars, and Davage the Vith would continue.

Davage rose and pulled the air gun from Tellerran's holster. Quickly he aimed and shot her in the face. The pellet hit her in the cheek, separated and, just like that, her face was covered in the black, sticky paste. She pawed at it, trying to clear her mouth, but it wouldn't give. She fell to the floor, crying out in muffled Conox.

He'd apologize to her later. "Ennez, Beth, get to Deck Seven! I thought I saw a Gamma Band opening there. They might be trying to deposit Berserkacides! Save them if you are able!"

Beth and Ennez exited.

"Com!' Davage yelled. "Beat to Quarters! Helm, bear 2:00pm of 9:00am and make rotations for full speed!"

The claxons went off and people began jostling around.

Davage engaged the creature nobody else could see. The first thing it did was open its mouth and commence a wretched "scream" of some sort. He recalled Tellerran saying something about the *Killanjo* casting spells that render one helpless. Kay, also, recounting the sordid details of his attack in the Grove, said that his attackers "bespelled" him, rendering him unable to move and defend himself.

Therefore, it was imperative to silence this beast. He fired the air gun again, hitting the creature in the mouth. Its face clotted with black paste and it gagged in surprise.

Davage unsaddled his CARG and came to grips with the monster. Despite his fierce appearance, he was surprisingly easy to defeat. In only a few cuts, Davage had him down, his legs, thrashing in a rhythmic fashion, went still.

As the ship heeled around, five more bizarre creatures dashed out of the Gamma Band. They were arrayed in all manner of depravities. None of them carried a Gamma device, and they could be seen plain as day. Upon seeing them, some of the crew began screaming.

Another Gamma band opened, and a clump of ten naked people were dumped out into a pale pile on the floor.

Monamas. They were clearly muddled in Head Swarm, as they were in the Crossland graveyard. The enemy is sticking to their favorite tactic, Davage mused—*Killanjo* and Berserkacide. He surged forward, trying to get between the grotesque brutes and the newly arrived Monamas. "Syg, take these people down, and do not allow them to speak!"

With a growl, Syg unleashed a brutal Sten, boxing in three of them in an instant with two managing the dive aside. The ones trapped in the box died in a storm of sparks. Syg held the Sten long past the need for it—she wanted them to suffer.

"For my son!" she roared with satisfaction.

Davage engaged a *Killanjo* man with three heads who fought with a blood-soaked spear in one hand and a red Berserkacide prism in the other. He aimed the air gun and fired at the Monamas over and over, covering them in paste, hoping to get them sufficiently covered to protect them from what was certainly coming.

The multi-headed man lifted his prism, and it began glowing red. Accordingly, a string of red lights around each of the Monamas'' necks blossomed in a rosy, rather festive glow. He was attempting to trigger the lot of them.

A crewman holding a chair ran up from behind hoping to break it across his filthy back. One of his heads opened its mouth and made a horrific sound that stopped the crewman in his tracks.

With a blast of Silver tech, Syg pulverized the head, and the *Killanjo* staggered.

The last creature, a skinned female, bounded her way toward the struggling Lady Tellerran, avoiding thrown bottles and chairs nimbly.

Syg loosed a blast of Silver tech and missed. Davage took a swing at her with his CARG, and she leapt over it, landing next to Lady Tellerran. She lifted a prism, setting it to a glowing cherry sort of red. She held it to Tellerran's paste-covered head. "Kill them all!" she tittered.

Nothing happened. The paste seemed to be working. The *Killanjo* shook her prism in shocked disbelief.

Elsewhere, Davage took down his three-headed foe. He put his CARG into his heart and dropped him.

He checked the Monamas. They lay where they were, out of their minds with Head Swarm, covered in a coating of tar-like black paste. None of them reacted. If they were Berserkacide, it should be obvious. Good!

Lady Tellerran became aware of the presence of the horrid woman and her prism. She flailed out with her hands, searching in the air. After a few moments, her hands found the woman's skinned, bleeding leg, and Lady Tellerran sprang. Moving with the agility of an enraged tiger, Tellerran attacked the woman, tearing at her with her claws, and breaking her bones with her Monama strength. The *Killanjo* woman dropped her prism and tried to get away, but Tellerran was on her fast. They rolled about on the floor in a mortal tangle. Before long, Tellerran, fighting with an age-old fury, had taken her tormentor apart, literally, having rendered her into pieces. For a moment, Davage wondered if she'd become a Berserkacide after all.

He knelt down and took her by the hands. "It's over, Lady Tellerran! She's dead. You've killed her."

Struggling for breath, her face covered with dried paste, she didn't seem to know who Davage was for a moment, and then she calmed and fell into his embrace, her long fingernails covered with blood and bits of flesh.

*   *   *   *   *

Outside, the Fleet fell under attack. The Sisters had alerted the captains and Admiral Carfax that an attack was at hand. The *Twilight* and *Halo Dawn* lowered into the atmosphere a little and opened their Battleshot ports. The *Bethel* and *Westerville* ascended and readied their Sar-Beams. Swarming around the huge vessels were just under two dozen Marine *Trelaines*, ready to overwhelm anything that might come against them.

From nowhere, a blast, like a colossal bolt of lightning, stretched out and struck *Bethel* amidships in a protracted hit. Listing and venting, she heeled to starboard. Another bolt struck her in the belly. Light ballasts flickering, trailing debris, and badly wounded, she rolled over and drifted, helpless.

With the Waft-lock in place to prevent boarding, Davage and Syg ran up to the *New Faith's* bridge. As they ran, Davage kept his Sight eye on the battle and the stricken *Bethel*. "Weapons Master!" he yelled into the air. "I want a full Sar-Beam set to 3:45pm mark 6:00pm of the *Bethel's* position. Fire when ready!"

A second or two passed, and the huge Sar-Beam emitters uncoiled a long, searing shot into the area Davage had specified.

Nothing happened; no damage was detected. The lances went off into space and, apparently, did nothing.

The *Westerville* and the *Twilight* took up station around the stricken *Bethel*, trying to guard her from further attacks.

As Dav and Syg entered the bridge, his Sight went wild. He saw bolts coming from open Gamma bands erupting all over.

Before he could say a word, huge bolts of crackling energy appeared from a number of different places. The *Westerville* was struck dead aft, while the *Halo Dawn* took a direct hit to the nose and starboard wing. The *Twilight*, banking hard, managed to avoid a bolt coursing for its belly. Three Marine *Trelaines* were caught up in a bolt and were destroyed in a violent flash.

Confusion. Secondary explosions from *Bethel*. The wires hot with panicked messages.

Davage ran to the helm and crewman Feran, Lord of the House of Six, the ship's junior helmsman, stepped away. Davage wrenched the helm and the huge, unwieldy-looking *New Faith* spiraled through the melee.

Sight: a bolt coming in from 2:00 pm. Davage hauled the ship around and spun away as the blindingly bright bolt seared in their direction, just missing the hull.

"Return fire on those coordinates!" he roared, bringing the nose of the ship about. A second later, two red-hot Sar-Beams burned into the area where the bolt came from, again with no apparent effect.

They were shooting at nothing.

Davage, his Sight fully lit, scanned the area. For a moment, he thought he could see something through the Gamma band, but then it was gone.

"Bridge!" came a voice over the Com. "Lt. Kite, 1st Marines! We are engaged with a hostile group of intruders, deck 22, section 4!"

"Engage with discretion, Lt.! If the intruders are Monama, endeavor to make use of the air guns and pellets provided to you and strike them about the head and shoulders. If that fails, then do what needs to be done, and ensure the protection of all vital areas!"

"Aye, sir!"

The scene around Hoban was chaotic. The Fleet and Marine ships were taking heavy damage from all quarters, and the status of the *Bethel* was unknown—her Com was out and the area around her was littered with life boats had been launched from her upper hull. Additionally, reports were coming in from all ships that they were battling groups of intruders in fierce confrontations who were boarding right through the Sisters'' waft-lock: Berserkacides.

Davage Sighted: a bolt was soon to be heading right for his

belly. Davage kicked the thrusters and wheeled the huge vessel around, the helm shaking slightly in his hands as he did so. The *New Faith's* wheel always shook, though nobody could ever explain why. A moment later a searing bolt came screeching past.

Davage then saw something strange. He saw the *Westerville* bathed in some sort of dim yellowish light. The ship didn't appear to be suffering structurally from the light, but . . .

He Sighted through the hull into the interior of the ship and was appalled. Inside, bathed in light, the crew were going mad: heads shaking, hands tearing, teeth biting. Even the Sisters aboard seemed affected.

Davage rammed the wheel and kicked the levers. "Weapons Master, I want an extended Sar-Beam placed at 5:50pm mark 4:45am. Fire and maintain—now!"

The Sar-Beams burst out of their banks and went where Davage thought was the source of the light. Nothing happened at first; then, the light flickered and went out. The *Westerville* was free—the crew now struggling to regain their sanity. Two quick bolts came in and slapped the ship across the back.

Davage Sighted: a beam of yellow light was heading straight for him.

He punished the wheel, pulling the *New Faith* into a gut-wrenching 12am climb. Looking behind, he could see a shaft of light following, struggling to bathe the ship in its radiance. After a few more seconds, the light went out, and Davage banked hard to his left.

The *Bethel* suffered a massive internal explosion that broke the superstructure and created out-of-control venting, scattering the litter of lifeboats blossoming around it. It heeled past the vertical, adrift and helpless, sucked-in like a tin can.

That was mortal, Davage thought. *Bethel is dead.*

Another round of bolts. The *Westerville* and *Halo Dawn* were struck yet again; only this time, the *Halo Dawn* managed to fire off five canisters in the direction of the bolt. They entered the Gamma Band and vanished.

Davage, seeing this, had a thought. The Hidden Wars. The Golden People and their slaves emerging from nowhere through feathery slits in the air. Atrajak venturing into the slits to face the enemy.

Sighting a nearby Gamma Band, he banked and plunged the *New Faith* into it, four *Trelaines* following.

The ship fell into darkness.

24—Dee

The *Goshawk* broke the haze over the Great Armenelos Forest and landed outside of Dee, a sea-side city northeast of the Withellwell River in the upper-reaches of Calvert.

Like all cities in the Calvert region, Dee was a small, but densely populated urban area that made most of its income from fishing and similar industries. Unlike Vith, Remnath and Zenon cities, which were very spread out and only sparsely built up, Calvert cities were tightly packed with narrow streets, clustered buildings and chaotic alleyways. The Calvert region of Kana was, traditionally, the least prosperous of the seven. The old Calvert tribe of long ago did not do well in the time of the Elders and was a general disappointment. Eventually, most of the Calverts migrated to Onaris, where they did much better, though they missed out on the Gifts of the Mind, and they became known as the Browns.

Dee was originally a city south of the Withellwell River on the eastern edge of the Great Armenelos forest. The old Dee was an unsavory place, rife with vice and corruptions of all sorts. The Sisterhood of Light, as they occasionally had to do with Calvert Houses and cities, got sick and tired of the situation and politely announced to the civic leaders of Dee in 000221ax that they were going to destroy the city, and all persons were encouraged to leave at once, lest they be destroyed right along with the earth and the stone.

They packed up and migrated north to the city's present location and, to their credit, cleaned up their act. Dee became one of the nicer Calvert cities.

The University of Dee was founded in 000391ax as an ecumenical school. One way to get back into the Sisters' good graces after an earth-scorching was to build places of learning, and the people of Dee did just that, eventually receiving praise from the Sisters as a nice, clean place where students from all over Kana could go and learn. Never considered one of the more elite schools, it nevertheless enjoyed a fair amount of steady success over the years and counted among its alumni a decent amount of well-known scholars. One of its most tenured professors, a Grand Dame Hanna-Ben Shurlamp, was well-known for her learned contributions, and, allegedly, for her rather ruthless methods of acquiring knowledge. The university was a sprawling place, built of brown sandstone buildings and grand patina-capped rooftops mixed in with broad walks and pleasant green spaces. Lon, wanting to attend the older, more prestigious Vith schools in Arden, turned his nose up at the place. This, he said, was a haven for liberal arts and nonsense. Science was best taught at science schools.

Finding a good spot to land, Phillip set the ship down, and they all got out, taking a short hike into Dee and the university.

The school was quaint and pleasing to the eye, with well-tended grounds and craggy buildings. Despite Lon's dismissal of the place, Kay, Phillip and Sarah thought it was a charming, approachable school. The students and staff appeared quite friendly as they passed them.

Beyond the main commons was the library. The library of the University of Dee was a huge rotunda with the large statue of a strange-looking dragon standing guard in the front by the main entrance. From the outside, the library appeared big and squat, topped with a vast green dome, like a huge mixing bowl turned upside down. Once they entered the library, the interior was breathtaking. Even Lon, who was continually disparaging the school, had to admit it was most impressive.

The library was apparently cut deep into the ground. The interior was twenty stories in total, rising to the huge ornate dome high above. The perimeter of the rotunda was a honeycomb of shelves, cubbies, reading areas, terminals and desks. Beneath the center of the rotunda was a vast open space that led down to an aqua-marine pool at the bottom.

They found a quiet place to sit down in privacy and began contemplating their strategy. Phillip plopped down on a comfortable couch by the rail, and Lon wandered into the maze of shelves, browsing.

"So, what are we supposed to be looking for?" Phillip asked.

"A silver device similar to the one we picked up in Rostov."

"Where is it?"

Kay looked around. "I'm not sure, really. The judge told me that it was in the library and that it will not be all that hard to find."

Sarah saddled up to a terminal and began looking at the posts. "You better start looking around then," she said as the holographic images orbited her head. "Meanwhile, I'm going to catch up on my reading—see what's hot out there. Take your time, Kay." The posts Sarah called up were the usual sensational stuff that she consumed in volume. The first post read:

PARAFLIES FOUND DEAD IN THE MILLIONS
IN CALVERT—FACE EXTINCTION

Dead? Extinction? He thought about the one Parafly that had helped save him after the attack on his life. "What's wrong with the Paraflies?"

Sarah read on. "Don't know. They're turning up dead all over the place. Says here their dead bodies clogged up the canal water in Bern."

"Ah, pity," Kay said. "I rather fancied them."

He allowed his Sight to roam. The giant library was full of a great many people, but the place was so big it appeared only modestly populated. He looked around, seeing the library clearly. He could see people walking around on the floors above and below them, including a few amorous couples kissing in quiet, romantic nooks. The underside of the dome overhead was etched with many images and shapes—the shape of a dragon being the most prominent. He could see through the dome as well, to the silty blue sky of Calvert above.

He looked down and instantly saw what he was looking for. "There it is," he said.

Sarah turned from her posts. "That was fast. Where is it?"

"Down there." Kay pointed down, over the rail to the pool below.

Phillip sat up, and they gazed over the railing.

The pool, from where they were standing, was four floors down. The water was a cheerful aqua-marine. Many students on the bottom floor were seated around the edge of the pool. Some sat with their books at the water's edge dipping their feet into it. Some seemed to be talking to the water—having a conversation with nobody.

"How deep is it?" Phillip asked.

"Deep, at least five hundred feet. There's an immense cavern under there that goes on for miles."

Sarah looked over the side. "What? Five hundred feet? That pool can't be more than five feet deep. You sure it's in there? I don't see anything."

"It's in there."

She smiled at him. "I guess you're getting wet then. Are you going to walk down and jump in, or am I going to get to toss you in from here?"

Kay continued to stare into the water. "Wait. I see something in the pool moving around. Something big."

Sarah squinted, lighting her Sight. "The water looks clear to me."

"Me, too," Phillip said.

"There's some sort of Cloak or Paint over it. Beneath the surface I see a lot of stalagmites, like what you'd see in a flooded cavern, and swimming through them is a large creature."

"A big fish?" Phillip asked.

"It doesn't look like a fish. It's bizarre. I don't know what it is."

Sarah was distressed. "Why can't I see it?"

Lon returned holding a book he'd pulled off one of the shelves. "What are we looking at?" he asked.

"Kay's found the device. He says there's a monster in the water," Sarah said.

Lon looked over the side. "Really? You sure, Kay?" "Yes, I am sure."

This sort of thing was right down Sarah's alley, and she was getting excited. "Describe it," she said.

"It's like nothing I've ever seen before. It looks sort of like a dragon with a green body, a long neck, a mane of long red hair like a horse, orange legs—splayed out like a gecko—and a long, thin pink tail with a woman growing out of the end."

"You're making that up," she said, cross.

"No, I'm not. I'd not make up such a thing."

Sarah, her imagination going haywire, strained to look into the pool—seeing nothing but the clear water.

Phillip took off his hat and wiped his brow. "So what are we going to do? I thought this one was going to be easy. No doubt if you jump in there, the creature is going to devour you."

Lon looked down and noted all the students casually sitting by the pool. "Nobody down there appears to be put off in any way."

"They must not be aware of the danger that lurks beneath," Phillip said.

Sarah started pushing everybody toward the lift. "Come on; we're going down there. I want to see this thing for myself."

Hurriedly they went down to the bottom. The bottom floor of the library was set up as a small café, serving light lunch fare to the students, a nice place to eat and read and gather with friends. They walked through the chattering noise of the café and soon stood at the edge of the pool gazing into it. Sarah, eager to see whatever it was, knelt down and looked into the clear water. Kay thought for a moment that she was going to pull her boots off and dive in—that was something Sarah would do without hesitation.

A small girl sat eating her lunch at a nearby table piled high with books. She saw Sarah and the rest gawking into the pool and laughed quietly. "You must be new here. Is this your first year?"

Lon spoke up, outraged. "We do not matriculate at this school, madam! I have been offered a full scholarship at the University of Arden, sciences."

The girl smiled and rolled her eyes. "Oh, I see," she said. "Arden, wow, you must be really smart then. Not smart enough to know what's in the water though, are you? None of those fancy Vith schools have what we've got right here in Dee."

Sarah walked toward the girl. "You've seen the thing in the water?"

"The 'Thing' in the water? Yeah, of course I have," she said in a slightly arrogant way.

Phillip interjected. "Well, then, miss, could you please inform us? What is it?"

She laughed. "Why don't you ask him yourself?"

"Ask him? How?"

The girl pointed at the other side of the café. There, perched at the water's edge, was the statue of a dragon-like monster. Sarah quickly made her way to the statue and looked it over, inspecting every inch. Long neck, dragon-like face with a mane of long hair, big beady eyes, splayed legs and a long, thin tail. "Is this what you're seeing in the water, Kay?"

"Looks like it," he said.

"It's hideous," Sarah remarked with wonder.

The girl at the other side of the café called out to them. "You're going to hurt his feelings with talk like that. Put some money in his mouth, and he'll talk to you—and be nice to him."

They looked at the girl for a moment; then, Kay slowly pulled a money purse out of his coat. He took out a Blanchefort hader and was about to stick it in the statue's mouth.

"Give him two, Kay—don't be cheap," Sarah said, wide-eyed with anticipation.

Kay scowled at her and took out another hader. He then put both of them in the statue's mouth. The coins fell in, rattled about a bit inside, and then emerged from its rear end, entering the water with a *plop—plop!*

A moment later, a beautiful, black-haired woman wearing a toga came walking out of the water.

They regarded her for a moment.

Kay Sighted her. She was some sort of molded, fleshy bit, like the tongue of a snapping turtle that resembles a worm.

Kay could see that this black-haired woman was the end of the monster's tail. Far below, the monster lurked in the depths of the pool, its tail stretching like elastic and ending with what appeared to be a beautiful woman. Kay sensed danger.

"Are you the creature in the water?" Kay asked.

"Aye."

"You're its tail, correct? We are currently talking to the end of a tail, yes?"

"That is correct," the woman said.

"Do you know why we're here?"

"No. Should I?"

Sarah didn't approve of the questioning. "I was expecting to see that," she said pointing at the statue. "What are you, the monster's slave?"

The woman smiled. "As the gentleman just pointed out, what you see is the end of my tail. I can will the end of my tail to be anything I wish. I feel like being a woman today."

"What are you?" Kay asked.

"All rudeness aside, I'm from here. There are many old and deep things living on Kana. When the builders of this library began digging, they dug up my home. I wasn't angry. I even assisted them in completing the library."

"And you've been here ever since?"

"I have. This is my home. I like it here. I get three free meals a day, and I help the students with their research. I have many friends. I'm even the mascot of this university. I am very proud of our brandtball team this year."

"What are you called?"

"Call me what you wish—I have no particular name."

"Mickey!" Sarah cried. "We'll call you Mickey."

"If you must."

Kay looked back into the water and saw the body of "Mickey" resting at the bottom of the cavernous pool far below.

"Mickey," Kay said. "There is a matter we must discuss."

"It sounds urgent. I am here. I am listening."

"There is a silver device resting at the bottom of your cavern. I am tasked to remove it from here. Do you know of it?"

"There are many items in here with me. I like shiny things. Can you be more specific?"

"It is a small silver object about this big," Kay said holding his hands out about a foot apart. "It is round with a hole in the middle."

Kay peered into the water and saw "Mickey" looking around, his long neck coiling about.

"Oh yes, I see that. It's over there. Very pretty."

"I need to take it from here. I am tasked to do so."

Mickey's tail, the woman in the toga, smiled. "There is a rule here—anything that falls into the water is mine. See," she said pointing at a distant sign carved into a stone pillar.

It read: "ANY ITEM FALLING INTO THE WATER BELONGS TO THE DRAGON. NO EXCEPTIONS."

As they continued to look around, they began noticing the dragon's motif everywhere, carved in the stone pillars, adorning vases and paintings; many students were even wearing clothing with a dragon stamped on the front. Even the food being served in the café followed the theme: dragon salad, dragon-tarts, dragon soda and dragon-tips.

Kay turned his attention back to the woman. "Mickey, I need this device. I have to have it. May we, perhaps, trade for it?"

The woman appeared intrigued. "What do you have to trade?"

"I have a purse full of Blanchefort haders."

The woman thought a moment. "I don't need any of those. What else do you have?"

They started looking at each other, trying to come up with something. The woman noted Kay's CARG. "That weapon will do. Let's trade for it."

Kay looked down at his CARG. "This weapon doesn't belong to me. It belongs to my beloved and is not mine to trade away, I'm sorry."

Sarah stepped forward. "What if we just dive in and grab the item? What about that?"

"Then, I suppose I'll have to devour you, and that's a shame as I just had breakfast. Why don't you try diving in later in the day, at around lunch time. I'll devour you then."

Kay continued. "It seems we are at an impasse, Mickey. There must be a way we can work this out to our mutual satisfaction."

The woman thought. "Why do you desire this item so?"

Kay sat down at the pool's edge, and he told Mickey. He told her as much as he could without going into too much detail as the students watching nearby were taking an interest in their conversation. She listened.

When Kay finished, Mickey spoke. "Well, you four seem like nice people. Why don't we try this: I'll play at a contest with each of you. If you win all four contests, I'll give you the device. How about that?"

"And, if we lose?" Kay asked, expecting some grim and horrifying punishment.

"If you lose, you lose. Big deal. Try again tomorrow."

They thought it over and agreed.

They sat down at a table and began—other students started milling about to watch.

The first contest was a game of Perlamum—an ancient board game. "I have to warn you that I'm pretty good at this game," she said producing a water-logged board and game pieces.

Lon, who was pretty decent at it as well, sat down, and they began playing.

Surprisingly, Lon beat Mickey in five moves. Mickey gawked dumbfounded at the board. "Wow, you're really good," she said. "One contest down, three to go."

Mickey rolled up the sleeve of her toga. "Next, arm wrestling." She put her elbow on the table and opened her hand. "Who wants some?"

Sarah sat down opposite her and rolled up her sleeve. Sarah had the Gift of Strength and was very strong. They clasped hands, adjusted their grip and then began.

It was over in moments. Sarah, using her Gift of Strength, literally threw Mickey into the pool—several students who were watching from a distance began clapping. Sarah, shocked at first, stood and slowly got that look in her eye that she often did when she was feeling rather happy about herself. "You all see that?" she said, brimming with haughty confidence. Some of the students bowed to her. She was eating this up.

Mickey waded back out of the water and smiled. "Boy, you're strong."

For the next test, Mickey sat back down at the table and said the contest was for someone to make her laugh. All they had to do was to make her laugh, and the contest would be over.

Phillip stepped forward. He racked his brains as he tried to think of a funny joke to tell. He settled on one he'd heard Sarah tell their mother about a Xaphan and three Monks on their way to the communal bath. Phillip told the joke in a rather stiff, un-humorous manner, and Sarah rolled her eyes.

Mickey sat there stone-faced; then, she began snorting, and, finally, started belly laughing.

"I get it; I get it!" she cried.

"You can't be serious," Sarah said. "Phillip butchered that joke. I should have told it to her."

"You already had your turn," Phillip replied, cross.

"It's funny, funny," she said laughing.

Phillip smiled and felt proud of himself. Three contests down.

It was Kay's turn. "So, what's my test to be?"

Mickey thought a moment. She turned and went back into the water. A minute or two later she returned with the silver device in her hands. She stood in front of Kay. "You need to take the device from my hand, if you are able."

"That's it?"

"That's it."

Kay looked at the device sitting in her hand.

"Be careful," Mickey said. "I'm pretty fast."

Kay slowly reached out and took the device from her hands. Mickey didn't try to stop him. She just stood there and let him have it."

"Were you even trying?" he asked.

Mickey winked. "It looks like you need this more than I do. Just don't tell anybody that I'm such a soft touch."

Kay looked at it again. "I—I feel I should give you something in return for this."

"Perhaps you'll come back and visit me someday—with your

beloved in hand. I would like that. I would like to meet her. That will be reward enough."

Kay stood there. "Mickey, thank you. I wasn't expecting . . ."

"You weren't expecting what? That I would be kind and reasonable? You thought you'd end up in some grand battle with me, did you? Such a thought assumes that the lords of this university would willingly subject their students and faculty to a dangerous beast, which is a little odd if you consider it carefully. You look to be a Vith, and Viths are always searching for a monster to fight. Just remember this simple thought as you continue on your travels: expect the best, but be ready for the worst. Sometimes, you get the former rather than the latter. Remember that, and you'll do well."

Sarah took her hat and duster off and, before anybody could say a word, dove into the water. After a minute or so, she surfaced, all smiles.

"Did you see him down there?" Kay asked.

She nodded, still smiling. She gave Mickey's tail a hug and swore they would return some day.

With that, they bade Mickey goodbye and left the library, each glad they'd come, even Lon. Clearly, none of those stuffy science schools in Arden could boast that they had a wondrous, guardian dragon swimming in the library.

25—Nowhere

The *New Faith* and four Marine *Trelaines* emerged on the other side of the Gamma Band. The other side was a dusty corner of darkness and swirling gases—the tell-tale signs of being deep within a nebula. At the navigator's chair, the holo AM/PM orientation wheels spun aimlessly, lost and without bearing.

Surrounding the *New Faith* were at least a hundred ships of various sizes. The ships looked like collections of bubbles, all pushed together and cast in gold. Some of the bubble-like ships were tiny, barely large enough for a single man-sized person to fit in; others were gargantuan in size, dwarfing even the huge *New Faith*. The larger ships were parked in front of the Gamma Bands, firing the bolts through. There was a clutter of wreckage floating about—apparently Dav's Sar-Beams and the canister from the *Halo Dawn* had got through and done a great deal of damage.

Hauling the ship around, Davage ordered his canister magazines opened.

The *New Faith*, hopelessly surrounded, fired Sar-Beams and canister off in random directions; the deep concentration of ships precluded the possibility of missing. The *Trelaines* stayed tucked in with the *New Faith*, firing their smaller Sar Beams.

These dozens of golden ships, though impressive and grand, were being scattered by the weight of the *New Faith's* firing. One shot seemingly deflated them, compressing them down into a deformed ingot of gold. Ship after ship suffered under Davage's guns. They also seemed to be having trouble maneuvering, the *New Faith* roaming around and through them at will. The Marines, seeing the situation unfold, broke and attacked, ranging through the crowd of golden ships, creating havoc.

In and out, diving and rolling, the *New Faith* put a merciless beating on the golden ships. They tried to maneuver around, to put a bolt on the *New Faith*, but they couldn't move fast enough. Some ships tried to shine a strange yellowish light on the speeding ship, but Davage, sensing extreme danger, kept away and focused his fire on them.

Eventually, the survivors pulled back and retreated—lumbering away and then vanishing, leaving only golden flotsam of the destroyed ships.

✳   ✳   ✳   ✳   ✳

There was jubilation aboard the *New Faith*. Just one Main Fleet Vessel and four Marine attack ships routed a massive force of enemy vessels. The enemy, whoever they were, had a massive offensive punch, but their ships were too slow and dainty to stand and fight effectively. Without being able to hide behind their Gamma Bands, they didn't stand a chance.

Reports began flowing in from all over the ship. The Marines had engaged and defeated a number of roving bands of intruders. Many captives had been taken. With Davage having alerted the Marines, they were able to arrive in time to meet the attackers as they stepped out of their Gamma Band holes.

More of the grotesque *Killanjo* creatures, as before, were fought and killed, and a number of bound Monamas with them as well. Using their air gun and paste pellets, the Marines managed to save twenty six male and female Monamas, while only having to kill eight that had been turned into Berserkacides. It was a huge victory, and the surviving Monamas, naked and gaunt, were taken to the overcrowded dispensary where Ennez and Beth checked them over and removed their collars. All of them, as Lady Tellerran had done previously, acted in a funk.

Head Swarm.

They were in abused shape but not beyond saving. All they needed was food and warmth, a regimen of vitamins, and the nourishing ground of Kana and they should be fine.

Kana . . .

Where were they exactly?

When the Golden ships vanished, so, too, did the Gamma Bands they had flown through. The *New Faith* and the four *Trelaines* were marooned in unknown, starless territory.

26—Dimples

The four made their way back to the *Goshawk* to await the next set of instructions. Kay held the silver device. Sarah, sopping wet, chattered about seeing the dragon.

"That was easy, Kay, just like you said," she added, wringing out her hair.

"Who knew there was a friendly dragon holding the device. I don't think he even tried in the contests."

"Oh, he tried all right; I was just too strong for him," Sarah proclaimed.

Two of three pieces held—these Trials weren't so hard.

When they got to the *Goshawk*, they were horrified.

The black ship was enveloped in some sort of golden gel.

"What is that?" Phillip asked in disgust.

Lon got out his goggles and adjusted the lenses. "Looks like amoebic protoplasm. We should get a sample. My mother would love to examine this."

Kay recalled seeing this type of creature the night the Trials began, created with Sam's NIGHTMARE.

He stepped forward. "Are you the final Judge?"

The protoplasm shot forward and enveloped Kay, drawing him into its golden interior, where he thrashed and kicked in the thick gel. Within, Kay could see bits of golden material and what looked like a sinuous skeleton floating about as a nucleus.

The Skeleton, though not "moving" per se, drifted toward him.

"I am the Judge of your final Trial," Kay heard a voice say.

Kay tried to say something in reply but couldn't. He couldn't breathe in this golden soup.

The skeleton bobbed near him. *"Two items collected, yet a third remains from sight. The final piece rests in a barbaric place, next to the bones of the fallen and the bodies of those who will soon be dead—a place of old evil and new revelations. The Temple of Ethylrelda of Waam, worn and threadbare, weary of malice, yet coiled and set to kill, a sea of Shadow tech knives waiting to dance at your throat. There you must go."*

A shimmering object appeared before Kay in the smothering golden protoplasm. It was unlike the two doughnut-shaped devices collected so far. It was rectangular and plank-like, articulated in a sharp curve at what was probably the top of the piece, and it bore, on one side, a deep ovular recess. Kay recalled from the Holo-net the machine looking like an archway; this last piece must be the cross-section. It bore a distinct resemblance in style to the first two pieces collected. It was twisting and organic in construction, like a vine made of silver.

"If you survive the horrors of Ethylrelda's temple, and you gather this piece, you will have completed your Trials. You will then return to your home and await additional instructions at that time. You will not see me again."

With Kay's lungs screaming for oxygen, the creature began to expel him.

It stopped, thought a moment, and then spoke again: *"Know you this. The enemy is upon you. They are the angels of the Horned God, and his temple deep in the ground gives them lease not only now, but in the past and the future as well. Their hatred and their pagan god provides fuel for the place. There you must go and there you must face them. That is not part of your Trial, it is merely an inevitability."*

On the verge of passing out, Kay was ejected, and the golden creature vanished.

✳   ✳   ✳   ✳   ✳

The Duke and Duchess of Oyln came running out of their huge, brand new estate as Phillip landed the old *Goshawk* on the fresh planted grounds. They were always happy to see their defacto nephews and niece.

Sarah and Phillip came bouncing out and hugged them both. This sprawling estate was their winter home, Peter and Lady Poe being given a whole wing to themselves in the northern sector of the manor.

Compared to the spired, multi-leveled sprawl of Castle Blanchefort, Grand Oyln Manner was a boxy, workman-like structure. It was built squat in the Esther-style. It was no more than four floors high, rather squarish in construction and built of a sandy-gray stone. To view it from overhead, it looked like a massive C, with a central courtyard that had been masterfully landscaped by the plant-loving duchess herself.

It was a wonder of Esther-style construction and would serve the House of Oyln well for centuries to come.

The Duke and Duchess were all smiles.

"What's the matter, Phillip? Is it too cold for you up there even in the summer?" the Duke asked tossing his hair.

"I like it cold, Uncle!" Sarah shouted roughly hugging him.

"I'll wager you do."

Kay and Lon came out of the ship.

Duchess Torrijayne, thick in pregnancy with her fifth child, gave him a big hug. "Well, will you just look at this handsome young man! Lord Kabyl, if I weren't happily married and madly in love, I'd just pick you up and carry you away!"

She gave him a warm kiss on the cheek.

The Duke shook Kay's hand and clapped him on the shoulder. "Good to see you, Lord Blanchefort—you don't come and see us often enough. They turned to Lon and shook his hand.

"Lord Probert," the Duke said cheerfully. "You traveling around with this sorry lot, now?"

"I am, sir," he said with a smile.

A distance away was a huge fountain in the central garden. There was a great deal of activity going on around it. Adorning the top of the fountain was a hideous, bronze statue. It was the likeness of the duchess, naked in all her glory and massively pregnant, dancing on one leg. Water streamed in a gushing, messy spray from her milk-filled breasts. Several staff members of House Oyln milled about, trying to figure out how to remove the statue.

The Duchess smiled. "Your mom did that, Kay, just in time for a large dinner party that we threw the other day. Actually, it's a pretty clever prank. I'm impressed. Of course, I'm going to have to retaliate, but . . ."

They all looked at it—Sarah having issues keeping a straight face.

The Duke laughed and shook his head. "Well, we and the kids

were just getting ready to sit down for lunch. Come on in and join us!"

Kay took Torrijayne's arm, and they went in to eat.

✶   ✶   ✶   ✶   ✶

After lunch, the three of them and the duchess went into the library. Lon had been corralled by the Duke. He wanted Lon to go through some of the specs of his new *Windhawk* starcraft, and they went down to the yard to have a look.

Like the many reading rooms at Castle Blanchefort, the main library at Grand Oyln Manor was huge and airy, full of books and busts and hung artwork. Unlike Castle Blanchefort, however, the library was heavily windowed, full of light and flowering plants, the duchess being a noted horticulturist in the area. It also had a multitude of obvious technologies—large, full-sized holo-terminals with not only a holographic gentleman to assist in locating data, but an elegant lady as well. There were elaborately illustrated databases and floating Silver tech automatons clattering about. The room smelled like new carpeting and fresh plaster and was decorated in the modern Esther style with lots of light.

Holding her pregnant belly, Torrijayne slowly sat down and brushed her black hair out of her face. "So, what brings you three all the way down from Blanchefort today—not that I'm not thrilled to see you?"

And they told her; they told her everything. They told her about Kay's Trial, about what happened at Rostov. They told her about Dee and the dragon. They watched the concern grow on her face as they told her about the hideous creatures who had attacked and nearly killed Kay.

And they told her that Kay was a Shadow tech male.

Torrijayne sat there a moment, then, swallowing, she sent out a streamer of Silver tech and closed the door to the library. She then created five Silver tech serpents which lined up in front of her and awaited their instructions.

"Guard the windows and exits and watch for eavesdroppers."

The serpents slithered off. The holo-terminals snapped off, and the Silver tech automatons drifted up toward the distant ceiling. Torri looked at a nearby brandy service with longing, but remembered that she was pregnant.

"And you've told all of this to your father and your mother?" she asked.

"Yes, Great Duchess," Kay replied.

"That's enough of the, Great Duchess" thing. Yes? To your barefoot, fountain-defacing mother, Kay, I'm, Great Duchess," but to you, I'm just Dimples—agreed?"

Kay smiled and nodded.

"So," she said, "you're a Shadow tech male? That's a rare honor. Take a bit of good advice, and don't go advertising that to just anybody—I'm serious. Being a Shadow tech male can be a dangerous thing."

"They say I can somehow control Shadow tech females," he said. "When I touched Bethrael of Moane's Silver tech, I . . ."

Despite her belly, Torri sat up bolt straight. "You touched Beth's Silver tech?"

"I did. She saved my life. The blood poisoning . . ."

Torri smiled. "And, how was it, Kay?"

"How was it?" Kay asked. "I don't understand."

"How did it feel?"

"It was a little strange."

"*A little strange*? I'll bet it was. So, umm, has Beth acted a little oddly toward you since then, Kay? A little touchy-feely, perhaps?"

"Yes, a little. Why is that?"

Torri reared back and laughed. "Come now, Kay, you needn't be shy—you can talk to me. I'm not a stuffy old grouch like your mom. Touching Beth's Silver tech was, quite probably, the best sex she's ever had by far, and she's had a lot if the gossip is to be believed. A Shadow tech female cannot resist the touch of a Shadow tech male. It drives us mad. Touch her Shadow or Silver tech long enough and she'll do anything you ask. She'd even kill if you told her to."

TELL ME WHAT TO STEAL!! TELL ME WHO TO KILL!!

Kay remembered and sat there, mortified.

"I'd give her some space if I were you for the time being, Kay. She'll be all right, although I'm certain the next few fellows she comes to grips with in the sack will leave her rather flat. I can picture it now: some upright lord, dressed in his best and unloading a fortune in dinner and entertainments on Beth only to have her fall asleep on him out of boredom. Nothing any handsome League Lord could do to her will come close to matching your touch. I'll bet she's thinking about you, even now."

Flex . . .

Torri again looked at the brandy service with longing. "I'm sorry, but I suddenly feel myself rather thirsty."

A Silver tech automaton came down and fetched a decanter full of orange juice. It poured four cool glasses and passed them around. It then glided back up to the heights of the ceiling. Torri took a few drinks. "Normally, I'd get it myself, but Lord Oyln in here is making things tough for me right now. My back and all."

Kay drank his juice and thought of Beth—remembering what it felt like to touch her Silver tech pulling him away from blood poisoning. He tried to put her out of his mind. "Dimples," he said, "the reason we've come today is to consult with you regarding our next task. We understand the final piece of the machine we are to retrieve is located in a Black Hat's temple."

Torri put her glass down. "Really? Which one?"

"Ethylrelda of Waam. We know you came from Waam and thought you could give us some useful tips."

Torri had always been open mouthed about her days as a Black Hat Painter, much more so than Countess Sygillis, who refused to talk about it at all, as she didn't want to share such a dark period of her life with her children. Duchess Torrijayne, on the other hand, typically offered a highly censored detailing of her days when she was known as Torrijayne of Waam, a vile and feared Painter. That fact, coupled with other things, kept alive the ongoing rivalry and animosity between Countess Sygillis and the duchess. For the sake of their families, which were very close, they could act in a civilized fashion, but make no mistake—they hated each other. Fortunately, that hatred didn't extend to Sygillis husband or her children. Torrijayne was a good friend of Captain Davage and Lt. Kilos, and she cherished Sygillis children, Kay most of all. Such was their relationship that Torri could poke fun at the countess, often doubling Davage and Kilos over with laughter. Davage, though he loved Sygillis beyond measure, had a good sense of humor regarding her. The horrid "shirt" incident that Kay uncovered in the curio shop was merely the latest shot fired in their ongoing conflict, and one for which the countess swore revenge—though Davage had secretly admitted he thought the shirts were the funniest things he'd ever seen. Apparently, with the fountain outside, Countess Sygillis had had her revenge.

She finished her glass of juice. "And you're going to do this, are you?" she asked, already knowing what the answer was.

"Yes, Dimples, we are."

"Certainly not an easy task, is it? You asked for my advice; well, here it is: don't do it. Going into a Black Hat's temple is just about the most dangerous thing you could ever try."

"If I don't, Sam will die. I promised her I would see these Trials through, and I intend to do just that."

Torri held up her empty glass, and an automaton immediately came down and filled it.

"Ohhh, you Vith," she said. "So heroic and brave all the time. So, what's your plan? Tell me."

"We were thinking we'd take the *Goshawk* to Waam, infiltrate her temple and get the piece."

"Ah, just that simple, hmm? Let's examine this point by point. So, you want to take the *Goshawk* to Waam. Do you even know where Waam is?"

"Waam is the largest city on the planet Gothan," Phillip said.

"Correct. Gothan is about a week's journey from here—that's a lot of Xaphan space to cover. How are you going to do it without being spotted and boarded—or worse?"

Sarah spoke up, beaming with pride. "Kay is going to Cloak the *Goshawk*. He can do that."

Torri's icy-blue eyes got wide. "I see. So, Kay, you're going to Cloak the *Goshawk,* are you? Let's see it. Let me see what you've got."

Kay set his glass down and tried to clear his mind. He felt rushed and pressured. He allowed his Cloak to well up, and then, after another moment or two, he Cloaked himself, Sarah and Phillip.

Torri, watching, burst into a smile and clapped. "Really good job, Kay—I'm impressed."

She started trying to pull his Cloak apart. She thought to have it down with a few simple tricks, found herself stumped, and then, with a cry, changed her approach, and the Cloak came down. Kay, Sarah and Phillip reappeared in their chairs.

"Wow, Kay!" she shouted. "Really good. Extremely good, actually. Come here and give me a hug!" Torri had always been a very huggy sort of lady. Kay got up and gave her a huge hug, making sure not to press too closely on her pregnant belly. He felt a bit shy at first, remembering what happened when he touched Beth's Silver tech. But no, he hugged her and didn't feel anything like what he had with Beth—Torri keeping her Silver tech deeply buried within, safely away from Kay's touch.

Sarah finished her orange juice. "We were hoping you could help Cloak the *Goshawk* for our trip."

"What for?" Torri said letting Kay go. "Kay's Cloak will work just fine. Truly. It's not quite a full Painted Cloak, but still, Cloaking a ship doesn't require an overly elaborate setup what with all that empty space to hide in. So, I'm sold. With Kay's Cloak I'll wager you'll make it all the way to Gothan without issue—provided the *Goshawk* doesn't break down on you along the way. Now, what are you going to do when you get there?"

Sarah again—apparently she was the author of their plan. "We were thinking we'd hide out in the ship while Kay goes into her temple, takes the Black Hat over and has her show him where the device is. Then he'd take it, and we'd be off."

"Oh, so you're just going to waltz into her temple and take her over, are you?"

"That's what we were thinking. Will the Black Hat not be subject to Kay's touch?"

Torri smiled. "Certainly she will, but touching a Black Hat will come with dangers unheard of." She turned to Kay. "Kay, are you certain you want to have an intimate encounter with a Black Hat, especially with an old and nasty one like Ethylrelda—because if you touch her Shadow tech, that's pretty much what you'll be doing. Does that thought distress you?"

"A little bit, yes. But what choice do I have? Again, Sam is depending on me."

Torri thought for a moment, then: "There is a lot of danger in what you're planning, Kay. For one, to be so intimate with Ethylrelda of Waam, an old and wicked Black Hat, could be overwhelming. She has lived long, knowing nothing but rage and hate, and you will be subject to every bit of that. You could lose yourself in the process. And, let's assume for a moment that you withstand the torrent and are able to command Ethylrelda. It is possible that you will make a 'friend'. She could become enthralled with you, Kay. Look at how Beth reacted—and, from what you've told me, you only touched her Silver tech for a few moments. Ethylrelda might just not be able to forget your touch, and she might come after you, provided that she lets go of you in the first place. And, by the by, Ethylrelda of Waam is probably the toughest Black Hat out there. She's on another level entirely."

"I heard she faced and killed the Grand Abbess of Kentaro in a fair fight," Phillip said.

"Yes, she did. It was a huge victory for the Black Hats."

"Then, well free her with our Sight," Phillip said.

"Assuming that Dav is not going with you, your Sight is not potent enough yet. But, let's say you do free her—then you'll have a love-sick, freed Black Hat that will want nothing more than to become a *Wandwilla* with Kay."

"What's that?"

Beth's arms around him, their flesh welding together.
Wandwilla . . .

"A *Wandwilla* is a creature that is result of a Shadow tech female and a Shadow tech male who have been allowed to join themselves together—basically the man and woman become one, locked together in ecstasy, forever. I've seen one myself, years ago. It looks like a huge leafless tree that creates a pod-like fruit that is very useful in certain Cabalistic recipes. Fall asleep next to one, and you're going to have a night full of sex-fueled psychedelic dreams like you've never had before."

Kay sat there and listened, white-faced.

Torri continued. "To become a *Wandwilla* is, at the same time, a Black Hat's greatest fear and greatest ambition. For a Black Hat, who has not touched a Shadow tech male, becoming a *Wandwilla* is something they most certainly do not want. But, touch her for more than a few moments, and becoming a *Wandwilla* with you is all she'll ever want again. Some Black Hats, who have lived for a very long time, like Ethylrelda, manage to develop a sort of consciousness all their own independent of the Black Abbess and actively seek out a Shadow tech male and *Wandwilla* with him, as a sort of reward for their ages of service. There is said to be a hidden world, known only to the Black Abbess, where a whole forest of *Wandwillas* grow—sort of like a Black Hat's version of heaven. I've heard there are a few located right here on Kana, located somewhere in the Tartan area. It's my goal of mine to locate these *Wandwillas* and ensure their safety."

Kay, Sarah and Phillip sat listening, open-mouthed.

"For that reason, Shadow tech males are killed without mercy or exception. Here, on Kana, safe and sound in the League, you are protected by the Sisters, and by your parents. You must realize that, because of what you could possibly do to a Black Hat, they would, should they become aware of you, not stop until you are dead. Waam has over a hundred Black Hats living in it, and their hordes of sniveling henchmen, the Spectres, are everywhere, always on the lookout for Shadow tech males. The sentence, should they find you, is death. So, touch her Shadow tech at your peril, Kay."

They sat there in silence for a moment. "So, Ethylrelda, huh? She's a tough one. One of the oldest Black Hats I know. My temple was in her shadow, though safely out of her way. In Waam, my temple was a large X-shaped structure, which has since been flattened. Hers is a huge sphere at least three thousand feet high, a lot bigger than mine was. It rolls around like a big marble, flattening everything before it. Kay, come here, and let me look at you."

Kay got up and approached her. She examined him with her huge blue eyes. "I just can't get enough of your face. All of your father's good looks, and only a little bit of your mother in there to mess it up."

"Dimples, I know that you and my mother . . ."

"Yes—stupid isn't it? That we can't just let what happened in the past go, that we hate each other still. In the old days, few Black Hats would have gotten between us—such was the sorry state of our relationship. But, that doesn't mean that I don't cherish her husband as one of my best friends, and her fine children. We are in full agreement on what matters most—your safety, your father's safety, our family's safety. I would stand side by side with your mother to defend our families to the death."

Sarah put her glass down. "Well, I for one think well do just fine. We did really well in Rostov, and we've our Gifts. Kay's Gifts are unbelievable now, Aunt Torri. You should see them. Those Xaphans won't be able to stand up to us."

Torri raised an eyebrow. "Really? Well, I admire your enthusiasm, Sarah, truly. However, you're overlooking one small thing."

"And what is that, Aunt Torri?"

"You are going to be in the city of Waam. Though we often don't give the Xaphans too much credit for competence, Waam is truly extraordinary. It is a great city—it could be a great League city as well. It is larger than anything here on Kana, and possibly larger than Inarri on Onaris as well. And her inhabitants are great, too. You have how many Gifts, Sarah?"

"I have two, Aunt."

"And Phillip?"

"Just one, I think, and Kay has three."

"The people of Waam are the descendants of the House of Clovis, and they have, on average, four Gifts per person, high or low. The only Gift they don't have is the Sight. And, on top of all that, they are evolved. They are on a slightly higher evolutionary scale than we are here in the League."

"How did they manage that?" Sarah asked, quite enthralled.

"There was once a great space station that orbited the planet as Gothan was being terraformed into a livable world, Zall-88; perhaps you've heard of it. The people aboard worshipped a mysterious feline goddess named Mabsornath who gave them great knowledge and enlightenment. The House of Xandarr then came along and coveted the knowledge to be had there and sacked the station, supposedly putting all aboard to the sword. However, it is said that a number of refugees from Zall-88 made it off the station and helped found the city of Waam, and there they performed a number of innovations meant to evolve the people living there."

"And how so?" Sarah asked.

"The layout of the city is odd, built at a topical level in a wheel configuration; however, a more detailed inspection proves it's more like a convex mirror meant to focus certain types of stellar energies. These energies are supposedly meant to bathe the body in radiance and assist it in rapid evolution. Likewise, there are odd constructs built up on the streets at various points that are as old as the city itself. Newcomers to the city often report that the constructs emit a piercing and rather unpleasant sound that the locals cannot hear. According to some, this sound enhances the senses, further accelerating evolution. Whole municipalities are built with the concept of torturing the flesh in the hopes of making it better."

Phillip set his glass down. "Aunt Torri, I've heard bits and pieces of what you mention, that Waam is a city in evolutionary transition; however, let us agree that such things can only be the worst sort of science, mad and misguided to an unheard of level, even for Xaphans."

"I really can't agree with you, Phillip. It sounds insane, and, probably, many aspects of it are; still, there is no denying that the people of Waam can do incredible things, and it is a good thing for the League that they are not more invested in the ongoing conflict with us as are some of the more war-like Houses. So, with that in mind, all four of you must tread with the thought that you are, at best, on par with the Waamites. You're not going to be, out-Gifting" anybody in Waam. That said, Kay, are you fully recovered from the attack in Grove? Please be honest."

"Yes, I believe so."

"Have you any theories as to the identity of the attackers?"

Kay didn't hesitate. "Lt. Kilos thinks that my sister, Lady Hathaline, did it."

Torri sat there and didn't react. Kay went on. "And, even though it sounds bizarre, I definitely have a feeling that the distorted, bleeding creature that attacked me was, indeed, my sister—somehow warped ahead a hundred years and perverted into a monster."

Torri's expression darkened. "Kay, have you ever heard the term *Killanjo*? Perhaps your mother's used it before."

"No, Dimples, I haven't."

"Figures—your mother was a Hammer, and they know nothing. It's a very great pity that the League and the Xaphans are enemies. If the two sides combined forces, there wouldn't be anything we couldn't accomplish. What the League knows and what the Xaphans know are two different things entirely. The League is mighty and strong, but its knowledge is flawed. Tell me, what is the driving intellectual force in the League?"

"The Science Ministry," Phillip said.

Torri shrugged. "Please, Phillip. The Science Ministry merely expands upon doctrines of thought pre-approved by the Sisterhood of Light. The Sisters determine what is known in the League and what is not. The Sisters are wise and ancient, and their knowledge of Elder-tech is truly astounding; however, they only choose to know certain things. They are decidedly ignorant on Pre-Elder and Non-Elder knowledge, and that is where the Xaphans" knowledge excels. The Xaphan Cabalists know of a creature called *Killanjo,* for they have been plagued by them for centuries. A *Killanjo* is a kind of monster that was once a loved one: a father, a mother, a—sister. Xaphan Houses sometimes were rocked to their core by these demons wearing the guise of loved ones. These Houses, so attacked, often imploded—

dying of broken hearts. A *Killanjo* is a terror weapon, a heart-breaking vision, and it is terribly effective.

"Lt. Kilos spoke of them. She called them Jennybacks."

"They have lots of names."

"Where do these creatures come from?" Kay asked.

"Don't know. Whoever is the driving force behind the *Killanjo* is our enemy—make no mistake about that. I have been a citizen of the League for over twenty years. I love the League for my husband and children, for the life that we've had the opportunity to build together. I will defend the League with my life. I've noticed that *Killanjo* are beginning to show up within the League in steadily growing numbers. They are spreading; I've been watching. I'm starting to see them pop up here and there, mostly on Hoban and some of the outer-lying League worlds but here on Kana as well with more and more frequency. Do you remember hearing about the collapse of House Williams on Hoban? I'm convinced it was a *Killanjo* who triggered that."

There was a thump at one of the windows, the Silver tech serpents reacting to it. They looked, and there, outside on the windowpane, was a huge bluish-green bug.

"And then there's these things—these huge bugs. They're everywhere. At night I can hear them buzzing in the marshes. They make an awful racket."

"They're called Paraflies by the Science Ministry. Do you think they are somehow connected to these *Killanjo?*" Sarah asked.

"Possibly—wherever the *Killanjo* show up, so too, are these Paraflies, by the thousands. A few days ago I found them dead in droves in the marsh.

"But why? I read about that."

"Don't know—they were just dead. And, they're not really bugs either. My daughter, Tulee, loves bugs and managed to collect a whole terrarium full the other day. I looked them over. I don't know what they are, they're just not insects." Torri turned to Kay. "Let me instruct you, Kay. Should a *Killanjo* come at you again, there are certain things you must be aware of. One: *Killanjo* can cast spells, rendering you helpless. I'm sure you already know that. You cannot let them cast a spell under any circumstance. Two: *Killanjo* carry a powerful stench with them. You often smell one before you see it. Three: *Killanjo* cannot bear the sight of their own reflection. You can use that as a defense."

Sarah was intrigued. "What is their purpose?"

Torri smiled. "What do you do when you face an enemy whose arm you cannot break, whose sword you cannot bend? Why, you strike at its heart, and so the *Killanjo*, a demon once a loved one, is sent to kill its House. Tell me, Kay, how does it make you feel that your sister, somehow warped ahead in time, did these things to you?"

"Words can't describe it."

"And your mother? Should she know the truth, how would she react?"

"She would go mad with grief."

A tear dripped down Torri's face. "Precisely."

27—Waam

Kay Cloaked the *Goshawk,* and they set out, first to Xandarr where they resupplied, then from 3PM of Xandarr, they soared into the dark night of Xaphan space.

It was a long, lonely trip.

Traveling through League space was alive with activity. There were often other ships flying at your side—transports, Fleet vessels, merchantmen, private yachts. These assorted starcraft created a small fleet of ships flying in a loose formation, as space travel, though quite safe in modern vessels, was best shared in groups. Should your vessel break down, help was close by to assist. And, should a pirate or raider rear their ugly faces, then you had the combined firepower of your "fleet" to send them packing. Also, even if you were travelling alone, you had the Aire-net and the holos—the broad-wave transmissions that allowed one, even in the abyss of space, to keep up on the latest gossip, to tune in on your favorite shows or talk to your loved ones as much as you wanted. Sarah constantly had the Aire-net on, even if she wasn't watching. If you tried to turn it off, she'd immediately turn it back on and give you a dirty look.

There was nothing like that in Xaphan space.

The Aire-net receptors offered nothing but static. A few boarder-area worlds had boosters that amped up the League signals, but, on the whole, the Xaphans had nothing that bound up the various worlds in their control and made them one. Each world, it seemed, was on its own, an island in space. Occasionally, as they neared various worlds, they tuned into bizarre religious transmissions spoken by monotone priests in black churches and other morose broadcasts that they would rather shutoff than watch.

They avoided the occasional Xaphan ships that they came upon, and there weren't many. They sometimes saw old *Merci* ships that had somehow survived the old League wars, and a few beaten up *Ghomes* that looked like beetles in the slow stages of death. They came across old derelicts and battered hulks lashed together with welded metal ties. They wondered about the poor souls inside, stuck in space in ships that appeared to be falling apart and trailing rads in quantity. Lon went into a poorly thought-out lecture on what rads at that level were doing to the tissues of those aboard, even if they were wearing protective suits. Kay, seeing Sarah's face, hushed him up.

Occasionally, they'd come across ships so bizarre they had no idea what to make of them. They were built in odd shapes, sometimes in squares, other times in triangles, polygons and other symmetrical shapes. Others were literally shapeless, looking like wads of chewed cud. And once, they spotted a huge ship in the shape of a naked woman, perfectly formed, like a giant statue moving through space.

Such sights had them scratching their heads.

Also, and this could simply have been their familiarity-starved imaginations, but space itself seemed *darker* in Xaphan territory. The various dangers of space travel, which seemed so distant when in League territory, were amplified in the sudden, lonely dark of Xaphan space. Alone in the lightless soak, nothing seemed to get closer even though they were moving at speed; all their gauges and instruments said they were moving, yet they seemed to be standing still. As the days rolled by, Sarah became increasingly paranoid and on-edge. Suddenly the *Goshawk* became not a hotrod designated for outings but a critical lifeboat carrying four desperate castaways. She stopped getting into her pajamas in the evening hours and just sat there in the cockpit nervously looking at the gauges, jumping at every sound she couldn't identify, gazing at the unfamiliar jumble of stars that didn't seem to be moving. Phillip made the mistake of mentioning that he thought that they had burst a helium tank—a rather minor thing to lose, but Sarah nearly panicked and insisted they set down and repair it. The closest place was Midas 6, a black, somber world of volcanic rock and fiery pits that was a former staging zone in the old days of the League/Xaphan conflict.

Sarah was deeply conflicted. She demanded they set down, but why did it have to be Midas 6.

"You know the old stories. The House of Bodice—weren't they

wiped out on Midas 6?" she asked in a shaky voice.

Phillip debated on whether or not to answer.

"Yes," Lon said. "They died on Midas 6."

Sarah slumped into a corner, openly full of dread.

Phillip put down in an uninhabited area, and Kay dropped the Cloak. As Phillip and Lon rolled up their sleeves and worked on the tank, Sarah stood there watching them with her Poltava drawn—the hand of loneliness that had nearly squeezed the life out of them in space was replaced by the cold feeling of being watched the whole time they were down there.

Sarah looked around, seeing the bleak sky laced with feathery plumes of volcanic ash.

The House of Bodice huddling in their fallen transport once looked at this same sky. The House of Bodice went extinct on this bloody world. Cursed world, lost dreams . . .

Phillip and Lon repaired the tank but announced that they needed to spend the night—the engines needed a rest and the tank needed to recharge. Kay Cloaked the ship, and they went inside and stayed there. Sarah, a normally bold adventurer, didn't want to leave the ship—somewhere out there was the ancient hulk of the Bodice's death ship—where they breathed their last.

She didn't want to see it.

Lon was actually the most eager to go exploring, and he and Kay set out for a bit, under Cloak, Sarah pleading with them not to go. They returned a few hours later, announcing that there was a dark city to the west. The news didn't go down well with Sarah as she expected to be attacked at any time. That night, as they peered through the cockpit glass, they occasionally saw Xaphan ships passing overhead, and they could see a dim, reddish glow coming from the city and from various erupting volcanoes nearby. Sarah swore she kept seeing figures lurking in the dark . . . *the ghosts of the Bodice.*

She swore she heard rapping on the cockpit glass.

But, all three of them Sighting could see nothing there. When they took off a few hours later, with the *Goshawk* nimbly climbing into the sky, Sarah was the happiest they'd seen her in some time.

Resuming their trip, Sarah kept checking their course, kept testing the AM/PM compasses and other navigational equipment. Everything was working correctly.

It just felt like they were lost, like they were making no progress.

The stopover on Midas 6 had not helped in the least.

On the fourth day, only a few hours away from Gothan, she put her face into her hands and began crying—Kay having to take her into his arms and comfort her.

Finally, like the voice of a benevolent spirit, their Aire-net receptors came to quiet but definite life, replacing the empty static that had lasted for days. Sarah, elated, put her ear next to the speakers and listened as the jumpy signal quickly grew in strength.

There were voices and laughter. Sarah listened to Xaphan comedies, and she laughed though she didn't understand some of the jokes. "I think . . . I think they're making fun of Black Hats!" she chirped, listening.

Then, like a tiny spit of land lost in a vast sea, there was Gothan, the fourth planet in the Omicron-Thetis system, as designated by League charts. It was a green and blue world, much like Onaris, with five uneven asteroids orbiting as moons. Gothan was a life-saver. Lit up by the cheerful-looking planet, they had light and sounds, and Gothan had a fairly interesting broadband that was half-way watchable. The programs they saw were racy, outrageous and rather pornographic in nature. Waam and Gothan around it appeared to be a rather uninhibited place.

Sarah, after watching a few undressed shows and listening to the happy voices, was instantly rejuvenated—the blood-shot scarecrow that she'd become over the last few days was gone.

Now that they were there, it was time to hash out a definitive plan. They'd had four days to scheme something up, but, in the dark night of the trip to Gothan, none of them had the energy to do that.

They'd brought a small holo-database regarding Gothan—Lon had thought of that and poured over it.

Gothan. Principality of the House of Clovis. Populated after an extensive terra-forming effort in 000021ax. A temperate world of ten continents and six major oceans. During the terra-forming years, which took two decades, House Clovis took up residence in a large space station known as Zall 88. After the planet surface was made ready for population, a small fragment of House Clovis stayed aboard Zall 88, where it is said they developed powerful technology that gave them access to true enlightenment. The station was attacked by the House of Xandarr some years later—Xandarr being jealous of the supposed technology to be had there. After they were unable to decipher the knowledge, for they had killed all aboard, the Xandarrs destroyed the station in a fit of spiteful anger.

The largest city on Gothan was Waam, a city ruled by a municipal parliament, which covered an entire continent in the northwestern corner of the planet. A popular place, over one hundred Black Hats made Waam their home.

The information in the holo-database was informative, yet fairly succinct and sterile, containing no hint of oddities in evolution or the "super-people" Torrijayne had warned them about. Perhaps she was exaggerating, or not remembering correctly.

Phillip rolled the *Goshawk* into a high altitude arc over Waam so that they could have a look at it through their powerful scanners. It was a long sprawl of tall and squat buildings all lit up in colored lights. As Torrijayne had mentioned, it was laid out in a wheel-like configuration with eight obvious spidery broadways all leading to the central core of the city.

"That is Waam-Core in the center, per the database," Lon said. Surrounding the core were various municipalities all irregularly sectioned off by roads. The differences in architecture between the various municipalities were obvious, even from high altitude. In the northern quadrant of the city was an inland sea. From the air, it was a lot cleaner looking and more orderly than they might have thought. They'd heard that Xaphan cities were a collision of mismatched design with little thought to proper planning or layout; their brief stop on Midas 6 had reinforced that notion. Waam, however, didn't seem like that—it looked like a decent place to live and visit—at least from the air.

Dropping down, they entered a bizarre layer of orbital shipping coming and going from the city. There were Xaphan ships of all kinds and colors mixed in with colossally huge ships that resembled great spirals, sort of like bacterium. The Spirals lazily orbited over the city with the smaller, more conventional craft flowing around them like tiny sperm cells swimming around a much larger egg.

"What are those?" Sarah asked as a large green spiral grew large in the glass. Larger and larger, it had a singular organic quality and offered no hint that it was a starship and that living beings populated within.

Lon came to the glass as Phillip carefully flew over the surface. "Those are ships built in Helixical Bondarism," he said. "It's an artistic design movement that started here in Waam. My father has a wealth of information on it back home. Has something to do with an effort to, 'stress' the flesh, to bend it in a pre-determined evolutionary path. A lot of nonsense, really, but the results here are quite remarkable. I was hoping to see it for myself, and one can't help but be impressed."

Sarah gawked out the glass as the *Goshawk* passed the end of the spiral. "You mean there are people in there?"

"Yes, it is a starship, though I understand the interior is quite brutal to try and live in."

Phillip dropped down, and the great city stretched out beneath them in a controlled mass.

Duchess Torrijayne had given them the approximate location of Ethylrelda's temple. She said it was near where her old temple had stood in the south-central area of the city. She also said that it, unlike other Black Hat temples, moved, rolling very slowly like a huge black marble, crushing everything in its slow, steady path. Over the centuries, it had moved in a steady southerly course of a few miles, the city withering and changing around it.

Black Hat temples were easy to spot from the air. They were usually black, geometric buildings devoid of lights or windows that were given a wide bit of space by the surrounding buildings. Some of them had dense, tree-filled lots surrounding them for literally miles. They saw an assortment of huge square temples, towering pyramids, ellipses, intricate polygons and spread out trapezoids mixed into the cityscape like a few black onyxes in a dumped out bag of colored stones.

The temple they were looking for was a huge sphere, at least three thousand feet high. Torrijayne had told them it was easily the largest in Waam, for its owner Ethylrelda was by far the oldest Black Hat in Waam. She was reputed to be one of the most powerful Black Hats possibly ever. She had fought the Sisterhood of Light more times than can be counted, and survived, putting her Hulgismen and the Stellar Marines facing her through a meat-grinder of ferocity seldom seen. Years back, she met in battle and killed the Grand Abbess of Kentaro—quite a feat.

Her temple wasn't hard to find—like a black pearl splitting the clouds and blotting out the sun for a long way in its vicinity. They looked for Torri's old X-shaped temple which was supposed to be nearby, but they didn't see it. It must have been flattened and built over since then.

So, now that they'd seen it, what was the next step?

There was a definite ring of decrepit buildings surrounding the temple for many blocks—the Black Hat apparently a bad neighbor, the coming of her temple bringing with it death and decay. They scouted out a tall building about a mile west of the temple, and Phillip put the *Goshawk* down on the flat roof. They piled out quickly and checked their surroundings. Everything appeared to be clear, and the ship was still safely Cloaked. There were several service doors on the roof which they barred and jammed shut. They then went to the edge and took a good look around.

They were about a hundred floors up. The building was vacant, old and dusty in the afternoon sun, but it was apparently sturdy and safe enough for the ship. Nearby, Ethylrelda's Temple soared into the clouds—its heights obscured in the afternoon haze. Its black surface was shiny and reflected the surroundings like an obsidian crystal ball. The area surrounding the temple was clear and neglected; again, the people of Waam weren't friends with the Black Hats and gave them plenty of space. In the distant cityscape, they could see two more Black Hat temples peeking through the buildings—a large black cube to the north and a spire-like tower to the west. Ethylrelda's temple was pressing up against half-destroyed buildings to its south, structures ready to be slowly crushed to dust by its ongoing, imperceptible roll.

Lon panned around with his goggles. "There's nobody around for at least several blocks—not that I can see. The large black temple ahead is featureless and windowless. I can see that it is moving at a steady but slow rate. Those buildings to its southern face are soon to be rolled over. I'd wager it progresses a few feet every year. The only opening I see is a large archway at its base which appears to lead into the interior."

"The Black Hat's open door—all their temples have such a thing. You go in, and you never come out," Phillip added.

Sarah drew her Poltava. "The piece we need could be anywhere in such a place."

She craned her head back to try and see the top of the temple, its towering heights making her feel immediately dizzy. "Kay," she said, clutching the ledge of the building for support, "what do you see?"

Kay opened up his Sight. Everything went to amber. He had to focus as his Sight tended to want to fade into the past. As it did, he saw Torrijayne's X-shaped temple rise up to the north. It was sinister to look at, knowing that Dimples, the smiling duchess was once a cruel Black Hat there. He could see Ethylrelda's temple, like a relentless juggernaut, roll backwards the way that it had come—its open door staying at the bottom, despite the movement.

Struggling, he focused his Sight back to the present and on Ethylrelda's temple. Its interior was surprising. Though huge, its internals were an intestinal tract of small, twisting passages that eventually wound their way to the top—like a huge sphere full of tightly compacted earthworms. He had thought that the Black Hat would be sitting alone somewhere near the top, as his mother was once reputed to do in her Black Hat days, but in the uppermost chamber, nobody was present.

He could see figures milling about mindlessly inside, filthy and naked: Hulgismen no doubt, a lot of them. The remains of many Hulgismen lay strewn about in various stages of decay, some freshly dead, others dusty skeletons. It was utterly barbaric inside, like an animal's den strewn with random detritus: no furniture, plumbing, lighting, or any other hint of the basic necessities a person would want in their home. This was Ethylrelda's home after all. It didn't need mentioning that there was no hint of art or decoration or any of the aesthetic accessories that intelligent beings tended to like to have. It was like a huge artificial cave.

He could also see a great deal of artifacts lying about here and there, forgotten. Kay tried to locate the piece of the machine, but, with so much lying about, he really didn't know what he was looking for or where to start, yet a further complication.

At the very bottom, peering out of the large open entrance that Lon had seen, was a solitary figure: small, female, clad in scarlet robes but just as filthy and ill-kept as the Hulgismen.

It was Ethylrelda herself—it had to be.

She moved about in a stilted, pre-programmed way, her arms held bolt straight at her side. Wearing her black, featureless sash, she gazed out at the sunshine and relative cheer of Waam. Seeing through her sash, she had a pretty, robust face with long brown hair that was matted with age and neglect. Kay felt rather sorry for her at that moment. Perhaps she longed for what was out there in the inviting city of Waam beyond the Black Abbess' Clutch; for the mundane, wondrous things she could never have.

He thought he heard a small voice enter his head, though he might have imagined it. He heard: *Hello, Kay.*

Kay looked away and quieted his Sight.

"Did you see her?" Sarah asked.

"I did."

"And did you see the piece we need?"

"I saw lots of items in there. This is going to be tough."

"It's the cross-piece, Kay—the arch of the machine."

"I know that; nevertheless, I didn't see it. There are miles of passageways in there."

Standing there on the roof of the abandoned building, the four of them were without a plan.

Sarah turned away, as the looming specter of the temple was making her dizzy, and she wandered to the other side of the building. She looked around. "Hey, you guys, what is all of this?"

They turned and joined her. Looking northwest toward the core of the city was a vast, eclectic collection of buildings framed by broad, well-organized skyways full of flowing traffic. There was an up and down smattering of tall, flat-topped, workman-like buildings mixed in with gilded treasures glittering in lights and spires. Here and there, in a rather surreal blend, were buildings in the shape of smiling faces, half-bodied busts and full-formed statues hundreds of feet high. There were oddities of nature, animals, flowers and more of the helix-like spirals seen in the skies above, only tipped on their sides.

"Does that building over there look like a fork?" Sarah asked pointing.

"These odd buildings are built in Mirrism, yet another, more watered-down form of Bondarism," Lon said. "According to my reading, it's just an artistic style of design meant to use common objects in unexpected ways."

"What's the point of all this?" Sarah asked.

"Evolution."

Kay headed toward the service door. "I feel more evolved already. Shall we?"

With nothing else to do, they decided to descend into Waam and scout out the surrounding area for themselves—just in case they had to make a break for it. Sarah and Phillip in their linens and black dusters didn't figure to stand out much, but Kay, with his Blanchefort coat and CARG, and Lon, with his long Probert coat, could be a problem. And then there was the hair—Sarah with her blue and Kay's purple might pose an issue. This was a Xaphan city, and they assumed the people would be sober and drab, conservative in the extreme. Kay removed his coat and borrowed one of Phillip's linen shirts. Lon, his pockets full of gadgets, including his CEROS, didn't want to be without his coat, so they agreed to let him wear it.

"What are you packing in there, Lon, just so I know?" Phillip asked.

He smiled and opened his coat. "I've got my CEROS—I never go anywhere without it. I've also got my spyglasses and goggles with an assortment of prisms and a no-Cloak freedom light and Meisha's Dirge Defeater. I've also got a sandwich, which is probably bad by now—I should throw it away. And, I've got a PITCOCK WONDER GUN."

"A what?" Sarah asked, half-laughing.

"A PITCOCK WONDER GUN. It comes from my mother's House, and this one here actually belonged to my mother in her younger days."

"Lady Branna of the Science Ministry used to carry a gun?"

"Yes, she did. My mother is a scientist, and sometimes in order to quest for knowledge, one must shoot one's way to the truth."

Kay thought a moment and tried to imagine Lon's mother, the tiny, blue-haired Lady Branna, dainty and elegant, packing a gun and using it as well.

Lon continued. "It's a sort of jack of all trades gun. It fires five large caliber shots which can perform a variety of effects, sometimes area-effecting, sometimes not." He pulled a large-barreled gun out of his coat with a rotating cartridge holding five, walnut-sized slugs. "I always load mine out with a nice combination of stuff: Perdition's Smoke round, a Hell-Fire, a Dragon-slayer for punch and a Sad Sampson No-Cloak. But, I've got a whole brace full of different ones." Lon put the huge weapon back into his coat.

Sarah clapped him on the shoulder. "Good to know, Lon, that you're armed to the teeth."

Making sure they had their small, trusty Poltavas safely concealed, Sarah and Phillip put their SAPPs on, and Kay debated on taking his CARG; it was an odd, elegant weapon and might draw attention.

"Don't worry," Lon said. "It looks pretty much like a sword, and I'll wager there will be quite a few swords roaming around on the streets."

Kay saddled his CARG, cocked his purple Poltava and stuck it in his pocket. They un-jammed one of the doors and went down the rickety stairwell to the street. The building was possibly some sort of multipurpose structure at one time, but now it was in ruin and slow decay. When they got to street level, they bore west of Ethylrelda's temple, its shadow looming over them. The immediate area surrounding the temple was devoid of people and urban animals; apparently, the presence of the Black Hat drove all life away.

"I feel like we're being watched," Sarah said, looking around at row after row of derelict buildings.

Kay looked around with his Sight. "I don't see anybody, Sarah. This area in the shadow of the temple is completely empty, except for us."

After several blocks of nothing, they emerged into civilization.

It appeared that their fears about sticking out were unfounded. The citizens of Waam, just like one found in any large League city, came in all styles and colors. There were stylish people wearing some sort of colorful Xaphan clothing mixed together with less-stylish folk in workmen's gear. Some carried weapons. Swords, staves, clubs and mounted axes and pistols of various makes weren't an uncommon sight. Hair color also wasn't an issue—there were lots of blue heads of hair bobbing down the street, along with an assortment of other bright colors; reds, greens, yellows, purples and blacks. Apparently gaudy hair colors were in style in Waam. Quite surprising.

As they walked about, they saw all sorts of people going about their business. Though they were Xaphans, they didn't seem much different from League citizens. People moved about, some laughing and talking with friends, mothers walking with their children, some carrying sacks of groceries and other sundries.

Flowing along at both ground level and in the heights was well-ordered traffic. The bulk of the traffic confined itself to the eight highways flowing toward the core, the nearest one being several blocks to the north. Much less traffic trawled the side streets. They couldn't help but be impressed with what they saw. League vehicles were very functional; they worked well with little thought to finery and aesthetics. These Xaphan vehicles were gaudy and self-indulgent in the extreme featuring shiny metal accessories that served no discernable function, over-stuffed plush seating, rim-rams, smoke and noise-makers and more. Other sky cars were built in geometric fashion, tumbling through the air in a seemingly random fashion.

There were more statues flying about with people haphazardly riding on them without the benefit of seats, harnesses or any other obvious safety accouterments.

And . . .

"Hey!" Sarah cried. "Did I just see somebody, flying" up there in the traffic?"

They looked up, Lon adjusting his goggles. "I don't see anybody flying."

"Aunt Torri's got you seeing things," Phillip added. "There's nobody up there."

Kay was impatient. "Come on; let's be on our way."

As they got father from the temple, the throng of people increased dramatically—the city chattering with life. The buildings were also transformed from abandoned and falling apart to occupied and well-kept. Waam was not a dirty city at all; in fact, the people seemed to carry themselves with a hint of civic pride. As they made their way down the street, people smiled at them and tipped their hats. The city appeared to be divided up into innumerable municipal districts, each with its own distinctive style and colors. The one they were entering was neat and tidy with baskets of colorful flowers built into the sides of many buildings. They came across a festive green and brown sign. It read: ENTERING AULD MUNICIPALITY. ALL ARE WELCOME HERE. WARNING: PROHIBITION STRICTLY ENFORCED AFTER THIRTY BELLS.

On the other side of the sign, facing in the opposite direction, it read in dark blue and silver: ENTERING HEATH MUNICIPALITY. DRINKING ENCOURAGED ALL 42 BELLS A DAY. BUDGES AND NEDERLANDERS NEED NOT ENTER ON PAIN OF DEATH.

"I guess we're in Auld now," Kay said leading the way.

"And I suppose that I'm still in Heath," Sarah said trailing, having yet to pass the sign.

"Auld?" Phillip said. "Why does that sound familiar?"

"Auld," Lon answered, chiming in, "was one of the twenty five Elders. Don't you go to church?"

Phillip shook his head, and they continued. Kay stopped and rubbed his ears. "You guys hear that? What is that?"

"What?" Sarah asked.

"That! That ringing. You don't hear it?"

They took a few more steps, and Sarah suddenly grabbed her ears. "Oh, now I do—that high-pitched wailing sound? Oh, I can't stand it!"

Soon Phillip and Lon were hearing it, too, and they weren't happy about it. The sound seemed to be coming from a rough-hewn gargoyle that was sprouting up in the center of an intersection. It was about twelve feet high and had a rather flowing lava-like appearance to it.

Phillip approached it. "I think this is what Aunt Torri had mentioned to us about the founders of Waam and evolution. This sound, I suppose, is intended to evolve us in some manner."

"Well, switch it off, Phillip. It's making me crazy!" Sarah ordered.

He examined the rather sturdy-looking gargoyle. "I don't see any way to shut it off."

Down the street an opulent green coach came down from the sky and landed. Several ladies in flowing green gowns and minty green hair got out and began sorting out stacks of papers amongst themselves. They then walked away in different directions up and down the street. One saw them and gave greeting.

Their coach then rose silently and climbed away. Kay noted it seemed to have no drive engine; rather, it was supported and propelled by four cables that went upward into the sky and vanished from view. He honed his Sight in, following the cables. They went up and up a surprising distance of tens of thousands of feet and ended at the base of one of the flying green spirals they had seen upon arrival high above in the thermosphere.

The woman approached. She held a stack of green parchments. She was pretty and smiling.

"Greetings, citizens," she said brightly in a Waam accent. "We have service several times a day in the Cathedral of Auld, and we bid you welcome." She pointed down the street to a large church with a steeple. "May we expect you this afternoon?"

Kay spoke up. "Perhaps, ma'am, if time allows."

She noted their discomfort. "Are you new to our city? You seem to be in a bit of distress by our Servitor here and the sound it creates. I assure you, in a few minutes you'll not notice them any longer. May I ask from where are you visiting us today?"

"Holly," Sarah said.

"Conwell," Lon said at the same time. Sarah scowled at him.

Kay jumped in. "We're from far away, ma'am. Our wits are a bit addled by this machine."

She smiled. "Well, please, welcome to Waam, good people. I again entreat you to join us this afternoon. I guarantee there will be singing and music and good fellowship. Also, though you do not appear to be in need, I will mention that a free meal will be served afterwards, available to any who wish to share it with us. I will look for you." She held out a parchment, and Kay took it.

Kay noticed the smiling woman in green was armed with a large wooden club hidden in the folds of her gown.

With that, she fell away and approached others.

"Seemed like a nice lady," Kay said.

"That was odd," Sarah said. "I wouldn't have thought Elder religion would be allowed to flourish on a Xaphan world."

"It's made a comeback in recent years, especially after the Battles at Mirendra 3 where the original Xaphans were defeated once and for all," Lon said. "Sure you don't want to go to church, Sarah and Phillip? Looks like you two could use a refresher."

Phillip gave Lon a good-natured shove.

"She was also armed with a hardwood club that looks for all the world like the MT CALM, the LosCapricos weapon of House Woolover," Kay said. "House Woolover is a League House."

"Recall your history, Kay," Phillip said. "House Woolover is a split Household—some of them went with the Xaphans to preach temperance, and some stayed in their ancestral lands south of Saga. Perhaps the lovely lady is a descendant of House Woolover."

Sarah looked around and smiled. "Say, she was right. I'm not hearing that damn noise as much."

"Good thing, too," Phillip added. "I'm not hearing it either."

Sarah suddenly tensed up. "Hey, you three, take a look."

Ahead they saw a large group of people clad in black robes slithering down the street like a patch of spilt oil. They appeared to be accosting the Waamites as they passed by. "Does that lot of toughs look like Spectres, or am I imagining it?" Sarah said.

"You're not imagining. They do look like Spectres," Kay said.

The group of Spectres rolled around the street in their black robes accosting random citizens as they passed by. They leisurely crossed the street, holding up traffic. They knocked a sack of groceries out of a lady's hands and pushed a small urchin to the ground. As in the League, they were a roving band of punks looking for nothing more than to create chaos on those they deemed weaker than themselves.

"The Spectres are the bootlickers of the Black Hats—they run their errands," Phillip said. He quieted. "Remember what Aunt Torri said, they search for fellows like you, Kay. We'd best avoid them if at all possible."

"I think we've gone far enough," Sarah said. "I think we should sit down, grab a bite, and figure something out. We can't stay here for long."

"How are we going to pay for our meal?" Kay asked. "All I have is a purse full of Blanchefort haders. That's something I forgot to anticipate. Probably won't go down too well in this Xaphan city."

"I have some unstamped gold," Phillip said. "You can pay me back later."

Sarah looked around. "I think there's a pub over there. Looks pleasant enough. Let's go in—I'm starving."

As they made their way to the pub, Kay stopped and turned red in the face. Across the street, one of the ladies in green was being accosted by a group of sniveling Spectres. They surrounded her, pushed her in the back and knocked her parchments from her hand where they scattered to the street. The Spectres laughed in their haughty fashion.

Before Sarah and Phillip could stop him, Kay was already marching across the street, Lon hot on his heels.

"Kay, did you not hear me?" Phillip hissed. "Kay!"

The Spectres saw them coming and awaited their arrival with anticipation. The crowd on the street formed a half circle to watch.

"What have we here?" one of them taunted in a cool, haughty voice.

"I believe you caused the lady to drop her parchments," Kay said in a commanding voice. "Please pick them up, and offer your apologies—immediately."

One of the Spectres went to step on the fallen papers, and Kay roughly shoved him down. The rest drew a set of slim, curved short swords from the depths of their black robes. Kay unsaddled his CARG, and Lon drew his large WONDER GUN, the Spectres eyeing it in dismay.

The Spectre grimaced in rage. "*Get on your knees!*" he yelled in a hideous Dirge voice, pointing at the street.

Something dampened the sound of his Dirge, and Kay and Lon

stood firm, resisting the command. The Spectres looked at each other a bit put off.

The woman in green approached Kay and Lon. "I thank you, citizens; however, I am not harmed and can attend to myself."

Kay and Lon didn't listen and faced the Spectres as Sarah and Phillip joined them.

"I see a throat aching to be cut," another Spectre said, drawing his swords.

Kay drew his purple Poltava and pointed it at the Spectre, who stared at it with obvious awe.

The woman put her hand on Kay's CARG, and she lowered his gun with the other. "Please, sir, it is time for service. There is no need for a confrontation. I shall take my leave. Auld's blessings be upon you all." Leaving her parchments where they lay, she walked down the street, joining a few other ladies in green, where they then went to the church and disappeared inside.

Kay and the Spectres stared each other down for a moment. "Done your good deed for the day, it appears," one of them said. "I fancy your gun."

"Why don't you go and lick the boots of some dirty courtesan," Kay suggested. "If I see you accosting anybody else again today, I will be glad to teach you a hard lesson."

The Spectre started to say something back, then bowed low. "Well then," he said as arrogantly as he could, "I suppose I have work to do." The Spectres turned and began walking away.

Kay lowered his CARG. "Ah," Lon said putting his gun away, "Meisha's Dirge Defeater gets 'em every time. I hate the Dirge." He patted his coat.

"What are you trying to do?" Sarah asked angrily. "I'm always up for a fight, but this isn't the place for it. Remember where we are and what we're here for."

"I can't abide bullies," Kay responded saddling his CARG. "They harassed that sweet missionary who was doing nothing but trying to spread good cheer." He saftied his Poltava and put it back into his pocket.

"She was armed with a MT CALM, Kay. She was far from helpless," Phillip added.

"I don't care."

The encounter over, they went across the street and entered the pub.

28—Thomasina the 19th of Waam

Inside the pub, they found an out-of-the way table and sat. Even in the enemy city of Waam, Sarah had a healthy appetite, and she ordered a lot of food, having no idea what she was selecting. Wary of eavesdroppers at first, it soon became apparent that nobody was interested in them in the least. People ate their food or drank at the large bar. Sportsmen plied their trade several tables down, and courtesans of varying degrees of pulchritude and cleanliness enticed prospective clients. As they ate their meal, they soon were deep into their planning, considering various methods and options. Using their utensils and condiments as visual aids, they arraigned them on the table, but no matter what configuration they came up with, nothing seemed promising. It was looking more and more that the only option available was to simply walk in and try to take over Ethylrelda as quickly as possible—a prospect Kay did not relish in the least.

After some time had passed, the door to the pub opened, and twenty Spectres came in. They spread out, occupying strategic locations all over the pub as people quieted down. Some people Wafted away in a blast, apparently wanting to avoid them.

Three of them slowly approached their table and, with a bit of theatricality, pulled out chairs and sat down.

They sat staring at each other in silence. They must know, Kay thought; they must know that he was a Shadow tech male.

"I wonder," one of the Spectres said after a long silence, "if you really think you're going to be walking out of here with that weapon."

Kay looked down. "My weapon?"

"Yes, that fine gun you carry. Looks rather valuable."

Before Kay could respond, Sarah chimed in. "Listen, Spectre, why don't you go home before you get hurt."

The Spectre smiled and pulled its hood back, revealing an attractive, blonde-headed woman. "We are not street urchins, like the wretched Milbrats you faced earlier—we are of the Drune. We are the elite Spectre order of Waam. Now, give us your gun, or none of you will walk out of here. We'll not ask again." She pulled her hood back down.

Kay was burning to give this Spectre a taste of his CARG, but he couldn't create too much of a scene. Questions might be asked. His status might be uncovered.

One of the other Spectres rustled. "Yes," he said in a sniveling voice, "and give us your money while you're at it, as well." The Spectre reached into his robes and pulled out a small prism. "Let's see what you got on you."

Just then, the door to the pub opened admitting the sounds of the street and the pinkish light of early sunset. The bells were ringing—thirty bells. Ten smiling women dressed in green and brown leather armor casually walked in. Many people, upon seeing them, groaned. Kay recognized two of them as the ladies in green gowns passing out parchments on the street earlier. Now they appeared like they were dressed for action, though they still smiled pleasantly.

Their leader walked in a moment later. She was dressed the same way as the rest, except she wore a visored leather helmet, her long green hair spilling out of a hole in the back. Her presence was commanding.

"Good evening, friends," the lead woman said in a lilting voice. She carried herself in a regal fashion. She was fit and well-formed with a slim torso, perfect hips, long legs and fairly broad shoulders. Her eyes were large and dark brown and glinted with a thoughtful light. A very attractive woman. "I trust everyone has enjoyed themselves tonight. However, I see that it is thirty bells, the sun will soon be down, and you've your wives and families to return to. I am afraid the pub will be closing shortly, and I advise all in attendance to head home in peace. Now."

She noted all of the Spectres present. "That includes you, Spectres, or shall we have a repeat of last week?" A few Spectres walked out obediently.

The barkeep threw his rag down in frustration. "Xaphan's Beard, Thomasina! This is a lawful establishment, and all my customers have conducted themselves in an orderly fashion—even the dammed

Spectres. The most notorious rabble-rouser I've had to contend with lately is you!"

Thomasina laughed and approached the bar. "Thirty bells, Ruben, you know that. And this . . . rotgut . . . that you serve in flowing quantity has yet to take its full effect. So, while things are still above board, while the minds of your patrons are still clear, why not end the evening on a positive note?"

A sportsman sitting at a game with a few Xaphan sailors was unimpressed and called for more booze. "Woman, the evening is young, there is mutton still to eat, ale yet to be quaffed and fools' pockets still to empty. I am going nowhere."

The woman in green armor looked at the man and smiled. Suddenly, a large wooden club, carved with glyphs, sat in her hand. All of the armored women in her entourage likewise produced clubs. MT CALMs, every one of them.

She approached the sportsman and gave his glass of strong spirits a tap with her club.

"If you spill my drink, I'll take it out of your hide!" the sportsman said. He picked up the glass and tossed it back.

His eyes bugged out of his head, and he spat out the liquid in a surprised spray.

"Water!" he cried in dismay.

"Indeed," the woman said laying the end of her club gently on the tabletop. "As I have said, this pub is closed. I'll not say it again, lest you'd like to walk home with your teeth in a bag."

Enraged, the sportsman pulled a small Laserlock energy gun from his coat. Moving like a green cat, the woman whacked the gun out of his hand with a blow from her club. She followed it up with a quick bonk to the forehead which seemed to utterly drain the sportsman of all his hostility. He oozed back into his seat, a contented grin on his stubbly face. The green-haired woman then, with strength belying her slender size, picked him up over her head, took a few steps and threw him out the door.

She turned to the other tables. "Again, and for the final time, myself and my Singing Ten bid you return to your homes lest you be chaperoned out in a similar fashion to that gentleman there! That goes for you, too, Spectres. Out!"

Resigned, the pub filled with the sounds of shuffling chairs and moving feet as the patrons began to empty—some Spectres mixed in with the rest. Appeased, the green armored women sang an Elder hymn and even passed out religious holo literature to the pub patrons as they exited.

As Kay and the rest watched, they noted in a bit of amazement as the rather simple-looking people exited the pub. Most walked out via the door while others casually walked up the side of the wall and went out a window.

A few even seemed to take flight and soar out the windows.

The leader, whom the barkeep had called, Thomasina", chatted with various patrons as they made their way out. Once or twice she got a small money bag out of a pouch in her armor and handed out several coins.

Like a mother hen overseeing her roost, she approached Kay's table and noticed nobody sitting there was in the process of taking their leave. She gave them a good hard look. "I told you to leave, Spectre," she said to the leader.

"We have business with these four that does not concern you," the lead Spectre said.

The other one holding the prism lifted it up and gazed through it. He stood up suddenly and was shocked. "Great Marilith!! Invernan!!—this one's a Shadow tech male!"

All eyes in the pub turned to Kay.

The Spectres looked at Kay, shocked for a moment, then they picked up their weapons and made to attack. "Kill this one!" the Spectre shouted. "Invernan! Gaaa!!!"

Some of the Spectres sprang to action. They vanished in a puff—all Cloaking themselves into invisibility.

The lead Cloaked Spectre attacked, and Kay unsaddled his CARG and let his Sight go. The pub interior went to the now familiar amber tint, and he could plainly see the Spectre standing there in front of him.

"Stand still and lift your chin!" she commanded with the Dirge.

Lon's Dirge Defeater squelched the sound of her Dirge and quickly he crossed her duel rapiers, which were headed for his throat. Sarah and Phillip lit their Sight and formed their SAPPs into long broadswords.

"Drunes!" Thomasina yelled. "Drunes!! Protect the people!!"

Cloaked Spectres attacked in earnest, some running with speed, some flying.

The armored ladies formed a defensive position, trying to protect the remaining patrons from Spectres that they couldn't see. They swung their clubs in precise, well-trained strokes, hoping to score hits. They seemed quite adept at combating Cloaked opponents, and several Spectres fell out of Cloak with a sigh.

One of the green ladies went down, slashed in the mid-section after a Spectre Wafted to her left.

As Kay battled the Spectre, his Sight wandered away into the near future. He saw her Wafting to his right and burying her rapiers into his neck. He Wafted to counter hers, and they got into a protracted Wafting duel, blowing Sarah's, Lon's, and several patrons' hats off. Two more Spectres Wafted in to overwhelm Kay—the four of them Wafting this way and that in a near continual blast.

He Sighted a flying Spectre swooping in for the kill. Sarah, Sight lit, cleaved him in two with her SAPP.

The remaining Spectres, in a sudden killing frenzy, began attacking anything in range.

Ruben, the pub-keep, cried out and went down, holding his bleeding arm. Thomasina jumped to his side, defending him with her club. As Kay went round and round with his three Wafting Spectres, he Sighted another Spectre Wafting in front of Thomasina, getting through her defenses and killing her.

"Phillip, Sarah, defend at the bar—quickly!" he shouted. "Lon, get under the table!"

Phillip and Sarah ran in that direction, but Sarah got intercepted along the way by a Spectre. In too close to get a good swing with her SAPP, she dropped it and engaged the Spectre hand to hand, the two rolling on the floor.

Phillip ran to Thomasina's side, his Sight lit in a silver stream. He engaged as the invisible Spectre Wafted in, using his SAPP in short, economical strokes. Soon, he had the Spectre down. More came in, the battle raging, Thomasina now anticipating Phillip's movements and lending her MT CALM into the action.

Sarah picked up her battered Spectre and threw him, literally, out the door.

Kay was very worried about poor Lon. He tried to keep an eye on him even as he soared about the pub with his Wafting Spectres in close pursuit. He'd sworn to Lady Branna he'd protect Lon.

Perhaps he needn't have worried. Lon stood, jumped on the table, and put on an odd set of goggles, adding a quick adjustment to the lenses. He then drew his CEROS from the depths of his coat—it looked like an ornate dinner plate. With Cloaked Spectres bounding, leaping and swooping in on him, he raised the CEROS to show it to them as was tradition; then, he loosed it, the hinged silver weapon howling through the air. He took down a flying Spectre, caught the weapon and then gutted another one. He assisted one of the armored ladies who had been taken off her feet, and downed another one on the return stroke. Kay was impressed. Lon might have been a shy and unassuming fellow most of the time, but his mastery of the CEROS was clear. With his CEROS, he stood tall, and was calm and dispassionate, picking his targets with care, using his weapon with lethal efficiency.

Elsewhere, Kay was a tornado of movement, Wafting across the floor, then up into the rafters, then down behind the bar, the three Spectres attempting to Waft with him. He could end this windy confrontation now and slay all three at a whim, but, as usual, his Sight wandered off into the future, and the things he saw gave him pause.

He glanced at Phillip and Thomasina fighting side by side near the bar, and he saw the future.

He saw Phillip and this green-haired Xaphan woman far away in time. He saw them in each other's arms. He saw them carving their initials on a tree in the Grove: P + R (R?? Kay didn't quite understand that). He saw the woman flying over the tree-lined horizon of the Telmus Grove and Phillip sitting on a blanket watching and clapping. He saw marriage and children. He saw Phillip happier than he'd ever seen him and the woman, this Thomasina, yet another odd but worthy addition to the collection of ladies from strange places having married into the House of Blanchefort. He thought he saw a few vague images of conflict along the way, but he didn't focus on those; he just looked at the end result: Phillip and Thomasina happy, he and his Xaphan bride, meant for each other.

And it all depended on what Kay did right at this moment. If Kay stayed in the heights and killed his three Spectres, that future would vanish, and Phillip and Thomasina would not be together. Both would be much less happy, the future much less bright, the two of them having, unknowingly, settled for somebody else. Kay saw Phillip as a dreary man in a dreary future, his potential not met. He saw Thomasina as bitter and fat, growing jaded in her long, lonely life as a Xaphan Matriarch. Without each other, both of their individual potentials were to be stunted fast and un-grown. Regarding a person's potential, Kay's mother was fond of saying that the mind sets the stage, and the soul provides the raw material, but it's the heart that truly inspires one to be his or her best, to meet his or her potential—and Phillip's heart, unmotivated, uninspired, unchallenged would fail him without this Xaphan woman at his side.

If he instead spared the Spectres and Wafted down to the bar right now, then Phillip, his cousin, his best friend, could have what, ultimately, everybody wants—a happy ending.

He thought about it for a quick moment as he only had a second to decide Phillip's fate, and then he Wafted down. *Here you go Phillip—my gift to you. Enjoy it.*

Kay appeared in a blast by the bar, the three Spectres appearing a moment after. He took a step back and tripped on a spittoon. He knew it was there but decided to play this out to the fullest. This was Phillip's moment.

✳ ✳ ✳ ✳ ✳

A cyclone of wind hit Thomasina square in the chest and blew her off her feet. She fell against the bar and hit her head.

The confused room spun a little. She saw the pub in a flurry of movement. She saw her Singing Ten fighting a desperate battle with a bunch of Cloaked, Wafting Drune Spectres. They often didn't see Drunes in this part of the city; Drunes were dangerous. She saw a small, pot-bellied boy in a long coat and goggles standing on a table with a strange weapon which he cast, slaying a number of Spectres in an impressive fashion. She saw a blue-haired girl wearing a black coat in a berserker-rage, fighting several Spectres hand-to-hand.

The fellow with purple hair and holding a silver, pipe-like weapon of some kind appeared nearby in a fast Waft and stumbled to the floor, tripping over Ruben's prize spittoon—legend tells that Princess Marilith of Xandarr, hero of heroes, once spit into that spittoon, and it became Ruben's treasure.

Him, the purple fellow—the Spectres said he was a Shadow tech male—and, if that's the case, then he is a dead man. The Spectres will come for his bones. She shouldn't get involved, for she had to think of her people.

And she saw the fellow in a black coat, which she'd briefly teamed up with, standing tall against the wind. The long split tails of his coat flapping in the breeze of the Waft, holding his black sword. He glanced back at her, his eyes glowing with a silvery light.

Glowing eyes. Elders teach that people with glowing eyes are favored, can see all that is hidden. She had never seen the Gift of glowing eyes—she didn't believe it really existed. But look, look at his eyes. What had Auld brought her today?

His soul . . . she could see his soul there in his light, all his thoughts and dreams laid out on a hint of silver tableau.

Here is a good man from far away, an honest man. A strong man, one strong enough to stand at her side. She saw herself planning elaborate schemes and complicated kidnappings—all intended to make this man with glowing eyes chase her and go to places she wanted him to go; always she was the prize, waiting at the end of the adventure with open arms. She felt an instant connection with him, a oneness—the two of them now linked via the silver causeway of his glowing eyes. *Auld wants this*, she thought; *the Elders have made this possible.*

Auld has brought this man to her.

He looked away and began fighting people she couldn't see. He could see them plain and true with his glowing eyes.

He skillfully swung his sword, and a Drune Spectre appeared on the floor, dead. He exchanged positions, moved his weapon a few more times, and another Drune appeared, bleeding, slain.

Clean fighting technique, short, fuss-free strokes. She approved.

And another, fallen, dead. He picked up the purple Shadow tech male, and they stood there together. She could feel the kinship between them, the closeness. She felt a hint of jealousy—she wished a kinship with him, too.

The berserker girl with blue hair arrived at their side. Who was she? What was her relationship to this man with silver eyes? She felt her stomach constricting.

She groaned rather theatrically, and the man with glowing eyes turned and helped her up.

✳ ✳ ✳ ✳ ✳

Lon saw a Spectre ready to kill a green woman. The CEROS howled, and the Spectre fell. Lon then put his weapon down and pulled a small prism from his coat. He set it on the table and turned it on. It cast a thin, pinkish light that feebly lit the pub. Drawing his PITCOCK WONDER GUN, he spun the cartridges, aimed at the rafters and fired with a booming report.

The capsule went up a bit and then exploded, filling the pub and rafters above with a fine red powder.

Suddenly all the Cloaked Spectres lit up like cats under a street light. Thomasina's group gave a battle cry and engaged the now plainly visible Drune Spectres, and they fell wholesale; the ladies" skill with their MT CALMs was clear. The MT CALM was a weapon noted for its ability to drain the fight out of anybody it hit and for its miraculous tendency to transform spirits and beers into plain water, a handy tool for the determined pub-rouster and prohibitionist. It was said to be made from the heart of a secret type of tree and was lathed with a supposedly enchanted set of gouges. One hit was all the ladies needed, and the Spectres dropped in a contented pile.

Soon, order was restored, and the city police came charging in. They spoke a few words to Thomasina and began pulling the Spectres out into the street.

Thomasina went to Ruben. He was wounded. She called for one of her ladies to fetch a local Cabalist to mend his wound. She then mounted her club in a brace at her back, approached Kay and grabbed him by the scruff of the neck. "My Ten," she said, "restore order here. I will deal with this lot myself."

She whispered into Kay's ear. *"If you value your skin, do nothing, say nothing, and come with me."*

Several of Thomasina's guard came and surrounded the four of them. Scanning, the Singing Ten reached out to disarm them. Sarah, still all pepped up from the fight, took exception. "Hey!" she cried.

"It's all right, Sarah," Kay said calmly and handed over his weapons.

Disarmed, Thomasina led the four of them out into the street. "They'll fetch a fair price, eh?"

There, waiting by the curbside, was a large open-air coach— green and brown and gaudy, just like their armor. It was similar to the one they'd seen earlier driven by cables trailing up into the vast sky. Thomasina threw them in, and the coach went up into the air. The coach moved smoothly with a great deal of silent acceleration up into the night, pinning them back into their seats a bit. They went up and over the tall, flat-topped buildings, covering a number of city blocks in just a few moments, and then began a quick descent into a large wooded compound below. There were at least twenty good-sized buildings situated within the compound and a central manor hall. Several of the buildings on the grounds were quite tall, rivaling the neighboring buildings in height. All of the buildings had a greenish tint to them. Between the buildings were nicely landscaped grounds including ponds, tree-lined paths and innumerable shrines to the Elders.

They were set down on the pebbled drive before a large manor built of serpentine and sandstone. They got out of the coach and were ushered in.

Green appeared to be the featured color, and it was everywhere, in the marbled floor, in the polished walls, in the jeweled ceiling. She led them into a large study plush with inviting couches, again mostly green. She removed her MT CALM and set it aside. She then pulled her tall brown boots off and put them in a corner. She flexed her tired feet and removed her helmet, allowing her long, green hair to come flowing out.

"Sit and be comfortable," she said. "Remove your shoes if you like. I'm sorry about pulling you out of Ruben's pub in such a fashion, but it wasn't safe. The Spectre announced that you are a Shadow tech male, and that is a very dangerous thing to be in this city with so many Black Hats around. The Spectres that grovel at their feet have standing orders to kill Shadow tech males upon discovery. They, even now, are most likely gathering their forces. Some of those were Drunes in the pub—quite a high-level order—very powerful, much more so than your average street-prowling Spectre. We don't see them very often here in Auld. No doubt they'll be arriving here in short order, demanding that I turn you over to them."

"With all due respect, ma'am," Phillip said. "We are not helpless—not against them or you."

Thomasina turned her gaze to Phillip and studied him with her huge brown eyes. She looked at him for a bit, apparently distracted, then continued. "I've no doubt, sir. It appears that we have not yet had time for formal introductions. I am Thomasina the 19th. I rule over this district, I sit on the municipal parliament, and I am also the local magistrate. It is a duty I take very seriously."

A servant entered the study and spoke a few words to Thomasina. "Refreshments for me and my guests," she ordered, and the servant left.

"It appears things are happening quickly beyond the compound walls, as I previously mentioned. Spectres from multiple orders will be here soon."

"Our business here in Waam need not concern you, Great Lady," Kay said. "We shall take our leave and spare you such an inconvenience."

"Is that a fact, Shadow tech male?" Thomasina asked with a rather unpleasant tone. "You fought rather well in the pub, but you would be four against thousands, and, should you somehow manage to put up a good fight, the Black Hats themselves would become involved, and nobody wants to see that. Black Hats roaming the streets is never any good for anybody. I suppose that honesty is your best course at the moment, as I can either be a great friend to you, or a terrible enemy, make no mistake, sir, and I like truth-telling. We can start with your names. I have already given you mine."

She pointed at Phillip. "You first."

Phillip looked around, clearly unused to being addressed ahead of Kay, who, in the family chain, out-ranked him. "My name is Lord Phillip of Blanchefort. And these are . . ."

Thomasina interrupted him. "I'm sorry . . . Blanchefort did you say? As in the League House of Blanchefort of Kana? As in the House of Captain Davage, the scourge of Princess Marilith?" She sat back and was rather annoyed. "I said that I wished for an honest discourse, and you set off with an outlandish lie. That does not bode well for us here right now, does it? If you didn't have such a handsome face, '*Phillip,*' I'd turn you out into the streets, let the Spectres have you."

Phillip continued. "It's not a lie."

"Oh?" Thomasina got into Phillip's face. As all noted, she didn't get up and walk around the desk; she *flew* over it, hovering in the air. She stared intently into his eyes, her feet not touching the ground. She seemed to be making a show, displaying her abilities for him to appreciate up close.

"I have a talent for discriminating truth from lie," she said. "Go ahead, *Phillip*, tell me again—to my face."

Phillip appeared quite bashful and looked to the floor. "I am Phillip of Blanchefort and . . ."

"Look me in the eye, please," she said interrupting.

Phillip looked up and locked eyes with Thomasina as she invaded his space, floating on air. He continued. "I am not lying. Captain Davage is my uncle. My companion here is Lord Kabyl of Blanchefort, his eldest son. He carries the CARG, though, of course, we have been disarmed."

Thomasina sighed. "You have the most remarkable hazel eyes, sir. Surely you've been told that before. Now, tell me, what is a CARG?"

"It's the LosCapricos weapon of House Blanchefort. It's a tube-like weapon with a hilt, rather like a sword."

Thomasina released Phillip from her gaze and returned to her desk, flying over it and settling back down. There, she pressed a button and sat back. "Just a moment, please," she said.

They all stood in silence. Thomasina's gaze was like a vise, and Phillip withered a bit in it.

Seconds worth of silence felt like hours. Phillip spoke, trying to break the tension. "Do all people fly in Waam?"

Thomasina seemed pleased and eager to talk. "No, not all. My father was a man of Bondar, where people fly. Can you fly, Phillip?"

"No, ma'am."

"And I can't make my eyes glow, so it's a trade-off."

An armored woman came in holding a large basket full of their weapons. The tubular shaft of Kay's CARG stuck out like a gangly lamp post. She set the basket down on the table and turned to leave. She stopped and went before Lon, where she curtsied. She then left the room.

Thomasina inspected the contents of the basket. "She offers her thanks," she said absently to Lon. "For assisting her in the pub. Now then . . ." She pulled Kay's CARG out of the basket and looked at it. "Is this it? Is this the CARG you mentioned?"

"Yes, my lady."

She carefully looked the CARG over, turning it about, examining it in detail. She noted with her fingers its smooth, tube-like shaft.

"Its balance is superb," she said balancing it on her fingertip. "It's nice and light, too." She saw the name etched into the shaft. "What's SAMMIDORAN?"

"'Sammidoran' is the name of Lord Kay's girlfriend," Sarah answered, having been unusually quiet through all of this so far.

"How quaint," Thomasina said giving Sarah a quick glance. She turned to a terminal on her desk and punched a few buttons—her large brown eyes going back and forth from the screen to the CARG and back again. After a moment she seemed satisfied. "It certainly looks like a CARG, but maybe you killed somebody for it. Maybe 'Sammidoran' is somebody else's girlfriend."

Kay got out his purse and flipped a Blanchefort coin to her, which she caught out of the air. She looked at it and flipped it back to him. "Again, you could have taken the fellow's purse as well." She glanced at Phillip. "You don't seem like a murderer to me, Lord Phillip—no murderer has eyes like that. I'll assume for the time being that you do not frequent company with the like as well. It seems we have esteemed visitors in Waam today." Again she turned to Phillip. "Where is your CARG, sir?" she asked looking into the basket. "The long black one I saw you fighting with in the pub? I don't see it in here."

"I am still training with the CARG. I prefer the SAPP. I was using a SAPP in the pub."

"The SAPP? What is a SAPP? I am not familiar with that weapon."

Phillip approached the basket and took out his SAPP—it looked like nothing more than a long, black scarf.

She seemed puzzled. "What is this?"

"It's the SAPP, Great Lady," Phillip said handing it to her. "It is the LosCapricos weapon of House Ruthven—my father's House. House Ruthven serves in fealty to another; therefore, we took the name of Blanchefort as is tradition—our mother is Captain Davage's sister, Lady Poe of Blanchefort. The SAPP is a type of cloth woven in secret and loomed using rare materials. It will bend to its user's will, shaping itself into virtually anything."

Thomasina examined the cloth, then handed it back to Phillip. "Really? Let's see. Make it do something."

Phillip took the SAPP, made sure he had plenty of room, then brought it to life. It twisted about for a moment like a snake, and then hardened into the form of a black sword. Thomasina smiled and clapped. "Yes, excellent! I've read about all of the various weapons the Great Houses of the League use, but I've only seen a few until now. I'm very impressed, Lord Phillip."

She handed Kay his CARG and began taking all of their weapons out of the basket, laying them out on the desktop. She gave a soft whistle when she looked at the Poltavas, at their beauty and craftsmanship. "These are works of art," she remarked.

She picked up Sarah's blue one. "Whose is this?" she asked. "That's mine," Sarah responded. "And that SAPP over there is also mine."

Thomasina smiled and gave it to her, butt first. She also gave Sarah back her SAPP. Thomasina then picked up Kay's purple one. "I'll wager this one is yours, sir," she said smiling to Kay. He nodded, and she handed it to him. He could tell by the weight that it was unloaded.

Her eyes bugged out as she looked at Lon's PITCOCK WONDER GUN. She picked it up, pointing the barrel at the ceiling. "Who belongs to this, please?"

"Yes, that's mine, Great Lady," Lon stammered. She winked at him and gave it back, its chambers empty. "Oh, and the CEROS there—that's mine, too," Lon added.

Thomasina whirled around and looked. "This?" she asked seeing the round, silver CEROS. "I thought it was a supper plate."

"No, Great Lady, no." She tossed it to him.

Thomasina then picked up Phillip's Poltava and held it. She noted its green and brown coloration—which matched her armor almost perfectly. She burst into a smile. "And, could it be that this belongs to you, Phillip? I'm sorry. May I call you Phillip?"

"Of course."

"I must say I like the colors. Green and brown. Very interesting."

"An odd coincidence," Phillip remarked.

"There are no such things. I think Auld has spoken to us," Thomasina replied. "You know what is said: 'One cannot go against the wishes of the gods.'"

"Yes, I—"

She held the Poltava up. "Go ahead, Phillip, take it. I give it back to you."

Phillip reached out, and Thomasina moved her hands. He moved his hand, and again she moved hers—their hands moving in a crazy zigzag pattern. Finally, she put his gun behind her back and pushed out her bosom. "Well, come on, Phillip. Take your gun." She stood there and looked at him invitingly, lips parted.

The servant returned with a tray of goblets full of rich, cherry-red liquid. Thomasina turned to address her, and Phillip quickly snatched his Poltava. She sighed.

"Ah," Thomasina said, "thank you, Garland." She picked up two goblets. "I've given you back your weapons as a demonstration of good faith—your ammunition will also be returned later, once we've established a few things. I'm not afraid of your swords, for I can handle myself against those, should you choose to raise them." She offered a goblet to Phillip. "Please, Phillip, try this. I'm certain you'll love it as much as I do."

She paused and looked around the room. "And so, I now know who you are, Lord Phillip, and who he is," she said pointing to Kay, "so who else do we have here? Is this attractive lady with the lovely blue gun your wife, perhaps?" she asked referring to Sarah.

"No, no, Great Lady. This is my twin sister, Lady Sarah of Blanchefort, and this fellow is Lord Lon of the House of Probert." Lon doffed his hat.

"Sister, ah, good, good." Thomasina smiled at Lon. "I was

greatly impressed with your skill, sir, and at your defeating the Spectre's Cloak in the pub. Very handy." She thought a moment. "Probert, Probert, why does that name sound familiar?"

"My father is the lead engineer for the Stellar Fleet, my lady."

"I see, so he designed those pretty vessels that constantly defeat our ships in space?"

Lon deflated a little, forgetting that he was speaking to a Xaphan. "I suppose so."

She laughed. "No need to feel bashful—I'm no great Xaphan patriot. My soul belongs to the Elders." Thomasina turned back to Phillip. "I am pleased to have met you all. Please relax and enjoy your drinks. I am not going to throw you out. You are safe here."

The drink was sweet and cold, clearly a fruit concoction. "Great Lady," Kay addressed her holding his glass. "If I may ask, are you perhaps, of the House of Woolover?"

She set her glass down. "Aye, we were once called by that name. I was born in the great helix floating above. It, the grounds and this very house has been in my family for centuries. I have never been away from Waam. I am rarely far from this sector of the city except when I go to Parliament. I am a Waamite, a Gothan and, by proximity, a Xaphan as well. I suppose, in the purest sense, that I am your enemy—geographically and politically speaking. However, I follow the teachings of the Elders, as I am sure that you do. My family has its ancient roots near Saga, in the Barrowlands of Kana— not too terribly far from Blanchefort if my geographical knowledge of Kana is accurate. So I suppose, in some regards, that we are neighbors, and that makes us friends."

Sarah put down her glass. "Then, how did you end up here, in Waam?"

"The House of Woolover has always been a high-minded and pious one. We have always closely followed the ways of the Elders and preached their tenets: sobriety, moderation, prohibition and self-sacrifice. During the Great Betrayal, under the leadership of Thomasina the 5th, we determined to put our preaching to the test. A fragment of the House followed the rebellious Vith Houses to the Xaphans. There, spread out in Xaphan space, we fought to bring news and the word of the Elders to these poor sinners, to demand moderation and enforce prohibition. We sacrificed ourselves—and have been here ever since. Even as the Xaphan influence faded, word of the Elders remained. We have done our duty. Please, don't misunderstand—I am not some abandoned soul longing for our ancient homeland. I am proud to be a Waamite. We are good people even though some of us might choose to sail and fight the League. We are an honest, simple folk trying to provide for our families."

She took a drink, then: "Tell me, Lord Phillip, do you attend regular services back home?" She seemed truly fascinated with Phillip and didn't appear to care much about any of the others there.

Phillip, who Kay knew couldn't remember the last time he'd set foot in church, blushed. "Err, no, my Lady, to my regret."

Thomasina leaned forward. "And are you a womanizer, sir? A drinker and slacker of duty?"

"No, my lady."

She smiled. "Then perhaps there is hope for you." She stood up, went around the desk and sat down next to him. She lifted her hand. "It is customary in Waam, when addressing a lady, to take her hand."

Phillip swallowed. "Lord Kabyl out-ranks me, my lady."

"Does he?" she said, not moving her hand. "Do his eyes glow, too?"

"No, but . . ."

Thomasina sat there holding out her hand. Phillip looked to Kay and finally took it.

Kay chuckled to himself. Having seen the future—the path he'd chosen for Phillip and Thomasina was already making itself felt in a small way. *You're going to thank me for this later, Phillip.*

Thomasina brightened. "So, what are you four doing here in Waam? Certainly, it wasn't simply to see me."

Kay stood and answered. He told her what they were up to—about Ethylrelda the Black Hat. It took quite a while actually, with Thomasina stopping him to ask several questions.

"So," she said. "You are here to save your woman, your 'Sammidoran' whose name is etched on your weapon, are you? How romantic."

"Yes," Kay said. "I offer my thanks for this respite."

Thomasina gave Phillip a sweltering stare. "You have quested in search of a lady, and you have found one. Do the Elders not work in wondrous ways?"

Phillip gulped.

"Do the ladies fly on Kana, Phillip?"

"Not without a coach, Great Lady."

"Please call me Thomasina."

Kay allowed his Sight to wander. Beyond the manor, he could see a contingent of Spectres headed their way, escorted by several armored females. "Spectres approach," he said.

Thomasina let Phillip go and returned to her desk. "I wondered what was taking them so long. Please, be seated. Now, before the Spectres arrive, let us be blunt. I could do one of two things—I could give you to them, where I'm certain a bloody battle would shortly ensue here in my home. And I've no doubt that you four could hold your own against an army of Spectres. Or I could shelter you, and nobody will be hurt. Then, at a suitable time, I could assist you in breaching Ethylrelda's temple and retrieving the item that you require. I personally have been in her temple many times assisting wayward souls whom she had ensnared."

"You'd help us?"

"Yes, I would—that is what the Elders teach, is it not? I have a price, however, one that I insist be paid."

"And that is?" Kay asked.

"We have church services here every morning at four bells. I insist that one of your party attend with me. It won't be bad, I promise. There will be joy and singing, and perhaps you will find inspiration. Perhaps you will find your faith renewed. What say you?"

They looked around at each other. Kay knew exactly who she wanted sitting in church with her. He hadn't considered the ramifications of what he did in the pub, now that this Thomasina the 19th appeared to be well on her way to falling in love with Phillip, and he didn't think she was going to be a passive participant in all of this. Something happened in that short moment when he descended to the pub floor with the three Spectres in pursuit—something profound. Maybe Thomasina was impressed by the way Phillip fought. Obviously she noticed him in a big way. In any event, Thomasina appeared to be walking happily down the path Kay had selected for her, so he only had himself to blame for any complications that may come, for he hadn't bothered to investigate those.

It'll be worth it—the complete man he saw Phillip become is worth it.

Suddenly, this was all the more complicated, but he vowed not to regret his decision.

Finally, Kay spoke, already knowing her response: "I will join you."

Thomasina didn't react. Kay felt a bit awkward. "Sarah, would you like to attend services in the morning?"

Sarah looked truly terrified and, again, Thomasina didn't react.

Phillip winced. "You said four bells?"

Thomasina nodded. "Yes, Lord Phillip, four bells."

"And it concludes at five bells, correct?"

"Incorrect, it concludes at eight bells. May I expect you, sir?"

Phillip looked like he was about to be eaten by a lion. Outside, Kay could see the contingent of Spectres approaching—they were just down the hall.

"Yes, Phillip will be honored," Kay said.

Thomasina's face blossomed into a smile. "I will look forward to the service tomorrow. I've never been to church with such a handsome man at my side."

Just then the doors to the study opened, and four Spectres came in, black-robed and hooded. They spotted Kay's group and pointed. "You are harboring a fugitive, Thomasina the 19th!" one of them rasped.

Thomasina turned to them. "Come now. Where are you manners? Announce yourselves, please."

The Spectres shrugged in a frustrated fashion. "I am Morge of the Drune. On behalf of the terrible Ruthinkiln of Waam, slayer of worlds and eater of children, we demand the living personage or dead body of the Invernan standing before us. You will give him up, or you shall die."

Another Spectre stepped forward. "I am Jessug of the Harms. I speak for the mighty Jennamaxx of Waam, douser of light and cracker of bones. She demands this Invernan be brought before her immediately, naked and shackled, where his body will be dismembered and his flesh cooked and consumed at her leisure. His genitals shall be the first to be consumed."

Thomasina winced. "Oh my," she said.

A third Spectre came forward. "I am Dez-Mortimer of the Gogan. My mistress, the fiendish and treacherous Wilhella Cormand-Grande of Waam, Queen of shit, Ruler of shit and Eater of shit, bids you go fuck yourselves and . . ."

"Watch your language, please, Gogan," Thomasina responded in a commanding tone.

Reproached, he continued. "The Mad Black Hat, Wilhella Cormand-Grande, demands the immediate and corporeal banishment of this Invernan." He drew a smelly, dirty-looking sword. "With this sword, which, for ninety moons has sat in the anal tract of the sacred Malulah beast, I am commanded to perform the action at once. He will then be burned, shat upon and then made into a statue to sit forever in the throne area of Wilhella Cormand-Grande's temple."

Thomasina rolled her eyes.

And finally, the last Spectre came forward. He stood there, quiet.

Thomasina stirred. "Well, sir, get on with it. Let's hear what you have to say."

The Spectre appeared shy and solemn—a very different attitude from the other Spectres. "I am Krotan of the Yard," he said. "I am compelled to offer greetings to the Invernan on behalf of my mistress, Ethylrelda of Waam."

Ethylrelda? Kay's ears pricked up, and he listened.

Krotan seemed bewildered by his own oratory. He continued: "Ethylrelda of Waam wishes it known that she has lived long in the service of the Black Abbess; may Her Darkness be troubled not by the Light of Dawn."

The three other Spectres mumbled something in response. Krotan of the Yard continued. "For centuries, Ethylrelda of Waam has fought the Sisterhood, killed the Sisterhood, fought the League and laid terror on the people of Waam. She has inspired nightmares and created incalculable suffering. My mistress is ancient and tired and has earned her reward—a reward she is eager to embrace. My mistress bids you welcome, Invernan, and she offers you safe passage to her temple on the sword of the Yard. We will conduct you there at speed. My mistress wishes to be one with you Invernan—it is her right."

The other Spectres were outraged.

Thomasina was shocked.

Kay was shocked.

"To *Wandwilla* is a blasphemy!" Morge shouted, drawing his swords.

Krotan drew his. "The Yard will kill any, be they Spectre, Black Hat, or unsuspecting fool, who tries to stop us! Ethylrelda of Waam will have her reward, and the Yard will deliver it to her!"

Thomasina, as if by magic, produced her MT CALM and

separated them. "As always, gentlemen, there will be no killing in my home," she said. "If you wish to kill, you may go out to the street and kill, where I and my Singing Ten will then arrest you for murder. So, is this all? I expected more."

"There are more!" Morge shouted with bile. "There are many more fools from this Order and that clamoring in the streets with claims to the Invernan, but, no matter. Their voices are weak and irrelevant, and the Drune laugh at them. The Invernan will die before the hideous gaze of Ruthinkiln of Waam!"

"Fuck that!" Dez-Mortimer yelled drawing his swords. "The Invernan's fate will be to become statuary in the shit-clogged presence of Wilhella Cormand-Grande, the Mad Black Hat of Waam!"

"No!" Jessug yelled drawing his swords. "The Invernan will be consumed by Jennamaxx of Waam, marrow-sucker and harlot-supreme!"

Krotan put his swords away. "The Invernan will *Wandwilla* with Ethylrelda," Krotan said quietly. He drew from his robes a black Shadow tech rose. "Which of you gentlemen is the Invernan? My mistress has a gift for him."

Thomasina sat back and smiled. "Don't you know which one it is? There are three gentlemen here to choose from."

"That fucking information has not been made plain. I will identify the prick," Dez-Mortimer said putting his swords away. He reached into his robes and pulled out a small prism. Before he could raise it up and look through it, Thomasina sprang. In four quick movements, she had the Spectres on the ground, all bonked in the head with her MT CALM. They lay there in contented bliss. She was truly a formidable fighter.

Thomasina thought for a moment, then she knelt down and spoke to the fallen Spectres. "You four will leave when you are able and return to your respective Orders. Then, you will each tell them that I have agreed to hand over the Invernan at twenty bells on the morrow. Oh, and Dez-Mortimer, you will also clean up your potty-mouth at once." She went to the door and motioned for her assistants to enter. They did and picked the Spectres up by the armpits. "Get them outside and separate them." Instantly, they dragged the Spectres off.

Thomasina returned to them. "The MT CALM happens to make

those struck by it very susceptible to suggestion. So, Lord Blanchefort, you will be either captured and killed, captured and eaten, captured, killed, pulverized and made into a statue in the Mad Black Hat's throne room—which isn't a place where I'd want to be—or your will live for eternity in mind-rattling sexual bliss with a four hundred year old Black Hat. Sounds like the forth option is the most pleasant."

Kay looked at the black rose resting on the floor and unsaddled his CARG. "There is a fifth option—we shan't wait for them. We will leave under Cloak and return to our ship. I will then enter the Black Hat's temple, locate the item and be off."

"But, if you do that, Lord Phillip will miss church. Please, you'll be fine for now. The Spectres will spend the rest of the day out on the street arguing amongst themselves. I have a great wealth of experience dealing with Spectres, and believe me when I say they will not be an issue until twenty bells tomorrow. Meanwhile, I have a secret system of tunnels that will take us all the way to the Cathedral of Auld, which is quite close to Ethylrelda's Temple. In the morning, we will simply use the tunnels and be off. I'll tell the Spectres that Lord Phillip here over-powered me and took his leave. By that point, you'll be gone." She winked at Phillip.

"Isn't lying something the Elders preach against?" Phillip asked.

"Why, I don't know. I suppose well find out tomorrow morning in church, won't we?"

✳   ✳   ✳   ✳   ✳

Kay spent a restless night. Thomasina had given him a small room in the uppermost floor of the manor, Sarah, Phillip and Lon in adjacent rooms. Outside, in his amber Sight, he could see a mass of black-robed Spectres surrounding the compound for blocks. As Thomasina said, they seemed to be having a hard time getting along. Kay saw a lot of angry confrontations between various Spectre Orders, and fights, including a few mortal ones, broke out with frequency. But, so far, they remained beyond the walls and didn't try to storm them. Apparently they felt he was safely boxed in. They even had an assortment of concealed rockets and missiles, in case he should try to fly off in a craft of some sort.

And what about Thomasina? He looked around the manor. There she was, in the opposite wing, sitting in her vast bedroom. Though it was early in the morning, she wasn't asleep. She was in her room wearing a robe, several of her Singing Ten milling about her. Some were doing her hair, others her nails—apparently she was already preparing for church with Phillip in a few hours. Several ladies held green gowns for Thomasina's inspection, and she didn't seem to be able to make a choice. They all talked and giggled.

You're welcome, Thomasina.

He got up, dressed and decided to put his new skills to the test. He Cloaked himself and then Wafted through the manor, high into the night sky. He passed a shell of flying Spectres, all looking down into the compound, not seeing him. Floating momentarily on his pillow of air, he could see the vast rectangle of Thomasina's compound with its tall buildings down beneath him and the pepper-grains of Spectres camped all around its perimeter. Beyond, Waam stretched out in a pleasing cityscape of colored, blinking lights and a smattering of honey-shaded clouds. Fairly close by, about five miles away, was the black pearl of Ethylrelda's temple. Though it generated no light of its own, it perfectly reflected the lights of Waam like a crystal ball. With his Sight allowing him to see all around at once, he headed off in the direction of Ethylrelda's temple, fast Wafting, moving through the night like an invisible bird, cushioned on a nest of wind. The temple got closer at speed, and Thomasina's compound faded to the rear. In only a few Wafts, he found the abandoned building with the *Goshawk*. The ship was still Cloaked safe and sound, though he could see through it with his Sight. It was black and bat-like, sitting on its cranked wheels, asleep.

He landed on the roof near the silent *Goshawk's* aft. He felt incredibly free and burdened at the same time. He could get out of this with no problem, but Sarah, Phillip and Lon were trapped; although, if he were gone, the Spectres would leave them alone. It was he that they wanted, not them.

He stood there on the roof and enjoyed the night air and the scenery. Looking back, he could see the distinctive greenish buildings of Auld, including the tall buildings of Thomasina's compound, mixed into the skyline. They looked homey and inviting as his tired, troubled mind began to settle into a sleep-ready mode.

He took a deep breath. What was going to happen here? Though quickly becoming tired, he focused on the temple and let his Sight drift into the numerous paths of the future . . .

Amber.

Kay standing there in the night. Something black coming out of the temple. Kay harpooned with a Shadow tech barb and pulled into the temple fast like a fish on the line.

Wandwilla.

Another vision. *Kay in the temple. Kay lost. A thousand Shadow tech spears pointed at his throat. No place to go. Ethylrelda.*

Wandwilla.

And another: *Kay in the temple. Kay cornered by Shadow tech. Kay seizing it. A battle of wills. Kay victorious. Kay exiting with the piece in hand. Ethylrelda soon following him back to Kana. Castle Blanchefort in flames, mother dead, father dead.*

Wandwilla.

Any way he looked, it was all the same: *Wandwilla, Wandwilla, Wandwilla.* Ethylrelda was too powerful to be denied.

He became so tired, so weary. Milling through the possible futures, he saw one last possibility, once small, but quickly gaining in strength:

Hunted, pursued, running through the streets of Waam. Flying people and cables from the sky.

Krotan.

Krotan of the Yard . . . and . . .

Something entered his mind, and his Sight fell away, pushed aside. *Wait—what was he about to see? It was important.*

Then he heard a voice.

I'm waiting for you, Kay. You needn't fear, I'll not allow you to be harmed. I know why you are here; you seek an item in my temple. You may have it. You may give it to your friends, and they may go in peace. You and I have our eternity to consider. We will Wandwilla, and become a creature of bliss and impassioned dreams. I have earned my reward. I want you, Kay. Let me touch you.

Kay thought he saw a reaching tendril of Shadow tech come snaking out of the temple, though he couldn't be sure.

He saw his vision coming true. Quickly, he Wafted into the air, and soared back to the manor and went to bed in the little room Thomasina had given him.

Safe, for now.

In the morning, Phillip clearly planned to "over sleep" and miss church; however, several of Thomasina's assistants came and got him out of bed. They barged into his room, and, giggling, they made him dress and follow them to the chapel.

Kay got up and dressed. He wasn't sure which fate troubled him the most: to be summarily killed, to be dismembered and eaten alive, to become a statue, or to become one with Ethylrelda. It would be easy to simply give in and become one with her—he still could feel Bethrael all over him—such pleasure. To experience such a thing forever, just imagine.

But, to fail Sam, to never see her again.

Sam, asleep in the protected chest of the metal man.

Sam, running from the demons, for him.

With Sam's face in his thoughts, he fought off the urge to give in, though his options appeared limited. One way or another, Ethylrelda of Waam was going to have her way.

He met up with Sarah—Lon hadn't gotten up yet—and together they explored the grounds. Tall, green buildings were mixed in with squat provincial manors, ornate Elder chapels, dormitories and workshops where MT CALMs were turned on mystical lathes, all bound together with trees, ponds and green, grassy spaces. Singing came from a nearby chapel, and they decided to peek in and see how Philip was doing.

Inside was a cheerful church, not unlike the churches one might find all over Kana, though this one was mostly decorated in green. Sitting inside near the front was Phillip, with Thomasina in a fine green gown to his right. They shared an over-sized song book, Phillip holding the left side, Thomasina the right, with her left hand lightly resting on Phillip's shoulder.

"I've never seen a lady as love-struck as this one. She couldn't take her eyes off him. Did you see that?" Sarah said, astounded. "And, if she's the kind of lady I think she might be, then I can't imagine her just letting him walk out of here."

Kay raised his eyebrows. "What makes you say that?"

"Just look at her. And, not only is she a Xaphan, she's a Woolover, too."

"What's that got to do with anything?"

"Woolovers, Kay—those obnoxious people from Barrow. They tried to get the Duke to impose stricter drinking laws in Esther a few years back. They made a big fuss when he told them to get bent. It's a mostly female House, and either they don't like men, or they don't know how to properly deal with men because they treated the Duke like a piece of garbage. If this Thomasina's got a shine on Phillip, then I think one of the biggest fights we're going to have is with her."

Kay had to agree. He hadn't anticipated this.

"Morning," Lon said emerging from the manor, pulling his coat on.

"Morning, Lon," Sarah said. "Sleep well?"

"I did—fine actually. Where's Phillip?"

"In church still."

"Oh." He thought for a moment. "I wonder what Phillip's going to do when we leave here, poor fellow."

"What do you mean?" Sarah asked.

"Well, clearly, he has an eye for our hostess. Correspondence with Xaphans can be rather difficult, and . . ."

Sarah twitched. "How do you know that, Lon?"

"Body language for one thing, and I happened to see them this morning before they stepped into the church."

"This morning?" Sarah said, shocked.

"Yes, I got up to seek the kitchens—I was hungry. Anyway, I rousted up a hearty leg of mutton and stepped outside to enjoy it. I saw Phillip and Lady Thomasina standing by the lake. They appeared to be sharing a rather private moment."

"The lake?" Sarah cried. "That's pretty far from the manor, right?"

"I was wearing my goggles. Zoomed right in on them."

Goggles? Sarah and Kay looked at each other.

When Phillip got back from church, Thomasina was hanging on his arm, clearly enamored.

Kay was fully ready to leave the premises as soon as possible, but Thomasina was maddeningly nonchalant. She made them sit down to breakfast and then took them on a guided tour of the compound, though the only person she talked to was Phillip.

Finally, with Kay ready to lose a gasket, Thomasina changed into her green armor and, along with ten of her assistants, descended into the bowels of the manor and slithered into the small dark mouth of an abandoned sewer. There, she gave them their ammunition back and watched as they loaded their weapons. With Kay Sighting up through the tunnel roof, he could see the throngs of Spectres sitting outside the compound. They moved east through the tunnels. Kay didn't really need Thomasina, but she followed anyway, as always standing near Phillip.

As they continued, a voice entered Kay's head.

Come to me, and let us be one . . .

He grimaced. "Black Hats cannot detect Shadow tech Males."

They all stopped and looked at him.

"Who are you talking to?" Sarah asked.

I have lived long and learned things untold to other Black Hats. I have known of your presence since you arrived. I can smell you, Kay.

"What about those I travel with?"

If you willingly join with me, I will give them what you came for and ensure their safety. I swear it.

Sarah shook Kay. "Who are you talking to?"

Kay continued. "I cannot—I am committed to another."

I have hope that you shall come to me of your own choosing, that our union will be something we both want; however, do not misunderstand. I will Wandwilla, and, if need be, I will take you if I must, though I would rather not. I bid you welcome, and all that I have is yours. Just remember . . .

Kay forced the voice out of his head. "Ethylrelda. She can sense me somehow. She says she'll give us the piece we need if I give myself to her."

. . . My patience will not last forever . . .

Thomasina smiled. "Well, now, it sounds like you're all set. If you follow this run, it will dead end at the Cathedral of Auld, just like I promised. Just pop out onto the street and you're there. Good luck with Ethylrelda. Now then, Phillip, please come with me."

Phillip looked at her. "What!"

"We just got acquainted, and you have a lovely singing voice. I insist you stay with me for a bit and be my guest. I promise that I'll make it worth your while."

Everybody drew their weapons, Kay, Sarah, Phillip and Lon facing off against Thomasina and her ten armored assistants.

Kay came very close to regretting his decision just then. The future he'd briefly seen was apparently coming true and gaining strength by the second: hunted, pursued—by Thomasina the 19th! Kay took a second to survey the surroundings. They were in a small area of the tunnel with not a lot of room to maneuver or escape. Apparently, Thomasina wanted them in close quarters before announcing that she wished to take Phillip.

The Singing Ten fanned out, covering any possible avenue of escape.

"Phillip can't stay here, Great Lady. He's our pilot. We can't leave without him," Kay said.

"What are you going to do?" Sarah said. "Hit us with your clubs and make us forget that Phillip came with us or something?"

Thomasina raised her MT CALM and crossed Phillip's SAPP. "Good idea, Lady Sarah. And I'm sure you'll muddle through, Lord Blanchefort, without Phillip to fly your ship. Come now, Phillip, I'd hate to have to rap you in the skull and carry you back, but that's what I'll do if I have to. I promise I won't drop you."

"You gave us our ammo back," Sarah demanded. "Why don't we just shoot you where you stand?"

Thomasina reared back and laughed. "Go ahead and shoot me, Sarah. You won't though, will you? You seem to like to talk tough, but you won't shoot me. You know I mean your brother no harm—quite the opposite. I wish to get to know him better is all and show him the wonders of Waam."

Phillip raised his SAPP and showed it to her. "This is all you're going to get to know, lady," he said.

"I enjoyed our kiss this morning, Phillip," she replied. "We can settle this between the two of us, right now, and we needn't involve anyone else. Come on, Phillip—let's fight, you and me, man to woman. You win, and you can go. I win, and you're coming with me. I'm eager to lay my hands all over you."

"Lady Thomasina, please," Kay said. "We have enough on our hands as it is. We do not wish to fight you and your lovely ladies here."

"Aw, you're no fun. In that case, Lord Phillip, start walking." She pointed back the way they had come.

Sarah extended her SAPP and pointed it at Thomasina. With a quick movement of her MT CALM, she had it out of Sarah's hand where it fell to the damp stone.

Kay had had enough. He concentrated and, after a moment, Cloaked all four of them. "Quick, back away from them," he said. "Don't worry; I've Cloaked us audibly as well. We can speak freely, and they'll not hear us."

They backed away as Thomasina and her band began swinging, trying to cover every possible avenue of escape with their clubs.

"A very impressive Cloak," Thomasina said looking around, moving her MT CALM in a whirl. "But, it's not like I've never faced a Cloaked person before, and, in this tight area, I'll have you down sooner or later. Come on, Phillip, I'm starting to get angry, and I'm really not an Elder-like person when I'm angry."

The ladies covered the ground well with their clubs. Any hit, anywhere on their bodies was enough to incapacitate them—the MT CALM was a frustrating weapon to face. And what could they do? Their weapons were meant to kill, and they certainly didn't want to harm Thomasina and her group.

Lon had the answer. He drew his PITCOCK WONDER GUN and spun the cartridges. He then fired upwards, where the slug fell out of Cloak. Thomasina, hearing the shell, quickly hit it out of the air with her club. She then zeroed in on Lon and got him in the shoulder. He immediately fell in a smiling heap.

The shell he fired burst open spewing smoke which quickly filled the tunnel.

"Don't let him get away!" Thomasina shrieked, her voice suddenly ugly and ragged with anger. Somebody got hit in a swirl of flailing MT CALMs and fell.

Kay, in his Sight, could see perfectly. Sarah, with her Sight lit, was dragging Phillip away from Thomasina, for she had got him in the face and was prodding about looking for him. Kay sprang and got Lon, who was on the ground with a huge, stupid grin. A lady blocked Sarah's path, and without hesitation, she punched her hard in the nose, knocking the lady down. Thomasina, hearing the lady fall, jumped in front of them and flailed away with her MT CALM.

Kay blocked it with his CARG; then, turning it, he cut the club in two.

Thomasina was quickly all over him. Before he knew what had happened, she put three fierce punches square into his Cloaked face, easily the hardest punches he'd ever felt. She then walloped him in the gut, again, all of this under Cloak in a smoke-filled tunnel. She could fight.

Sight—She was going to try a blind leg sweep.

Kay jumped over her armored leg, as it came sweeping in and then returned the favor, socking her in the cheek. He expected her to go down, but she didn't—she was one tough Xaphan. Not having any other choice, he hauled back and socked her again, this time sending her down into the clouds of billowing smoke.

Not wasting a moment, Kay grabbed Sarah and led her out of the area, she using her Gift of Strength to easily drag both Phillip and Lon.

"Phillip!" Thomasina yelled, searching for him. "Phillip please! PHILLIP!!"

Soon, with great effort, they got away from Thomasina and her Singing Ten. They decided that staying in the tunnels might be too dangerous, as they didn't figure on Thomasina giving up any time soon. Fortunately, she didn't know where they had parked the *Goshawk,* so, at least, that would keep her guessing. And, as the smoke cleared, they could see the Singing Ten break into small groups, each looking in a different direction. They even heard one of them saying something about watching the temple for their arrival. That was a disadvantage, for she knew that was where they ultimately had to go. Now that they weren't boxed in, their Cloak would be much more difficult to defeat, but it looked like the Singing Ten were going to give it an A+ effort. Suddenly, the brooding Black Hat Ethylrelda and her windowless temple seemed less a threat than the love-struck magistrate and her band of club-wielding ladies.

They searched for an exit before Thomasina could get them cased—which wasn't going to be long by the number of ladies that were filtering into the tunnels. Thomasina called them her "Singing Ten", but there seemed to be quite a bit more of them than just ten. There appeared to be hundreds.

After a bit of searching, they found a cover to the street and went out into an alley. There they'd regroup, allow Phillip and Lon time to recover and hash out some sort of plan. Sticking their heads out into the street, they were clearly in a different municipality; the streets and buildings looked different. Kay panned around with his Sight and saw the more familiar buildings of Auld a few city blocks to the north. He even saw the tall buildings in Thomasina's compound; once they appeared charming and homey, now they seemed sinister and prison-like. He had a thought that Thomasina might have a few ladies stationed on the tops of her buildings, scanning the streets. Sure enough, there were several ladies on the rooftops looking around with high powered binoculars.

They took a moment to catch their breath. "What are we going to do, Kay?" Sarah asked. Her eyes were wide and eager. She was clearly enjoying this. "Did you see me hit that lady right in the face? Dropped her with one punch."

"I saw it. Great punch. Let's move across the street and get a few city blocks between us and them. Come on. We're under Cloak and should be fine."

They hauled Phillip and Lon and stepped out into the street.

A cable tipped with a strong net came down from the sky in an instant and had them pinned fast to the street. "What in the name of Creation is this?" Sarah yelled, struggling with the net.

Kay was tangled. He tried Wafting through it and couldn't, it seemed to be Waft-locked. The ends of the net were barbed, and the barbs had sunk deep into the street, holding the net fast. Traffic floated past them.

"Waft-locked!" he said in frustration. "This must have come from Thomasina's orbiting Helix ship."

"How'd it zero us?"

"I don't know!" He had a thought. "Wait, check your pockets! I wonder . . ."

Kay felt through his pockets and, sure enough, there was a small green device sitting innocently in one. "They've got us rigged!"

"Oh, Feature! How are we going to get out? And it better be fast 'cause I'm certain she's on her way."

Kay tried to draw his CARG, but he couldn't free his hands enough. "Sarah, power up and pull this net off us! Hurry, will you?"

Sarah began the process of hardening into Full Strength. It usually took her about a minute. Kay lay there in the net. His Sight wandered away. He saw a huge vehicle come blundering down the street ready to plow into them. It wasn't long before it would be there.

"Sarah, hurry!"

She pulled on the ends of the net. The cords stretched and groaned. Down the street a large Xaphan barge came floating into view.

Sarah pulled one of the barbs free. They'd need at least three or four more free to slide out.

"Sarah, you see that barge heading right for us? Do you?"

"Shut up, Kay, or I'll wrap these cords around your neck!" Two more were yanked free.

The net had loosened enough for Kay to unsaddle his CARG. He jostled it around and sliced through the cords of the net. They pulled Phillip and Lon away from the oncoming barge which hit the cable square, ripping the remaining barbs out of the street with a great commotion.

They moved south desperate to get off the street.

Sight.

"Sarah, jump aside!"

Another cable and net from above came screaming down, and then a third, all of them clamping down fast onto the street. Carrying Phillip and Lon, they made it off the street under an overhang. Sarah gasped and stared at the open sky. "That stupid ship up there is really annoying me!" she yelled.

Kay Sighted. "Sarah, check your pockets again. You've got three rigs on you, Phillip has about ten in various places, and Lon also has three."

Sarah went through her pockets, finding the small green devices in abundance. They pushed them into a pile. "Is that all?"

Kay looked her over again. He sighed. "No, you've got a few in your stomach, too. As do I, and Phillip and Lon as well. She must have rigged our breakfast this morning."

Sarah looked down at her stomach. "That conniving Shocktyte!"

His Sight wandered off into the future again. He looked skyward. "Sarah, hide Phillip and Lon and then get against the wall! Hurry—we're about to have company!"

Sarah picked Phillip up and tossed him down the alley several feet. She then tossed Lon, the two of them lying there in a heap. She quickly joined Kay and pressed up against the wall. "What are we doing?"

"Shh!"

A few moments later, a fast descending cable came down from above. The end of the cable had a small platform and rails, just wide enough for two people to stand. Two ladies in green hopped off and moved into the alley. They were both carrying rifles tipped with darts. They discovered the pile of discarded rigs and kicked at them in frustration. One of them lifted a scanning device of some sort and waved it around, moving right past where Kay and Sarah were standing. Cloaked, Kay quickly moved to the other side of the alley, Sarah following. The lady with the scanner turned around once or twice and finally put her device away. She ran back to the waiting cable, climbed onto the platform and was gone; the both of them pulled skyward as quickly as they'd arrived.

"Well, that was a near thing," Kay said. "Good thing the proximity of all these rigs fouled their scanner readings. Come on, let's get these two and keep moving."

Even though they had a whole city to hide in, Thomasina's ladies seemed to be everywhere. They prowled the streets. They rode about in green coaches suspended from cables, their MT CALMS drawn, many with large binoculars stuck to their eyes. Spectres, too, were out in force, many roving on foot, some in a mish-mash of vehicles. They were in such a hurry they didn't even bother to harass the people as they passed by.

The hunt was on. Some were hunting for Kay, others hunting for Phillip.

Though Cloaked, they felt very exposed. They decided to try taking a circuitous route to the temple. Instead of going straight for it, they circled around it to the south, always keeping the black pearl of Ethylrelda's temple to their left. Dragging Lon and Phillip, they entered a seedy municipality called Nilpop. They couldn't stop and rest for the Singing Ten were right on their heels, in some cases, entering alleys and streets moments after they had departed. They looked about with their binoculars, and others waved scanning equipment, one of them finding the fresh drag marks made by the heels of Phillip's boots where Kay had pulled him along. They were relentless, and they were thorough. With this latest piece of information, they hit their communicators, and the hunt was on afresh.

They continued south, bearing slightly to the east. They entered the municipality of Stove and then bore due east into an ugly place of industrial warehouses and fallen lots called Ferd. They stopped to rest near a dumpster full of mannequins. Carrying Lon and Phillip both for most of the way, Sarah was exhausted.

"You doing all right, Sarah?" Kay asked.

She settled down near the dumpster with her knees pulled up into her chest. "I'm fine. Just need a few minutes." She patted Phillip on the cheek. "When do you think these two will start coming around?"

"I'd hoped they'd be recovered by now."

"Check the future. Seriously, Phillip's getting heavy."

Kay casually consulted the near future, seeing a vast number of possibilities sort themselves out in front of him. "What do you see?" Sarah asked.

"I see a couple of things. We could do this the hard way or take an easier route—it's up to you."

Sarah sighed. "Let's take the easy way, please. I'm too tired for anything else, right now."

"In that case, just stay where you are." Kay got down next to the dumpster and peered around the side.

"What are you looking for?" she asked.

"One moment."

As they rested, an odd vehicle came floating in from the west. It appeared to be the black statue of a robed woman in a demure pose. The statue was about three hundred feet long. It possessed no apparent power source, control surfaces or other accessories that would allow it to fly; it simply looked like a floating statue toppled over on its side. It moved smooth and silent through the air. A host of Spectres milled about on the statue's back, standing wherever they could find a decent purchase on its irregular surface. Light came out of the statue's mouth and palms, panning around. After another few minutes, it moved on, flying silently to the south. Sarah watched it soar away.

"Those things are actually pretty cool. Just out of curiosity, what would the hard way have been like?" Sarah asked.

"Oh, we would have continued on, and they'd have spotted us, and we'd have gotten into a shootout."

Sarah was a bit put off. "Well, I'm sorry we missed that, actually. Perhaps next time."

After a few more minutes, Phillip and Lon recovered. They were finally able to stand on their own again.

Phillip was smoking hot as they crouched near the dumpster. "Can you believe the nerve of that woman?" he yelled. "What was I to be? Her prisoner—her slave?" He hit the dumpster with his fist.

"Well, gee, Phillip, after a round of face-sucking this morning I'd have thought you'd be happy she wishes to enslave you!" Sarah said, her eyes flashing.

"How do you know about that!" he raved.

"Lon caught you red-handed, so don't try and deny it!" Phillip glared at Lon, and he backed away a bit.

"I guess she didn't want you to leave, Phillip. I guess she likes you," Sarah said pinching him on the cheek. "You're just so adorable."

"Got a damn funny way of showing it, doesn't she?"

"Why didn't you just fight her?" Sarah said. "You could have saved us all this fuss."

Kay shook his head—remembering the love taps Thomasina had given him in the tunnel. "I don't know. She's pretty tough; she hits like a man, a big man, and has probably been in a lot more scrapes than Phillip has. I think she might have won that fight, had you accepted her challenge."

Phillip gritted his teeth. "She is a rude and imperious woman, and I will gladly knock her teeth out should we encounter her again. What's our status?" He looked around, seeing the seedy warehouses and the ever-present round mass of Ethylrelda's temple in the distance to the northeast.

"We are being tailed. We have all ingested a number of rigs for the purposes of their zeroing in on us."

"She fed us rigs this morning for breakfast?" Phillip was horrified.

"She did, along with larger ones placed in our pockets, which we've already eliminated. With those, she was able to zero in on us from her high-flying spiral ship floating above with great effectiveness. The smaller ones inside us don't appear to have as much range."

"Well, that's something anyway," Phillip said.

"What about your lip-lock with her this morning?" Sarah asked.

"What about it? We shared a moment; I kissed her. I didn't expect one kiss and a few songs in church to grant her an invitation for abduction, mayhem and rigging."

"You don't just smooch a Xaphan and walk away from them, Phillip. What's wrong with you?" Sarah yelled.

Kay, despite the situation, laughed. "Perhaps she lacks a bit in couth and basic manners, but I don't think she had it in her mind to harm or enslave you. And, she was quite the picture in her armor, don't you agree?"

"I don't recall what she looked like," Phillip said.

"She was very attractive," Lon said. "You thought so as well, or you shan't have kissed her."

"May we please move on from that? I don't care. Any good will I might have had for her is gone and done. She has revealed herself as a despot and a lunatic!"

"Ha!" Sarah exclaimed.

Kay shook his head, knowing better. Though their situation was "unusual" to be sure, Kay now felt certain that they selected the correct path—that there was hope for coming out of this successfully. He no longer saw the many *Wandwilla* futures with Ethylrelda—most of those had vanished. Still, he was sure a large confrontation was in the offing, as the image of Krotan of the Yard was still floating about in his mind.

"Oh, come on," Sarah said checking the streets. "You've always said you like them a bit wild."

"Wild, yes," Phillip cried, "but not insane, maniacal and slavering." He stepped away from the dumpster and looked around. "Are we certain we didn't tell them where the *Goshawk* was landed because I can picture that green-haired fool staking it out and waiting for us there."

He suddenly turned white. "What if she finds it and vandalizes or destroys the ship? What then?"

Sarah couldn't resist. "What if she suddenly materializes out of thin air with blood-shot eyes and dripping fangs, Phillip? Look!!"

Phillip whirled around, ready to kill with his SAPP. Sarah laughed.

"This is not funny! Kay, is the *Goshawk* still Cloaked?"

"It's still Cloaked, Phillip. Relax," Kay said, amused. Phillip was normally such a calm, clear-headed fellow. Now, he seemed on the verge of panic.

"Are you certain?"

Kay reached out with his Sight. He could see the *Goshawk*, miles away, sitting Cloaked in the afternoon sun. Nobody was around. "Yes . . . And why are you so upset? All you've got is a love-struck, green-haired hogtie gunning for you. Me—I've got a 400 year old Black Hat, who probably hasn't bathed since we've all been alive, wanting to merge into a bizarre, sex-crazed creature with me, and several others waiting in line wanting to either perform atrocities on my dead body, use it for arts and crafts or devour it whole!"

"No, the guy said she wanted to start with your genitals first," Sarah corrected.

Phillip shuffled his feet and paced, unimpressed with Kay's dilemma. "Does anyone recall mentioning, or even *hinting* at the *Goshawk's* location?"

"Shut up!" Sarah said.

"I don't recall it coming up in conversation," Lon said.

Lon rubbed his chin. "The only issue is that Lady Thomasina knows what our goal is—Ethylrelda's Temple," he said pointing at it in the distance. "Therefore, she will most likely assume that our vehicle is somewhere nearby. Due to the size of the temple, that's a lot of area to cover, but, still, I don't think I'd put it past her."

"Yes, well, we need to hurry." Phillip shuffled them along. "Lon, that Super Gun of yours . . ."

"Wonder Gun," Lon corrected.

"Whatever. Get it fully loaded—and shoot to kill if you have to!" Phillip was crazed with fear.

"Boy, Phillip," Sarah said egging him on. "Feeling pretty happy about yourself, aren't you? She's probably got some other fellow enslaved by now."

"We need to continue," Phillip said again.

"Wait a minute, Phillip. What's our plan going to be? What are we going to do when we get to the *Goshawk*? I believe Ethylrelda's Temple has become a bit of an afterthought at this point," Sarah remarked.

"We're going to lift her off and move her, far away, in some random direction. Kay can then Waft into the temple on his own."

Phillip considered what he just said and appeared a little ashamed of himself. "I'm sorry, Kay. That was a selfish remark. Does that sound possible to you? Can you Waft that far at speed?"

"Sure I can." He looked around, not seeing anybody suspicious. "I don't think there is a continued need to Cloak ourselves. Doing all four of you and the *Goshawk* is giving me a slight headache. And, it doesn't really matter given the fact we're rigged," he said.

"No, no—we need to be Cloaked. She'll spot us and drag me back to the love nest. If we're not Cloaked, I'm not moving!" Phillip said.

Love nest, if you only knew, Phillip . . .

Kay laughed and Cloaked everybody again. They headed east, leaving the low and dingy cityscape of Ferd and entering into the upper-scale municipality of Marilith. Apparently, Princess Marilith of Xandarr was a big celebrity in Waam. There were statues dedicated to her, streets named after her, and the ladies walking down the street even did their hair in the long, short banged style she wore. Odd, statue-like vending machines in Princess Marilith's form, selling everything from junk food to sex protection and procreation-defeating gels, stood on every corner bathed in flashing lights. The breasts of the statutes were convex monitor screens granting access to Waam's version of the holo-net. Traffic in Marilith picked back up, and Phillip eyed each passing vehicle with suspicion, no doubt imagining that each was filled with maniacal green-haired women.

And some were. Green and brown, waving scanners, supported by cables going up into the sky.

After a few blocks, they plunged into the dead zone around the temple and headed back to the *Goshawk*, which was probably a good four miles away at this point. They suspected that Thomasina had staked out the perimeter of the temple, and, sure enough, as they moved on, Kay saw the now familiar green and brown armor of Thomasina's Singing Ten hidden in various buildings.

"They're up there," Kay said, "scoping the area with scanning devices."

"Are they detecting the rigs we swallowed?" Phillip asked.

Kay gazed upward. "They seem to be reacting to our approach, but I can't tell if they've good enough a signal to lock on. Their actions don't seem to indicate that they've established a lock."

"What are they packing?" Sarah asked.

"Rifles armed with darts. I suppose Thomasina's not giving up, and she's not playing around either."

Fortunately, since he could see the ladies plain as day, they skirted around the Singing Ten placements, using the dead buildings as cover. He watched for any signs that they may have spotted them, but, outwardly, they looked tired and bored and probably wished they were elsewhere.

Finally, after making their way building by building, they got to the correct one. After first checking to make sure there were no ladies waiting for them upstairs, they went in and made their way to the top. Kay couldn't remember when he'd seen Phillip moving so fast—he wanted out of Waam in a bad way. They really couldn't leave, though, as they hadn't secured the final piece of the Machine. As Phillip had rather rudely suggested, they'd move the *Goshawk* possibly several hundred miles away to another part of the city and let Kay Waft in. It was the best plan he could think of. It would cut down on the fuss and bother of Thomasina, leaving only the fuss and bother of Ethylrelda.

This was the good path; Kay was certain. He had a chance to get out of this with Sam's item and with his soul as well. He wasn't certain how, though. The situation simply needed to play out.

They got to the open sunshine of the rooftop and Phillip thanked his maker for his deliverance and went into the ship—the *Goshawk's* familiar interior never looking so good.

29—The Brand

As they piled into the comforting confines of the ship it was déjà vu; they were horrified to discover a person sitting quietly on the back couch waiting for them.

Phillip drew his Poltava, ready to fight to the death. It was Thomasina! It had to be her!!

It wasn't Thomasina sitting there but rather a black robed Spectre.

"Greetings," Krotan of the Yard said.

They drew their weapons. Krotan appeared unfazed. "Please," he said in a calm voice. "There is no need for your weapons. I am here to assist you."

"How did you find us?" Kay asked, holding his CARG at the ready.

"My mistress knows much. She told me where your ship might be found. She is eager to join with you, sir, whichever one of you is the Invernan."

"She's not getting him," Sarah said. "We are going into that temple, and we are going to take what we came for."

"You will be killed instantly. However, my mistress is tired of death; she is tired of everything. For centuries, she has gazed out of her door to the sights beyond, not understanding what she was seeing—such is the Clutch the Black Abbess holds over her. She has come to know that there is more than just the darkness around her. She simply desires to have her reward, to *Wandwilla.*"

"That is not going to happen!" Sarah yelled.

Krotan rustled in his seat. "Perhaps we can agree upon an alternative, mutually beneficial course of action."

Kay lowered his CARG and sat down. "What do you propose?"

Krotan looked down at the floor, then began. "I am of the Yard—I have served our mistress for years doing her bidding, standing in her terrible presence, living while all else died around me. I suppose that, despite it all, I worship Her Mightiness; nay, I love her, truth be told. Though she is powerful and terrible, she is, at her core, an innocent and is full of dreams that little girls dream. I want to make her dreams come true, and I want to share them with her. I propose that I take your place. I wish to *Wandwilla* with Ethylrelda. You don't want it—I do!"

"Are you a Shadow tech male?"

"I am not."

"Then how do you propose to proceed?"

"We of the Yard have made a great study of Invernans. I know more about you than you do yourself. If I may—which one of you is the Invernan?"

Kay hesitated, then he admitted it. "I am a Shadow tech male," he said.

Krotan smiled. "Thank you. It is probably not known to you, but, among the many things you can do, you have the ability to brand another male."

"Brand? I don't understand."

"You may create another Invernan. Invernans are not just born; they can be made as well. A branded Invernan is not as potent as a born one, but, regardless. I am asking you to brand me. I will then *Wandwilla* with Ethylrelda. It is my wish. I want it like nothing else. And, to reward you, I will give you the item you seek. You may then go on your way."

From the depths of his robes, he produced a fairly large bundle wrapped in a cloth.

"I can feel that you are people of character, people of your word—that is an admirable thing. I offer you this, the wondrous item you came for, and, in exchange, you will brand me."

Kay took the bundle and unwrapped it. There, shining up at him was a twisting, organic-looking rectangular object, about two feet long, shining in silver. "Lon?" Kay asked. "Is this the piece we need?"

Lon accepted the piece and scanned it with his goggles. "Yes, yes, this does appear to be the piece, yes indeed."

Kay stared at Krotan: sinister-looking, intense, but apparently sincere. "I thank you for giving us the item we require. I must be perfectly honest, I do not know how to do what you ask."

Krotan stood. "I will instruct you. Do I have your word?"

Kay thought for a moment and looked at Lon holding the final piece of Sam's machine. There it was, right in front of him. Sam's salvation was at hand. Here was the last piece of her *Olonol*.

"Yes, you have my word."

Krotan stood up. "Then, if you are ready, we must go outside, in the fresh air."

Everybody, except for Phillip, went outside into the afternoon sun—he couldn't be dragged out. Krotan removed his hood, revealing a heavily tattooed bald head. He then stripped to the waist and threw his small swords aside. He lay down on the dirty surface of the roof. "Now, sir, please, what is your name?"

"My name is Kabyl."

"Thank you, Kabyl. Now please lie on top of me and place your Mark on my right eye. That might sound a little confusing, so simply lay your right temple on my right temple, yes?"

Tentatively, Kay lay down on Krotan and placed his temple against his—they almost appeared to be kissing.

"Now, and this is the distressing part, we must both be run through with a sword or other sharp weapon. We must both be pierced and made to feel great pain."

"Are you insane?"

"It must be done. The Brand will save us from death. When we are run through, the Brand will begin. Then, after a minute or so, we may be separated, and I will be an Invernan—though not as powerful as you."

Kay lay there, wondering what to do. Then: "Sarah," he said. "Take your SAPP and run us through. Be careful to pick a spot where you will minimize puncturing my vital organs."

"By Creation, Kay, I'm not going to run you through with my SAPP! We have the piece; let's go!"

"I gave this man my word. Now, I must be true to it. According to him, well not be harmed. Come on, Sarah, we haven't all day."

Sarah huffed and formed her SAPP into a thin, spear-like shaft with a wickedly sharp point.

"Use your Strength, Sarah—let's make this a nice clean thrust."

Sarah hardened up. "You ready?" she asked, holding the SAPP against his back.

"Yes, yes, hurry up."

Sarah then ran the SAPP through the both of them and skewered the roof beneath Krotan. It was easy. The scalpel-sharp SAPP cut through their flesh like nothing. She even didn't need her Strength.

Kay and Krotan writhed in agony, like skewered fish on a hook. Kay had never felt pain like it before, and he hoped he never would again. He tried to raise his head, but Krotan held him fast.

"Do . . . not . . . break the . . . connection!"

Kay's Sight spun in a carnival of past and future events.

Sam . . . asleep inside the metal man.

Phillip and Thomasina holding each other, that future now set.

A dark place of pagan idols.

People suffering . . . fire and oil. Lightning from above.

Sam being tormented before a Horned God . . .

Carahil in chains . . .

Clawed hands at his throat . . .

SAM!!

POW!!

He couldn't concentrate. Everything was falling apart.

And his Cloak fell. Suddenly the big, black *Goshawk,* with Phillip sitting inside, appeared on the roof top.

In his agony, he trained his Sight, forced it to obey his pain-clotted mind. And he saw what was about to happen.

"Down!" he shrieked. "Sarah, Lon, get down!"

Sarah let go of her SAPP, and she and Lon hit the roof, just as a cloud of fired darts came whistling in from all quarters.

The Singing Ten had spotted them. Now, it was on in full! Thomasina herself would probably be arriving in no time.

Lying on the roof top really wasn't any cover, as some of the Singing Ten were perched on taller buildings quite a distance away. Rolling away and just missing a dart, Lon stood and drew his CEROS. He presented it as was customary and moved it just in time to block a dart that was heading right for his throat, ready to administer a knock out dose. These Singing Ten were crack snipers.

Lon depressed a hidden trigger, and the CEROS expanded, doubling its usual size. He then donned his goggles, adjusted the lenses and began a skilled dance, protecting Sarah, Kay and Krotan from the hail of incoming darts, his long coat and buckle shoes adding a comical edge to his masterful skill.

There was a lull. Kay could see the Singing Ten reloading for another volley. Lon lined up a shot and let the CEROS go at a howl.

"Lon!" Sarah cried. "You aren't planning on killing any of them are you?"

The CEROS went about a quarter mile at speed and bisected one of the Singing Ten's rifles as she reloaded it. It then returned to him as always. "That one was in too good of a position," he said. "She would have had us before long."

Kay writhed. "Sarah—cables! Cables from above!"

As if from nowhere, three cables pierced the surface of the roof from the spiral ship in orbit above and held tautly. Moments later, three ladies in green armor came screeching down the cable length in a controlled fall. They carried dart-tipped rifles.

Sarah was on the first new arrival. She grabbed the barrel of the rifle before she could aim and hit the lady in the face with a powered up punch. The lady went limp, and Sarah took her weapon.

The other two sprang into action, one rolling into a protected firing position near a stairwell, the other taking flight. As Sarah and the Singing Ten maneuvered around on the rooftop for cover, the sky darkened. Glancing up, she saw a strange silvery cloud rolling in from the east, like a rain cloud alone in the sky on a sunny day. It had a distinct animal shape, sort of like a great, flippered seal performing a trick. As Sarah watched, the odd cloud seemed to grow "whiskers", as a number of black cables appeared through it. Thomasina was sending down cables from her ship above en masse, trying to skewer the *Goshawk*. The cables seemed to be having a hard time passing through the layers of the cloud, losing their speed and power coming down limp and ineffectual.

The Singing Ten on the rooftop lined Sarah up with her rifle and fired.

The shot was blocked by Lon's thrown CEROS. Sarah promptly returned fire and darted her in the leg. Sarah's victim fell forward, unconscious.

The flying lady came around from the north and lined up Sarah for a shot. Lon drew his impressive PITCOCK WONDER GUN and spun the chamber. Before Sarah could say anything, he fired with a bristling report. A large slug hit the lady in the chest and exploded in a spray of shards, apparently stunning her and throwing off her aim. "That's Mad Molly's Crystaline load!" he said with pride. "Hurts like the devil!"

"Lon!" Kay shrieked, still impaled atop Krotan. "I see another volley coming in!" Sarah moved to get the stunned flying lady out of the way for good and shot her with a dart. It hit her in the side, and she immediately plummeted past the edge of the building and down to the street far below.

"Oh, Creation!" Sarah cried. "I didn't mean for that to happen— I thought she'd land on the roof first, then pass out! Gods—she's going to be killed!"

Lon went to the edge, aimed his WONDERGUN and fired. A large slug came skittering out, covering the distance fast and opening up into a billowy cascade of web-like strands that enveloped the plummeting woman. Sarah watched with relief as the web-like mass with the lady safely nestled within landed far below soft as a baby. "Great shot, Lon. Thanks!"

Then Sarah saw the mass of approaching vehicles. "She's here! She's here! They're storming the building! Slam the door and wedge it!"

Five float cars arrived, carrying at least fifty ladies. They piled out of the cars and entered at a run. Some bounded up the side of the building, while others flew.

More cars arrived, a motley bunch—Spectres, dozens of them. They streamed out of their cars like a box of black mothballs dumped out, only to be met by other Spectres of the Yard who had been hiding in the adjacent buildings. In a mass of shouting and black robes and bloodied swords mixed with green armor and whirling clubs, they fought a pitched battle with Spectres of other Orders and with the Singing Ten both on the ground and in the heights.

The battle for both Kay and Phillip was on in earnest.

Sarah made her way to the service door. The other service doors went nowhere—this one was the only one that mattered, and with Lon covering her, she braced it as best she could.

Kay, still locked together with Krotan, had more bad news. "Creation—rockets! Incoming Laser-Lock rockets! They're going for the *Goshawk*!"

Inside, Phillip freaked. He began trying to start the ship up—it was a long, intricate process. He pulled handles, tugged on gauges and set the pumps. The landing lights came on, and the engines slowly cycled, coming to life at a maddeningly slow rate.

The Singing Ten, camped out all around, were done messing about. They were readying a cache of rockets. The rockets appeared to be fairly small, two stage models that probably couldn't do serious damage, but they could probably punch large enough holes in the *Goshawk* that it wouldn't be going anywhere without repair.

About a mile away, one of Thomasina's ladies lined her target up, lazed it, and fired. The rocket jumped out of its tube with a small launch engine; it then ejected the spent motor and fired its main rocket. It appeared to hover in the air as it did so.

Howling, Lon's CEROS cut it in two, touching off a colorful propellant fire in the now useless pieces. Again, Lon was deadly accurate with his CEROS, and it returned to his hand.

No time to bask. "Lon!" Kay cried. "Many incoming Laser-Locks. Northeast quarter!" Kay appeared to be on the verge of passing out.

"They're here!" Sarah screamed, holding the door shut with her Strength. "I can feel them on the other side!" Armored fists banged on the door from within, and Spectres and Singing Ten swirled up over the side of the roof in a confused mess.

The *Goshawk* made a puff of ionized gas and died with a sputter—Phillip had messed up the startup sequence. He emptied the tanks, reset the levers and started all over.

A shadow passed overhead. The black statue crawling with Spectres they'd seen in Ferd was back, punching through the silver cloud, now dissipating. Standing on its back, shoulders and extremities, they rained projectile shots down onto the roof.

Rockets from the Singing Ten lit into it from all sides, peppering its length with tiny explosions. The statue endured the small attacks, seemingly impervious to them. The rockets the Singing Ten were using appeared to be meant only to cause moderate damage. The Spectres standing all over it returned fire. Some were struck by incoming dart fire from the Singing Ten, tumbling away and falling off like fleas from a gigantic dog.

As Kay cringed and watched helplessly, Lon adjusted his goggles and saw a Spectre standing on the statue hoist a deadly-looking shoulder-fired rocket.

The Spectre locked on and fired in a blast, his hooded cloak fluttering.

Lon spun the cartridges of his gun, selected a fiery red one, aimed and fired in return.

The large red slug, an Inferno round, skittered out of the gun at a fairly slow speed. It went about three hundred feet, corkscrewing slightly, then exploded in a cascade of fire. The fire formed an expanding curtain between them and the incoming Spectre rocket. The rocket entered the fiery veil and exploded in a nasty ball of blue flame that expanded all the way to the exterior of Ethylrelda's temple. That was a killer explosion, and, had it hit the rooftop, everything on it would have been killed or destroyed.

"Lon, he's reloading!" Kay cried.

Lon searched his coat for another Inferno round.

Too late. The Spectre, robes billowing, was already leveling his rocket launcher and lining them up.

Cables came down from the sky in a taut cloud, barbing fast into the flying statue and holding it suspended in mid-air like a marionette. One of the cables even bisected the rocket-firing Spectre. He dropped his rocket launcher, and hung there, impaled like the statue he was riding on.

Kay, in agony on the rooftop, considered the irony. Only moments earlier, the Singing Ten were their opponent. With the arrival of the Spectres, they were now tacit allies against a common enemy.

The rocket fire of the Singing Ten coming in from all quarters took effect, and the black statue crumbled, breaking apart in arms and legs suspended from the sky, dumping off the remaining Spectres. A few began flying and were engaged by other Spectres of the Yard and the Singing Ten, some Wafted and others fell to their death.

Lon raised his gun in triumph. "Here's to the Singing Ten!" he cried, and then fell as a dart pierced his neck right on the button and dosed him. He was out.

The alliance, now that the Spectres were mostly out of the way, was over.

"They're beating on the door—they've got something on the other side. I can't hold it much longer!" Sarah cried. Without Lon to defend her, a dart pierced her leg, and she immediately fell unconscious.

At that moment, cable cars rose and the door burst open. Thomasina and her Singing Ten gained the roof in a howl of triumph, both through the service doorway and over the side of the building. A volley of ten Laser-Lock rockets came in, this time passing through the hanging meat of the destroyed Spectre statue ship. They headed for the *Goshawk*. Those rockets wouldn't destroy the ship. They would do just enough damage to mess it up and keep it where it was.

And the black pearl of Ethylrelda's temple came to life. Like a massive black octopus, innumerable tendrils of Shadow tech came snaking out. They seized the incoming rockets, held them burning in air, and then crushed them. More tendrils slithered up to the roof top.

There, they gently picked up the fallen Lon, his WONDER GUN, and Sarah and placed them within the open hatch of the *Goshawk*. The tendrils also latched onto the struggling Thomasina and her ladies and lifted them into the air along with a number of Spectres. They whacked at the black tentacles with their clubs and swords, but it did no good.

Then, a final tendril came and gently pulled the SAPP out of Kay and Krotan. It picked Kay up by his shirt and, again, placed him inside the *Goshawk*, where a frantic Phillip shut the hatch. He purged the tanks and began restarting the ship for a third time.

Krotan rose amid the waving forest of Shadow tech stalks blooming with rockets and Singing Ten. Arms spread in welcome, he serenely walked to the edge of the roof. He stepped off into thin air, where Shadow tech tendrils came up to support his feet as he did so. More tendrils came down and gingerly, tentatively touching him— they throbbed and tremored at his touch and he was born away, down into the mouth of the temple far below where Ethylrelda awaited him.

There was a muted explosion within. The air around it shook with their combined ecstasy, a moment of passion that will last an eternity. The perfect sphere of the temple wrinkled, and sucked-in like a dried prune. The striating tendrils of Shadow tech set Thomasina and her ladies down and retreated into the roiling mass of the temple.

$$\ast \quad \ast \quad \ast \quad \ast \quad \ast$$

Inside the *Goshawk*, Phillip furiously worked the controls, trying to start up the ship. It was a complicated process. He had done it so many times it normally wasn't much of an issue anymore.

But now, with his enemy outside the ship, he fumbled with the controls, fouling the tanks, over-priming the engines, mis-starting the ship. He'd failed twice now.

Finally, tanks properly primed, it cranked to life as Sarah stirred, the gauges winding to a ready state. She shook her head, groggy from the dose she took, and checked Kay, who was out next to her. Lon, too, hit in the neck, was out fast. She checked Kay's back, and couldn't find the hole she'd made in him, just the tear in the fabric of his shirt and nothing more.

Phillip finally had the ship ready, and it thrummed to life, the engines purring steadily, ready to go. The floorboards vibrated as they normally did.

He glanced out the cockpit glass as he finished his work, and there she was.

Thomasina the 19th.

She stood there in the sunshine in her green armor and visored helmet—an incredibly attractive, yet imminently scary lady. Outside, framed in billowing smoke and dangling appendages from the destroyed flying statue, she was smiling and statuesque. Thomasina walked slowly up to the *Goshawk*. She stopped at the cockpit glass and lightly rapped it with her MT CALM.

"Phillip . . ." she cooed. He couldn't hear her, but he could see her lips moving. Just a few more preparations, another lever or two, and the ship would be ready to go. The engines powered up to idle.

She tried the hatch. It was locked.

Suddenly, she reared back, eyes bugging, fists bolt straight at her side. "PHILLIP!" she screeched. She ripped her helmet off. Her green hair was an angry tangle around her face.

Phillip engaged the pan—finally, the *Goshawk* was ready to sail. All he had to do was grab the sticks, raise her up and fly her off.

Huffing, she went around to the back of the vessel, out of sight, and started messing around with the ship. They could hear her clanking about outside.

"She's . . . going to do the *Goshawk*!" Sarah cried, groggy.

"Oh yeah?" Phillip said with a sadistic grin. He raised his hand and calmly pressed a button. A blast of air jarred the ship and Thomasina, rolling head over heels, was blasted away along with several of her Singing Ten, their released MT CALMs bouncing, some going over the side of the roof.

Phillip smoothly lifted the *Goshawk* and spun it around over the edge of the roof, hovering to face her.

He had to do it—something made him do it.

She stood, and they stared at each other for a moment. Phillip augured the nose down and they were eye to eye. She threw her MT CALM at the cockpit glass, where it bounced off with a harmless thud. If the glass hadn't been there, the throw would have been right on the mark. He then yawed the ship, free as a bird, and let it soar down the sheer side of the building where he joyously buzzed the armored ladies and surviving Spectres standing at street level, causing them to dive for cover. Leveling and gaining slow altitude through the metal canyons of Waam, Phillip was all smiles. A cable came down from the heavens, hoping to skewer the ship, and then another. He easily evaded them.

He rolled the ship. He looped it. "Creation, that felt good! See ya', Thomasina! Goodbye, and good riddance!"

"What are you doing, Phillip?" Sarah asked crossly, still trying to collect her wits. "Are you showing off? You're showing off for Thomasina, aren't you?"

∗ ∗ ∗ ∗ ∗

As Waam fell back into the distance, Kay awoke.

Sarah was sitting next to him. "You ok?" she asked. He nodded and sat up.

He Sighted into Ethylrelda's temple. Inside, he could see a great portion of the twisting passages had broken away replaced by what looked like a gigantic, leafless tree. Soon, the tree, the new *Wandwilla*, would burst through the cracked sphere of the temple and reach for the sun.

It had worked—both Ethylrelda and Krotan had gotten what they wanted. He could only imagine the joy they were feeling now and forever.

And he had what he wanted, too. He checked the back of the ship. There were the two pieces of Sam's machine, and, sitting on the couch still wrapped up in its cloth was the final piece they'd come for, the three pieces together for the first time in centuries—the *Oberphilliax.*

Olonol. The Machine.

It's done, Sam; it's over. I did it, Cerri-Tela!

Kay had passed the Trials.

EPILOGUE

The Skull in Reverse

We're going after the Horned God, Hath, you and me.

Lady Hathaline chuckled and clapped as she watched the scene unfold on the *Goshawk*. She'd watched most of Kay's adventures throughout the trials. She'd seen him grow in stature and power and was very impressed and proud of her brother, and her cousins as well. She wished she could have gone with them and flown the *Goshawk* through Xaphan space, or maybe one of those weird statue ships in Waam, those looked fun to fly. She couldn't wait to see him again alive and well.

She was leaning over a Vith fountain in the Grove—the same one her aunt, Lady Poe, had created Carahil in years ago. He had told her much about this fountain. He had brought her out there through the tangle of beech trees and shown it to her; it just seemed like an overgrown fountain, an old Vith ruin. Carahil said that some of the material used in his creation was still there, sopped up in the cracks and pores of the stone like cooking oil in a well-seasoned iron frying pan, waiting to be activated.

As he showed her, it was an easy process to bring the fountain to life. All she needed was a little bit of cool water from the lake and pour it into the basin, just enough to create a bit of depth at the bottom. That done, all she had to do was peer in. Images formed in the shallow water and she could see things beyond the confines of the Grove. She could see anything she wanted, the surface of the water alight with images. Carahil instructed her to focus the images to see specifically what she wanted to.

As she concentrated on the fountain, she often heard whispered laughter in the beech trees and saw soft flashes of green light.

"That's the enemy," Carahil told her. "Hidden behind their veils. Don't worry about them—I'm here to protect you."

Dubious, but trusting in him, she returned to her work. As Carahil directed, the object of her attentions was a curious skull sitting in a library on the 50th floor of Xyotel Tower. It was her cousin Sarah's "Mystery Library" a sort of clubhouse where she, Kay and Phillip liked to hang out. She had only been in it herself once or twice. Sarah was very particular about the place and made a nasty fuss whenever she entered as she wasn't on the "WELCOME" list, neither was her sister Lady Kilos—in fact she had been on the "FORBIDDEN" list for a long time. So, she generally avoided the place.

There was a bleached, partially fossilized skull sitting on a shelf in the library surrounded on either side by books. Sarah proudly proclaimed that it was a Berserkacide skull and that Carahil himself had asked her to guard it years ago while she was still in training pants. Given Sarah's habit for exaggeration, Hathaline had always thought the story was either a half-truth or a complete fabrication.

"That skull in Sarah's library belonged to the Horned God's Secret-Talker. All the gods have one," Carahil said. "It's an individual whom we entrust all our secrets, hence the name. We can't achieve our full measure with the universe without a Secret-Talker, they're sort of like a safety-valve and paper-trail, I guess, and that's how the universe likes it. The gods have lots of secrets, and if you're a god and you're messing up and doing things you're not supposed to be doing, the Secret-Talker is going to know and have a complete memory of it. That's how the gods are supposed to police each other, by having access to the secrets held by the Secret-Talker. That's the theory, anyway, however in practice it's very difficult getting to a god's Secret-Talker, because we take great pains to ensure they're well hidden and protected—you wouldn't believe where we've got some of these poor people stashed sometimes. I have my Secret-Talker and she's very dear to me and nobody's going to find her—she never stays in one place for very long, it was her idea."

Carahil winked at Hath. "What we need to do is get to the Horned God's Secret-Talker and find out his secrets. I'm pretty certain the Horned God and his damn temple is the root cause behind much of the weird stuff that's happening here on Kana, and if we can get his secrets we can be rid of him for good."

Hath had a question.

"Yep—you won't have to worry about becoming a monster, The only things you'll have to worry about, Hath, will be your bowling average and what to wear on a Saturday night and which lucky fellow to court first."

Hath said she hated bowling and didn't care about wearing clothes and courting boys. She wanted to fly and join the Fleet.

Carahil laughed. "Ahhh, all in good time. Now, here's the thing, if you're a god you really need to keep your Secret-Talker happy, otherwise bad things can happen. If you mistreat or abuse them, then their loyalty might waiver or change all together, and I think that's where the Horned God has slipped up. I think he, being rather confident in himself and the fences he's created, forgot about his Secret-Talker in the depths of antiquity and sort of left him there in limbo, and his Secret-Talker was very sad, for a long time. I can feel the loneliness permeating the bone and hollow spaces of that skull—whoever this person was, he wasn't very happy and that's for certain. I would never allow my Secret-Talker to be neglected to point of misery like the Horned God did his, and that's where we can make our move."

Hath asked who the Horned God is.

"He is the, Boogey-Man" of the gods. He's a criminal who goes around terrorizing the younger folk, making them worship him, making them kill for him. It has long been suspected that he is one of us, a member of the Celestial Arborium in disguise, and the quest to uncover his identity has been going on for centuries. Most recently, Anabrax was accused and convicted of being either the Horned God himself or in league with him and she was sent to the Windage of Kind. I recently visited Anabrax and she told me she was framed, and I believe her. She told me that the Horned God is none other than Bathloxi himself.

"Who's Bathloxi? He is a beloved senior member of the Arborium, well-respected and above reproach. He is a friend, giver of laws and mentor of many gods. He is wise and very kind—or, is he? I think, over the course of his long existence, the rigid constraints of the very laws Bathloxi wrote began to wear on him and he, like many beings, yearned for something more—something his sadistic alter-ego, the Horned God, could deliver to him in earnest. Maybe he thinks the laws he wrote don't apply to him and he has lease to do whatever he wants. Or, maybe, the ravenous Horned God who has tormented Sam and her people for ages is who he really is and the calm, reserved Bathloxi sitting at the top of the universe surrounded by his friends is the alter ego. Perhaps he really is the Devil. I don't know."

Carahil was lost in thought for a moment, lamenting the possibility.

"So," he said, "let's look to it. Sarah's skull in the Mystery Library is the key. Obviously, since it's just a skull, the Secret-Talker is dead. Been dead for a long time, but times the whole thing, isn't it and he's alive somewhere in the past with the secrets we need. Here's what we're facing—Bathloxi has placed four significant protections around his Secret-Talker. The First Protection proclaims that no god or other member of the Older Folk may interface with him, ok? So, that takes me and everybody else from the Arborium out of play. By the way, technically, his First Protection goes against the rules of Universal balance since the whole point of having a Secret-Talker is for accountability amongst the gods, but nobody's ever called him on it—I suppose status and familiarity speak for themselves, don't they? Here's the Second Protection, Bathloxi's got him stashed away in a time loop somewhere in the distant past—nobody's quite sure where or when. So, even though the Secret-Talker today is just a skull, he's still getting fed current information in the past; I'm not quite sure how it works, but it does. That's the Second Protection."

Carahil blinked. "Still with me, Hath, 'cause here's where it gets tricky."

Hathaline nodded and listened.

"Good. The Third Protection is that Bathloxi's Secret-Talker can only be located in the past by one of his servants—and, when I say one of his servants, I don't mean the cute little creatures up in the Arborium that help us out with this and that, I mean his, *servants"*; the Golden People, the *Killanjo* and, by default, the Monamas. If anybody else tries to look back into the past with a magic mirror or other such time-seeing device, they're not going to see anything. Here's where you come in, my lady. You, Hath, are one of the Horned God's servants; you don't want to be his servant and you haven't been converted into one yet, that's still years off in the future, but you still fulfill the criteria. I checked on it. Bathloxi's protections around his Secret-Talker, like any magical contrivance, only work as well as they're written. The Third Protection is the most porous and poorly thought out of the four, and that's because gods, like him and I, don't really understand the mechanics of how time works any better than anybody else does—we're bound by the flow of time too. The Golden People who serve Bathloxi have a vast understanding of time—they ride it like mariners across the sea. They created the Time Loop used in the Second Protection and helped Bathloxi write the Third Protection and assured him it was sound and he listened to them. They're his loyal servants, after all, but I think they made the Third Protection a little vague intentionally so that they themselves could get at the Secret-Talker whenever they want. Why, I don't know. In any event, the Third Protection is flawed because it doesn't say you have to be a *current* servant, it just says *servant*, and that's what you are, a future servant of his. Thanks to that loose wording you should be able to focus on that skull, look into the past and see Bathloxi's Secret-Talker. It's a loophole the Golden People wrote and Bathloxi doesn't seem to be aware of it."

Carahil blinked and gazed down at the calm water in the basin. "Now, here's the Fourth and final protection, and this is the toughest one. Bathloxi's Secret-Talker won't give up his secrets unless you know his name. So, even if you locate him back in time and he wanted to tell, he couldn't unless you first say his name. He can't tell you what it is—you have to say it to him first. Ok? I've done all the research I can and his name is lost to the ages—it's just not written down anywhere, there's no lore or songs or oral histories with his name hidden within—there's nothing. And, it's really frustrating too."

Hathaline stood there listening. Carahil gave her a little nudge with his silver noggin. "So, your task, in a nutshell, is to use this fountain, focus on the skull in Sarah's library, locate the Secret-Talker in time and then observe him until you discover his name. If we have that, then we have the Horned God and we will take him down. And, best of all, since we have the Secret-Talker's skull well be able to use it to mess him up if he tries to come at us. It's our ace-in-the-hole, and he doesn't know we've got it, but first we need the name. That's the key."

$$* \quad * \quad * \quad * \quad *$$

And Lady Hathaline set to her work. Every day she went to the fountain, standing over the old basin and peering in, concentrating on the skull in Sarah's library as Carahil watched.

The water came to life. There was the skull, sitting on the shelf, bleached white and smooth. At first, nothing happened, she simply stared at it, wondering what she was supposed to be seeing; the tedium of standing there was killing. Few children her age could have stuck with such a test of endurance for very long, but Lady Hathaline was stalwart. Carahil said the skull was vital, so, she'd come out and stare into this fountain all day every day if need be.

Day after day passed with similar results—a skull on a shelf. Every so often Carahil left her side, saying he needed to go and "Look after Sam", and "See how Kay's doing", and he'd vanish, leaving her alone in the Grove. He didn't leave Hathaline defenseless, however. He gave her a handful of little blue figurines shapes in his smiling likeness. "If you hear or see anything disturbing, use one of these," he said. "Just toss 'em."

Needing a break, she occasionally used the basin to check in on Kay herself—she was quickly becoming adept at its use. She saw him far away and she heard his thoughts. He seemed to be doing fine. Look at the things he could do now. What a strange city Waam is.

She checked in on Sam. She was sealed inside a gigantic metal man riding on a pewter chariot through the ether. She saw Carahil flying by her side lending his protection. Just an all around nice guy Carahil was.

She also looked in on her father and mother in their Fleet ship over Hoban. It was lots of tedious stuff, then there was a flash of confusion, and then she lost them and didn't see them again. Odd.

And there were the voices and the tittering jibes coming from the trees. "*Hath!*" she'd hear. "*Hath, we're going to get you . . . We're going take you, do things to you . . . Make you one of us . . .*"

. . . make you one of us . . .

She stood tall though and trusted to Carahil and the little figurines he'd left her, throwing them in the direction of the sounds, and they would quiet down for a time, leaving her in peace. His protection worked.

✶　✶　✶　✶　✶

Hathaline continued on with the skull, and her persistence paid off. In the shallow water time changed around the skull, moving backwards into the past. Slow at first and then accelerating, events unfolded in reverse. She saw the skull gone from the shelf being given to a tiny, pig-tailed Sarah by Carahil on her mother's birthday some fourteen years ago. "Take good care of this for me," Carahil had told her, and, hugging it with both arms, she promised she would, mouth open and pigtails jangling.

So, Sarah hadn't been exaggerating after all.

Events in the fountain were flying now, moving steadily backwards in time. Watching actions in reverse, Hath had to re-train her thoughts and how she processed information; not in normal time progression, but watching from end to distant beginning. It was bewildering to see things in reverse. As a growing pilot, her father had taught her how to process information quickly and in concise order, a skill that was a must have for a person flying such a fast and potentially unforgiving craft like a ripcar. He taught her to clear out a familiar spot in her thoughts and then place pertinent, concise information into that clean space in precise order, first A, then B, then C, all organized and available for immediate recall when needed. With her thoughts working in such an orderly manner, she could remember vast amounts of detail: pitch, yaw, speed, altitude, landmarks, hazards, and recall them perfectly in the short term. Now, she was seeing everything happening in reverse; Z, then, Y, then X. She forced herself to concentrate, to adjust, to correctly process what she was seeing and not miss a single detail.

This was for Carahil, and her brother . . . and for herself.

Continuing back in time, she saw the skull being dug out of the ground in a heavily wooded area. Carahil had dug it out, holding it in his mouth, dirt caked up around his muzzle like a beard, and flying away holding it in his teeth, a rare and eagerly sought after prize.

She felt his excitement. Faster and faster into the past it went, events turning into a blur.

**The skull stayed in the ground for a long, long time—ages passed, stuck in a vein of coal, to compacted peat, to dry earth.

**The skull unearthed in ancient times, sun rising and falling, resting before a headless skeleton on a pile of filthy rags in a primitive, fallen down hut, the skeleton's hands crossed over its heart.

**Now, deep in antiquity, there was the skull no longer a skull. Now it was a face and muscle and skin and a body, alive and breathing.

There was the Horned God's Secret-Talker.

**Clawed hands clasped with another's—a final moment of solace and shared comfort after ages of solitude.

**The figure sat alone in the woods, head down, garbed in black rags. It sat there by itself for a long time. It had a string of bone beads around its neck, which it fingered with clawed hands and toyed with, the bone rubbed smooth. It was all alone, deep in time. Watching through the waters of the fountain, Hathaline could feel the Secret-Talker's loneliness.

So lonely, longing for what once was.

"I think the Horned God's forgotten about his Secret-Talker in the antiquity of time . . ." Carahil had said, and he was correct.

She couldn't help but feel sorry for it.

Hathaline studied the figure, taking in every detail. It was a woman (not a man as Carahil had assumed), and, from the looks of it, she was a Monama woman. She had the characteristic chalky white skin, the bursting mane of ankle-length black hair and the tell-tale large black eyes. She looked a lot like Sam. She was full and strong, the face of an angel, fierce and proud.

Wait—four arms. The Secret-Talker had four arms. She was a Berserkacide.

**All alone.

**All dead, mate and child, kin hand in hand. All dead. All gone. The last of her kind, denied the simple gift of death. The Horned God had done this to her. Full of His secrets. All His fault. She walked away from the temple and returned to the woods, her ancient home now empty and unfamiliar. She would never see the temple again.

Time continued backwards.

**The Golden People, wearing stolen forms of the aliens of jade and sapphire, became the Horned God's new angels of death. They hated her. She hated them back.

**New beings came from the temple, shapeless and golden. They routed the accursed aliens of jade and sapphire, chased them from the planet and stole their forms. They came to her to steal her form as well and she killed them with her claws.

**All the dead who could not be replaced, turning to bones where they lay.

**They breed like grass. No end to them. Giving birth to ten or twelve heretic two-armed children at a time, while she and her people were managing just one. Outnumbered.

**Battles. Two-armed Monamas wearing the jade and sapphire aliens clothing fighting the woman and a primitive band of four armed Berserkacides in rags and furs. Death and savagery. Hatred. Ripping each other apart—each the anathema of the other.

**Two-armed heretics emerging from the alien cities in the north at last, wearing their clothing, speaking their language . . . sharing their beds and turning from the Horned God. A blasphemy! Look at them! Kill them!! Sacrifice them!!

**Rivers choked with dead, pale four-armed bodies. Botched experiments. Flotsam.

**Jade and sapphire aliens in northern cities where it was too cold for them to reach, more capable than the Horned God had anticipated, ensnaring her people and dragging them inside the walls. Experimenting on them. They called this place Ka-Na.

**Aliens, soft and weak wearing clothing of jade and sapphire, lured in from the stars by the Horned God for his angels to kill. He always brought them creatures to hunt and play with. To sacrifice them in the temple. They lived for blood and sacrifice. These aliens were merely the latest and their blood shall be spilled in the temple. They were doomed as they stepped out of their armada of vessels, looking at the landscape with wonder. They thought they'd discovered heaven when instead they were in Tevlapradah—hell.

**The four-armed woman, receiving a gift from a gigantic monster standing on two hooves, shaggy, wearing a horned crown of lightning. The Horned God giving her the gift of immortality and sharing his secrets, becoming his Secret-Talker. Such secrets he had to share. An honor.

**The four-armed woman standing on a platform of blood for decades, oiled, feathered, wearing her bone necklace, holding sacrifices and burnt offerings in her four strong hands. A high priestess to the Horned God in his temple, he watching with cross-armed approval.

**A temple of blue stone being built and hacked out of the ground by her people. The Horned God watching, impatient for the suffering to begin.

**Primitive and proud, the woman shook totems and strings of beads in worship. They killed everything around them, collecting the skulls and fashioning little altars of skulls, anointing them in blood and smoking clouds of burning animal fat. They were covered in the blood of the slain. All for the Horned God. He was very demanding.

**Something came from the sky and watched them from the woods. They were afraid of it. She took the head of a slain woodland creature and presented it to the thing in the woods as an offering. The first bit of blood offered to the creature they would come to know as the Horned God. He had found Tevlapradah.

**The woman roaming with her people through the woods and plains, unshod, filthy, clad in furs and crude, stinking skins. Beautiful, yet fierce and terrible, they killed everything they encountered, dragging their prizes back to their woodland hovel to be torn apart and devoured raw. She was part of a group, a war party bounding across the countryside ever seeking their next victim. This was to be alive—to hunt and kill with her kin. This was Tevlapradah.

**In a rare moment of peace, the woman received a necklace of bone beads from a war-like four-armed man. She accepted the beads—some sort of primitive marriage ceremony.

Hath wondered what all this was leading to. She'd seen epochs of time, the coming and passing of the Horned God, the creation of the modern Monamas in now lost alien cities, and the building and anointing of the Horned God's temple. And, the four-armed woman, how she'd gone from being a warrior-hunter, to a high priestess in the Horned God's temple, to his immortal Secret-Talker and then the last of her kind.

Nowhere in all of that, in the shouting and dying and ringing of weapons and beating of drums did she hear her name uttered. Did she even have a name?

But wait . . .

Time continued backwards. She saw the woman and the man she would "marry" alone in a pool, nude and bloodied, full of entrails from a recent kill having a contorted round of sadistic, animal-like sex—furs cast aside, their pale bodies tangled together, pitted with cuts and clouding the water with blood.

The male was shouting something. Grunting it. The woman was latched onto his neck, mangling it with her teeth.

Hath strained to hear.

"On . . . ., On . . . c.a, Ond.c . . ." he cried in primitive ecstasy.

What? What was that?

"Ondecca, Ondecca, Ondecca!"

The Horned God's Secret-Talker was named Ondecca.

Mission accomplished.

Author Information

Ren Garcia, author of the League of Elder series, graduated from Ohio State University with a degree in Literature. When he has free time he enjoys playing volleyball and ice hockey. He lives in Columbus, Ohio, with his wife and their four dogs.

Publisher Information

VISIT THE LOCONEAL BLOG AT

www.loconeal.com

Breaking News Forthcoming Releases
Links to Author Sites Loconeal
Events